Totally Bound Publishing books by Amy Craig

Single Books
Lost in LA
The Devil in the Deep South

I0598051

THE DEVIL IN THE DEEP SOUTH

AMY CRAIG

The Devil in the Deep South
ISBN # 978-1-83943-782-3
©Copyright Amy Craig 2022
Cover Art by Kelly Martin ©Copyright March 2022
Interior text design by Claire Siemaszkiewicz
Totally Bound Publishing

THE DEVIL
IN THE
DEEP SOUTH

Dedication

To my sister, Brittany, who never reads my books
but might laugh if she did.

Chapter One

"O beautiful for spacious skies..." Taylor Lenore sang along with the first-grade class occupying her bookstore. Rows of eager children filled the community space. Their seersucker shorts, ruffled cuffs and monogrammed collars reminded her of her idyllic childhood, and she loved Ronan's tiniest performers as much as she loved books.

The pudgy kid in the front row stuck his finger up his nose.

She stumbled over a verse but continued singing. Watching the kid made her nose itch, but she kept her hand pressed against her side, wrinkled away the sensation and exaggerated her participation. *"From sea to shining sea!"*

The kid sneezed and sent a green glob flying across the open space. The emission landed in front of the audience of grinning parents, doting grandparents and special guests.

Clapping, she rushed forward and placed her shoe over the snot. "Fabulous! Aren't they just the sweetest?"

The audience lowered their phones, clapped and nodded.

The children shuffled on the risers.

She scanned the crowded store, but everyone looked happy so she exhaled. After her engagement to Josh had fallen apart, returning to Ronan felt like a smart move, but she'd struggled to envision her future. Her mother Nancy wanted to coddle grandbabies and her father Jack wanted to protect her. She wanted to go to bed each night knowing she made a difference in her tiny corner of the world. Maybe she should let the kid wipe up his own snot. She glanced at her shoe and smiled. *We all have room to grow.*

Looking toward the pastry case, she sought out Plucky's encouragement. Her friend wore her shiny black hair cut in a chin-length bob. Long bangs swept over one eye like a brush of feathers tinged with blue. *I liked the pink tips better, but she never could settle.* Plucky's response to the performance would tell her whether the bookstore had displayed Ronan's germ-caked darlings to their full advantage.

Plucky grimaced.

They tried. Taylor swallowed and raised her eyebrows.

Plucky mimed gagging herself.

She slashed her hand across her throat. *I get the point. I tried to do a good thing!*

With a wink, Plucky turned back to the pastry case.

Clapping her hands together, Taylor turned back to the parents who were gathering their things. She inclined her hands toward the first-grade teacher's black curls. "I just want to say that Mrs. Jenkins did an amazing job teaching the kids. I never knew that song had so many verses." Avoiding her mother's gaze, she extended her hands toward the children. "Y'all are so impressive!"

Her mother, the elementary school librarian, stood near the nonfiction section. Plastic reading glasses hung from her neck, and a soft purple cardigan accented her bright-blue eyes. Risking a glance, Taylor saw her raise her chin. *She caught that fib about the song all right. I sang every verse at my first pageant.* Brushing her bangs out of her eyes, she ignored Nancy's reproach and focused on the stars of this show. "Kids, thank you so much for coming to our little bookstore and brightening our day."

Mrs. Jenkins squeezed the shoulders of two first-graders. "Thank you for having us. The auditorium intimidates some of our special friends, but everyone loves Ronan Reads."

She clasped her hand against her chest. If the elementary school wanted to utilize her space for a spring performance, who was she to turn away the free publicity? "Why, thank you!" She let the performance's spirit wash over her and exhaled. Nerves kept her on edge, but the little darlings charmed her. "Plucky has cupcakes for the kids and coffee for the adults. Everyone, please stay and visit."

The students leaned toward the sweets.

Mrs. Jenkins smiled. "Go, you little hellions! You earned it."

The orderly rows dissolved into chaos. Elbows flew, and several children stepped on their classmates' toes.

Holding the tray of cupcakes like a shield, Plucky skewed her mouth and turned her head to the side.

"Me first!" the pudgy kid yelled.

His suspender-strapped belly strained his shirt buttons, but he made his way across the room with admirable speed. A muscled little bruiser overtook him, snatched the first cupcake and shoved the icing into his mouth. Taylor covered a laugh.

"That one was mine!"

"Hog!"

The children crowded around Plucky.

"Charles Brannon hit me!" a girl cried.

"Did not!"

"C.B., mind your manners." Mrs. Jenkins's sing-song voice cut through the noise.

Charles Brannon mumbled an apology, but he gave his classmate side-eye.

Taylor sympathized with the girl. The first time she'd called that kid 'Charles', he'd shaken his head and turned his brown doe-eyes to his mother. "It's okay, Mama. She doesn't know me yet." The mixture of innocence and sincerity charmed Taylor, but she wondered if the little tyke would throw her under the bus for a slice of cake. Today's kids were so much worldlier than the kids from her dirt-tinged, polyester youth. *Good thing I didn't call the little tyke 'Charlie'.* Trusting Plucky to handle the first graders, she turned from the fray and keyed up the music.

Housed on the main floor of an old, three-story brick building, Ronan Reads offered everything from thrillers to obscure local publications. Online sales kept the balance sheet healthy, and a casual space in the middle of the store let customers read, nibble cookies or linger over free Wi-Fi.

She envisioned the bookstore as a gathering place and a hotspot for book releases. After a year of business, her dream felt naïve, and she struggled to keep the store afloat in the digital age. Sparrow

County's population topped sixty thousand, but only a few thousand people lived within the city's limits, and even fewer of them cared for books. Bankers and health-care workers toiled away in the Historic District, but Thirsty Thursday remained an Atlanta gimmick. Given free time, Renan's residents spent their hours praying, gossiping or binging television shows. Taylor could never pin down the right order.

Nancy walked up to her side. "How many verses does that song have, Taylor Lenore?"

She swallowed and met her mother's gaze. "Three?"

Nancy raised an eyebrow.

"Four?"

Nancy nodded.

She focused on the children's shrieks and laughter. Despite Nancy's public-facing job, she was an educator and an introvert who hid behind picture books and manners. Once strangers broke through her prim exterior, they found a loyal woman who loved her job. Taylor loved her, too, but she never had the luxury of distance. "I wanted to flatter the kids for a job well done."

"Do they look like they need your flattery?"

She considered the kids wreaking havoc in her store. Two boys finger-painted chocolate icing on the floor and a pair of girls chased each other with napkins. Their parents clustered around the coffee urn and exchanged pleasantries over cream and sugar. *They might not need my flattery, but I'm going to need a few hours to put the store back together.* "No, they're doing just fine without me."

"*Those who flatter their neighbors are spreading nets for their feet,*" Nancy said, quoting the Bible.

After two-and-a-half decades of experience with Nancy's wisdom, Taylor wisely nodded. *I love Jesus, but the Bible doesn't get into detail about running a bookstore, balancing the bottom line and maintaining the goodwill of the online community.*

Nancy pushed her glasses up her nose and picked up a new release. She flipped through the first few pages. "You did good hosting the concert, but you don't need sweet talk to turn a profit."

Setting her phone on the table, she let a playlist direct the tracks. "Mama, I'm running a business."

Nancy looked up from the book. "Goodwill will come back to you in spades."

She frowned. "I don't recognize that verse."

"I made it up."

Exhaling, she met her mother's gaze. "Mama, please..."

"Is this book any good?" Nancy asked.

She considered the question. *Llama Serenade* was the story of a couple who abandoned their one-bedroom apartment in New York City for seventy-five acres in Flagstaff, Arizona. In poetic, reverent detail, Bunny and Brunswick Kissimmee explored their relationship with the llamas they raised, the land they owned and the clothing-optional hot tub parties they hosted in the desert. "I'm not sure 'new-age mecca' is quite your style."

"People have alienated themselves from the animals that feed them."

Her mother raised chickens but not the kind kids cuddled for backyard photo opportunities. "True."

Nancy turned to the back cover. "Whew. Twenty-four dollars. The authors think highly of themselves."

"Publishers set the price," Taylor said. "You know you get a twenty-percent discount."

"You're a good girl." Nancy tucked the book under her arm and walked toward the coffee urn.

Am I? She considered her mother's admonishment about flattery. Instead of waking to a cartoon alarm clock, she'd spent her first eighteen years opening her eyes to Nancy's steady inspiration. After she moved out for college, Nancy's inspiring messages came by text, but she often liked their comforting support, responded with an emoji and went about her day. *Now that I'm back, a little less maternal influence would be nice.* Remembering her bookstore audience, she shook off her personal issues. "Oh, Mama?"

Nancy turned.

Lifting her shoe, she revealed the green mess. "Would you do me a favor and get the sanitizing spray from the cleaning closet?"

Nancy stared at the glob and wrinkled her nose. "What is that?"

"Snot."

"Oh, my," Nancy said.

"Aren't children precious?"

Nancy smiled. "You were."

Her heart and her stance softened. "Thanks, Mama."

The door opened, and Ronan's city manager stepped into the bookshop. Jonathan O'Connor meant well and smelled pleasantly of cigar smoke, but he rarely ironed his shirts. A local dry cleaner offered him discounted services, but he'd shrugged off the offer. "If I wanted pressed shirts, I would have married a woman who liked to iron." Instead, he'd married a woman who spent most of her time getting her nails done, and they both seemed happy with their arrangement.

He was a decent enough manager for the city, but Ronan's citizens expected him to submit budgets, shake hands and cut ribbons. If they needed someone at the bargaining table, they redirected their figurehead and turned to their lawyers and the board of commissioners.

"Peaches!" Striding across the room, he stopped short and looked at the icing-smeared chaos running rampant through her bookstore. "What on earth is going on today?"

"School performance." The old nickname irked her, but her fourth-grade reign as Little Miss Georgia Peach Queen had delighted the town. "Did we forget to invite you?"

He frowned and patted his empty pocket. "No, no… It's just we have a special visitor."

"We?" she asked.

"Ronan."

"Ahh-h." In her experience, silence yielded answers.

"Christopher Durand is here." O'Connor checked his pants pockets. "All the way down from Atlanta."

She smiled. "I'm sorry, but who is Christopher Durand?"

"Owns Ocelot." Smacking his lips, O'Connor rolled his tongue across his teeth and patted his pants. "Heavy machinery and big bucks."

If he keeps digging in his pockets, I'll have to turn my back. "Sir, can I get you something?"

He looked up. "I ran out of nicotine gum. Do you sell that stuff?"

"Oh." Laughter slipped past her lips. Amid the screaming kids and chattering parents, the city manager's dependency reminded her why Ronan's residents banded together. When a family hit hard times, neighbors and church members stepped in to help. If O'Connor wanted to quit his cigar habit, she would help. "Is that all? I'm sure the pharmacy's open."

He shook his head and exhaled. "No time. Durand's on his way here from the chambers."

She frowned. "Why?"

"Dog and pony show touting Ronan's charm. He wants to build a new factory, and Ronan's in the running."

A little boy tugged O'Connor's pants. "Hiya, Mr. Manager."

He patted the boy's back. "Hiya, Smith. Where's your mama?"

"At work. My mamaw's here."

Making a face, O'Connor nodded and sent the boy back into the fray. "Hell of a day to have the kids over for snacks."

She crossed her arms. "Nobody told me the great Christopher Durand wanted to tour my bookstore. He doesn't like kids?"

"The kids aren't the problem." O'Connor lowered his voice and leaned in. "He's supposed to be incognito."

The rich, lingering cigar smoke used to intrigue her, but now she worried about his health. The man was active with the Kiwanis Club, the Salvation Army, the Historical Society and Uncle Brent's church, but his common sense went the way of his ironing board. "So, take him somewhere else for coffee and local-interest books."

O'Connor glanced at his watch and shook his head. "No time."

The door opened, and three adults stepped into the bookstore. She recognized the department directors in their power suits and high heels, but the man in jeans looked as inconspicuous as a cougar on a playground. A hat obscured most of Christopher Durand's face, but his bronzed cheeks and strong jawline cut a nomadic cowboy's striking, cinematic profile. Trying not to be rude, she looked away from him but risked a second glance. His weathered skin had bypassed Hollywood's warm glow, but if the sun's heat had hardened it to armor, he wore the look well.

Scanning the room, Durand looked at her.

She returned his stare, but his hat's shadow disguised his eyes' color. *Are they blue?* She watched his face for signs of emotion. Not a tic. "No time, indeed."

The girls chasing each other with napkins rounded a bookshelf and collided with Durand's legs.

Little Cecilia Williamson looked up, locked eyes with the man and screamed.

Every person in the bookstore turned and stared.

Durand frowned but stood resolute.

If the man wanted to go incognito, he picked a fine day to do it. Abandoning the slimy mess beneath her foot, Taylor strode up to the trio of adults, pulled the precocious girl against her legs and crossed her arms over the child's vibrating chest. "That's enough, Cece."

The girl looked up and quieted.

She smiled at Durand. "Welcome to Ronan Reads."

He removed his hat, placed it on the counter and inclined his head.

His eyes were as gray as a roiling thundercloud.

"Quite the welcoming committee," he said.

"Well" — she waved her hand toward the crowd — "we weren't expecting tourists."

"I'm not a tourist."

She tilted her head. "Who are you?"

"Peaches, this is Christopher" — the department director swallowed — "and we told him your store stocks local-interest books."

She kept her gaze locked on Durand. "Is that so?"

Cece's mother stepped up and reached for her daughter.

Taylor released the first grader and patted her shoulder, but she felt Durand's condemnation and refused to fold beneath his scrutiny. "Well, we aim to please, Mister..." She raised her eyebrows.

"Durand," he said.

At least he doesn't lie. "What types of books interest you, Mr. Durand?"

He rubbed his thumb along his lip. "I hardly know. Show me what you have."

His quiet concentration turned the request into a command. *Who doesn't know what type of books they like?* She opened her mouth to sass him, but the intensity of his stare sent a chill racing up her arms. Glancing over her shoulder, she considered her audience. Half of the first graders were barefoot, short one shoe or trailing laces. Their parents tilted their heads, offered slight smiles or whispered to their neighbors. Standing tall, she plotted a course through the crowd. "When in Ronan."

He cleared his throat. "I believe the phrase is 'When in Rome'."

"Hmm-m." She managed a smile. "I'll remember that fact."

Falling into step, he followed her through the crowd.

She strode past O'Connor. "You owe me."

The city manager nodded. "You're the best, Peaches."

Smiling, she found her gait, skirted the tables in the center of the store and led Durand to the local-interest books.

"Are you?" he asked.

She missed a step. "Excuse me?"

"Are you the best?"

Straightening her shoulders, she paused. "Ronan Reads is a community resource. We offer a variety of new and used titles, educator discounts, community events, bulk orders and book trades."

"I asked about you," he said.

Two children raced down the aisle.

Immune to her tension, the tumble-bumble first graders turned the corner and rolled through the store.

She wished she could slip away as easily, but she felt every inch of the stakes. Catching her reflection in the window, she saw the stiff-shouldered silhouette of a confident woman. *Or one who took too many dance classes and tried to live up to her parents' expectations.* Looking up, she met Christopher's gaze. His gray eyes intrigued her, but the sheen of steel-kissed flint looked too intense for life in Ronan. "I try my best."

He inclined his head.

If I had warning, I could have staged this tour better. She picked up a large-format book. "Ronan looks sleepy, but the city has a vibrant past and a promising future. General Dick gave one of the most important pre-war Secession speeches from Ronan's courthouse steps, and Georgia's largest Confederate training camp occupied the site of the new high school."

"You condone slavery?"

She bristled. "No! But the historic city reflected the state of the nation." She frowned. "The state of the South. One of the first paved sections of the Dixie Highway passed through Ronan, and our farmers pioneered advances in modern Southern agriculture."

"When was this? 1856?"

She swallowed. "1888."

He yawned and covered his mouth. "How modern."

She moved deeper into the shelves and reached for another book. "Textiles."

"Spare me." He scanned the crowd milling in the center of the store.

Devoid of front-row tickets, the parents and special guests had resumed their chatter.

Gripping the books against her chest, she tilted her head. "Why are you here?"

He shrugged. "The tour's part of the show. Local representatives lead me around town and show me the best and the brightest stars the town offers." He cleared his throat and looked at her. "Usually, they pick an up-and-coming lawyer with corporate ambitions."

She shelved the books. Freed from curt responses and a keen audience, his voice rippled like windswept grass. Amid her treasured books, their hushed conversation felt far too intimate. His rolled r's spoke of intense meetings held beneath a midday sun, but his cultured drawl left room for the horizon. Judging by his tailored shirt, speed and efficiency meant more to him than her idealistic notions. "Lucky you."

"Indeed." Reaching across her, he pulled both volumes from the shelves.

His woodsy aftershave and masculine warmth smelled better than the fresh-cut paper.

"I'll take these. Ring me up, please."

The please sounded like a caress. Needing space, she slid past him.

"Ronan intrigues me."

Turning, she tilted her head. "Why?"

He shifted the books to one hand, reached toward her and skimmed her upper arm.

"What are you doing?" She kept her voice to a whisper.

Holding up one finger, he smiled and held up his finger. "You're wearing chocolate."

Her cheeks warmed. "Thanks."

Pulling a handkerchief from his back pocket, he cleaned up the mess.

At least he didn't lick off the icing. Did I want him to lick off the icing? She swallowed. "Do you always carry a handkerchief?"

Folding the soiled cloth, he slipped it into his back pocket. "Are you always the center of attention?"

"No." Clearing her throat, she wondered what had possessed O'Connor to bring this man into her bookstore. *The devil himself would have been easier to ignore.* "You picked a special day to visit. Despite the chaos" — she glanced at two boys tousling on the story-time rug — "Ronan is a lovely town."

"I don't need lovely."

The admission stopped her from fleeing into the crowd. "What do you need?"

"Hard workers, reliable transportation and progressive tax policies."

She swallowed. "I can vouch for two out of the three."

He raised an eyebrow. "Can you?"

"The state empowered Ronan to levy property taxes on real and personal properties within its boundaries." She recalled a recent news article. "The state also empowered the city to extend its corporate limits by annexation. I promise you, when the roads get bad, the borders shift."

"Hmm-m." He glanced at O'Connor. "How often does that happen?"

She smiled. "Whenever the governing board deems it appropriate."

"And how would you run the town?"

The question caught her off guard. Scrambling for an answer, she wondered how long O'Connor would stay in his position. *Ronan's commissioners make that decision. If the town thought I was prepared and capable of filling the role, would I take on that challenge?* She shifted her weight. "Tell me, Mr. Durand, will your factory be inside or outside the city limits?"

"The factory doesn't exist yet, Peaches."

"It's Taylor."

He rubbed his lip. "And if I asked you to dinner, who would join me? Taylor, the savvy businesswoman, or Peaches, the town darling?"

She raised her chin. "Taylor."

"Give me your number, Taylor."

"No."

He frowned.

"I don't date overgrown boys who drive lifted, diesel-guzzling trucks."

He laughed. "The lady does me wrong."

She frowned.

He dipped his head. "I drive an electric truck."

Suppressing a smile, she scanned him from head to toe and tried not to show her approval. "I've heard the towing's a little" — she chewed her lip — "lackluster."

Laughing, he scanned the store but returned to her gaze. "I promise you that my truck hauls ass and tows like a fiend."

Heat bloomed in her core, but she raised her chin and scrambled to avoid a diplomatic disaster. "I prefer not to mix business with pleasure."

"But you enjoy pleasure?"

Her stomach flipped. "I'm sure I don't know what you mean."

He scratched his lip.

The wrinkles near his eyes deepened into laugh lines. No wonder the Atlanta newspapers published his charismatic smiles.

"No, I'm sure you don't," he said.

"You're welcome to follow Ronan Reads on social media." She brushed her hair out of her face. "Let us know what you think of the books."

Giving her a curt nod, he turned and preceded her through the crowd.

Social media? How lame am I? She charged ahead, rounded the sales counter and smiled.

Placing his books next to his hat, he pulled out his wallet and examined the crowd.

He's probably guarding his back against first graders. She scanned the books' bar codes, slid them across the counter and tried to repair her failed diplomacy. "The books are on the house."

"No." He pushed his credit card toward her. "I don't accept handouts."

"Oh, don't worry." She winked. "I'll bill the city manager."

His laughter drew curious looks.

"Goodbye, Taylor," he said.

She smiled. "Mr. Durand."

Shaking his head, he walked through the crowd, donned his hat and nodded to the department directors. "Thanks for the tour."

The stone-faced directors returned his nod.

O'Connor yawned, peeled himself away from his cronies and trailed the trio. Stopping in the doorway, he fixed his pants and walked into the sunlight.

Taylor exhaled.

Cutting through the crowd, Nancy came around the counter. "Who was that?"

Frowning, she tried to summarize the man. His weathered exterior and rigid command made sense for an executive who manufactured heavy machinery, but his laugh lines left her at odds. "He owns Ocelot."

Nancy arranged the pens in a cup. "What's Ocelot?"

She chewed her thumbnail, caught the uncouth habit and shrugged. "Chunks of metal that move dirt?"

"Oh," Nancy said. "*That* Ocelot."

Watching Christopher's silhouette cross the street, she shook her head and left herself a note to bill O'Connor for the books. "That man doesn't belong in Ronan."

Nancy set aside the cup. "Who does?"

She surveyed the kids and their families. Some people wore dresses and pants from big box stores and some wore precious outfits from boutiques, but every child had a cupcake and a chance. In her small town, that chance mattered, and she refused to budge from her foundations. "I do."

Nancy patted her hand. "Of course you do."

Pulling free of her mother's tender touch, she found Plucky near the pastry case.

Plucky snapped her tongs.

Biting back a smile, Taylor reached for a roll of paper towels. "Give me a hand, Mama. I have a mess to clean up."

Chapter Two

Sitting in the back seat of a chauffeured car, Christopher replayed his day in Ronan and stared out of the window at the looming Atlanta skyline. His head hurt, his body felt heavy and the tightness in his back and chest made him consider calling his physician. *How do I tell the difference between a heart attack, indigestion and uncertainty?* Each of the diagnoses felt as improbable as the rest. Ignoring the symptoms, he focused on his day. Ronan had merit, but the new plant decision matrix had already listed the town's assets and assigned it a score. Unfortunately, all the other towns had scored in the same vicinity. Until he'd walked into Ronan Reads, he would have had a hard time differentiating the contenders.

Then he'd seen Taylor Lenore. Her dimples, blue eyes and honeyed hair looked sweet, but her willingness to step up to the plate had earned his respect. The city manager looked like a newspaper editor from the eighties, and the department directors checked their talking points before opening their mouths, but Taylor had faced down the lion.

If he were a kinder man, he would have purred. Instead, he'd glowered and maintained his army stance. She'd held her own. Bridging his fingers over his chest, he slouched on the car's soft black leather and closed his eyes. *Taylor would make Grandmère Durand proud, the crazy old bat.*

The driver braked hard, and the books from Ronan Reads flew to the foot well.

"Sorry, Mr. Durand," the driver said.

He nodded and scooped up the books. The cover of the Ronan history book featured a God-awful bronze statue of General Dick, but the book on textiles intrigued him. He flipped through the Chapters and let the driver cover the miles. The removal of the Creek Indians shamed the state, but it created opportunities for cotton cultivation and the emergence of textile mills. From the 1830s onward, cotton mills mirrored Georgia's economy. *Where do we go from here?* He flipped through pages on industrialization, segregation and workers' rights. The book covered the subtleties missing from high school textbooks. *Taylor Lenore stocked this book, so she doesn't shy away from grit. What else did I misjudge about her?* Setting aside the book, he picked up his phone and opened a social media app.

Ronan Reads' profile had close to one hundred thousand followers. *Metro Atlanta has six million people. One hundred thousand followers are chump change.* He checked Ocelot's account and found a follower count near eighty thousand. *Ocelot generates billions of dollars of revenue from construction and mining equipment, diesel and natural gas engines, industrial gas turbines and diesel-electric locomotives. What does Ronan Reads generate?*

Landfill waste and smiles? His shoulder pained him, and he rubbed away the tension. *Definitely indigestion.*

Most independent bookstore accounts used satire, activism and engaging tweets to build customer loyalty. Their long-winded posts ended with event links and five percent discount codes that no one ever used. Scanning the feed for Ronan Reads, he realized Taylor took a fresh approach. Between book reviews and industry articles, she posted inspirational memes, Bible verses and small, fuzzy-animal GIFs. *Fluffy, ridiculous comforts in a crazy world.* He added his account to the sea of admiration. *What's one more follower in a swarm of nerds?*

To cover his tracks, he liked a few extra Ronan businesses. As he tapped the screen to follow the local brewery, he realized he'd opened his personal account instead of the Ocelot one. Pausing, he set down his phone. *How much trouble can she be?*

Taylor was the type of blushing woman that his brother William would have loved. William had been dead for a decade, but his presence haunted their family meals and Ocelot ownership meetings. Admiring Taylor's dimple was one thing but selecting Ronan for the construction project should have nothing to do with her.

The driver pulled up to his house on Ridgewood Road.

He climbed out of the car, stretched his back and walked into the house. It boasted enough rooms to qualify as a Buckhead bachelor mansion, but he left the press at the front gates and spent most of his time in his home office, downstairs gym or infinity-edge pool. Finding a note from his housekeeper Greta next to his tuxedo, he smiled. He pulled out his phone, texted her and promised to tell her if he spilled anything on the fine fabric. Ten minutes later, he was back in the car and headed toward the hotel.

Buckhead hosted charming buildings with pristine facades and discreet, unnecessary signage. Locals knew the location of every luxe-wear brand and mom-and-pop gem anchoring the Atlanta suburb. Visitors could fend for themselves or turn tail and head back to downtown.

On Friday nights, an array of fine-dining establishments and upscale shopping malls brought the entertainment district to life, but gossip traveled along the paths of Chastain Park. Tennis courts, baseball fields, a golf course and a private horse park catered to families, but Buckhead's blonde huntresses knew him on sight. If he wanted exercise, he knew better than to set foot on the park's manicured paths. He also knew better than to disappoint his mother

Looking up, he took in the floodlit stone edifice of the Mainstay Hotel. His lower back ached from riding around in the car all day, but the indigestion seemed to have passed. Straightening his bow tie, he nodded at the valet and stepped from the vehicle.

A newspaper photographer recorded his entrance.

Walking past the press and the security guards, he made his way to the Astor Ballroom for the Diamond Ball. Beyond a thick-carpeted threshold, sparkling chandeliers gleamed and flowing, golden curtains draped floor-to-ceiling windows. Each round table held a centerpiece dripping with crystals and candle wax. The cream-and-white flowers preened for attention, but the women circulating the ballroom stole the show.

Sequins and hair shone against spray tans, false eyelashes and enough surgically enhanced cleavage to keep a silicone factory in business. Striding through the groups, he ignored the jewels and furs on display and headed to the bar. *Never mind the outside temperature hovers in the low eighties.*

This year marked Ocelot's tenth year of sponsoring the Diamond Ball. The event benefited his mother's favorite foundation, and it had raised over ten million dollars for research and local programs. Every year, the evening offered Georgia's elite a formal dinner, live music and vibrant auctions. Tickets came in pairs, and after handing over five figures for the privilege of claiming a table, the dancing and drinks almost felt complimentary.

Settling in at the bar, he signaled for a beer and watched the crowd swirl. He doubted he would stay long enough for speeches, but he smiled for a brave photographer and traded small talk with the acquaintances who came up to say hello.

He checked his phone for instructions from his mother. The absence of commands worried him, but she knew how to find him. Seeing the social media app for Ronan Reads open on his phone, he paused and read a recent post.

Sweet angels visited the store today! I can't show you their smiling faces, but I guarantee you they sang like angels.

He smiled and decided to respond to her post with a direct message.

Sugar-fueled Tasmanian devils.

He'd meant to leave a lighthearted comment, but the open bar and the monotony of small talk loosened his fingers. *Maybe I should add one of those dinky red heart emojis. Don't they fix everything?*

I believe Tasmanian devils live in Tasmania and New South Wales, but I'd be happy to recommend a book on Australian fauna.

Shaking his head, he tipped back his beer and gave the woman a point. Despite the bookstore's chaos, her unflappable smile had prevailed. *Except when I wiped off the icing. If I'd licked it off my finger, she probably would have slapped me.* He grinned. *I would have deserved it.*

"Christopher, dance with me, please."

Turning, he found his ex-girlfriend Rebecca wearing a lavender evening dress. Diamonds dangled from her ears, and he wondered if he'd given her the gems. "I'm not in the mood."

She took the beer from his hand, set it on the bar and pulled him to standing.

Because they'd known each other as children and dated as adults, he let her. Sighing, he followed her through the crowd and smiled like the bemused man his peers expected.

Rebecca had grown up in Savannah and attended the prestigious, all-girls St. Vincent's Academy. The granddaughter of a former state senator, she inhabited the same moneyed circles that filled his parents' social calendars. Long before she'd moved to Atlanta to report the news, she'd known the fastest route from the airport to her favorite five-star hotel on West Paces Ferry Road.

He remembered sitting next to her during a high school fundraiser and asking what she did for fun.

"Oh, it's October," she'd said. *"I'm helping plan the Annual Tour of Homes and Tea. It's a self-guided tour of the original 1845 convent building and private homes in the Historic District."* She'd tilted her head and smiled.

"Proceeds from the tour and the tea benefit the preservation and restoration of the convent."

"No, I mean, like sports and music. Do you like movies?" he'd asked.

She'd blinked. *"If the tea was good enough for Winnie Davis, it's good enough for me."*

Exhaling, he'd turned his attention to the lame fundraising speaker. Winnie, the daughter of Confederate President Jefferson Davis, had attended St. Vincent's Academy, but he preferred emulating modern mentors.

Choosing a spot on the edge of the Diamond Ball dance floor, she held up her arms.

He sighed and stepped into position. Dancing came as easily as breathing, but his partner's alabaster skin and defined lips looked unnatural. "I assume you have a reason for ignoring my wishes." Listening to the music, he caught the flow, stepped forward with his left foot and joined the waltz.

"I wanted to talk to you," she said.

"You have my number."

She looked over his shoulder. "I called. You never check your voicemails."

"Leave a message with my assistant."

"Christopher, you fired your assistant."

He missed a step, corrected and stepped back with his right foot. "You're right. She couldn't take ownership of a guinea pig."

Rebecca swatted his back. "You're supposed to train her, Christopher."

"My bad. I thought I was supposed to run the company."

Rebecca shook her head and looked over his shoulder.

See something good?

"You've been busy?" she asked.

He focused on the woman in his arms. She smelled the same. Her perfume came in a rectangular red bottle. For a year, he wondered if she enjoyed the hints of flowers and spice or had purchased the bottle to match her hair. When the question and her ambitions had ceased to amuse him, he'd given her the boot. "I have."

"Doing what?"

Meeting her gaze, he sensed the reason for the dance. "Working."

"You're always working. That's why our relationship failed."

"Hmm-m." He looked over her shoulder. *That's not why it failed.*

He came from a long line of achievers, but he wondered if his ancestors had picked the low-hanging fruit. His grandfather, James M. Durand, had founded Ocelot, served as Georgia's governor and run for President. Like most southerners, he blamed his national loss on Yankee intervention. His father, David Durand, retired to the links, but family narratives painted him as an ideal son. He'd grown the company to a national scale and produced two heirs. When William had died in 2005, the loss shook the family, but Christopher had filled his older brother's shoes. *Am I going to be the disappointment that sends Ocelot Enterprises racing toward public ownership?* He'd implemented procedures to tighten record keeping and accounting. Strict financial policies and internal controls prevented fraud and mismanagement, but nothing prevented poor decisions. *Hell, I can't even choose the 'right' wife.*

"You look tired." Rebecca toyed with his hair above his collar. "Tell me what's keeping you up at night."

A secret electric test fleet in the research lab. Soon, fully electric powertrains for heavy equipment will be a tight race. He smiled. "Wouldn't you like to know?"

The music stopped.

Her unblinking stare remained constant. "I would."

"Rebecca, you'll have to wait for the press releases like everyone else. Ocelot is a family company. We don't issue shareholder reports."

"But shares trade on secondary markets," she said. "People care."

"People care or people want to know whether they'll get paid?"

She frowned. "Is there a difference?"

He sighed. *In your world, no. Every person holding a share depends on my discretion and success.* Running Ocelot felt like a sharp knife against his throat. One wrong move, and he would bleed out, but thriving under pressure reminded him that he lived. "We'll announce our developments when we're ready."

Pouting, she pulled in her arms.

"Don't give me that shit, Rebecca. If your daddy wants to know what's happening, have him call my dad."

She raised her chin. "He did."

Biting back a smile, he nodded. *Well, point for ole Dad. I didn't think he could hold out.*

Dropping her hand, Rebecca scanned the room.

She's probably looking for her WSB-TV scoop.

He pulled out his phone.

Looking at my inventory list and imaging book lovers around the world bonding over favorite books. Who's the bookplate to your back matter?

You're novel. I'll give you that.

Swapping puns with a bookseller ranked low on his entertainment list, but the banter held a colloquial charm. He rubbed his hand over his face. Next week, he'd be frying chicken. *What the hell am I doing? Definitely no more emojis.*

"Are you paying attention to me?"

He looked up. "Huh?"

Rebecca pulled his phone from his hands. "Oh! What are your bids?"

He rolled his eyes and pulled it right back. The live auction merited big-ticket items and ludicrous, alcohol-fueled rivalries, but the scale of the silent auction brought in the cash. Mobile bidding kept guests engaged with immediate outbid text notifications. The Diamond Ball crowd could afford every restaurant and homegood in town, but they dropped cash for autographed memorabilia and limited access experiences. Basically, the hardest to get, the higher it went. "I'm not bidding on a thing."

She crossed her arms and tapped her foot. "Your mother expects you to buy something."

"What would you like?"

Her eyes lit up.

"The trip to China would bore you, you've already been to the Mayan Riviera and you don't gamble, so Vegas is out."

She pouted. "Vegas has more to offer than slot machines."

He laughed. "How about the stunning bedroom remodel from Guavacado House Interior Design and the $10,000 home accessories shopping spree?"

She tugged her earring. "I think you're mocking me."

Smiling, he dismissed her. "Yes, Rebecca, I am." His phone vibrated. He pulled it from his pocket and saw a message from his friend, Chao Yung Dong. "Sorry... Quick text from C.Y."

Rebecca nodded.

He'd met C.Y. in Iraq and lured him stateside with the promise of a fat position. China may have 'won' the Iraq War by refusing to participate, but the China National Petroleum Corporation had invested copiously in post-Saddam Iraq's oil industry. C.Y. had spearheaded oil and infrastructure projects. Now, he spearheaded Ocelot projects as the company's Vice President of Energy & Transportation.

Before Christopher put away his phone, he peeked at his feed.

Atlanta might think it's the soul of the South, but for a taste of home, come to Ronan and experience the joy and familiarity you need.

He frowned. *What do I need?*

Rebecca yanked the phone from his hand. "What on earth are you doing?"

Crossing his arms, his patience grew thin. "For a modern woman, you're surprisingly cavalier about personal space."

She stuck out her tongue.

Twenty years of watching the same gesture softened his stance. "Becca, give me my phone."

Looking up, she frowned. "You follow bookstores?"

"Sometimes." Ocelot's three-hundred-thousand-square-foot generator production facility would land in the continental United States. If Ronan were lucky, the town would land the factory and three hundred quality employment opportunities. Close to the world's busiest airport, the community's large labor pool and local training facilities made economic sense. To negotiate the best deal for Ocelot, he needed all the leverage he could muster, and ignoring Taylor Lenore was the smartest course of action. *Mooning over a southern belle won't help me run my family's company.* "I'm scouting towns for a new factory and making nice with the locals."

"I knew it!"

He took the phone from her hand and slid it into his silk-lined pocket. The weight felt right, but the unanswered post lingered in his mind. Taylor Lenore's sincerity slid under his defenses and lingered like an itch he could never reach. *Nobody can be that good and that serene.* Remembering her tensed, pert little mouth, he modified his description. *She's definitely not serene.*

"That's why you've been working dusk to dawn?"

Startled, he found Rebecca still standing in front of him. Faking a yawn, he nodded. "You're right. I'm beat." She nodded, but her tight expression looked skeptical. "Early day of meetings tomorrow."

"You're hiding something, Christopher Durand, and I aim to find out what's keeping you up at night."

He shrugged. "You're the reporter."

She raised her chin. "Ronan is a little Podunk town. The last time it made the news, it flooded."

Her long, red hair and toned arms no longer roused his interest, but he nodded. Even when the sex had bored him, the conversation had kept him sane. Rebecca was sharp as a tack, and she knew it. "I'm aware of the risk."

She narrowed her gaze. "Are you?"

A buried memory surfaced. He recalled staging backyard reenactments with William. Two years older, his brother knew the allure of washed-out roads and smashed bridges. Now he was gone, and Christopher struggled to understand why Ronan's flood risk had evaded his research team. "Night, Rebecca. Sleep well. Go buy yourself a spa day on my account."

"I don't need you to buy me a spa day."

He winked. "But you'll do it anyway."

"Christopher Durand!"

Raising his hand in farewell, he left her standing on the dance floor, grabbed a beer from a passing server and took a long pull. He stepped onto the balcony overlooking the pool, pulled his phone from his pocket and reread Taylor's post. His fingers hovered over the screen.

I can't decide whether ripping off Alabama lyrics is sacrilegious or brilliant.

As long as we're not proselytizing Uncle Remus, we're in the clear.

Her post came in response to his comment. No longer aimed at the general audience, she'd responded directly to him, and he grinned.

I'll aim for sweet potato pie.

And I'll shut my mouth. Goodnight, Mr. Durand. Thanks for visiting Ronan Reads.

Goodnight, Taylor.

He left the familiar sendoff for the world to see and upped his bid on a luncheon package he would give to his executive assistant. *Fuck, I fired the woman, didn't I?* Shaking his head, he jogged down the staircase leading toward the pool, hopped the fence to the main entrance and tapped the window beside his driver.

The man startled and spilled coffee on his shirt.

Swinging open the back door, Christopher settled into the seat and drummed his fingers on the black-leather armrest. He texted the head of Human Resources and demanded a new assistant to keep track of meetings, manage the company's social media accounts and free him to focus on hard decisions. *Like where to build this factory and how to deploy a fleet of electric machines.* Unsettled, he eyed the hardcover books from Ronan Reads and rehashed the town's pros and cons. No matter how much he focused on taxes and utilities, his thoughts circled back to Taylor Lenore. Something about the woman's clear, blue gaze held his attention. She rose above the fray, and for a moment, he thought he could rise with her.

Terrifying, bright young women aren't really my thing. Wishing he'd met her under different circumstances, he turned on the overhead light, opened the first page of the textiles book and read the topic sentence. *If anyone asks, I'm doing homework.* Glancing out of the window, he watched illuminated high-rise towers flicker behind a row of trees. *What am I hoping to learn?*

Chapter Three

Taylor savored the lazy afternoon and the familiar guests perusing Ronan Reads' wooden shelves. Her friends and neighbors leaned against red-brick walls, watched dust motes dance in the air and yawned with the complacency of mid-afternoon shoppers. *The kids were cute, but I love sleepy afternoons in this bookstore.* She stifled a yawn. *Maybe not so sleepy would be better for business.* Picking up a pen, she shifted her weight on the black swivel stool and drafted a menu for the pastry case. "Everybody likes scones."

"What?" Plucky asked.

Looking up, she found Plucky cleaning the pastry-case shelves. "I'm thinking about the menu."

Plucky put down her rag. "No more of that gluten-free-keto hybrid shit."

"Plucky!" She glanced at the corner of the store featuring picture books. A mother and her children lounged on beanbags and turned pages beneath a sunlit window. The youngest child blissfully sucked her bink and listened to her mother read. *All good.*

She checked the group of retirees lingering over coffee and newspapers in the common area.

Nobody looked up.

James, an old friend and the owner of a local IT service company, browsed the sci-fi books.

He looked more interested in the blurbs than Plucky's outburst.

Why am I so jumpy? I need to get back to the three C's — Christ, community and coffee. She put down the pen and pulled up the day's sales. The morning coffee run had turned a profit, but she doubted the mother-daughter pair would purchase a book. *Most of their collection came from the bookstore. Not every day has to be a transaction. As long as I can pay the bills, I'm content to blur the lines between a library and a bookstore.*

The pen rolled off the table and clattered on the wooden floor.

She startled, reached for the pen and banged her head on the counter.

"Rough night?" Plucky asked.

Rubbing her head, she nodded and blamed her sleepless night on a combination of snot and surprise diplomacy.

"You look ragged."

"Thanks." She'd known Plucky since kindergarten. Their friendship depended on proximity, shared secrets and healthy competition. "I know I can always count on you to lift my spirits."

"I have concealer in my bag."

"That's okay." She swallowed. "Wait! Do I look that bad?"

Plucky nodded.

She sighed. Christopher Durand deserved most of the blame for her sleepless night. He intrigued her, but she bore a scar from the last man who'd commanded a stage and caught her attention. Instead of tossing and turning, she'd spent the early morning hours drafting a series of posts about Old Testament covenants. *Even Mama can't fault me for reading the Bible.* Straightening, she tapped her phone and posted a message from her draft folder.

God is faithful and promised Noah he wouldn't destroy the world with a flood – Genesis 9:11. Tired of fighting your computer? Be faithful to your local bookstore. We can't promise to praise you, but we'll hook you up with a little R&R.

"What did you say?" Plucky asked. "After you post, you always look smug."

A dozen pithy responses sprang to mind, but she swallowed every one. Feeling petty, she blinked and considered her friend's comment. *I don't want to appear smug. What would Mama say to Plucky's comment? She'd turn the other cheek and keep actin' like a lady.* She smiled. "I hope the post brightens someone's day and sends us new business."

Plucky nodded, sprayed the glass shelf with cleaner and wiped off the streaks. "I'm sure it will."

Fumes from the astringent cleaner and the dark-roasted coffee obscured the soft papery smell of books that she loved. Wrinkling her nose, she scanned the GIFs and supportive comments trailing her online post. *Pride is a sin, but I am making a difference in the world, aren't I?* She refreshed the screen and saw a new comment from Christopher Durand rise to the top of the conversation.

Plenty of ways remain to destroy a world.

She dropped her phone on the counter, and it clattered on the glass. "Ugh! He's so cynical. Doesn't the CEO of Ocelot Enterprises have better things to do than rain on my parade?"

Plucky closed the pastry case and brushed her bangs out of her eyes. Walking to the counter, she peered at Taylor's phone. "That's the guy from yesterday?"

She nodded.

"Man, you have all the luck."

"What does that mean?"

"Well, if a hot billionaire walked into my coffee shop, I wouldn't say no to a night on the town." Plucky brushed her bangs from her eyes. "Or a trip to his bed."

She widened her gaze and scanned the customers. "I shouldn't have told you about the date." She dropped her voice to a whisper. "Plus, he was rude. He didn't really want to be here, much less invite me to his bed."

"Why don't you just, like…ignore him?" Plucky asked.

She frowned. "His responses rise to the top of my feed."

Plucky popped a piece of bubble gum into her mouth. "Stupid algorithm."

"Exactly!" Needing to move, she twirled on her black swivel stool. She would never admit to googling the man, but Christopher Durand regularly made the front page of *The Atlanta Journal-Constitution,* and the Internet offered plenty of eye candy. Sometimes his dates smiled like pageant queens, but who was she to cast the first stone?

The first time he'd responded to her post, she'd felt the warm glow of recognition, but other commenters had carried the banter, and Durand had gone silent. The second exchange had left her speechless. *Doesn't he have better things to do than talk to me?* His jaded attitude had persisted, and she'd given him the last word. "Doesn't the algorithm know we aren't friends? Atlanta's like an hour away from Ronan!"

"Your posts probably rise to the top of his feed, too," Plucky said.

She gripped the counter and tilted her head. "I only have a few thousand followers."

Blowing a bubble, Plucky popped the gum and cleared her lips. "Check again."

She swiped to the top of her profile and swallowed. "I guess my follower count grew."

"The post about banned books and the biblical canon went viral." Plucky stretched. "People dig your inspirational messages. Online sales are up fifty-five percent. I'm glad one of us paid attention during Sunday School."

She considered the nearest shelf. White recommendation cards fluttered below staff favorites. Some people might mount a plasma screen in the room's corner and cycle through book covers, but she preferred the ambiance of tape and flashcards. More than once, a customer had ripped a card from the shelf and thrown it onto the counter with a competing review. She welcomed the discussion. "Durand's just so jaded."

"I mean, he's right. Weren't there seven plagues?"

"Plucky!"

"What?" Plucky shrugged. "Maybe he forgot to eat breakfast."

She drummed her fingers. "I doubt a scone would soften his attitude."

Meeting her gaze, Plucky burst into laughter.

"What?" Throwing up her hands, she tried to keep a straight face. Twenty years of friendship sidestepped her practiced polish. "You already said you'd do him."

"I would. Wouldn't you?"

I'd fantasize about his body. A smile tugged at her lips, but she flattened her expression. "Not with his attitude." *For all I care, he can stay in his high-rise tower and be miserable.*

Plucky rolled her eyes. "Right." Shaking her head, she headed toward the stock room.

Abandoned in her own bookstore, she glanced at James. His long trench coat could hide a book, but she knew his patterns. After an hour or two, he would choose a world to explore, and she would cheerfully ring up his purchase.

Sure enough, he rounded the tables in the middle of the room and headed toward her carrying a book.

A retiree looked up and intercepted him.

Leaning over the table, James helped the man with a crossword puzzle clue, laughed and glanced at her.

She appreciated his good nature and the whiff of technology he brought to Ronan's economy, but his status in 'friend' territory was about as deep-seated as her love of fried chicken. Still, seeing two generations of Ronan residents connect validated the bookstore's existence.

Placing a paperback on the counter, James flapped back the edges of his trench coat and smiled. "Heya, Taylor."

She smiled and pulled the book toward her. "Hi, James. Find something good?"

He looked at her breasts. "I think so."

I would roll my eyes, but he wouldn't see the gesture. Turning, she scanned the barcode on the back of the science fiction novel. "That will be eight-eighty."

He slid a ten across the counter. "What are you doing this weekend?"

Slipping the book in a brown paper bag, she made change and placed his items on the counter. "I'm hosting a celebration of free speech at the bookstore. Didn't you see the flyer?"

He glanced toward the cork bulletin board. "I had my mind on something else."

"The celebration's a tradition." She filled up her coffee cup and took a sip. "In 1938, Alma Lovell distributed religious Bible tracts to her friends and neighbors. A police officer said a city ordinance required prior permission to distribute literature, and he arrested her."

James scratched his head. "I kind of remember that case from civics class."

"The case went all the way to the US Supreme Court." Taylor put her cup behind the register. "The court found the city violated Alma's First Amendment and Fourteenth Amendment rights. We're celebrating freedom of speech!"

He frowned. "But you stock sci-fi and romance books, too."

She laughed. "I don't care what people read."

He puffed his cheeks and exhaled. "What about the next week? I can get, uh, tickets to a baseball game."

She bit her lip. A lifetime of polite encounters trained her to avoid saying 'no', 'that's a bad idea' or 'you're out of your freaking mind'. Declining dinner invitations or illicit puffs merited the same reaction. She just felt mean. *I guess he's not coming to Alma's party.* "That's really kind, James, but I'm not into baseball." She smiled. "You know who likes baseball?"

Frowning, he stared.

"Katie Jesse."

"Nope. She's my employee. I can't take her anywhere."

Leaning on the counter, she checked that her shirt hid her cleavage and cleared her throat. "Who wrote your website text? *'Tech-inspired makes technology work for your business. We deliver complete customer care through collaboration, forward thinking and innovative solutions. Bridging the gap between people and technology is our specialty, and we can't wait to meet your needs.'* Don't you think she deserves a reward for increasing your customer base?"

He scratched his head. "You memorized our pitch."

Well, Katie clutched an oat-milk cold brew and repeated the pitch thirty times until it sounded right. Then you left your business card with it on the bulletin board. How could I ignore it? Straightening, she nodded toward the cork community center. "Things get slow around here. Sometimes, I wander around and read more than books."

"Yeah, I guess so."

She chewed her lip. "So...Katie?"

Picking up his book and his change, he exhaled. "I'll tell my mom about the Alma thing."

"Awesome!" She clapped her hands.

Shaking his head, he walked out of the front door.

"Another strikeout?" Plucky leaned against the counter. "He can't resist your blonde hair and pretty blue eyes." She blinked and pantomimed a half-wit wonder.

Taylor laughed. "Awkward! I can't imagine dating him."

Plucky yawned. "You had no qualms about throwing Katie under the bus."

"I know she has the hots for her boss." She wrinkled her nose. "Plus, James and I went to the same daycare. We're practically related."

"Whatever."

She swallowed the remainder of her defense. After breaking off her engagement to Josh, the thought of dating another person from Ronan turned her stomach. Every time she saw his family, she felt like an imposter. *I can't envision my future beyond these brick walls, but I love this town.* Watching the tree branches sway beyond the front door, she rubbed the small scar at the corner of her eye and wondered if returning to Ronan had been the right choice. *Maybe I should have gone West.* Looking at the haven she and her father had built, she knew she could never duplicate the store.

Plucky rummaged through a drawer. "I shoulda known you would have the inside scoop about Katie Jesse. I don't know why the *Ronan Daily News* bothers to publish a newspaper."

"It's quaint?"

The phone rang.

Plucky looked at the retro cat phone mounted on the brick wall. "So's that phone. Don't worry. I'll get it."

"Thanks." Picking up a rag, Taylor drifted toward the retirees to pick up plates and brush crumbs from empty tables. Making small talk with the men and women who pulled the strings at the bridge club, she caught snippets of Plucky's conversation.

"Well, she met him yesterday." Plucky spit her gum into a napkin, tossed it in the trashcan and straightened a rack of postcards. "Nah, she'd never go for that."

Mr. Higgins lifted his white ceramic mug. "Peaches, would you mind getting me more coffee?"

Taylor blinked and looked at him. He owned the farm next to her parents' house, and she'd grown up traipsing through his cotton fields. He liked to whittle wood, and she liked to cast tall shadows from his front porch. "Of course."

Walking to the café area, she pulled the urn spigot toward herself. Hot coffee splashed her hand. "Dammit." Turning her head, she found every person in the bookstore staring. Half of them were church elders, and the other half probably had her mother in their contact list. "Sorry, folks... I wasn't paying attention."

Mr. Higgins raised an eyebrow.

"Sure... Come on down. We're open until six." Plucky hung up the phone.

"Who was that?" Taylor asked.

"A reporter from the *Constitution*."

"What did they want?"

"Your inspirational messages caught the editor's eye," Plucky said. "The paper wants to do a news piece on Ronan Reads."

"Today?" She dropped the mug, and it shattered on the wood floor. "I need time to prepare!"

The toddler in the corner laughed.

Getting to his feet, Mr. Higgins ambled toward the coffee urn. "Peaches, you're lookin' a bit piqued. Maybe you ought to close shop for the day."

She shook the liquid from her hands. "What a pleasant idea."

He bent and picked up a piece of broken ceramic.

"No! I'll get that." Reaching across the bar, she grabbed another mug and filled it with fresh coffee. "Take this and let me take care of the mess."

He handed her the shard and accepted the mug. "A day might not be enough. Take your mama into Atlanta."

"Good idea." *I love that woman, but she's about as fun as a lace doily.* Forcing a smile, she watched Mr. Higgins reclaim his seat. *This passive communication style has to go. I can't close up the bookstore. A reporter wanted to profile the business. I need more customers, not fewer!* Smoothing her tunic, she regretted choosing leggings and ballet flats for comfort. "I need to get dressed! I need to clean." She glanced at the floor. "I need a mop!"

Plucky reached for her arm. "Slow down. The reporter won't be here until five." She cleared her throat. "Why don't you send out another message and offer half-priced cookies? We have dough in the freezer, and a bustling crowd will look good in the paper."

Gripping her friend's elbow, she exhaled. "You're the best."

Plucky winked. "Aren't I?"

She grabbed the mop bucket and turned on the hot water. Wordsmithing the next message would eat up time, but Plucky's plan to fill the store deserved a chance. Pouring cleaner in the hot water, she watched the bubbles form and cut off the water before the iridescent show stole her momentum. She plunged the mop in the bucket and wrung out the water. *So much for a slow afternoon.*

After picking up the ceramic shards and cleaning up the spilled coffee, she poured dirty mop water down the drain and rinsed the mop. Wiping her hand across her forehead, she inhaled and savored a moment of satisfaction. *Just do the next right thing.* Pulling her phone from her pocket, she posted another message on the store account.

The world is a wonderful, diverse place. Don't wait for divine intervention to break down your walls — Genesis 12:1-3, 22:15-18. Get up, go to your local bookstore and read! Half-priced, warm chocolate chip cookies until five o'clock!

She exhaled and watched a few local accounts like the post. *I should wear the navy dress with the round collar. Doesn't everyone look better in blue? Why isn't Katie Jesse here to help me with talking points?* She moved to set down her phone, but the screen lit up.

I doubt the Babylonian empire would trade their culture for chocolate chip cookies.

"Of all the" — she bit her tongue and exhaled — "literal things for that man say."

Plucky set the rolls of cookie dough on the counter. "Problem?"

"Of course not." She smiled. *One big, handsome problem.* "I'm going upstairs to my apartment to grab clean clothes."

"Maybe some makeup?"

"Good call. I'll be right back." She scanned the store. "You have this?"

"Of course." Plucky smiled. "Get freshened up!"

She mounted the first stair and paused. "I haven't done laundry in two weeks. I'm wearing these pants for a reason."

Plucky laughed. "Swing by your folks' house. You have time."

Rubbing her face, she nodded. "Of course." She grabbed her keys and her purse, let herself out of the back of the building and walked to her white, late-model car. A hula girl grinned on the dashboard. She started the engine and cranked up the air conditioning. A blast of cooling air hit the air freshener and filled the interior with the smell of sheets drying in the sun. *Crisp linen and blue skies would brighten anyone's day.*

The car engine died.

Frowning, she turned the key and listened to the fast-paced *ruh, ruh, ruh* noise. The last time she'd driven, she'd noticed the car's sluggish morning starts, but she'd blamed the engine's long, dragged-out coughs on age. *My starter isn't going. It's gone.* Dropping her head to the steering wheel, she exhaled and picked up her phone. "Mama?"

"Hello, my love," Nancy said.

She sighed. "I need some help."

"What's wrong?"

Her mother's unflappable tone soothed her anxiety. *She's been an elementary school librarian for thirty years. Of course, she's unflappable.* "I spilled coffee on myself, a reporter's coming from Atlanta to profile Ronan Reads and I haven't done laundry." She cleared her throat. "Can you bring me a clean dress?"

"Oh, is that all? I thought something might have happened."

"My car won't start."

"Your daddy will fix it," Nancy said.

Straightening in the seat, she gave thanks for her father's carpentry and mechanical skills. "I know. He can fix anything."

Nancy laughed. "Well, don't ask him to fix a pie or a drink. That man's cooking skills stop at peanut butter and jelly. Did you know George Washington Carver didn't invent peanut butter? The earliest reference goes all the way back to the Ancient Incas and the Aztecs."

She smiled. "Mom, I need that dress."

"I know, Peaches. I'll swing by the house and be at the shop in fifteen minutes. Do you want me to steam it?"

She closed her eyes. "I'm sure you've already pressed it."

"Oh, you're right. It's probably as good as new. Fifteen minutes."

Exhaling, she considered whether to close her eyes or go back to the bookstore. Plucky deserved her help, and without air conditioning, the car would roast her. "Thanks, Mom." She ended the call and climbed from the vehicle.

Past the brick buildings, pine trees swayed in the breeze, and fluffy white clouds floated across a cerulean sky. *I may not smell like fresh linen, but I couldn't ask for a prettier sky.* Turning, she entered the bookstore and watched Plucky hand a receipt to the mother.

The mother waved to her and ushered her children out of the door.

She waved back and turned to Plucky. "You made a sale."

Plucky shrugged. "I told her we only had one signed copy left."

"But we have two."

Walking toward the children's corner, Plucky cleared her throat. "My bad."

She exhaled and considered the lie. *I have bigger fish to fry.* Pushing in the chairs at empty tables, she grabbed the glass cleaner and advanced on the windows as if her life depended on seeing her reflection. Paper towels piled up at her feet, but each swipe and squeak ratcheted down her stress. *Ronan Reads is an asset to the community.* She closed her eyes and tried to remember the copy on her store's website. *I should have paid more attention to the buzzwords.*

The door opened.

Nancy entered carrying the navy dress draped over her arm. "Peaches?"

She waved.

"Oh, that glass is flawless," Nancy said.

"Good." She shook out her arm. "Although I've probably worked up a sweat and will smell so bad that the reporter will turn tail and run before they finish the interview."

Laughing, Nancy shifted her load and revealed a small cosmetics bag. "I brought some of my makeup, dry shampoo and a few baby wipes. Baby wipes cure –"

She reached for the items. "Everything. Thanks, Mom. Plucky's pulling cookies from the oven. Why don't you grab one and head back to school?" Her mother's smile faltered, and she felt her cheeks warm. "If you want."

"You don't want me to stay for the interview?"

"Of course, but I'm sure you have better things to do." She gestured toward the tables but feared her mother's scrutiny. Her entire life, she had performed her role, but no longer had a child's latitude. If she stumbled on camera with the reporter, she would lose face but ask for a second take. If she stumbled in front of her mother – she swallowed – Nancy had a long memory. "Mr. Higgins went to the restroom, but he'll be right back. I'm sure he'd love to discuss the new school board members and their transgressions."

Nancy stepped backward. "Actually, I have an after-school art class using the library. I'd better go see if they need any help."

She leaned in and kissed her mother's cheek. Nancy's soft, sweet scent made her smile, and she pulled back to meet her mother's gaze. "Thanks, Mama."

"Good luck, Peaches. You'll do great."

Careful not to wrinkle the navy dress, she slipped into the white, tiled bathroom and shucked her stale, coffee-stained outfit. Pulling the dress over her head, she zipped the back and looked at herself in the mirror.

Baby wipes might cure everything, but blush and lipstick definitely help. She fixed the round, white collar, brushed her hair and pretended she'd majored in broadcasting instead of library science. *Who says I don't have screen presence?* She lifted her chin. *Peaches to the rescue!* Opening the bathroom door, she walked across the wood floor.

Plucky whistled.

She rolled her eyes.

"Shoes," Plucky said. "You forgot shoes."

Looking down, she exhaled. "Ballet flats will have to do."

"But they're black." Slipping off her hot pink heels, Plucky offered them.

She pulled off her flats and made the switch. "You're the best."

"Aren't I?" Plucky asked.

Smiling, she heard a customer open the front open and turned to greet the first wave of office workers. These men and women had left their desks at four-thirty, smoothed their khaki pants and reported for cookies. They deserved her attention. Steadying her walk, she made her way to the counter.

Showtime.

Plucky manned the pastry case and snapped the tongs.

Sitting back in his chair, Mr. Higgins crossed his arms and watched the parade of people filling the bookstore.

He looked as skeptical as she felt.

Taking a deep breath, she greeted each guest by name and traded bits of small talk. For the women who resisted the smell of butter and brown sugar, she fired up the popcorn machine and filled small boats with white, popped kernels.

"What's the occasion?" a man asked.

She smiled. "I have a new recipe I wanted to try."

He took a bite out of his cookie. "I liked the old ones better."

"Yes, sir." He walked away, but she continued smiling for the next customer. "Hello, Ms. Meyers."

"I want the cookies, but give me the popcorn. I can't stand this diabetes." She reached toward the warm, oozing sweets but stuffed her hand in her pocket. "When I was young, I would have eaten twelve."

"Me, too."

The woman laughed. "Peaches, you're the definition of young."

Am I?

A woman entered the store and paused. Her long red hair and bright, lemon-yellow dress drew looks from the crowd. White sandals showcased her ankles, and large pearls decorated her ears. Taylor shook her head. *She must be the reporter. Nobody in Ronan wears white before Easter.*

The woman walked up to the counter and smiled. "You're Taylor. You look just like your profile picture." Tilting her head, she smiled. "I'm Rebecca."

She walked around the barrier and shook the woman's hand. "Thank you so much for coming down."

"Oh, we were in the area. A crash has I-75 blocked in both directions. The traffic is horrendous."

"We?" Taylor asked.

The door opened, and a man toting a video camera scanned the shop.

"I thought the *Constitution* sent you," Taylor said.

Rebecca brushed her hair over her shoulder. "The ties between the newspaper and WSB-TV run deep.

Everyone loves a special interest piece. Where can we set up?"

Frowning, she scanned the tables and the shelves. *If a newspaper article is good, a television segment must be better.* She looked for Plucky, but her friend manned the espresso machine like a focused black belt. She forced a smile. "The local section has large-format photography books on stands. I'm sure they'd made a vivid background and give the authors a little extra exposure."

The cameraman nodded. "Perfect. You two will look great in front of the brick. Navy, yellow and red will pop. Y'all make my job easy."

Rebecca grinned. "Don't we?"

Taylor saw Plucky clapping tongs and pretending to pinch the fingers of a small child. "Plucky only works Tuesdays and Thursdays, but she does a lot for the bookstore. Would you like to interview her, too?"

Rebecca tilted her head. "Sure."

Did Plucky know she'd agreed to a broadcast piece? Glancing at her borrowed pink shoes, she took a deep breath and wondered how many newspaper photos featured shoes. If Plucky joined the interview, Taylor would insist they swap back their shoes. She beckoned her friend to come closer. "Plucky?"

Looking up, Plucky wrinkled her nose and shook her head. "Nah, you go ahead."

I wanted to own a bookstore. Now is the time to own it! Taking a deep breath, she positioned herself in front of the shelf she had in mind. "How's this?"

"Great." The cameraman set up a light screen and nodded.

Straightening her shoulders, Rebecca turned to Taylor and smiled. "I'm here with Taylor Lenore, owner of Ronan Reads. Ms. Lenore also posts inspiring messages the residents in our greater metro area love to share. Tell me, Ms. Lenore, what prompted you to start a bookstore in the digital age?"

Keeping her gaze focused on the reporter, she smiled. "Independent bookstores serve individuals and foster collaboration. Their contributions are invaluable, and online retailers can't replicate their ambiance."

Rebecca gestured to the bookshelves. "But so many books! Who reads them?"

Thanks for the support, Vanna. "We serve our community, tourists and remote customers who trust our recommendations and excellent customer service. In my family, literacy runs deep. My mother is a librarian, and my father helped renovate the building."

"Have your inspiring messages boosted sales?"

"What an interesting question," she said. "For as long as I can remember, sharing positive messages was part of my life. I owe the success of Ronan Reads to the help of friends and family, but I can't say whether the messages drive book sales. I simply love to share the Good Word."

Rebecca tilted her head and smiled. "But the messages have certainly extended your reach! How does sparring with Atlanta's most eligible bachelor feel?"

Taylor bit the inside of her cheek.

The red light on the video camera blinked.

Feigning confusion will only make me look ignorant. She widened her smile. "I hope our messaging brightens Mr. Durand's days. Everyone inside and outside of I-285 deserves a smile."

Rebecca laughed. "Oh, I'm not so sure about that fact. Mr. Durand's leadership roles stem from extensive industry and international experience. Do you think he finds your messages quaint?"

"Quaint?" she frowned.

"Rural?"

"I know the meaning of the word!" Smoothing her dress, she kept her elbows pinned to her sides and hoped the navy fabric hid her sweat stains. *We're not live, are we?* "My mother taught me messages matter more than circumstances. Surely, with all that international experience, Mr. Durand has seen the world's beauty."

Raising an eyebrow, Rebecca smiled. "Based on his posts, he doesn't share your view of the world. Who do you think is right?"

"Scripture isn't right and wrong," she said. "Books aren't right and wrong. When you pick up a book, you take a gamble. Sometimes, the book changes your life."

"And other times?" Rebecca asked.

She lifted her chin. "You pick up another book and try again."

"Oh, I believe in trying again."

Rebecca's whispered statement fell short of the cameraman's microphone.

Taylor shifted her stance. "One more thing."

The reporter frowned.

"On Saturday, we're hosting a celebration of free speech at the bookstore, and we love visitors. We invite your viewers to make a day of the trip and explore Ronan's picturesque downtown. The Georgia Municipal Association gave Ronan a Live, Work, Play Award. Come see what's we're all about!"

"Charming." Turning to the cameraman, Rebecca nodded. "We're good."

He slashed his hand and lowered the camera. "Pretty as a picture."

Rebecca shimmed her shoulders. "Thanks, Jeff." Turning to Taylor, she smiled. "Can I get a coffee?"

Her pulse raced. Realizing she held her fists at her sides, she released her hands. *Where would the world be without books? Every pithy, crafted message I post pales compared to a well-thought-out book. Wait! She wants coffee?* "That's it? You don't want to hear about our author events and book clubs?" She scanned the patrons savoring their cookies and their front-row seats. Searching for a way to validate her airtime, she focused on the reporter. "What books do you enjoy?"

"Well, bless your heart. I'm afraid I have little time to read." Rebecca checked her cell phone and looked up at the cameraman. "Traffic's clear. Let's go!"

He nodded and handed Taylor a business card. "If you want a copy of the piece for your website? Call me."

Taking the card, she tried to slip the white paper into her pocket and came up empty. *Stupid dress. I should have stuck with my leggings and called it a day. Thirty seconds of airtime wasn't worth that amount of stress. I could have filmed a better clip with Katie and James.* She watched Rebecca walk toward Plucky, accept a cup of coffee and head toward the door. "Wait!"

Every person in the room turned to look.

Throwing back her shoulders, she walked to the reporter. "Are you acquainted with Mr. Durand?"

Rebecca smiled. "We dated for several years, but nothing came of the relationship." She shrugged. "Who really knows Christopher?"

"I've hardly met the man," she said. "I would prefer to focus the piece on Ronan Reads."

"Would you now?".

"You must have actual news to report." She glanced at the men and women pursuing the shelves. "Atlanta has more than a dozen independent bookstores. Ask their owners about their social media plans. I'm not the only person posting on the platform."

Rebecca glanced at her shoes. "Well, you're certainly the sweetest." Clutching her coffee, she looked at the cameraman and jerked her chin toward the door. "After you."

Left standing in a crowded room, Taylor forced a smile and turned to face her customers. "Well, the show's over! That's a wrap."

The retirees at the round tables clapped.

Chairs shuffled, and a few patrons lined up at the counter.

Taking her place by the register, Taylor buried her doubts. "Thank you for stopping by. It's so nice to see you. What a great selection." Each platitude depleted her reserves.

At closing time, Plucky turned the sign on the door and released the blinds.

The profound silence gave her permission to breath. She exhaled and met Plucky's gaze. "Did you know the reporter wanted to film a video segment? Did you know the reporter wanted to rile me up and trigger a reaction to Mr. Durand's cynical posts?"

"Yes," Plucky said.

She let her mouth drop. "Why? Why didn't you tell me?"

"Gee, I dunno. I figured all those choir performances, leads in the school play and speech competitions conquered your stage fright."

She has lost her mind! I was sweating bullets in front of the camera. "I have a terrible voice!"

Plucky laughed. "Exactly."

Taylor braced her hands on the counter. "The piece wasn't about Ronan Reads." Looking up, she met Plucky's gaze. "The piece was about *him*."

Leaning against the doorframe, Plucky toyed with her cuticles. "They wanted you and Mr. Durand to debate the future of the metro area, but I said you wouldn't do it. Everyone loves watching the church mouse go head-to-head with the industry titian."

"As if." Recalling the man's cynical presence and his tuxedo-clad newspaper photos, she shook her head. "Debates require mutual respect. We have nothing in common."

Pushing in a wayward chair, Plucky shrugged. "You're right. You're polar opposites, but any publicity is good publicity for the bookstore."

"That's not true. The newsroom's editorial team could edit my responses and make me look like a rube."

Plucky laughed. "Rube or not, every time you post or bat your pretty, blue eyes, online sales increase. I'm happy to fulfill the orders." She brushed a speck of dust from the shelf. "What did you expect from the reporter? She's not your high school English teacher. She's here to generate ratings and sell ads."

Slipping off her borrowed heels, she handed them to her friend. "The entire exchange felt mercenary."

Plucky returned her flats. "That's life."

Is it? She slipped on the soft leather shoes, walked to the wall and flipped the light switches. Darkness descended on the red bricks and shiny dust jackets. Making her way through the space that she'd fought to refurbish and develop into a community asset, she paused and looked at the soft spring twilight illuminating the city streets. *I love God, my family and this town. I should be thankful my success doesn't depend on ratings.*

Plucky offered her an arm. "Margaritas?"

Sighing, she nodded. "God knows I want one." Her phone buzzed, and she stumbled mid-stride. Her mom had sent a message inquiring about the interview. Dropping the phone back into her purse, she looked over her shoulders at the orderly merchandise and charming seating areas. *I have so much. What else could I want?*

Chapter Four

Sitting in his darkened corporate office, Christopher listened to Ocelot's project manager tout redesigned plans for the Ronan site. She stood in front of a high-resolution presentation screen, but the figures on the screen meant more to him than her facial expressions. The engineering firm hired to assess the site played up its green features, but the elevated structure looked like a jack-up rig, and the project manager knew it.

From the small table in the corner of the office, his new assistant, Dillan, took notes on his laptop.

Christopher watched the man loosen his tie. *Who wears a tie anymore? My father told me to dress for the job I wanted. Then again, he wears golf shirts and conducts meetings from the greens, while I sit through the presentations.* Unbuttoning the top button of his cotton piqué dress shirt, he rolled his head and blamed the tension in his back on the prolonged meeting.

Dillan stood and stretched his hips.

That kid's is going to plateau in HR. The kneejerk reaction brought him up short. The nation debated 'toxic masculinity', but he'd run through his toddler years like an assertive little asshole, and he'd never slowed down. Losing William and witnessing the war firsthand had improved his emotional vulnerability, but he worked hard to include a range of personalities on his team Accepting his assistant's rhythmic hip rolls, he focused on the project manager and watched her advance her slides.

She stepped in place and swallowed. "Ronan offers a number of strategic advantages."

He scanned the slide's bullets. *No changes from the pre-read. Why does she look like she's smuggling Largemouth?* "Skip to the redesign."

"You had concerns about flooding."

He nodded.

Advancing the slides, she directed the mouse cursor to a floodplain map of Sparrow County "When seasonal flood waters come over the riverbanks, they flood parts of the Ocmulgee Heritage Trail. The county treats the trail like an urban buffer. Boat ramps along the river, including at Amerson River Park, close until water levels go down."

"How high?"

She paused and made eye contact. "Excuse me?"

"How high do the waters get?" He enunciated every word.

Clearing her throat, she looked at a project team member.

The team member dodged her gaze and looked at his notes.

The project manager swallowed. "Since the construction of the Lloyd Shoals Dam on Lake Jackson, the river hasn't risen above…"

"How high?" he asked.

She chewed her lip. "Annually or peak?"

He gave her points for the feint. "Peak."

She straightened her shoulders. "In 1994, a near-record flood of sixty-eight thousand cubic feet per second occurred on the Ocmulgee River. At the dam, the maximum water surface elevation in Lake Jackson reached five hundred and thirty-four feet." She cleared her throat. "On July seventh, the river reached thirty-five feet."

Looking at the printout on his desk, he frowned. "I thought flood level was seventeen feet."

"It is."

Dillan stopped typing.

His new assistant took copious notes, but Christopher hoped Dillan had enough discretion to omit facial tics and colorful reactions from the transcript. Shaking his head, he crumbled the paper and shook his head. "We're done."

The project manager stepped forward. "The power company has better controls in place."

He raised an eyebrow. "The power company can control tropical storms? I remember the 1994 flood. Every television set in the state broadcast the roiling, brown water." He shook his head and set the crumpled paper on his desk before he shot it into the wastebasket and destroyed the project manager's confidence. "I doubt the power company will pay Ocelot's insurance premiums. The Ronan site won't work."

She crossed her arms. "Berms and pumps."

Her pose reminded him of a spirited bookstore owner, but he shook his head. "If the Ocmulgee reaches thirty-five feet" — he raised an eyebrow — "or higher, damage to buildings, electrical systems and mechanical equipment will occur. Ocelot will lose product. Worst-case scenario, we'll lose people."

"The site redesign places the manufacturing floor above thirty-five feet." She slapped another printout on his desk.

"And below it?" he asked.

"Parking facilities and maintenance."

Taylor's dimple and the town's eager officials sweetened the deal, but not enough to compensate for a flooded facility. *Hell, what if the dam breaks? Ocelot is a privately held company, but we're responsible to the public.* "I don't even want to know the price tag." Shaking his head, he gestured to his assistant. "Turn on the overheads."

Dillan pushed a button and flooded the office with light.

Well, he learned that trick. Jerking his head toward the shades, he watched Dillan race to raise them.

"Ronan's out?" the project manager asked.

Turning to her, he nodded.

Her shoulders sank. Packing up her materials, she paused. "The flooding's your only concern?"

"Yes. You did a good job." His answer should have softened the blow. *Who can out-engineer the weather?*

She exhaled. "The 1994 flood was a freak event."

"Accidents happen. Dams break, tropical storms stall and"—he thought of his brother's funeral and exhaled—"well...a berm won't save us from tragedy."

Nodding, she picked up her handouts.

The project team left his office. As the door closed, he heard the project manager compliment her team. *I asked for an impossible task, and she offered a solution. I should send a commendation to her supervisor. Without the* shuffle of papers and fidgeting employees, the ensuing silence felt like a disappointment.

Dillan coiled the power cord for his laptop.

He scrolled through his Friday calendar availability and shook his head at the back-to-back meetings headed his way. *How the hell did Dillan get all these people scheduled on a Friday afternoon?* Dreading the eager smiles of town officials hoping for a site deal, he placed his phone on his desk. "Cancel all my appointments."

Dillan skewed his jaw and frowned. "All of them?"

"Every last one."

Nodding, Dillan opened his laptop. His hand hovered over the track pad. "You're aware several of your appointments traveled to meet with you? On a Friday afternoon?"

Turning his chair, he looked over Ponce de Leon Avenue. The thoroughfare hosted twenty-four-hour donut shops, dive bars and greasy-spoon diners, but the other side of the building looked over a fountain-studded park. *Looking west, at least I can see the people and their vices.* Above the traffic, steely clouds filtered sunlight. A cluster of tornadoes hammered Birmingham, but once the weather crossed into Georgia, forecasters predicted diminished storm activity. "I'm aware of their interest."

"And I should send them home empty-handed?"

Keeping his face to the window, he smiled at his assistant's polite reproof. Raised in Genteel, Dillan seemed capable of handling his moods with measured patience. *I would, too, if a single mother and five sisters raised me.* "If you're feeling put out, take everyone out to dinner."

"I'm not worried about my feelings. I'm worried about..."

The door opened.

Turning in his chair, he dropped his chin and waited to see which impetuous, white-shirted asshole felt brave enough to barge into his office. *I doubt the project manager's coming back for round three.*

C.Y. waved a familiar printout from the project team. "Guess who I saw in the elevator? Been busy?"

Dillan pouted. "Mr. Durand informed me he would like to cancel all his appointments."

C.Y. held up his hand. "Leave off, Dilly. Dickhead already made up his mind about the location of his dinky generator facility. Listen to the man and cancel the appointments. They're a waste of time."

Raising an eyebrow, Christopher crossed his arms, leaned back in his chair and met his friend's gaze. *The man thinks on an imperial scale, but I wouldn't call eighty million dollars a 'dinky' investment.* "You're wrong. The Ronan presentation went south. I haven't made up my mind about the facility's location."

Shaking his head, C.Y. tossed the printout to the desk. "You don't do second chances, but you had the Ronan team re-configure the site drawings. You want them to succeed."

He itched to yank the paper from the desk, crumple it and toss it in the wastebasket. "Unfortunately, the redesign didn't pan out."

"So, choose Montgomery," C.Y. said.

"No."

C.Y. crossed his arms. "Decatur."

His jaw twitched.

C.Y. raised an eyebrow. "Clayton."

"Are you done yet?"

"Actually, no." C.Y. jabbed the printout. "You're biased toward the Georgia site, and I'm calling your bullshit."

Dillan backed toward the door.

Standing, Christopher walked around his desk and stood next to C.Y. Genetics gave him a foot of height advantage, but his friend rarely backed down. *Best hire I ever made.* "The decision matrix erases bias." Sliding the printout from C.Y.'s reach, he smoothed a creased corner. "On paper, Ronan makes sense for the company, but risk modeling eliminates it from contention."

C.Y. rubbed his temples. "The site's in the middle of a flood plain."

"I'm aware of that fact."

"I'll, um…just cancel the appointments." Dillan eased the door closed.

"We engineer the best machines in the world," Christopher said. "Asking the project team to reevaluate their proposal isn't insane." He replayed the project manager's solution set. "Unfortunately, they came up with pumps, berms and a payback period long enough to choke my father."

C.Y. faced him. "You knew how the presentation would play out. Why did you waste their time?"

He crossed his arms. "My grandfather started his company in Georgia. Every other city in the nation increases transportation and labor costs. Why deviate from the momentum of a local asset?"

"Insurance. Labor relations." Narrowing his eyes, C.Y. ticked off his objections on his fingers. "The Ocmulgee River."

He smiled. "Afraid of gators? You need to spend more time in the country, city boy."

"Compared to compared to Beijing and Shanghai, Chengdu *is* the country." Wrinkling his forehead, he mimicked Christopher's directive. "You need to spend more time in the country, city boy."

Laughing, Christopher picked up the printout and stared at the site schematics. He saw the project team's vision, but he questioned their ability to protect the site. "You're right. Ronan's a bust. I wanted that site to work."

"I know." C.Y. pulled up a chair and sighed. "You're loyal to Georgia."

You have no idea. Settling in his desk chair, he felt his watch vibrate and scanned the texted weather alert.

Tornado Watch. Be Prepared! Tornadoes are possible in and near the watch area. Review and discuss your emergency plans and check supplies and your safe room. If a warning is issued or you suspect a tornado is approaching, be ready to act quickly. Acting early helps to save lives!

A curscry alert. The Storm Prediction Center routinely issued watches for the counties where tornadoes might occur. The large watch areas typically covered numerous counties or states. Growing up amid Georgia's pine trees, he'd practiced sheltering in windowless hallways and listening to drill sirens wail. Without thinking, he checked his competitors' stock prices and scrolled through his notifications.

We all learned the Golden Rule — Exodus 19:5-6. A priestly people exists not for itself but for the sake of others. How can you make the world a better place? If paper feels old school, go digital. Your local bookstore knows the best apps and the best reader groups. ¡Viva la tecnología!

How could any person be that encouraging? His thumb twitched. *I have to stop responding to that Pollyanna. William would have fucking loved her, but he's not here, is he?* The doses of religion meant little to him, but he appreciated how she blended them into her messages. If her followers took something from the bits of scripture, more power to them, but he had better things to do with his time.

"What are you looking at?" C.Y. asked.

"Tornado outbreak." The lie came too easily between friends. Looking up, he made eye contact. "Tell the officials in Denham Springs they can have the generator production facility" — he tapped his fingers on the desk and held up one finger to stop C.Y. from leaving — "if they reduce the property taxes by two-thirds."

C.Y. grinned. "Now we're getting somewhere!"

The door opened again.

Do I need a vacancy sign? He watched Rebecca waltz into the room and frowned. *No wonder the receptionist balked.* His ex-girlfriend had a way of bulldozing her way through propriety. "To what do I owe the pleasure?"

Walking around the desk, she leaned down and kissed his cheek. "Lovely to see you. Too tired to stand?"

Gesturing toward C.Y., he shrugged. "Pull up a chair."

"I don't think so."

Worried you'll wrinkle your white linen dress?

Walking toward the door, Rebecca leaned into the hallway. "He's in here!"

He straightened. A cameraman walked into his office and hovered near the doorway. *Smart man.* He met the man's gaze and shook his head. "Out."

The man retreated.

Grabbing the cameraman's hand, Rebecca pulled him back into the office. Crossing her arms, she lifted her chin and stared at Christopher. "Let's talk about your plans for the new plant."

He met C.Y.'s gaze.

The man shook his head.

Walking to Christopher's desk, she sat on the edge and smiled. "Oh, he would never betray you."

"Huh." C.Y. rubbed his chin. "I thought you were just pretty."

She clutched a hand to her chest. "Why, thank you!"

C.Y. smiled. "It wasn't a compliment."

She frowned.

Laughing, Christopher picked up his phone. *The afternoon is already looking up. As soon as Rebecca leaves, I can beg off and hit a few buckets of balls.* "Rebecca, I told you when we select a site for the plant, I'll issue a press release."

"Aren't you tech savvy?"

He brushed away the backhanded compliment. "I have appointments. Go pester someone else."

"You're not too busy to read the posts from Ronan Reads."

Looking up, he frowned. "Excuse me?"

She shrugged. "Every time Ms. Lenore posts an inspiring message, you respond."

"So does half of Atlanta." Frowning, he saw the cameraman hoist his camera and shook his head. "Don't you have real news to cover?"

She rubbed her thumb along the edge of the desk. "The girl's sweet, Christopher. I met her yesterday." Looking up, she smiled. "William would have loved her."

Hearing his brother's name no longer sent a searing pain through his chest. Ten years ago, a drunk driver had changed everyone's lives. Christopher had returned from Iraq and assumed his brother's position at Ocelot Enterprises. His father had retired, and his mother had thrown herself into advocacy work to memorialize her son. *Time doesn't heal all wounds. It gives people the chance to build calluses and protect their nerves.* "Leave William out of this discussion."

"Oh, but the way you talk about him" — she smiled — "I think you're trying to live his life." She rubbed together her lips. "But you don't really know what you want, do you?"

He stood. "Out, Rebecca."

"Chris—"

He picked up the phone. "Security, please escort Ms. Rebecca to the front door."

The cameraman paled.

She stood. "Tell you what... You give me the scoop on the new plant, or I'll run the Ronan Reads piece without you." She smiled. "Unless you'd also like to film a response to Ms. Lenore?"

Raising an eyebrow, he crossed his arms.

"Everyone loves her." She yawned and covered her mouth. "If you want to run for governor, softening your image wouldn't hurt. She would make the perfect first lady. Sweet little thing." She raised an eyebrow. "Isn't that what you want?"

Rebecca's description of a 'sweet' woman covered everything from a twelve-year-old girl to a four-hundred-pound grandma. "You realize we're never getting back together."

She sighed.

The head of security walked in the door, looked at her and shook his head. "I'm sorry, Mr. Durand."

"No more free passes, Michael." He glanced toward Rebecca. "For you or for her. The next time someone barges into my office, I'll fire you, the receptionist and Dillan."

C.Y. laughed. "Oh, come on. Not Dilly!"

Suppressing a smile, Christopher kept his gaze locked on the head of security and channeled his former commanders.

"Yes, sir." Michael swallowed, cupped Rebecca's elbow and led her toward the door.

She looked over her shoulder. "You don't know what you want, do you?"

He raised an eyebrow.

Pulling free of Michael's grasp, she cleared her throat and led the security guard and the cameraman through the door.

"Charming woman," C.Y. said.

Shaking his head, Christopher settled into his chair. "You have no idea."

"Nice ass."

"Go for it." He picked up his phone and looked at the last post from Ronan Reads. Rebecca's observations stung. *Treat others as you want to be treated. I chose to take William's place, but is the choice erasing me? Would I have asked him to make the same choice?*

Stop the guilt. You're a salesperson. I sell equipment. You sell books...and cookies.

Don't worry. I saved several for you.

Her sass summoned a smile. Over the last few days, the bookseller had responded to his rebuttals, but she'd never lost her cool. *Rebecca's wrong about the woman. Taylor's not the sweet little thing people imagine.* Looking up, he found C.Y. watching him. "I don't pay you to sit around my office and bullshit."

"Don't you?"

He raised an eyebrow.

C.Y. stood. "Denham Springs?"

Putting down his phone, he sighed. "Let me think about it."

"You know she's right." Walking toward the door, C.Y. paused. "If you want to run for governor, you do need to improve your image. 'Surly second son' isn't a good campaign slogan."

"I'm not surly." He frowned. "And who said I want to run for governor?"

"The last time we went drinking, you said it yourself."

Christopher exhaled and watched C.Y.'s expression soften. Beneath his tailored suits, C.Y.'s hardened muscles testified to his attitude toward life. His days started at five with a workout and ended at nine with a whiskey. Lately, Christopher had made the workouts but failed to show for the whiskey. "We need to hang out."

"And the governor thing?"

He exhaled. "One day."

"Start an exploratory committee." C.Y. consulted his phone. "Rebecca would be happy to lead it and drain your war chest."

Rolling his eyes, he spun a pen on his desk. "You just want to get rid of me so you can have my position."

C.Y. made a noncommittal noise. "The thought has crossed my mind."

Shaking his head, he stopped the pen and met his friend's gaze. "Focus your attention on splitting the Energy & Transportation segment into two divisions. Electric power generation is the future. I won't let Ocelot live in the past."

"The past makes money," C.Y. said.

"Money isn't everything."

C.Y. jammed his hands in his pockets. "Isn't it?"

He uncapped the pen. "Solid-state battery technology has applications in construction, energy, storage, transportation and mining. Oil, gas and marine applications aren't going anywhere, but instead of huffing diesel fumes and looking over my shoulder, focus on your damn job."

"I know how to do my job."

"Do you?"

C.Y. raised his eyebrows. "Fuck off and focus on your shit list."

"Oh, did you want to play nice with the HR department and labor relations?"

C.Y. winced. "You are a bad-tempered and unfriendly asshole."

Raising the pen, he pantomimed throwing it.

Laughing, C.Y. extended his arms. "Only you would save my life so you could nail me with a fountain pen. I was wrong. You're not surly. You're diabolical.'

Flipping him the bird, he turned his back.

Christopher responded with the expected laugh, but when C.Y. closed the door, he let the pen clatter on the polished wood. *They're both right. How long can I fill*

William's shoes? Looking over Ponce de Leon, he sighed. Dark clouds shadowed the donut shops, dive bars and greasy-spoon diners. Winds pulled leaves from shady elms and forced walkers to clutch their packages to their chest. *A storm's coming.* He reached for the presentation handout and smoothed out the wrinkles. The Ronan design looked space age, but he had to stop living in the past.

Chapter Five

The Lenore farmhouse's faded wallpaper and single-paned windows took Taylor back to her childhood. A pot of chicken simmered on the stove in a rich, peppery broth. Next to the stove, dough rose in an old ceramic bowl, and a thin kitchen towel kept off the breeze. She could almost forget about the interview.

Nancy lifted out the dough and rolled it flat for dumplings. Dropping the scraps back into the bowl, she handed it to Taylor and nodded toward the back door.

She carried the bowl on her hip, opened the door and tossed the scraps to the backyard chickens. The dusty, feathered frenzy brought a smile to her face. Turning into the wind, she let the humid, evening breeze rustle her hair. A bird pecked at her feet. Seeing an opening, she stoked the animal's soft feathers. The hen tolerated her gentle strokes, but Nancy would put away her flock, and they knew who buttered their bread.

Lifting her face to the cloudy sky, she breathed in the familiar mix of sharp clay and crisp pine. *I love Ronan and I built the bookstore of my dreams, but did I make the right choices? Was refusing Josh the smartest or the stupidest thing I've ever done?* Her college memories tasted as bitter as dandelion greens. Shaking off the introspection, she looked beyond the yellow porch light where towering Cherokee rose bushes bloomed and filled the air with a soft, sweet scent. *In the grand scheme of things, my problems are insignificant.* Reaching off the back porch, she plucked a white bloom, inhaled the scent and carried the bloom into the kitchen. As the door clattered in her wake, she filled the scrap bowl with cold water and cast the flower on the surface. *I'm thankful for my blessings.*

"Nothing like the calm before the storm." Nancy pulled a water glass from the kitchen cabinet. "This old farmhouse has been here since the 1890s. I'm sure another spring thunderstorm won't matter."

She replayed the tap-tap-tap of hail hitting the metal roof. Sitting on the front porch as a girl, she'd loved to watch rivers of water fill the porch gutters and cascade over the eves. "You're right, but I love a good storm." Leaving her mother in the kitchen, she walked to the basket of laundry in the living room, picked up a faded chambray shirt and watched muted news coverage of Birmingham tornadoes.

"Go ahead." Jack lowered his newspaper. "Turn it up."

She upped the volume.

"*Several ingredients came together for tornado development.*" The meteorologist pointed to an area map. "*A strong surface low pressure system in north central Tennessee set the stage. The low pulled unseasonably warm and most air north into central Alabama. A surface dryline, or push of dry air from the west, bulged into Alabama and sparked the instability characteristic of strong March weather systems."* The meteorologist shook her head. *"One tornado causes destruction. An outbreak causes chaos."*

The broadcast cut to flattened houses, crushed cars and smoking fires.

Turning from the scenes of destruction, Taylor set down the work shirt and reached for another garment. *I meant I love the kind of storm that cleans the air and leaves everything fresh and green. I don't have room for chaos.* She considered the schedule for the upcoming celebration. *I wonder if the neighboring restaurant owners planned specials. Maybe we could distribute samples.*

Nancy walked into the room. "Oh, look, honey. Peaches is on the TV!"

"What?" Pivoting, she stopped folding her father's shirt and peered at the flat screen.

He set down his newspaper.

Hearing the papers crumble, she wet her lips. *Here we go. How bad could it be?*

Pumping up the volume, Nancy settled in her pink gingham glider.

Taylor waited to hear her voice. At her first utterance, she winced. *I sound like a bubbling helium addict.* Rebecca prompted her onscreen, and her responses sounded increasingly coherent. The segment aired for less than a minute, the news anchor made a transition and relief flooded her system.

"The navy dress was perfect!" Nancy lifted the remote and rewound the DVR's temporary recording. "I bet you'll be swamped for tomorrow's event."

She nodded and set down the shirt. "I couldn't have done it without you." Despite Nancy's needling, she appreciated her love.

Nancy re-watched the interview. "Oh, you're just being modest. Look at my girl, all grown up."

The minute Daddy found out I was going to be a girl, he ordered that pink gingham glider for the nursery. Since then, Mama has sat in it every day of her life. Am I always going to be their little girl? Edging toward the front door, she smiled and wondered how many times Nancy would watch the interview. "I should get a good night's sleep. Plucky's meeting me at six to finish setting up for the event."

Nancy's pleased expression faltered. "You could stay here. I keep your room made up."

She reached for the door handle. "I have to water my plant."

Jack coughed and scratched his late-day whiskers.

Slipping out of the front door, she leaned against the wood and exhaled. *I should take Plucky out to dinner. The news piece wasn't bad!* Shimmying her shoulders, she bounded down the front steps and opened her car door. Remembering the bum starter, she bit her lip and considered her options. "Daddy!"

The front door opened, and he walked down the steps carrying a screwdriver. "I figured you wouldn't get far."

Glancing toward the yellow light spilling from the old farmhouse, she considered staying the night instead of climbing the stairs to the small apartment above the bookstore, but she needed space to stretch out. "I appreciate the help."

Wiggling the screwdriver, he bridged the positive starter terminal and the solenoid terminal. The old trick bypassed the starter relay, sent a direct current to the solenoid and started the engine. Straightening, he brushed dust from the top of the car. "Your new starter should arrive in the morning. I guess they don't stock parts for this model." He scratched his chin. "Maybe we should buy you a new car."

"I'm an adult. I can handle it." Opening the driver's side door, she slipped into the familiar interior. The cloth seats and remnants of sun-washed linen made up for the car's age. "The car's still good."

He palmed the door and paused. "Your mother..."

She's not sick. Nothing's wrong. A strong breeze swayed the pine trees, and the slightest hint of ozone drifted through the heavy, evening air. *She can't be sick.*

"...misses you."

Just good, ole fashioned, Southern guilt. Biting her lip, she nodded. "I'll be back for Sunday dinner. As soon as I close up the bookstore on Sunday, I'm free."

He nodded, closed the door and banged the roof.

Hearing the familiar sendoff, she smiled, cleared the gravel driveway and turned onto the county road.

Unlocking the bookstore's back door, she let her phone illuminate the steps and opened her apartment door. A ticking clock marked her presence. Groping the wall, she turned on the lights and headed toward the droopy Christmas cactus sitting on the coffee table. Unwilling to make herself a liar, she turned on the kitchen tap, wet her fingers, and sprinkled cold water over the plant. *Now grow!*

Collapsing on the cold, leather sofa, she pulled up the news site and replayed her interview. None of her tension and nerves came through the piece. *Thanks, Mama.* Flipping through apps, she wondered if James had taken her hint to call Katie Jesse. *He sits down the hall, but he probably texted her. If it works for them, who am I to argue? I'm just living my dream.*

Wind shook the old windows, and the second-story loft felt empty. *Maybe I should adopt a cat.* She pulled up the bookstore's account.

What are you reading? Quality in and quality out – 2 Samuel 7:12-17, but don't knock romance, science fiction and space odysseys. Cool mornings are lovely, but wouldn't your morning be lovelier with a honey-butter biscuit? Join us Saturday morning for a free-speech celebration and a piping-hot coffee!

Listening to the wind, she revisited her mental task list. Her phone screen flashed. Opening the social media app with a notification, she pulled up her direct messages and found a new one from Christopher Durand.

Your followers should listen to the weather forecast, stay indoors and skip your knock-off version of Banned Books Week.

Local counts.

Only if you've never left town.

Why are you so angry?

Why are you so naïve?

I know Ronan is a blip on his radar, but I can't imagine a sweeter, more loving community. Why does he have to be so negative? She threw the phone into the corner of the couch. After bouncing off a throw pillow, it clattered to the floor. *I'm so glad I sprang for the padded* case. Picking up the device, she placed it next to her and stared at the black screen. *Black like his heart. My mother taught me to care for things, whether they're a year old or a hundred years old. How old is the devil from Atlanta?* Skewing her jaw, she picked up the phone.

'Naïve' might be relative, but traditions count. The long-established customs and beliefs we pass between generations keep people alive. The warmth of bookstores and small-town gatherings can improve lives, even yours. Come on back, Mr. Durand. We'll try again.

Funny, I thought technology and antibiotics kept people alive. I believe in science, machinery and the research that improves people's lives. If you're brave enough to stock this nitty-gritty book on Georgia textiles, you do, too.

You read the book!

I had nothing better to do.

How droll.

She waited. *Ha! He probably had to look up the word.* Crossing her arms, she leaned against the back of the couch and smiled.

A minute passed.

Opening her eyes, she eyed the phone. *He's right. He has better things to do than banter with a bookseller.*

The device lit up.

Snatching it to her chest, she opened the notification.

Take a break from the parochial covenants and get back to your book reviews and recommendations? What are you adding to the discussion?

She swallowed.

Covenants are like theological glue binding a book's pages. Without covenants, the path from promise to fulfillment would scare the stoutest believer. I'm sharing the light at the end of the dark, twisting path.

Are you the type of person who reads the ending first?

Squeezing shut her eyes, she considered how to respond to his question. Posting scripture and messages made her feel productive, spread the Good Word and drove book sales. Before her engagement had ended, she'd believed in all kinds of covenants. She believed the aspirational messages the town leaders shared with the youth. She believed her parents' dreams for her future. Now, she exhaled and wondered if the covenants governing her life were platitudes in disguise. *Stay calm.*

No.

Liar.

I believe in happily ever after.

I'm sure you do.

She seethed and wanted to debate face to face. *Are we talking about books, religion or weather?* She scrolled through their posts and responses. His comments infuriated her, but her follower count climbed before her eyes and topped a hundred and twenty thousand. *"Bad company ruins good morals." One naysayer shouldn't undermine my message. Instead of sinking to his level, maybe I should block him, take my ill-gotten gains and run.*

The only twisting path you should worry about is the one on radar. Dual-polarization weather radar saves lives, but only if people heed notices and take shelter.

Doesn't everyone have to power to make their own choices?

Haven't you ever heard of unintended consequences?

Tilting her head, she exhaled. Although God made a good world, humans chose good or bad deeds. *A celebration of free speech can't be a wicked deed. Who could suffer?*

I hope you'll join us on Saturday.

I hope you'll cancel the event. 'Love thy neighbor more than thyself.'

That isn't a commandment.

It should be.

Ridiculous man. She buried the phone under a pillow and considered her entertainment options. The television beckoned, but if she wanted to live other people's lives, she would open a book. Downstairs, her slim portfolio of Shakespeare's sonnets waited by the cash register, but tackling the stairs seemed like too much trouble. A bottle of wine sat on the countertop. Remembering her fight with the margaritas, she shook her head. *Well, at least I have a bed.*

Ensconced in soft, cotton sheets, she trailed her fingers across her collarbone and thought of the men in her life who'd caught her eye. Nobody in Ronan came to mind. Thinking of Atlanta, she remembered Christopher Durand dressed in a tuxedo on the front page of the newspaper. *Strong jaw. Stubborn pride.* Shaking her head, she flung her arm over her eyes. *He might be as handsome as sin, but I'm not that desperate.*

* * * *

On Saturday morning, Taylor eyed the stale bagels in her refrigerator. *I should have stayed with my parents.* Closing it, she bit into the boiled bread and sighed. *Mom's eggs and bacon would keep me going, but I can buy bacon and eggs, too.* She trooped down the stairs, eyed the pastry case and reminded herself not to eat the inventory.

Boxes of red, white and blue decorations waited on the round tables. The combination of burlap and patriotic colors made the decorations look vintage. Semi-circle bunting would hang over the windows, and strings of pennants would ripple between the exposed beams, but she only had an hour to hang them.

Pulling the ladder from the storage closet, she picked up the first piece, held a pushpin between her lips and climbed the rungs.

Plucky came through the back door. Looking up, she tilted her head. "Who are you channeling? Betsy Ross?"

Pulling the pin from her mouth, she tacked the first pennant string to an exposed beam. "Better than margaritas! Grab the other end of the bunting and help me get ready for Alma's day."

"Doesn't her name mean, like...*ghost*?" Plucky unfurled the rest of the patriotic streamers. "It's a Spanish name."

Pushing the pin into the wood, she exhaled. "Soul."

"Oh, yeah. I should get one of those."

Laughing, she climbed down the ladder and picked up the next decoration. Forty-five minutes later, she surveyed the bookstore. "Okay, let's go over the agenda."

Plucky grabbed a copy of the flyer and read it aloud.

9:00 a.m.: Virtual Q&A with the author of *Manners Don't Win Beauty Pageants*

10:00 a.m.: Panel discussion on the censorship of LGBTQIA+ stories

11:00 a.m.: Censored book title bingo

12:00 p.m.: Readings on Black voices, racism and systemic brutality

Taylor grinned. The older she grew, the more she enjoyed taking risks and challenging other people to call out her audacity. She'd grown tired of stealing kisses, speeding down empty roads and courting conflict in the name of free speech, but she wondered when her liberties would amount to more than terse conversations and gallons of sweet tea. "Well, that agenda should make for a lighthearted day."

Plucky laughed. "Go big or go home."

"Exactly." She checked her watch. "The kids' activates start after lunch. I figure the littles are napping, and the emerging readers need something to do."

"What about the kids who like margaritas?" Plucky asked.

Laughing, she checked the nametags. "The closest you've come to South America is the tortilla machine. You need a new hobby."

"A girl can dream."

She stared out of the window. For all the talk of storms, the distant, dark gray clouds looked like any other rainstorm. The news had proclaimed Saturday a 'Weather Warn Day', and the storm center had issued a tornado watch and a flash flood watch through two o'clock in the afternoon. "One day, we'll all have the vacations we need." She reached for the posters describing historical First Amendment cases. "Even Shakespeare took vacations, right?"

Plucky rolled up a spare decoration. "Ew-w. I can't stand the codpieces and the stuffy, grammatically correct phrases. Who the hell says 'whence'?"

She opened her portfolio to the bookmark and wondered if Plucky had flipped through her book. "From whence at pleasure thou mayst come and part, and even thence thou wilt be stol'n I fear. For truth proves thievish for a prize so dear." *Maybe we can dig into Sonnet 48 after the event.* "I know relating to history can seem difficult, but the work is worth the prize."

Plucky laughed. "The only prize I want is a platinum credit card."

"What would you buy?"

"A yacht. Three hundred and sixty-five pairs of shoes. A maid."

She frowned. "You can't buy a person."

Plucky rubbed together her hands. "I can try!"

She shock her head at the improbability of a millionaire's life, put down the posters and watched the clouds. Everyone in middle Georgia knew the weather drill. Two-to-three inches of rain would fall in punishing, wind-whipped sheets. Anyone living along creeks, streams and rivers would closely monitor the water for quick rises. After the clouds passed, the songbirds would return. *Won't they?* "That jackass in Atlanta is right. I am running a business." Exhaling, she considered the power of social media. "If we can sell cookies with a spur-of-the-moment post, we can postpone Alma's day, too."

"What?" Walking across the room, Plucky gripped her shoulders. "No! This is *our* event! You sent flyers to every business in town. I posted paid advertisements. What about the panel speakers? The people who come to the event will stay for lunch and poke through the downtown shops."

She bit her lip. Like the old farmhouse, Ronan had survived many storms. The city owned its early success to railroads and cotton, but it had survived the Civil War, Reconstruction, a boll-weevil infestation and the Great Depression. When imported textile goods had threatened to tank the local economy, city leaders had diversified and proven the persistence of the residents' grit and mettle. *I doubt Christopher Durand will read the sequel to his textiles primer.* A proud resident of Ronan, she nodded. "You're right. Let people make their call. Worst-case scenario, we'll shelter in the basement."

"Exactly!"

Eyeing the door to the basement, she swallowed. The old brick building, completed in 1910, had once housed city council chambers, a fire hall and city offices. After the city modernized, the building had sat vacant, the roof deteriorated and water damaged everything within reach. Her father had bought the building for a dollar and a pledge to rehabilitate it. For years, she'd helped him repair neglect, refinish floors and paint trim. She knew every inch of the space and trusted its integrity. *How long can the old guard's infrastructure hold?*

One source of strength outlasted all others. Pulling her phone from her pocket, she fired off the last of her drafted messages.

I'm struggling today, but I know God will lift me up — Jeremiah 31:31-34. From the least to the greatest, we all want hope and love. Bring a friend to the Alma Celebration. Clang a cymbal. Bang a gong. This year, Easter is late, but He comes! — Hebrews 8:7-13; 9; 10:11-24.

"Taylor?" Plucky asked.

Looking up, she met her friend's gaze. "Huh?"

"You want coffee or not?"

"Coffee. Definitely coffee." Her phone vibrated. Expecting an urbane, surly response from Durand, she steeled herself to weather his cantankerous, capitalist remarks.

The National Weather Service in Peachtree City, GA has issued a tornado warning for Carroll County in Northwest Georgia until 7:30 a.m. EST. At 6:56 EST, a confirmed large and extremely dangerous tornado was located 4 miles west of Carrolton and moving southeast at 25 mph.

She swallowed. "Geez, the storm line's headed right down I-20."

"Any touchdowns?" Plucky asked.

She pulled up a new app. "Not since Birmingham." The flattened homes and flipped vehicles on last night's news broadcast flashed through her mind. "Atlanta can't take a hit."

"Probably petering out," Plucky said. "Nothing has happened in the last twelve hours."

A second notification lit up her phone. *What? They couldn't fit the doom and gloom on one screen?*

This is a particularly dangerous situation. Damaging tornado confirmed from trained spotters. Flying debris may be deadly to those caught without shelter. Mobile homes will be destroyed. Considerable damage to homes, businesses and vehicles is likely and complete destruction is possible.

Carroll County is too close. "Maybe we should cancel the event."

Brushing her bangs out of her eyes, Plucky yawned. "Do you hear sirens?"

She frowned. Somewhere in Carroll County, the cloudy skies, raging winds and NWS alert would have to trigger more than a yawn. Someone would have to receive the alert, confirm a localized threat and pressed a proverbial 'red button' to activate the civil defense sirens. The eerie, pulsing wail of the sirens would alert residents until the threat expired.

Walking to the front door, she lifted the shade and scanned the roofline of the bank. Above the prized concrete gargoyles, a painted siren presided over the Historic District. For now, the siren remained quiet. Unlike broadcast messages, the county designed the warning devices to go off in specific towns, not throughout the county — and certainly not throughout the region. "You're right."

The phone screen faded to black.

Relieved, she set the device on the table. Turning her back, she surveyed the bookstore. Within minutes, regular customers and interested attendees would fill the tables and peruse the shelves. Her phone vibrated. She jutted forward her chin, picked up the device and scanned the notification. *Enough with the NWS alerts!*

Which part of your religion recommends sacrificing your friends and loved ones? Pay attention to modern technology and cancel the Alma thing, Taylor.

She wanted to lash out and defend her event. *Alma wouldn't be silenced, and neither will I!* Swallowing her bile, she frowned. *What am I trying to say to the world?* She reread the message. *He used my name.*

"What's wrong?" Plucky asked.

She looked up. "I can't shake my misgivings about the storm."

"Oh, for the love of God." Yanking her phone from her hand, Plucky tabled the device. "How many times have we practiced tornado drills? How many times have we laughed over safe rooms and dug through old preparedness kits? Did we ever use the N-95 masks for a storm? No. We used them for that damn pandemic."

"Shh-h." Pulling her friend into a hug, she rubbed Plucky's back. Her dad succumbed to the virus, and nothing she or her neighbors did would lessen the loss. "You're right. I'm overreacting, but I can't stop thinking about the kids and the elderly. How fast can we move a herd of octogenarians? What if we're not fast enough?"

Sniffling, Plucky collapsed against her shoulder. "We can never be enough." She pulled back and wiped a tear from her cheek. "I'm sorry I pushed you. You love this city and this bookstore, but you love the people more. Of course, we should cancel the event. The storm's just a piss shot away."

She laughed and released her. "Everyone can stay put. We'll celebrate Alma tomorrow. Who cares whether we have panel discussions and bingo?" She scanned the book-filled room. "We have this space!"

Plucky wrinkled her nose. "Isn't she lovely?"

Putting her hands on her hips, she wished her friend offered the type of camaraderie, shared knowledge and absolute acceptance she craved. *Most 'brick homes' in the county were wood-frame structures with 'brick veneers'. But this old building?* She felt like banging the sturdy, old walls to prove a point. *Rock solid.* "If you'd spent more time sanding banisters and less time polishing the quarterback's dick, you'd appreciate the store."

Laughing, Plucky leaned over and slapped the table. "I didn't think you had it in you." She waved her hand toward the shelves. "By all means, cancel the love fest! Let's set up the projection screen, watch X-rated movies and rate the actors' asses."

She looked at the plate-glass windows and wished she'd invested in blinds. *I'll save ass-judging activities for myself, thank you very much.* Durand's ass came to mind, and she squashed the thought. A cloudy sky hovered over the city and few cars traversed the quiet streets. Shaking her head at the thought of senior citizens rapping on the glass, she exhaled. "Let's not go overkill. Flip over a poster and practice your best sorority bubble letters. The event's off, but we're still open for business."

"You know I wasn't in a sorority."

She winked. "But you were curious."

"I'm curious about a lot of things." Plucky tucked a poster under her arm and rummaged in a drawer for a large-format marker. "Curious is a long way from covetous."

"What?"

Plucky waved off her question. "Go cancel your event."

Sighing, she considered what to say. Without time to select a quote or search for the perfect verse, she fell back on good manners and simple pleasures.

Due to the threat of severe weather, the Alma Celebration will occur on Sunday. The employees of Ronan Reads suggest grabbing your favorite book, making a hot cup of coffee and savoring the last of the cool weather. Summer's coming, and it'll be a hot one! Stay safe!

Finally, common sense.

She wanted to ignore him, but if she climbed the church steeple on a clear day, she could see the county line. Birmingham had succumbed to the storm, and I-20 led right to Atlanta.

Stay safe.

Her heart beat once.

You, too.

She pulled a shot of espresso and warmed whole milk in the microwave. Boxes of new releases waited in the stock room. Grabbing a dolly from the closet, she loaded the lift tray and wheeled it toward the front of the store. A gust of wind blew last year's brown leaves from the elm tree. Spring's bright, green buds stayed put and tested the gray-blue sky. *The clouds look darker.* She frowned.

Plucky taped the poster to the front door, turned and eyed the cardboard boxes. "New releases?"
Throwing up a quick bun, she nodded. "I love the first pulse of summer reads. The big hitters come out in the fall, but the summer reads make people happy." Sipping her quick latte, she read back covers and skimmed Chapters. Thunder rumbled. She looked up and caught a flash of lightening. "The weather's beginning to storm."

Yawning, Plucky reached for a purple book. "People'll take shelter until the lightning stops."

She nodded. Setting down her book, she reached for her coffee and found the mug empty. Lightning cracked nearby, and she started. Looking outside, the sky had darkened to a heady, green-tinged twilight. Light rain fell, and the elm tree's smaller branches succumbed to the wind, snapped off the main limbs and skittered along the sidewalk.

Watching the tumbling foliage, she frowned. *The leaves are blowing around kind of funny.* The sky darkened further. She pressed her hand against the cool glass and peered between buildings to catch sight of the horizon.

A limb snapped off the elm and blew against the thin, old glass. The pane shattered beneath her touch, and she screamed and squeezed shut her eyes. The wind lashed her face and blew raindrops along her cheeks. Their erratic landings scored her exposed skin. She felt the sharp stings, but afraid of the glass minefield littering the floor, she held fast.

"Taylor! Are you okay?" Plucky asked.

Nodding, she opened one eye and faced the storm. *Nothing more.* "Startled, is all." She surveyed the damage and sighed. "Let me call the hardware store and see if they'll bring over some plywood."

The wind shifted, and she felt pulled toward the opening. The tree fought the wind, and she wondered which force of nature would win. "Plucky?"

"I'm getting the broom." Plucky opened the closet door, and it clattered against the brick wall. "Get someone over here before we lose all our inventory!"

Lifting the phone, she scrolled through her contacts. Before she could find the hardware store, Jack's call claimed the screen. *Does he have eyes everywhere?* She raised the phone to her ear. "Daddy, I'm fine."

"Get to the basement."

"It's just a broken window."

"Mr. Higgins doesn't like the look of the sky!"

His clipped intensity claimed her attention. *He doesn't know about the window.* "What do you mean?"

"Basement, Peaches. Go!"

She met Plucky's gaze. "Daddy wants us to take shelter."

"From a thunderstorm?"

She stared at the gaping hole in the storefront and the water pooling amid the shards of glass. "Mr. Higgins doesn't like the look of the sky."

"Peaches!"

Jack's entreaty punctured her indecision. Grabbing Plucky's arm, she pulled her toward the basement stairs.

Plucky planted her feet. "Do you hear sirens?"

She yanked harder and vowed to apologize after the storm passed. "Let's go."

"Humpf." Plucky shook off her grip. "I'm coming. A whole county full of police, fire and trained spotters, but we're listening to the damn farmers."

A section of shingled roofing blew down the street, and she felt the pressure change. "Now!"

She and Plucky clamored down the wooden stairs, but the rising wind drowned the sound of their footsteps. Racing for the oldest part of the basement, she crouched in the corner and pulled Plucky down beside her. The lights flashed and went out.

"Mother of God!" Plucky said.

Feeling Plucky against her side, she wrapped an arm around her shoulders and listened to the rising wind.

The basement door flapped and blew off the hinges.

Squeezing her eyes shut, she recognized the symbolic shattered glass and thanked God for the warning. Somewhere beyond the confines of the old brick building, a storm threatened Ronan, and the only thing she could do was pray. "God, protect us from all storms and lightning. Christ went through their midst in peace."

The winds gusted. Above the howl, lightning cracked and sporadic debris hit the building. The pressure in her ears shifted, and a loud rumble like a heavy tractor plowing the fields shook the building. "I always thought it would sound like a freight train!"

Plucky buried her head against Taylor's shoulder.

Lifting her chin, she watched the dust-choked doorway above the stairs and prayed the dim rectangle of light would not be the last thing she saw in this life.

Within minutes, the fury subsided, and she heard her heartbeat above Plucky's whimpering sobs. "We're okay."

The warning sirens wailed to life.

Plucky lifted her head. "A bit fucking late."

Closing her eyes, she exhaled and gave thanks she lived to experience the joy of another day. "Forecasting isn't an exact science."

"Tell that to the farmers! I owe them like…a cow or something for saving my life." Struggling to her feet, Plucky smoothed her shirt and held her palm to her chest. "I'm moving to the tropics."

"Hurricanes," she said.

Plucky shook her head. "They have to be easier to bear."

The banter lightened her steps, but she replayed the driving fury of the twister. Someone in Ronan had succumbed to the storm, and the sobering reality tempered her exuberance.

Gripping the railing, she tested its strength. *Thanks, Daddy.* She climbed toward the hazy light and braced her heart for the damage to the bookstore. Stepping onto the main floor, she felt a chill. The western side of the building lay in ruin. Books and broken bricks littered the floor, but she inhaled and nodded. *We'll rebuild.*

Stepping over the rubble, she made her way through the rain-soaked building and peered through the dusty twilight. The elm lay on its side, uprooted like a loyal sentinel afraid to leave its post. She stepped through the window opening and reached for the soil-caked roots. *I'll plant another tree.*

The siren quieted.

Looking up, she felt the wind shift and gasped. Broken silhouettes presided over the street, debris littered the pavement and smoldering fires spiraled smoke into the steel-gray sky. Pushed against buildings, cars rested on their sides. The fire hydrant spewed water, and a lone dog howled. She searched for a landmark at the edge of her vision and spotted the bell tower on Central Alley. In the other direction, her uncle's church on Chapel Hill lay in ruins. Between the two icons, people stumbled to the street's hazy safety, and she felt lucky to be alive.

"Good God." Plucky wrapped her arms around her waist. "I can't believe we survived."

Biting her lip, Taylor nodded and wondered who she would count among the dead.

Chapter Six

In the basement of his home, Christopher powered through an early morning workout and pushed his frustration into his repetitions. Sweat dripped down his back, and he thrust the air from his lungs. *Can't a man get a breath of fresh air?* Thinking of the destruction in Ronan, he closed his eyes. *Is Taylor Lenore alive?*

"Go easy on yourself," C.Y. said.

"Fuck off." Reversing his grip on the pull-up bar, he restarted his count. Two hours of high-intensity training had done nothing to erase his guilt. *I told her to cancel her event, but I should have told her to take cover.* Since last Saturday, the bookstore's account had remained dark.

Every year, the National Weather Service issued thousands of warnings, but the F4 that had destroyed Ronan's downtown had slipped under the radar like a third of all events. In their nine a.m. EST outlook, the Storm Prediction Center had identified a thunderstorm barreling toward the Atlanta area, but they'd missed the independent supercell that had spawned Ronan's destruction. Well ahead of the main storm system, the flurry of energy had torn buildings to pieces and claimed seven lives.

What a dick move, spouting off about technology while the entire system failed the woman. Gritting his teeth, he closed his eyes and continued his count. *Failed Taylor.* In the early morning hours, he'd scoured the Internet to locate her name among the list of survivors. There she was, shining from the archive as Little Miss Georgia Peach Queen, reigning over homecoming from a glossy convertible and leading story-time while mischievous children mugged for a local reporter. Unable to speak her name, he shredded his muscles and let the images sear his brain. He doubted she would rise from the ashes like a fucking phoenix, but he struggled to find her name listed among the dead. *Wouldn't Ronan's pride and joy take center stage?*

Since touchdown, every aid organization in the country had descended on the small town, and he'd found himself unable to avoid the news coverage. Rebecca had spearheaded the morning news and balanced sober facts with human-interest stories. He'd ignored the redhead and watched the segments for signs of Ronan Reads. *Nothing.* Watching the coverage became a penance, and he understood the militant pilgrims who whipped themselves for their sins. *I should have kept my advice to myself. I have the bookstore's number, but I need Taylor's personal line. Why doesn't Rebecca have it?*

Pushing his body through an aggressive workout, he watched his form in the mirrored wall. *What good am I? What can I do?* His muscles tightened and burned. Instead of lifting weights, he used his body as resistance. *All the training in the world, and I can't do anything but sit back and watch destruction unfold.*

C.Y. switched to hanging reverse crunches.

His bare chest rose, fell, and taunted him into more repetitions. Sweat dripped into his eyes. Losing his grip, he fell to the matted floor. Lying beneath the lights, he wanted to return to the simplicity of Iraq, where he took orders instead of giving them.

"You ever heard of moderation?" C.Y. crouched beside him. "How's beating yourself up going to help you win in a complex world?"

He threw a hand over his eyes. "Save me the army bullshit. If I wanted to regress to Fort Benning, I'd throw my ass in the car and drive to Columbus."

"You're about as pathetic as a new recruit."

Shifting his weight, he knocked C.Y. to the ground and pinned him. "What do you suggest, pretty boy? A massage?"

C.Y. laughed and pushed off his weight. "If that's what you need, I'm happy to schedule it."

"Don't give me your fucking sloppy-seconds."

Laughing, C.Y. reached for a towel. "Unlike you, I don't pay people to get laid." He flicked on the television and muted the coverage of Ronan's destruction. "What's the upkeep on the redhead?"

Rising, he shook his head. "She's too much trouble for you."

C.Y. slung the towel over his shoulders. "I'm feeling rich."

He ran a hand through his sweat-soaked hair. "Buy a boat. I'm going to run and grab a shower. Tell Greta to make breakfast."

Nodding, C.Y. pressed a button on the intercom. "Two omelets."

"Yes, Mr. Dong," Greta said over the intercom.

He bit back a smile. Greta traced her roots to the Sea Islands Gullah community. She'd started as his nanny, whispered of juju and never left his side. He wondered if her disdain for C.Y. stemmed from second sight or a subtle war between two influencers. His friend was always 'Mr. Dong' to his face and 'that dick' to his back. He struggled not to laugh, but Greta's humor molded his attitudes as much as her cooking. As long as he had Greta and C.Y. in his life, he would be all right. *Unlike the people in Ronan.* His smile dissipated.

"Have you picked a site for the generator production facility?" C.Y. dropped to the mat and braced his arms for pushups.

He grunted and started the treadmill. Five miles at a punishing pace should do the trick. He pounded the belt, but the sweat pouring down his back refused to carry away his concerns.

Sitting back, C.Y. worked his jaw. "Ronan's obviously out."

Looking down, he met the man's gaze and slowed the belt. Every jackass with an Internet connection could follow his quips to Ronan Reads. Since the tornado, Taylor's silence grated on his nerves and apprehensions. For the past week, his short-tempered retorts scared away everyone in the office, but C.Y. stood by his side. *Why hasn't he called out my bullshit?* Clearing his throat, he came to a stop. "Ronan seems unlikely."

"Montgomery."

"No."

C.Y. leaned on one arm. "Decatur."

His jaw twitched.

C.Y. raised an eyebrow. "Clayton."

"I told you, Denham Springs was my next choice." He felt like punching something. C.Y.'s attention to the bottom line usually thrilled him, but in the face of community destruction, Ocelot's success felt excessive. Standing in the basement of a six-bedroom mansion, he exhaled. *Where is Taylor?*

Rising, C.Y. grabbed a towel and wiped down the mat. He chucked the towel toward his chest. "You're like a dog with a bone."

Catching the towel, he climbed off the treadmill and considered responding with a punch. His muscles ached for violence and a solid release. He wondered if an old-fashioned wrestling match would obliterate his concerns, but ineptitude felt like a heavy mantle. *I'm too old to play.* Exhaling, he tossed both towels in the hamper. "I'm getting dressed and heading to the office."

C.Y. frowned. "What about the omelets?"

He rolled his eyes. "You can have mine."

"This was great." C.Y. braced his hands on his hips. "Let's do it again sometime."

Raising his finger, he gave his friend the bird.

* * * *

An hour later, showered and shaved, he jogged down the oversized front porch and climbed into his truck. A long driveway led to the main road and a straight, twenty-minute shot to downtown. Buckhead sat along the east side of Interstate 85 and the west side of Interstate 75, but compared to the mess in Ronan, the neighborhood might as well be on the other side of the world.

Instead of punishing himself for failing to act, he hit the pedal, felt the truck lurch into action and chose recovery. "Call Dad."

The hands-free system broadcast a ringtone.

"Boy!" his father said.

Boy. The nickname rankled. *We were interchangeable to you, weren't we?* "Dad."

"You coming out to play the course?"

He gripped the steering wheel. After stepping down as president, Richard had built an estate next to an excellent Marietta golf course. The Atlas Coast Conference often chose the pristine, rolling course for a tournament location. Sprawling estates, Civil War sites and groomed trails surrounded the holes, and fans came out to watch. *Like my father has ever set foot on a dirt trail. He prefers shaving off strokes and gloating to the caddies.* "Busy, sir. I'm taking equipment down to Ronan."

"Oh, yeah? The local dealer put in a rush order?"

"Nope. Ocelot Enterprises is chipping in on the recovery effort." He switched lanes and wondered how long his father would let the silence stretch.

"Unnecessary. The Ocelot Foundation invests in the US Annual Disaster Giving Program."

He nodded. The company's annual contribution helped the Red Cross open shelters, provide meals and assist residents displaced by disasters, but it kept Ocelot out of the fray. Pooling Ocelot's funding with other corporate funding sources made sense and an immediate, scalable impact, but it did nothing for the itching fear keeping him awake at night. "I'm aware."

"The people running the aid organization have it covered, Boy."

"I want to do more." He waited for another long pause.

"Trust me. Responding to individual disasters is a PR nightmare. Every time a disaster strikes, the affected community will expect Ocelot to scale up our response efforts. If you go down to Ronan, you're setting a dangerous precedent."

He stroked the steering wheel. "Who runs the company, Dad?"

Richard cleared his throat. "You do. You don't have a boss."

"Great. I'm going to Ronan. I'll deal with the fallout."

"I don't like the moves you're making. The company's growing, and you deserve credit, but maybe it's getting too big for our family. Maybe we should hire outside executives with proven track records."

He laughed. *Outside executives don't work for privately held firms where former executives think their voting rights are a free pass for micromanagement.* "You going to pay their salary out of your share of the profits?"

Richard snorted. "Last year, most of our competitors sold off non-essential business segments and took accounting write-offs to bolster their financial statements."

"They want to go public." Knowing his father would never relinquish control, he let the statement sink in. He'd begrudgingly taken on Ocelot, but the company thrived under his leadership, and he knew better than to lose their lean maneuverability in stacks of regulatory filings and legal briefs.

"Tell me what Ronan does for the company."

He thought about the scenes of destruction and the constant tension between rural and urban populations.

Georgia often felt like a slow, burning fuse. If business leaders and politicians kept looking away, the tensions would explode. "Watch the news, Dad. The town needs help. We should do more than pay taxes and claim write-offs from our disaster fund contributions."

"We keep people employed!"

"In this economy, that's not enough."

"Boy, you're turning into a socialist."

Richard practically spit out the word. Ice clinked in a glass, and Christopher wondered if he'd misjudged his father's location. For years, his father had muttered about foreign influences. Immigrants, socialists and secularists rose to the top of his bully list, but Christopher had tuned out the rants and focused on the bottom line. Ocelot's employees needed a basic quality of life to thrive, and the company was profitable enough to compensate them. *I want people to work hard, do a good job and come back to work the next day. We've cut attrition by thirty percent. That's not socialism, it's common sense.* "No, sir, but I'm the one handling grievances and profitability reports. My neck is the one on the line."

"Is this about your greenie weenie prototypes? William wouldn't have been this idealistic and pigheaded..."

He shook his head and ended the call. The gesture pained him, and he worried that his drive to modernize would destroy what little family he had left.

* * * *

"Dillan!" Christopher tossed his belongings on his desk.

Rising from the table in the office's corner, Dillan nodded. "I'm here."

"The trouble in Ronan…"

"Terrible."

He glowered. *Why couldn't HR find me a tech-savvy fifty-year-old project manager who's counting his days until retirement?* "I know it's terrible. I don't need you to summarize the news."

Dillan swallowed.

He exhaled and rubbed his temple. *What did the media coach tell me? Try to be more approachable?* He focused on his assistant and wondered how his father would handle the situation. Based on Richard's philosophy, Human Resources had three functions — payroll, hiring and pink slips. Christopher knew times had changed, but he regretted letting the HR department manage his assistants. Most employees imagined the HR department as benevolent purveyors of health insurance and paid time off, but Richard's generation viewed employees as the resources requiring management. Fifty years ago, Ocelot's equipment, factories, capital and employees had bowed to the company's needs, but times, jargon and leadership had changed. Under Christopher's watch, onboarding, balanced scorecards, cultural integration and the eighty-twenty rule drove patience and performance. He smiled. "Tornadoes rarely strike downtown areas."

"Ronan is hardly a large city," Dillan said.

Thanks for stating the obvious. Exhaling, he fired up his computer and summoned patience. "Tornado paths can go anywhere. In less than a century, four different tornadoes have hit St. Louis, Missouri. Given our national footprint, we should prepare Ocelot Enterprises to respond to crises near manufacturing centers. The quicker employees meet their needs and their families' needs, the quicker they can get back to work. Where better to start than in our backyard?" He looked up from the computer. "I'm talking about Ronan."

"You want to write a check to speed the recovery? The Ocelot Foundation invests in the US ADGP. We're already funding part of the disaster response."

He narrowed his eyes. "I know where my money goes. We're putting boots on the ground."

"Yes, sir." Dillan nodded. "Neighboring dealers and organizations supported by the Ocelot Foundation will spring into action. Excellent photo opportunities. I'll inform Mr. Dong."

He shook his head. *C.Y. knows me too well, and he'd give me shit for caring about a woman I've barely met.* He could spin his decision a million different ways, but he had to know if the lion tamer lived. "You, Dilly. You and I are going to Ronan." His assistant paled. He tried not to laugh. "We're going to be like really good neighbors."

"But what will we do?" Dillan loosened his collar.

"Drive equipment. Shovel rubble." He raised an eyebrow. "You can drive, can't you?"

Dillan nodded.

"Great." He stared out of the window. "Call the dealer in Sparrow Country. They're on the scene in Ronan, but tell them we're bringing reinforcements." He'd done his best to expedite orders for traditional skid steers, but his factories moved at predetermined rates. Terse calls could shift delivery priorities, but they couldn't manifest machinery out of thin air. Falling back on relationships, he'd called area dealers and asked them to trade priorities and release prior claims. Undoubtedly, every dealer in the country empathized with Ronan's plight, but they had companies to run, too. Fortunately, he had his research fleet.

"Isn't this setting a dangerous precedent?" Dillan asked.

Smiling, he faced his assistant and cocked his head. *If he's smart, he'll learn to recognize this look and back down. Times might be changing, but I learned a few tricks from my old man.* "Funny, my father asked the same question."

"What'd you say?"

He cocked his head. "I hung up the phone."

"Right." Scratching his head, Dillan frowned. "How many reinforcements?"

Cracking his knuckles, he reached for the hard hat he kept behind his desk. "Lots."

Dillan's eyes widened.

He grinned. "You have two hours to pack a bag."

"But" — Dillan cleared his throat — "you have commitments on your calendar. Surely we could go tomorrow."

Placing the hat on the edge of the desk, he sat next to it and crossed his arms. In a strong job market, HR staff members were purveyors of big-hearted recognition, and every Ocelot employee felt valued, significant and well-compensated. When the economy changed, management did their best to avoid cuts, but the same people who handed out discounted theme-park tickets collected employee badges and passed out COBRA flyers. Dillan was a newbie. He'd probably heard tales of terminations, but they sounded like things that happened to other people. He suppressed a smile. "You like your assignment?"

Dillan nodded.

The military's chain of command has multiple benefits. Growing up, how many times did I hear my father's booming expressions as I ran to do his bidding? "When I say, 'jump', you say, 'how high?'" Dropping his chin, he channeled his father's authoritative expression. "Pack your bags or tell HR to send me a new assistant."

"But, Mr. Durand, you've already run through the onsite pool."

"Not my problem."

"Umm-m."

He raised an eyebrow. "You're replaceable."

Sighing, Dillan packed up his laptop. "Sure, two hours, and we're off to Ronan."

He stood, picked up the hard hat and tried not to smile. *Smart kid.*

* * * *

"I feel like I'm riding in a parade," Dillan said.

Christopher laughed and looked over his shoulder. A convoy of eighteen-wheelers trailed behind his truck. In their beds, they carried light towers, excavators, generator sets and compact construction equipment fresh from the research lab. At first glance, skid steers and compact track loaders looked like the same machine with different drive mechanisms, but their unique advantages proved their worth, and he couldn't wait to see them perform.

"The Ocelot Enterprise family is behind this effort." He gripped the steering wheel and repeated the line in his head. *Even if the Durand patriarch has his doubts.* "If you want to throw koozies and wave, go right ahead."

Dillan scanned the backseat. "You brought koozies?"

He rolled his eyes. *This kid is going to be the death of me.* Behind the big rigs, paid drivers kept rented RVs in a neat formation that occupied the highway without causing a traffic jam. The vehicles would house the Ocelot crew and keep his staff from the strain of multi-hour commutes. *The last thing I need is a traffic accident on my hands.*

Slowing for traffic outside Ronan, he saw battered Ocelot loaders clearing county roads. Piles of debris lined the medians, and their neat construction shielded the storm's scars. Each mangled pile of wood, bricks and steel used to be a home or business, but the tornado demanded another iteration. Farther down the road, families scratched their heads and stared at their slabs, likely wondering how they would reconstruct their dreams from savings, insurance and FEMA claims. No matter the answer, they needed heavy equipment before they could rebuild.

Guiding the trucks to the parking lot of a flattened county high school, he followed a signaler's flags toward parking spots drawn with spray paint. Stepping out of the truck, he watched the eighteen-wheelers align like members of a well-trained squad. *Well, that makes me the staff sergeant.*

Shouldering the responsibility, he hoped the gleaming, next-generation, black-and-cream electric equipment could do the work of hundreds of laborers and skip diesel emissions. Alongside firefighters and other first responders, Ocelot's machines would help families dig through rubble and find glimmers of possibility. *But will we find Taylor?*

He exhaled. *Fuck, let's do this before I lose my nerve.* "Set up the generators away from the building. We'll charge the batteries at night."

Dillan nodded.

"Keep the camp perimeter tight. I don't want anyone wandering around the equipment or the staff. If press or visitors don't have a badge, they can check in at the main entrance."

"Who's manning the entrance?" Dillan asked.

He smiled. "You."

The signaler directed the RVs to the sports field. Dropping his flags, he lifted a radio.

Christopher turned and surveyed the high school. In the past week, municipal crews had cut utilities and fenced off the destruction, but the remaining structure required heavy demolition.

"She was beautiful," a woman said.

He turned and found a middle-aged woman standing next to the signaler. An elastic held her straight, black hair in a low ponytail, but he wagered she wore it styled like a helmet when she faced an auditorium of high school kids. He stuck out his hand. "Principal Levatino."

She shook his hand and smiled. "The kids call me Bettina."

"Do they?" he asked.

She grinned. "Keep your friends close and your enemies closer."

"What does that make me?"

"Time will tell."

Laughing, he nodded. "Thank you for allowing Ocelot to stage in the parking lot." He beckoned to Dillan. "My assistant might look like a newbie, but until we leave town, he's my right-hand man. You let him know if you need something."

Dillan grinned.

Bettina extended her hand. "Pleasure to meet you."

Her meaty grip swallowed Dillan's polite handshake. He looked away. *Giving the kid a hard time in private might be fun, but he'll have to find his way in the world. Ronan's not a bad place to start.*

Bettina turned to him. "I can't tell you how much we appreciate the assistance." She fanned herself. "We won't finish the school year on site, but as soon as we clear the rubble, we're one step closer to rebuilding." She exhaled and dropped her hand. "At least, that's the plan."

"I can only do so much," he said. "I wish I could do more."

She laughed. "Oh, the legislature will pony up. Federal disaster funds and insurance money will cover the rest." She patted his cheek. "But aren't you the sweetest?"

"Hardly."

Dillan choked back a laugh.

She eyed him. "Early last week, our state senator toured the campus with Governor Bentley. Wasn't much of a tour" — she raised an eyebrow — "if you know what I mean."

Dillan nodded. "Yes, ma'am."

Christopher smiled. *Now he's learning.*

Bettina shook her head. "If the tornado had struck a few hours later, the kids would have been onsite for sports and meetings. Whatever hand guided that tornado" — she whistled — "I'd like to think it did us the favor of funding a new facility with zero cost of life."

He scanned the horizon. "Seven fatalities."

"Mostly from the trailer park on the outskirts of the city. Too many people asleep and too little warning." She sighed. "When National Weather Service issues a tornado warning, they explicitly tell people to flee mobile homes."

"They didn't issue a warning," he said.

Her gaze softened. "I know."

"And downtown?"

She raised an eyebrow. "No amount of money can rebuild Ronan. Have you seen it?"

He shook his head.

"You ex-military?" she asked.

He nodded.

"Good. Go." She sighed. "The county officials will deploy your Ocelot troops. Go see what we lost. In comparison, rebuilding the high school will feel like a hiccup."

Glancing away, he buried his fears. *Georgia has hundreds of small towns. Each one is special, but each one doesn't have a proselytizing bookworm who looks like an angel.* "And yourself?"

She smiled. "I'm off to strategize with the school board. General Stephen Townsend has nothing on this old girl."

"I thought y'all were all fans of General Dick."

Her eyes widened, but she slapped her thigh and laughed. "Get on with you."

He winked.

Driving away from the flattened high school, he looked in the rearview mirror and exhaled. He understood the frustration and anger of witnessing war without any sense of control. So many of his peers had returned from Iraq with post-traumatic stress disorder, depression and substance-use disorders. Unable to handle what they saw, they threatened physical violence, destroyed property or fought to release their anger. He chose humor and locking horns with his father, but when those strategies failed, he pushed his body to its limits. Some soldiers required more help. Subthreshold PTSD existed, and cognitive behavioral therapy barely scratched the surface of what his peers needed to process their emotions. *What will Ronan's citizens need?*

He wondered if the indiscriminate destruction of a natural disaster removed the frustration so many survivors felt. After the storm, a trail of victims remained, but no commanders stood behind a podium to accept the blame.

* * * *

"Good La-wd!"

Dillan's exclamation matched the destruction Christopher saw. He slowed his truck and tried to separate the rubble into discrete buildings. Every ambitious, wood and brick edifice bore signs of damage. The red-brick building housing Ronan Reads leaned on its neighbor. Stretched taut across ragged rooflines, blue tarps rippled in the wind. The dry, sand-caked Iraqi destruction had stolen his breath, but the familiar, crumbled, turn-of-the-century buildings broke his heart. "The news coverage doesn't do it justice."

Pressing his hand against the window, Dillan nodded.

He put the truck in park and grabbed his hard hat. Wind had crumbled the buildings, but water had claimed the remains. Inventorying the structures, he hoped the mom-and-pop businesses were too small to self-insure. Instead of hiding behind an organized police line, men and women scrambled over jagged debris, caught bites near smoking barbecue pits and sipped bottled water in scarce shade. "The local dealer said he's working from the corner of Central Alley and Drake."

Dillan climbed down from the cab. "But there aren't any streets signs."

He slammed the driver's side door and walked around the hood. "That shouldn't stop us."

Nodding, Dillan closed his door and followed suit.

His assistant carried his hard hat like a live grenade, but Ronan laid in repose.

Slipping on his hat, he pulled it low against the sunlight and picked his way through a cleared path in the middle of the street. On the edge of the twelve-foot swath, debris loomed like rusted snowbanks. Someone had run a skid steer through the wreckage, and he hoped that someone worked for Ocelot.

An older woman walking a dog in the opposite direction paused. "You lost?"

Her flowered housedress and pink slippers worried him, but the white terrier lunging for his ankles could do more harm. "Yes, ma'am. I'm looking for Central Alley and Drake."

She cocked her head. "You're not from around here."

Atlanta is hardly Yankee country. "No, ma'am, but I'm here to help."

"You from the power company?"

He shook his head.

"Haven't had power in a damn week. Ain't nothing going to help." Spitting on the ground, she walked past him. "We're done."

"Ma'am?"

She dropped the dog's leash.

The dog turned, looked at him and attacked.

Dillan screamed.

Scooping up the twenty-pound terror, Christopher held it at arm's length. "Ma'am, does your dog bite?"

She scratched her scalp. "No, child, don't be a fool."

Child? He lifted the dog to eye level and raised an eyebrow. "Have you eaten?"

The dog growled.

"Dillan, go buy a hot dog."

"But I'm not hungry," Dillan said.

"The food's for the dog."

His eyes wide, Dillan nodded.

Holding the terrier against his side to keep its jaws from finding flesh, he walked up to the woman and offered his unencumbered arm. "Where's your family from?"

She took his arm. "Washington."

Washington? Which Washington? "Can't say I've been there."

She peered. "Up near Athens."

He nodded as if he'd won second place in the school geography bee. Tugging her into motion, he set an easy pace toward the people milling for food. "And what brought you to Ronan?"

"My husband found a job down here. Glad he didn't live to see this mess." She planted her feet. "He's dead."

"I got that."

She gave him a side-eye.

Her pearl earrings were as big as lima beans. *She may not be poor, but she's lost.*

The dog whimpered.

Adjusting his grip, he tried to hand off the animal.

She shook her head. "You look like you can handle him."

"Well, aren't you the sweetest..."

Dillan thrust a hot dog in his face.

He pulled the bun from his assistant's fingers, broke off a piece of meat and gave the offering to the dog. The animal snapped at the offering like a trap in the woods. *Why do people keep these animals as pets?* Grateful he'd kept his fingers out of harm's way, he fed the dog bits of meat until it licked his fingers. Satisfied, he handed the animal and remains of the hot dog to Dillan. "Feed it the rest."

Jostling his load, Dillan mumbled about an MBA and retreated to the shady side of the street.

The lady watched him go. "He likes pulled pork."

"I'll keep that in mind. And you? What are you eating these days?"

Shading her eyes, she grinned. "I guess I could eat. You going to eat with me?"

"No, ma'am, but I'll see you settled. You live around here?"

"Just up the road. I came into town to see the show. Nobody needs me for rescue attempts, cleanup and ass-o-ci-ated activities." She wobbled her head, mocking the seriousness of the efforts. Losing steam, she let her shoulders slump and sighed. "Ain't nothing else to do but worry and keep Roger out of harm's way."

He eyed the terrier nipping at Dillan's fingers. "Roger."

She smiled. "I named him after my husband. He's certainly less trouble." Releasing his arm, she walked up to the smoker. "Peaches, gimme one of those pulled pork sandwiches."

His heart stopped.

The woman wearing a baseball cap and a stained apron nodded. She stood behind a plastic table bearing condiments and disposable dishes. Smoke blew across her face, and she lifted the cap, brushing sweat and hair from her eyes. "Be ready in a minute, Ms. Tina."

Giving thanks he'd already handed over the dog, he let himself breathe. Georgia might be full of beautiful women, but he recognized Taylor Lenore on sight. No longer smiling from a stage or presiding over shelves of colorful books — hell, of course he'd watched the interview — she looked about as enigmatic as a horsefly. *Just another pretty, small-town girl who grew into a lovely woman. William wouldn't have looked twice, and neither would I.* Drawing a deep breath, he rocked back on his heels and suppressed a grin. *Except her mind's quicker than half the people I know, and her heart's twice as generous. Now that I know she's safe, I can get back to work.*

"And one for my friend, too," Ms. Tina said.

Taylor looked up and frowned. "Durand... What are you doing here?"

He felt so relieved to see her that he released the grin. "Just another volunteer happy to help."

"He's a greenie." Ms. Tina yanked the sandwich from Taylor's grasp. "Not a scratch on his pretty hard hat. Probably bought it at a convenience store." She bit into the meat. "Probably has an ugly head."

"I do not," he said.

Both women stared.

Clearing his throat, he stepped away from their stares. "Well, I'll get back to the helping."

Taylor frowned. "You don't belong here."

"You're probably right."

She planted her hands on her hips.

He swallowed.

"Did you come to kick us when we're down?" she asked. "Are you trying to negotiate for a better deal on the new factory?"

Ms. Tina paused with the sandwich halfway to her mouth. "What new factory?"

"Ma'am, I came—"

Taylor skewed her lips. "What? Tired of playing putt-putt? You came south for a bit of disaster tourism?"

Maybe the grin was overkill. He squared his shoulders. "I brought reinforcements for the cleanup efforts."

Scanning the rubble-lined street, she raised an eyebrow.

"The equipment's at the high school." He swallowed. "I brought skid steers."

Tilting her head, she stared. "Unless that's a cut of meat, we probably have it onsite. I've seen every piece of machinery from the tri-county area. We don't need more exhaust and more tread marks. We need repairs."

Her eyes were so blue that they bordered on violet. He had a chunk of amethyst in his library, but her eyes outshone the stone. "We'll make a dent in the cleanup efforts and leave…"

"After your publicity photos. I get it." She turned back to the worktable. "I already met your friend, Rebecca. She's a piece of work."

He frowned. "I was going to say, we'll leave you in a better spot."

Shaking her head, she reached for a bun. "Good luck with the press tour."

"That's not how it is. I came to find" —he exhaled— "out whether Ocelot's equipment holds up to our motto. *Tomorrow's solutions for today's earthmoving challenges.* I'll be onsite for a week, maybe more."

She nodded and laid out buns for sandwiches.

Ms. Tina wiped sauce from her face. "You two know each other?"

He shook his head.

"I never seen Peaches this rude." Shrugging, she reached for more pickles. "What would your mama say?"

Pausing, Taylor bit her lip and sighed. "Stop running your mouth and get back to work."

Ms. Tina slapped her thigh. "That's right."

The housedress parted, and he swore he saw a lace-edged slip.

"Now tell me about this new factory. I swear, these kids think they can run the town. The old guard's here for a reason!"

Taylor bit back a smile.

The flash of humor reassured him. *Taylor's right. I shouldn't be here. Let a small-town boy sweep her off her feet and impress her with his carpentry skills. Hey, baby, you want to see my lathe?* He cleared his throat. "I'll leave you two ladies to your work."

Grabbing another sandwich, Ms. Tina offered it to him. "Peaches forgot her manners, but you and your factory are welcome in Ronan." She bit into the sandwich and chewed. "Or what's left of it. We're looking a mite sad, but now that you're here, we'll keep you. Eye candy never hurt the soul."

He accepted the sandwich and the compliment. "Thank you, ma'am."

Taylor slapped meat on the first bun. "Don't get your hopes up, Ms. Tina. He'll be back in Atlanta before the sun sets, counting his money and patting himself on the back for a job well done."

"And you'll be slinging sandwiches." He cocked his head. "How retro."

She wiped her hands clean and glared.

He wondered if he should back up a step.

"My daddy stayed up all night cooking this meat." She squared her shoulders. "Where were you the last week? Where were you when the hospital overflowed, and we patched up the injured and made coffee for the grieving? Where were you when we buried animals caught in the storm and mourned the people we lost?" She blinked and cleared her throat. "Ronar's a small town, but it's *my* town, and I don't have time for city boys who roll in, eat my daddy's sandwiches and bat their eyes for the press."

"You done?" he asked.

She blew out her breath. "Hardly. Go back to your mansion, pretty boy."

The command spiked his pulse, but he leveled his voice and set his hard hat on the table. "I brought what I had. You haven't posted from your acccunt. How should I know what you needed?"

"The storm took out the communications tower!"

Her voice wavered, and her chest heaved. He might look like a fool, but he would rather see her angry than verging on tears. Sensing she would rather match wits than accept a hug, he held her gaze. "Get a sat link."

She threw a bun at his chest.

Catching it, he set it on the table. "Welcome to the twenty-first century, Ms. Lenore."

Leaning forward, she jutted her chin. "Go home."

He crossed his arms and considered his tactics. Coming from the Army and a company that manufactured heavy machinery, he respected the problem of workplace sexual harassment. The #MeToo movement, media coverage and victim testimonies caught every executive's attention. Before the surge in public discussion, he would have stood by Ocelot's record of accomplishment for responding to complaints. After the surge, he knew every HR champion in the company, and he'd personally empowered staff to report cases without fear of retaliation. The shelves behind his desk housed highly regarded books on management theory and, damn, but he'd sat on a panel or two himself. Yet, faced with a pissed-off woman, all he wanted to do was throw her over his shoulder and swat her ass. *Some impulses die hard.* He narrowed his gaze. "I'll stay."

"Nobody invited you."

Her steely response brought out his grin. *Pretty as she may be, she won't buckle.* Relief never felt so good. Considering the nearest collapsed building, he appraised the crumbled bricks and adopted the persona she expected. "Think of the photo opportunities."

Ms. Tina dabbed a napkin at her lips. "Honey, I'll take your picture any day of the week. Just watch your feet. Half the people on this street have stepped on nails."

Tilting his foot, he displayed his steel-toed boot.

She laughed. "Oh, you'll do."

He winked. "Such a sweet welcoming committee."

Grinning, she looked at Taylor. "We aim to please, don't we, Peaches?"

Taylor tightened her apron strings. "Whatever."

Her dismissal scalded his pride but being in Ronan cleared his senses and highlighted his choices. *We're here to do good.* For the first time in a while, he felt like dirtying his hands.

Sure, confirming her presence lightened his heart but Ocelot remained a priority, and he had a fleet to validate. The company's equipment drivers would push the limits of the research machines, report on their performance and recommend improvements. Ronan's citizens? They would benefit, too. Taylor should admit her needs and accept help wherever she found it. He narrowed his gaze. "Your attitude's fine by me, but at the end of the week, you'll recognize Ocelot's contribution, and you'll thank me."

"The good I can muster from this community is worth more than your mechanical envoy." She laughed. "They'll need more than a day to get their bearings and stop chasing their tails anyway."

He crossed his arms. "Ms. Lenore, based on your social media feed, I didn't take you for a betting woman." He cocked his head. "Wouldn't that be a sin?"

Ms. Tina reached into her dress pocket, pulled out a twenty and slapped it on the table. "I haven't set foot in a church in years."

Biting his lip, he kept his gaze focused on Taylor. The spark of defiance in her gaze would keep her saner than a cascade of tears. *She's exhausted and frustrated, but she's not broken. I thought money and pedigree made the man but she has neither, and she's standing on her pride. What does that make me?* He shook off the comparison. "You know Ocelot's scanning sites for a new factory. If you're right, the townspeople deserve recognition. I'll put Ronan at the top of the list."

Ms. Tina whistled.

Taylor tilted her head. "And if *you're* right?"

He grinned. "Your next Ronan Reads post will be a confession. You're running a business, and you'll admit the verses, memes and feel-good GIFs are a means to an end."

She raised her chin. "I don't need your money."

He nodded. "I believe you, but faith, hope and love won't rebuild this town."

She wiped her eye.

Feeling like an ass, he wanted to wrap his arms around her and tell her everything would be fine.

She met his gaze. "This community is worth rebuilding."

If it produced someone like you, it must be. "Your neighbors feel the same way. On my way into town, I saw trucks and signs belonging to need organizations, churches, food banks and grassroots supporters."

Exhaling, she nodded. "The aid's coming. We just have to" — she sighed — "get through each day."

Ms. Tina rubbed her back. "My money's on you, Peaches."

He picked up his hard hat, slid the twenty in his back pocket and inclined his head. "Either way, the town wins." Heading back to the truck, he slowed his stride and waited for Taylor to claim the last word.

She slammed a box against the table. "Arrogant asshole."

The sound of jostling plastic cutlery brought a smile to his face. Scanning the street, he found Roger asleep at Dillan's feet. Instead of calling the man's name, he released a shrill whistle.

Dillan snapped up his head, and the dog ran for its owner.

"Come on, Dilly. We have work to do."

Chapter Seven

Taylor's eyes felt dry, and her body ached. No amount of pork, caffeine or buttermilk pancakes could revive her spirits. She stared at the faded wallpaper in her parents' house and braided her hair. The screen door slammed, and she startled. Looking at the single-paned windows, she added a hair tie and exhaled. *Have the windows ever looked this flimsy?*

"Good morning, Peaches." Nancy stepped through the back door and pulled eggs from a basket.

She adopted a bright smile but wondered if the expression made it to her eyes. "Good morning, Mama. I didn't see you go out."

"You looked lost in your own little world." Nancy inspected an egg. "Your imagination always took you to places the rest of us couldn't see."

Frowning, she gripped her coffee cup and replayed her youth. Church, school and sports had kept her going, but country life left a lot of downtime. *I turned to books, but I wouldn't call myself lost.* Downing her lukewarm coffee, she rose and set the mug in the old, white enamel sink. "I'm headed into town to help Ms. Tina put the blue tarp back on her roof."

"Oh, let someone else do it. You've been working yourself to the bone. You look weary."

She gripped the edge of the sink. "Who, Mama? Who's going to do it?"

Nancy set down the eggs, placed her hand at the small of Taylor's back and rubbed.

The soft, comforting gesture once helped her fall asleep, but the moment she stepped from Ronan Reads, she realized her nightmare's extent. Nancy's simplicity and devotion chaffed, but her mother deserved respect. *Just because she's lived in the same county her entire life doesn't mean she has nothing to say.* "I'm okay. Once this coffee kicks in, I'll be raring to go."

Nancy dropped her hand. "Are you sure?"

She turned and smiled. "Perfectly!" The lie felt as smooth as home-churned butter. "Have you seen the website Plucky set up?" Pulling her phone from her pocket, she navigated to Plucky's new page and held up her phone. "'*Founded in the wake of the Ronan Tornado, the Ronan Recovery Foundation exists to provide aid to those suffering catastrophic losses after a natural disaster.*' I'm sure Katie Jesse helped her with the text."

Nancy held out her palm.

Placing the phone in Nancy's grip, she knew the images and narratives would be enough to divert her mother's attention.

Nancy scrolled down. "'*Through a combination of survivor requests and feedback from those serving the victims of natural disasters, the Ronan Recovery Foundation compiled a list of items helpful to disaster survivors.*'" She shook her head and handed back the phone. "Survivors need more than bleach and bottled water. 'So do not fear, for I am with you. Do not be dismayed, for I am your God. I will strengthen you and help you. I will uphold you with my righteous right hand,'" she said, quoting Isaiah 41:10.

"Mom, she's doing the best she can. Plucky's good with all the technology stuff." She looked at the neatly ordered items on the screen. "Formula, dishes and box fans. She's giving out the supplies from her garage as fast as she receives them. I wouldn't have thought about needing that stuff."

"But you thought about Ms. Tina."

She swallowed. "Well, she paraded down the street in her house dress. I would have redirected her, but he got to her first."

Nancy leaned on the kitchen counter. "Who?"

She slipped her hands into her jean pockets. "The big shot from Atlanta who wants to make a splash in the local papers." When she'd looked up and recognized Christopher Durand, she'd hid her visceral pleasure. Amid the destruction, he'd looked like a sun-warmed desperado, but he had no place in her town.

"Was he from the government?"

The note of suspicion in her mother's tone summoned a smile and tamped down her vulnerability. "No, he's the guy who makes heavy equipment. I'm sure he's already back in Atlanta where he belongs."

Nancy yawned. "Well, helping Ms. Tina was good of him."

She reached for her keys. "Nobody's all bad."

"Ride with your father."

Shaking her head, she walked toward the back door. "He already left. Said he'd swing by the hardware store in the next town and see if they'd received any more tarps or ropes."

Nancy cracked an egg. "That's what Plucky needs on her wish list."

"Good call." She eased shut the door.

Free of the farmhouse, she closed her eyes. Tears welled behind her eyelids, and she swallowed. *I'm not lost in my own little world. I'm living it, and if you left the farmhouse, you'd see how much work rebuilding this town will take.* She loved her mother, but her jaw ached and her chest felt tight. *Why can't she step out of her comfort zone and face the world – or let me scream without saying everything will be okay?*

A tear slipped down her cheek. The day after the storm, her uncle had held up his Bible and preached. Listening, she'd sat in a folding chair beneath a clear blue sky, kicked her legs in the grass and wondered what she'd done wrong. Disasters stemmed from human sin. God allowed evil and suffering, but the Bible called for practical aid, empathy for the hurt and overcoming injustice. The mission had given her a focus to keep her fears at bay. Like her uncle standing behind the pulpit, she believed God worked with believers to produce good from bad situations, but she wondered if she had the stamina to keep finding hope amid the destruction. Wiping away the tear, she pulled open her car door and stuck the key in the ignition. When the engine roared to life, she smiled. *Well, at least Daddy fixed the starter.*

On the edge of town, Ms. Tina's house marked the spot where the tornado had hesitated. Seemingly spent of its devastating energy, the winds had ripped off sections of the roof but left the house's white columns and temple-fronted facade. Built right before the Civil

War, Ms. Tina had used the gable-fronted porch and wide front lawn to host reenactments and weddings, but she rarely opened her doors to guests.

Today, she stood in front of the rose bushes with clippers in her hand while Roger snoozed in the shade. A worn, canvas apron shielded her faded jeans, but at least she'd dispensed with the house dress. Taylor stopped the car, stepped out and waved.

"I waited too long," Ms. Tina said. "As soon as the forsythias bloomed, I shoulda gone after these thorny things."

She looked at the pile of stems strewn along the brick walk. Based on the litter, Ms. Tina had made up for lost time. "I'm sure a good whack will encourage growth and rejuvenate the shrubs."

Shading her eyes, Ms. Tina looked at her roof. "Maybe I should rip out what's left and start fresh."

Fearing Ms. Tina would take a wrecking ball to the old home, she rushed up the walk and lifted the clippers from Ms. Tina's hand. "Nah, you wouldn't want to start from scratch. Think about the strong roots waiting to push up fresh growth." She guided the woman to a rocking chair, set down the clippers and sat on the front porch steps. "How'd your night go?"

Ms. Tina gripped the rocking chair arms. "About as expected. I heard every croak and groan. It's a damn nightmare."

"It's an old house." She braced her hands on the step. "It settles."

"Taylor, there's a hole in the roof. I couldn't sleep a wink."

She looked up at the stately roofline. "I'm sorry the last tarp blew off."

"Distracted teenagers." Ms. Tina rocked. "They tried, but they didn't know their ass from their elbow."

"Daddy and his crew will be here shortly." She soaked up the morning sun. "We'll get you patched up. I'm sorry it took so long."

Ms. Tina rattled the second rocker. "Come up here where I can see you."

Standing, she approached the chair.

Roger raised his head and growled.

"I'm good."

Ms. Tina pulled a pack of cigarettes and a lighter from her apron. "Don't mind that old dog. He ain't got teeth."

She tilted her head. *Funny, I could have sworn I saw a flash of white.*

Jack's dusty truck pulled up and parked behind her car. Before his boots touched the pavement, a line of mud-splattered vehicles rolled into place behind his truck. Men and women climbed from the vehicles, stretched their backs and sipped from insulated travel mugs.

She waved and jogged down the steps. "You're right on time."

He nodded, but he stared at the house. "Johnnie, grab some plywood. We might do better than a tarp."

"Sure thing, Jack."

Johnnie had moved to town a few years ago. He was dependable and clever, but he had a lot to learn about construction. Stepping back, she followed her father's gaze and looked at the hole in the roof. The second floor had surely suffered water damage, but until plywood and shingles reclaimed their rightful places, the house remained vulnerable to the elements. "No luck with supplies?"

"You'd think the world forgot how to make polyethylene fabric." He sighed. "I can't find a bolt of blue for a hundred miles."

She nodded and looked at his clean-shaven skin. *He's probably been up since five. He's no spring chicken. How long can he run at this rate? When Mama brings lunch, I'll ask her what she thinks.* "I'm sure Ms. Tina appreciates the help."

He nodded. "Let's get moving." Turning, he beckoned the crew toward the house.

Ms. Tina stood and planted her hands on her hips. "You need to get in the house?"

"You offering?" He grinned.

"Hell no!"

"That's okay. We'll slip in the back while you're busy murdering roses." He pointed the crew toward the side of the house.

Ms. Tina snapped the shears. "I'm pruning them."

"Whatever you say, ma'am."

She gave him the bird.

Laughing, he followed his crew.

Taylor glanced at the scattered clippings and knew her daddy poked the old woman to liven up her day. *The beauty of a small town is neighbors knowing neighbors. They know when to lift you up, and they know when to put you in your place.*

Johnnie and his wife unloaded plywood.

Crew members whose houses had escaped damage walked around Ms. Tina's house, shook posts and flagged damage spots with blue painter's tape.

She grabbed an extension ladder from Jack's truck and carried it toward the house. *At this rate, Ms. Tina's grand ole house will look like those blue-and-white china plates she loaned to the library.* She found a spot of even ground and laid the ladder in the grass. Raising the top end of it, she walked it upright hand-over-hand. Once the ladder stood nearly vertical, she grabbed a thigh-high rung, lifted the ladder and walked its base away from the house. She could hear her daddy's voice in her head telling her to do it right. Judging the angle, she grabbed the rope and raised the fly to the top of Ms. Tina's house. She made sure both rung hooks locked securely onto a rung of the ladder, tied off the end of the rope to a lower rung, and wiped the dust from her hands. Turning, she met Jack's gaze.

"You ready to go up?" he asked.

She nodded.

"Stay away from the edge of the roof. Let Johnnie transfer the plywood."

"Daddy..."

He walked away.

You win the arguments you never hear. Rolling her eyes, she grabbed both rungs and climbed the ladder. The breeze and the view from the top of the house should have thrilled her, but it broke her heart. Ronan's historical district slumped, and the flattened high school would devastate an entire generation. *One way or another, everyone took a hit.*

Johnnie paused near the top of the ladder. "Peaches, you back away from that edge before your daddy tears my hide."

She inched up the gray, weathered shingles. To her right, a gaping hole revealed pink carpet and sodden bed sheets, but she trusted the remainder of the old roof. *At least they took down the asbestos shingles in the seventies.*

Johnnie threw his leg over, straightened and hitched up his jeans. "I wish my Jeannie Mae could get over her fear of heights."

She pinched closed her lips. *Jeannie Mae didn't have any problem climbing the water tower to neck with her high school boyfriend.*

"Grab a seat while I get this plywood loaded up."

She watched him stack sheets of plywood and marveled at his strength. *What does a sheet of three-quarter-inch plywood weigh? About sixty-four pounds? He hauls them around as if they're foam board.*

Knowing his pride would keep her from helping, she watched Ronan's citizens move through the debris like industrious ants. Having a mother for a librarian came with a love of books, but it also came with a wealth of knowledge. Desperate to settle the land by 1850, leaders gave away acreage using a lottery system. Nearly every two-hundred-acre 'win' went to farming, and the farmers' goods went to market via wagon. By the time the first steam engine hissed, groaned and slowed for Ronan's stop, a small group of townspeople waited on the platform. They had thrown their hats into the air and cheered. *What would this land look like if people had never set foot in Georgia?*

Johnnie wiped the sweat from his brow and peered over the edge of the roof. "About time!"

Turning, she walked to his side and came face to face with Christopher Durand's shiny hard hat. The sinfully handsome man had no reason to be in her town, but here he was, climbing the ladder she'd erected. "You!"

He pulled himself over the edge and tipped his hard hat. "Well, good morning to you, too, Taylor."

"What on God's green earth are you doing here?"

Bracing his hands on his hips, he stretched his back. "Imagine my surprise this morning when my crew and I mobilized and found an army of pickup trucks focused on this grand, old house." He peered into the tattered hole, looked at her and smiled. "I offered to put the plywood on a work platform and raise it to the roof. Now you have a nice, flat place to work."

Sure enough, the whirl of a motor filled the air, and a work platform loaded with materials rose to roof height.

She wanted to kick something. Standing on the roof in the bight morning sunlight, he looked too vibrant to be a neighbor and too convenient to ignore. The city needed help with everything from sanitation to shoes. *Why does he look like he has never had a better day in his life?* She licked her lips, frowned and denied that she wanted to taste his vitality. Chalking up her attraction to the allure of normalcy, she shook her head and waited for him to climb down the ladder.

Johnnie stuck out his hand. "Man, I appreciate it."

Shaking Johnnie's hand, Christopher grinned. "Saved you a few hours?"

"You bet."

She cleared her throat. "You two going to stand around and yak or let the rest of us get to work?"

Christopher cocked his head. "I never expected to find you on top of the house. Who knew Ronan's booksellers had so many skills and talents?"

"The locals," she said. "Everyone else can shove off."

He winked. "I'll just add those saved hours to my tally sheet."

Johnnie scratched his head. "Peaches?"

She jerked her thumb toward Christopher. "My friend from Atlanta thinks his machinery can outperform our tradespeople."

"Well, of course it can," Johnnie said. "That's why God invented machines."

Christopher laughed. "If God invented them, my father has a few questions about our research and development budget."

She grabbed a pry bar and removed the old shingles surrounding the hole. *Of all the luck. Why can't he leave us in peace and lord over the people in his city?* She turned and frowned. "Johnnie, you going to gab all day or pick up a hammer and help?"

Taking a knee, Johnnie nodded and used his hammer's claw to remove errant nails. "I'm getting to it."

Christopher crouched, pulled a hammer from his leather tool belt and tackled the other side of the gaping hole.

She squeezed shut her eyes. The storm had destroyed her town, but it had also tattered the politeness she held dear. *Just tell him to shove off.* "Manners separate us from the animals grazing in the fields." *Nancy's admonishment lingered in her subconscious like a buzzing mosquito.* She looked over the landscape. *Didn't we all suffer the wrath of wind and rain?* Fed up, she put down the pry bar. "No."

Christopher looked up. "No?"

"We don't need your help." She faced him. "Johnnie and I have it covered. We'll have this hole fixed before long. Go find somewhere else to earn your scout badges."

Standing, Christopher brushed his hands on his jeans and looked over the roof's edge. "Maybe you'll get it done, but the sooner you're finished up here, the sooner you can get back to the ground and help the people caulking holes in the banisters." He whistled. "Shoot... Looks like they're replacing a few too."

She struggled not to look. *Did the damage stem from the storm or general neglect? Roger passed away a decade ago. How long has Ms. Tina needed help?* She forced herself to stay focused on her work.

"Why don't you like me?" he asked.

She ground her teeth. "I like you just fine."

"Liar."

Setting down her tools, she shaded her eyes against the sun. "How would you feel if someone rolled into town and pointed out your flaws? I haven't heard you say a nice thing about Ronan."

He cleared his throat. "The air's clear."

Johnnie choked and slapped his chest. "Sorry. Swallowed a bug."

"I bet." She shook her head and turned her back on both men.

"You don't want statistics," Christopher said.

She picked up the pry bar.

"My neighbors wouldn't do this for me," he said.

Frowning, she imagined a world where neighbors hid behind Boxwood hedges and Eagleston hollies. "I'm sure they would find a way to help."

"No." He took a knee and braced his hand on the roof. "They wouldn't."

She turned. "None of them?"

"Not the ones I've met."

"Maybe you need to get out more."

He smiled. "I'm here."

She shook her head and levered a sheet of shingles. "Fine. You can help with the roof."

He laughed. "Well, aren't you generous?"

"Go get a circular saw and cut out the damaged plywood." She shifted away from his long-legged bulk.

Looking up, he raised his eyebrows.

"Please."

He smiled.

She tilted her head. "You do not how to use a circular saw, don't you?" His face reddened, but he sat back on his heels and watched her. She smiled. "Try to avoid cutting the rafters."

"Ma'am, I can use any tool you have on hand."

"I doubt it."

Johnnie shook his head. "Man's just trying to help."

Hearing the censure in Johnnie's voice, she exhaled and knew he spoke as a friend. "I know. I appreciate the help." The lie burned her throat. Right now, the only things she appreciated were natural gas, humming generators and hot coffee. "I haven't slept well." She swallowed and met Durand's gaze. "Ms. Tina and the town appreciate your help."

"And you?" he asked.

She looked away. His online comments' elusive camaraderie and curt derision remained fresh in her mind. She appreciated matching wits, but the tornado had upended their circumstances, and the change felt like too much to bear. Looking at him, she followed the lines of his biceps and the tension of his thighs against denim. *Admiring a handsome man feels normal, but what right do I have to be normal when so many people lost so much?* She cleared her throat. "I appreciate the help."

"Happy to help. Now, where can I find the saw?"

Johnnie stood and stretched his arms over his head. "I'll go get it." He swung his leg over the edge of the roof and climbed down the ladder.

"Nice guy," Christopher said.

She smiled. "The best." Prying up a shingle, she tried to play nice. "So, Mr. Durand, how'd you learn to play handyman?"

"Peaches, play nice!"

Johnnie's avuncular warning tone carried over the sloped roof. Her cheeks warmed. "You know we're the same age!"

"I also know your dad!"

She shook her head. "Sometimes, this town feels too small."

Christopher laughed and tossed a loose shingle onto the work platform. "Every summer, my dad sent me into the field. If an internship was good enough for new hires, it was good enough for me. What's your excuse?"

"I spent every summer working with my dad too."

"Commercial or residential?"

She pried out a nail. "Both. Whatever needed doing."

"But you run a bookstore."

Hitting nails into place would feel a hell of a lot better than prying them out of damaged wood. "Library science degree, like my mom."

"The apple doesn't fall far from the tree." He stacked damaged shingles. "We both followed our parents into work."

She looked up. "If I had a brother, things would have been different."

His smile faltered.

"I mean, a son would have palled around with my dad and left me in the kitchen." She flicked a fallen leaf from the tip of her finger and waited to hear a line about strengths and weaknesses.

"Parents can only manage to love one kid at a time?"

She grinned. "I was a handful."

Laughing, he pried loose a nail. "I bet. What kind of mischief did you find?"

"Same old stuff." She adjusted her stance on the sloping roof. "Lazy summer nights and weekend swimming pools. These old towns hardly change." She looked over the town. "Isn't that the charm? People go to Savannah, Augusta and Darien to relive the past, tour stately homes and revel in a slower pace of life. Ronan's no different. We're just a little more country."

He shaded his eyes. "Large, beautiful Greek Revival homes won't revive Ronan. From what I hear, the town's heyday fizzled out with the railroad."

The truth stung, but she refused to deny it. "What does that mean?"

"I read the book you sold me. The cotton farms led to a textile industry, but embezzlement and competition killed the mills. Throw in a few race riots, shattered windows at the bottling plant, lost opportunities and you have" — he drew a deep breath — "the history of most small towns. I don't find it charming. I find it inefficient and full of decay."

She stood and planted her hands on her hips. "Did you come down here to give me a lecture or help rebuild a town? I've lived here my entire life. When you're down, the town lifts you up." She wanted to kick her hammer off the roof, but she worried who worked below. "Of all the arrogant, opinionated things to say to a local."

"Should I have complimented your eyes?"

"No, you should have stayed in Atlanta! We don't need big businessmen to bail out our economy, fix our roofs or compliment our eyes."

Setting aside his tool, he stood and braced his legs. "So you'll tell the elected leaders to return every cent of the government money headed to this town? You'll rebuild the high school with scraps of wood and reclaimed pride?"

She threw her arm wide. "Does it look like we're trying to build skyscrapers?" Wobbling, she closed her eyes and searched for balance. A steady hand gripped her upper arm. She glanced at the strong contours of his hand looked into his eyes. "Get your hands off me."

He released her and shook his head. "You'd be happier falling off the roof."

"I got myself up here. I can get myself down."

Pulling off his hard hat, he rested it against his hip, ran his hand through his hair and looked toward downtown. "I'm on your side, Taylor. Small towns like Ronan have never seen a time like now, and neither have I. Running Ocelot doesn't keep me out of touch with my workforce. Interest rates are low, deficits seem meaningless and expansion feels like the only way to compete. You're feeling the pain in Ronan, but the cost of rebuilding this city won't register on the national stage. Bigger bailouts, mounting debts and loose financing make the headlines people read." He looked at her. "Ronan's a sympathy case."

She gasped.

"Don't let your pride bankrupt your recovery. The world has bigger fish to fry."

Sitting, she bowed her head and rubbed her scalp. "'Socialism for the rich and capitalism for the poor.' The only thing worse than riding around in my dad's old truck and listening to fifty-year-old hits is listening to his fifty-year-old politics."

He settled beside her. "Well, now they're calling it 'Socialism for the rich and capitalism for the rest.' Your dad and my dad would probably get along."

She wiped her hair out of her face and turned her head. "And which one are you?"

He rubbed his neck. "Rich."

Startled, she let his honest answer draw a smile on her face. "Exactly."

"Look... I'm not discounting your pain or the long road ahead of Ronan, but you seem to think I'm here to make fun of you. I'm not."

She exhaled.

"I see Ronan's equation from a few angles. Right now, government intervention does more to stimulate the financial markets than the blue-collar economy. Middling productivity limits opportunities, choices and income gains. I want to see the people of Ronan thrive."

"So you can get richer?"

He laughed. "Well, yes."

She rolled her eyes. "Christopher doesn't suit you."

"What name would be a better fit?"

She stared. "Lucifer."

Laughing, he slapped his knee and let go of his hard hat. "Ronan's recovery isn't the ticket to my bottom line."

The plastic tumbled toward the edge of the roof, and she lunged. "Heads up!"

Gripping her arm, he held her fast.

She pulled against the constraint. "Go back to Atlanta where you belong."

He released his hold. "Atlanta is hardly Hades, and you're hardly Persephone."

She wanted to spit nails, but the classical reference intrigued her. "People misunderstood Persephone..."

Johnnie hoisted the circular saw onto the roof. "Damn, this thing weighs a ton, then you go and drop a hard hat over the edge." He rubbed his head. "Take it easy on me."

Christopher nodded and offered him a hand. "My bad. You should have used the lift."

Shrugging, Johnnie threw a long, blue extension cord over the edge of the roof. "Seems like a waste of energy. My legs work just fine."

She kept her mouth shut and wondered if five more minutes would have given her the upper hand on the debate. Once the blue cord hit the ground and a neighbor connected it to the portable generator, they would be up and running, and circular saw's noise would negate further conversation. Turning her back on the sun, she focused on cutting out damaged plywood, replace rotten two-by-fours, and secure new framing to the rafters. *I almost had the upper hand.*

"If we could enter the attic, nailing two-by-fours to the rafters would be a lot easier," Christopher said.

Johnnie laughed. "Don't even think about it."

She wiped the sweat from the back of her neck. Thanks to Ocelot, a stack of plywood waited to cover the hole. After cutting the plywood decking to the right size, they would secure the decking to the framing, add tar paper and shingles, and tell Ms. Tina she was good to go. Without the lift, they would have spent the morning hauling sheets up the side of the house, and the job would have stretched into two days. *Maybe I should thank Christopher instead of mocking his efforts.* She wrinkled her nose. *The man's not an altruistic hero. He's running a business.* She frowned and glanced at him. Side by side with Johnnie, he could have been any overly developed high school quarterback turned handyman. Her attraction to the man and her annoyance with his circumstances felt like ambivalence, and that emotion never sat well with her.

A horn beeped.

Looking down, she spotted her mother carrying two brown paper bags brimming with food. "Lunch is here!"

Christopher looked up. "But we're not done."

Johnnie laughed. "Oh, everybody stops for Mrs. Lenore's chicken salad. The flock just about lays down their heads. It's that good."

She swallowed. Having helped her mother thin the flock once or twice, she preferred not to burden Johnnie with the specifics. Gripping the ladder rails, she swung her foot over the edge of the roof and walked down the rungs. *Saved by chicken.*

The lift lowered, and Johnnie and Christopher waved on the way down.

"Don't eat my sandwich!" she said.

Johnnie laughed.

Christopher rubbed his lip, but when he dropped his hand, he smiled.

Too tired to keep fighting, she sighed. *I'm onto you, rich boy. You want to play* The Prince and the Pauper? *Welcome to Ronan! We'll kill you with kindness until you can't wait to plunk down a wad of cash for a Greek Revival pile or turn tail and run back to Atlanta.* Dropping her tool belt near the ladder's base, she walked toward her mother and accepted a brown paper sack. "I'm so happy to see you!"

Nancy's gaze widened. "You are?"

Tearing open the bag, she settled onto one of the old railroad ties Ms. Tina used to line her flowerbeds. "I'm starving." Biting into the cool, rich sandwich, she looked down the length of the tie, saw her friends and neighbors working together and replayed Christopher's digs. *We've never been stronger!*

Christopher plopped down beside her.

Without tar paper's pungent odor, he smelled like a pine forest. She scooted an inch to the left, but the scent remained. Unlike the woody, sharp resins left by a lawnmower, he smelled like the woods themselves. She would take his airy, transparent warmth any day of the week. Not trusting her nose, she scooted to the side and added space to clear her senses.

He unlaced his boots.

"New shoes?" she asked.

He shook his head. "I forgot to pack socks" — peeling back the tongue, he revealed a raw blister — "and my assistant took my truck. I figured he would be back by now, but he can't seem to find his way to a super center without GPS."

She lowered her sandwich. "You have an assistant."

He nodded, slipped off the boot and winced.

His foot looked as golden and sun-kissed as his face. *Come on. Why couldn't it be pasty and hairy?*

"Christopher!"

Taken aback, she looked up to see Rebecca charging across the lawn. Her bright, blue sundress flared around her narrow waist, but the station cameraman lugging equipment looked like he needed a cool drink of water.

Nancy stepped in front of the pair. "Well, I heard we had a celebrity in town."

Rebecca stopped and blinked. "Aren't you sweet?"

"Sandwich?" Nancy held up the offering.

The cameraman nodded and reached for the sweet, white bread.

Smiling, Rebecca bypassed Nancy and walked right up to Christopher. "I found you!" She beamed. "And you found Taylor. How perfect! The viewers will eat up the two of you working together."

Standing, Christopher shook his head. "Rebecca, I'm here to test drive a few pieces of equipment and help Ronan. I'm not interested in giving an interview."

Hearing him call the woman by her first name, Taylor stood. "Me neither."

Rebecca smiled at Christopher and blinked. Some unspoken communication passed between the pair, and Taylor felt left out. "How long have you two known each other?"

Glancing at her, Rebecca smiled. "Oh, honey, we go way back, but everyone in Atlanta knows Christopher Durand. Why do you think your online skirmishes drew so much attention?"

"But-t." She replayed the popularity of her posts. *Had the likes gone up before or after he started leaving comments?* She exhaled. "I'll leave you two to chat."

"No...stay!" Rebecca said. "You're the perfect foil."

"I hardly know the man."

Christopher shifted. "Don't you think that's a bit harsh? I just spent a morning with you pulling nails. Surely, I get a nod of recognition."

She plucked a sweet from her lunch, tossed it to him and smiled. "Have a cookie."

He caught it, but his gaze widened.

Rebecca laughed.

Suppressing a smile, she walked toward her father. "Oh, come on... Fuck!"

Hearing Christopher's exclamation, she turned and found him standing on one foot, squeezing shut his eyes and gripping his bare foot in his hand.

He pulled out a roofing nail and swore.

I've done that. She moved to offer him comfort.

Rebecca reached him first. "Oh, Christopher! Are you okay?"

He nodded. "Just stupid."

Taylor wanted to leave the couple to sort out their lives, but responsibility niggled at her consciousness. Stopping, she exhaled and licked her lips. *I just wanted to eat my lunch and feel good about doing something for Ms. Tina. I was even going to let the man hang around a while and not sass him.* She cleared her throat. "When's the last time you had a tetanus shot?"

His gray eyes widened, and he mumbled under his breath, "A while ago."

Taking pity on him, she nodded. "Come on. Grab your boot and I'll give you a ride to the clinic. They can patch up your wound and save you from lockjaw, public shaming and a painful death."

He lowered his foot. "I thought you didn't like me."

She straightened her shoulders. "I thought you didn't like me."

Glancing from left to right, he took in the activity. "I'm here, aren't I?"

Her cheeks warmed.

"A ride's unnecessary," Rebecca said. "I can take him."

Looking up, Taylor raised her eyebrows. "Aren't you here to report on the recovery?"

Rebecca lifted her chin. "Something like that." She turned to the cameraman and jerked her thumb toward the house. "Let's get B roll while I figure out how to spin this stuff into an update."

The cameraman looked longingly at his sandwich.

Taylor felt sorry for the man, but she had enough problems.

Picking up his boot and his sandwich, Christopher ambled toward her. "A lift would be great."

She nodded and headed toward the car. Johnnie's wife, Jeannie Mae, ran up. Her thick, auburn ponytail swung behind her head.

"Peaches, you going to the clinic?" She thrust out an envelope. "Drop this at the post office? I swear, I keep meaning to mail it, but it's been festering in my purse." She dug in her pocket. "I'm sure I have change for a stamp."

Taking the letter, Taylor smiled. "Don't worry about it."

"You're the best, and people know it!" Jeannie Mae grinned. "In the middle of all this upheaval, I'm glad Ronan Reads can still send out online orders."

She stilled. After she and Plucky had climbed from the basement, checked on their families and triaged their neighbors, they'd sorted the books that had survived the storm. Damaged titles went on her insurance claim, and salvageable books went to storage. The laborious process felt like torture, but leaving the books exposed to the elements would have hurt more. "We haven't shipped orders since the storm."

Jeannie Mae tilted her head. "Oh, but I saw Plucky at the post office with a whole heap of boxes."

"Before the storm?" Taylor asked.

"No." Jeannie Mae puffed out her cheeks and exhaled. "After."

She frowned for a moment but connected the dots. "Those must be deliveries for her relief foundation."

Jeannie Mae laughed. "Of course! What a sweetheart."

Nodding and picking up their lunches, she walked toward the car and tried not to admire Christopher as he hobbled at her side.

"So, about this nickname." He reached for the passenger door handle.

She blinked to clear her mind and looked over the roof. "Ignore it."

"Can I still have a ride?"

Beneath the noon sun, his smooth, bronzed cheeks and strong jawline looked menacing, but she heard nothing but compassion in his voice. *Maybe a little pain.* Having started the morning on pins and needles, his persistence and good humor had shaken her out of her funk. She tossed the lunches on the back seat. "Get in."

He opened the passenger door.

She put the key in the ignition.

Dropping onto the faded upholstery, he reached for his seatbelt. "Who's Plucky?"

His question had too many nuances. She dropped her shoulders and rolled her head. "She works at Ronan Reads. You probably saw her when you came to visit."

"I only had eyes for you."

She frowned.

He cleared his throat. "But you're not shipping out books."

She put the car in drive. "I know."

"So, what is she doing?"

Checking her mirrors, she cut away from the curb "Taking donations for storm relief. I haven't seen her in days. I'm sure she's busting her butt."

"Does she get a tetanus shot, too?"

She laughed and glanced at him holding pressure on the puncture wound. "No, but you're going to have a hard time talking smack and living down that little boo-boo."

"This? This is nothing."

Navigating the sparse traffic of rubber-neckers, joy-riding locals and county vehicles, she looked at his long frame and admired how he filled the passenger seat. If she took him at his word, he had mobilized a small army of equipment and deployed it to a ravaged cotton town. She understood moral imperatives and bottom lines, but his motives held shades of gray that she struggled to understand. *He said this banter means nothing, but I'm paying way too much attention to the man. If it's not nothing, what is it?*

Chapter Eight

Sitting in the passenger seat, Christopher rubbed his foot and wished he had sucked up the pain of the blister and left his boot in place. *A misstep like that could have killed me in Iraq.* Watching the pine trees along the side of the country road, he thought of the tall, slender towers he'd seen in the desert. At each mosque, a *muezzin* had stood on the balcony of the minaret and called Muslims to prayer. Like so many of the wind-ravaged pine trees, the towers had succumbed to superior forces. He missed their cry and the siren call of the desert winds, but Iraq would never be his home.

"Does it hurt?" Taylor asked.

He kept his gaze trained on the view. *Pain isn't the right emotion. The human and financial cost of the conflict left behind a mind-numbing sadness and a sense of guilt. We should have done better. I should have done better.* Forcing himself to relax, he dropped his shoulders, plastered a good-natured smile on his face and dropped his muted phone in the cup holder. "Nah, just a minor wound. If you weren't so particular about doctor's orders, I'd still be swinging a hammer and accomplishing work."

Glancing at him, she snorted. "Yeah, right. Without me, you'd be standing on the curb, scanning the horizon for signs of your assistant and searching your phone for the nearest urgent care clinic." She slowed the car and made a left. "It's halfway back to Atlanta."

Probably. He scratched his lip. *The sass is back, and I like it.* He glanced at the dancing hula girl. *How old is this car?* "What's wrong with having an assistant?"

"When the two of you strolled into town yesterday, I thought he was your partner."

He frowned. "Ocelot Enterprises is a family-owned company."

She laughed. "Not that kind of partner."

Recognition warmed his cheeks, and he rubbed his forehead. *Apparently, my flirting skills are as rusty as that old nail.* He stilled his hand. *Do I want to flirt?*

"I mean, I'm fine with your choices. You and Dillan do your thing. Love who you want to love."

He laughed. "Well, aren't you liberal?" Watching her open her mouth, he took mercy on her pink cheeks and decided to cut off her defenses before she dug a hole deep enough to swallow the day. "Dilly works hard, but trust me, I prefer blondes."

She demurred from his pointed stare and chewed her lip.

Noting how the pink lingered on her cheeks, he grinned, but he questioned whether he wanted her attention or he wanted to win. William had brought home a succession of simpering sorority girls who'd gone to church every Sunday, crossed off their to-do lists with fruit-scented ink pens and known how to spot the difference between personal monograms and couples' monograms. *I should go home.*

He'd dated Rebecca and her pedigreed, lily-white ambitions, but the minute he'd caught her surfing wedding websites, his stomach had flipped. *I don't know why she wanted to book the cathedral. She spent most of the church services whispering about what the other women wore.* Watching Taylor grip the steering wheel at two and four, he imagined her chin lifted in adoration and her voice joining a congregation of believers. He struggled to wrap his mind around that kind of devotion. Surrounded by performative Christians, he had no problem with religion, but he felt little need to embrace it. *Let's be honest. Taylor wouldn't be in the pews. She'd be in the choir. She's running me to the clinic, and she doesn't even like me.* He thought about her on Ms. Tina's roof and frowned. *She genuinely cares about people. Who else do I know who fits that description?*

"The clinic's just ahead," she said. "We're lucky the post office chose Ronan for a regional sorting facility and moved the main branch out of town."

He tried to focus. "Lucky?"

She glanced at him. "Otherwise, it'd be a pile of rubble."

"Right." He cleared his throat.

She waved her hand toward the scenery. "After the government built the sorting facility, savvy local investors plunked down a cluster of businesses. The clinic used to be a grocery store."

"Wait! You let people build strip malls in Ronan?"

She glanced at him. "Um, the post office moved in 1920."

Spotting the short, brick building and a gas station with a rusted sign, he laughed. "Which direction is the nearest super center?"

She pulled into a cracked parking lot, dodged a pothole and parked. "East."

By now, Dillar's probably in Florida. He climbed from the car and put weight on his foot. Wincing, he tried not to hobble toward the clear, glass door marked with gold lettering. He shifted his weight to his heel, but friction rubbed the blister. He tried the side of his foot, but the pressure squeezed the wound. *Hell, I might as well hop.* Taking a deep breath, he ignored the pain and aimed for the clinic door.

Breezing past him, she opened the door and held it. "Dr. Greene?"

He felt a blast of cold air and stepped into a tidy office that smelled of antiseptic and furniture polish. A man wearing khaki pants and a white, button-up shirt stepped out of an exam room. His creased, dark skin and the white-flecked black hair demanded respect, but his ramrod-straight posture gave away his military training.

Before landing in Iraq, Christopher had thought he had good posture, but the Army had drilled his form until it shaped his life. The moment he'd returned to Georgia, his mother had dried her eyes, brushed lint from his shoulder and told him to stop crossing his arms. Calling the posture 'command presence' had failed to sway her opinion, but a decade later, he recognized the doctor's body language and grinned. "You were a combat medic?"

Dr. Greene nodded and extended his hand. "Vietnam, but these days, I deliver babies, set casts and sew sutures."

He nodded. The war was the first conflict after the civil rights revolution of the 1950s and '60s. Even though Executive Order 9981 had desegregated the armed forces in 1948, many units had remained segregated until 1954. By most accounts, Vietnam soldiers had shared supplies, told stories and jokes and offered each other the empathy needed to survive active duty. When they'd returned to domestic soil, equality had shattered and race relations had mattered. *I would love to share a beer with this man and see what he says about life in Ronan.* "Not many babies on the battlefield."

Cracking a smile, Dr. Greene crossed his arms and jerked his head toward Taylor. "Combat soldiers and Sparrow Country's youth came to me for help, but the soldiers didn't give me lip."

She stuck out her tongue.

Dr. Greene laughed. "Well, you seem fine." He turned to Christopher. "What's your story?"

He cleared his throat. "I need a tetanus shot."

Dr. Greene raised his head and nodded.

"He stepped on a nail," Taylor said. "You should probably look at it."

Christopher crossed his arms. "The wound's not bleeding. Just give me the shot."

Dr. Greene handed him a clipboard. "Sign the last page and give me a copy of your insurance card."

Pulling his wallet from his back pocket, he sighed. *I should have taken Dilly's socks.*

Ten minutes later, he sat on a paper-covered exam table and watched Dr. Greene tweeze debris from the wound. Each pinch felt like a cut, and he wondered if lockjaw would have been an easier outcome.

"So, what brings you to Ronan?" Dr. Greene asked.

"Recovery aid," he said.

"Publicity," Taylor countered.

Raising his head, Dr. Greene looked up. "After the storm, I patched up several injuries." Applying a thin layer of a topical antibiotic cream, he added a heavyweight bandage. "Some people got off lucky."

"Some didn't," Taylor said.

Dr. Greene turned on the swivel stool. "You doing okay, Taylor?"

She ripped out nails as fast as I did, and she looked good doing it.

She met the doctor's gaze. "I can't sleep much."

Her voice wavered.

He wanted to take her hand and steady her.

The doctor nodded. "You talked to anyone?"

She shook her head. "Everyone's been busy."

"My door's always open."

Dr. Green looked like the kind of man who accepted life in all its messy, broken forms and still loved it. Christopher wanted to be that man.

She smiled. "Thanks."

He frowned. *She lost her business and half her town. Of course she's bent out of shape. What kind of jackass am I, giving her a hard time?* Swinging his legs over the table, he rolled up his shirtsleeve and exposed his arm.

Dr. Green swabbed his skin and administered the shot. "Give the nail wound a few days to heal. Keep it clean, change the bandage after showering and watched for signs of bacterial infection. Tetanus isn't about rust. It's about penetration." He removed his gloves and tossed them into the trashcan. "Only fools let wounds fester."

Nodding, Christopher rolled down his shirtsleeve and hopped off the table. Landing on both feet, he closed his eyes and bit his lip. *Next time I decide to play handyman, I'll pack an entire bag of socks.*

"How're you feeling?" Taylor asked.

He smiled. "Peachy."

She shook her head and followed Dr. Greene out of the exam room.

"How's the town's recovery going?" Dr. Greene asked.

She tucked her hair behind her ears. "Good. The weather's warming up. We'll need a fleet of portable air conditioners to get through the summer."

Christopher made a mental note to see what his logistic coordinator could find. Sliding his credit card across the counter, he watched Dr. Greene print out a receipt for an office copay. "I'm surprised you're in my network."

Dr. Greene laughed. "I'm not. I gave you a discount."

"You didn't have to do..."

Taylor took his arm and steered him toward the door.

Despite the heavily air-conditioned clinic, he felt the warmth of her touch and the steely pressure she exerted on his arm. *Fine, you can be the boss of your town.* Looking over his shoulder, he met Dr. Greene's gaze. "Thanks."

The man nodded. "Any time."

Free of the clinic, he wanted to finish the lunch he'd started, kick up his feet and enjoy the pleasure of a cold beer. He closed his eyes for a moment and envisioned the heady freedom of relaxation. In his midday fantasy, Taylor leaned across the blanket, her breasts peeking from a flowered sundress. Cue the record scratching sound effect. Blinking, he opened his eyes and found her staring. She wore a braid, sensible denim and a long-sleeved work shirt. *I can still hold out hope for the sundress.*

"Are you sure he gave you a tetanus shot?"

A smile tugged at the corner of her mouth. He cleared his throat. "I slipped him a tip and asked for the good stuff."

She laughed.

Her lighthearted response died too quickly.

Turning her head, she exhaled. "I need to see what Plucky's up to."

Shit, I forgot about her friend's mysterious packages. "Do you want me to wait in the car?"

She shook her head. "Ronan can't keep a secret. If she's up to no good, the entire town will know, so I might as well know first and help her untangle the mess." Squaring her shoulders, she walked toward a concrete building. Above the gold lettering, a relief of an eagle in flight crowned the entryway.

A bell tinkled, and he blinked in the dim light. Brass and warm wood anchored an oasis of civilized efficiency. Each polished mailbox waited for an old-fashioned key. Behind an older man wearing a postal worker's blue uniform, a grid of neat pigeon-hole message boxes stood guard over tablets and digital tracking systems. The cubbies' uniform precision suggested a readiness to step into action, but he heard mechanical mail sorters whirring behind the brass screen.

"Can I help you?" the postal worker asked.

Taylor approached the counter, set down her keys and leaned on her elbows. "Hey, Jeb."

Jeb nudged forward a tray of plastic-wrapped suckers. "You're too old for a lollypop but have one anyway."

She laughed.

Christopher smiled. *I'm not sure if she plays her part or trains everyone in town.*

"Mail dried up after the storm?"

Jeb scratched his silver hair. "Advertisements and magazines don't care for the weather forecast. Most people have gone to online bill pay. Short of packages, the biggest excitement I see is a load of wedding invitations or hand-written thank you cards." Glancing at Christopher, he smiled. "Life still brings me surprises."

He nodded.

"Plucky been by?"

"Sure," Jeb said. "She picks up Ronan Reads deliveries and drops off orders on her way home."

Taylor cleared her throat. "I'm surprised she had time to get them together. The town's a mess."

Jeb shrugged. "Unless the contents are hazardous, liquid or perishable, I don't question the packages."

"I think she might have mixed up the boxes for the store and the boxes for her new foundation," Taylor said. "Could I pop back there and see what's in the biggest box?"

"Now, Peaches, you know you can't go in the sorting room."

She straightened. "But, Jeb…"

"Don't 'but Jeb' me. I'm not about to risk my pension for a pretty girl."

"What about a pretty boy?"

Jeb laughed. "You shut your mouth."

Christopher watched the pair banter and felt like a neglected boyfriend at a girls' lunch. "You two planning to go on vacation soon?"

Taylor laughed and placed her friend's letter on the counter. She dug through her purse, fished out two quarters and slid them to Jeb. "Jeannie Mae sends her love."

"What a sweetheart," Jeb said.

Taylor nodded and backed out of the room. "I can't wait until she and Johnnie have babies."

Christopher cleared his throat.

Backing up, she laughed and shrugged, but the bell tinkled, and an older man walked into the post office. She backed right into him.

The man swore, and a pile of mail hit the ground.

She turned and gasped. "Mr. Nelson! I'm *so* sorry!"

Christopher crossed his arms and decided he should have waited in the car.

"Here! Let me help you." She crouched and scooped up the letters and magazines that had fallen from Nelson's hands.

The man's long limbs tangled with Taylor's helpful scoops, and he swore. Looking up, he met Christopher's gaze and swallowed. "Sorry for the foul language."

Caught on the perimeter of the room with no purpose and no escape, he nodded and let Taylor untangle the mess.

She stood, brushed off her knees and reached for a final envelope. Holding it in her hand, she frowned "What's this?"

Nelson snatched at the envelope, but she held it fast

"Why's the rosin factory sending mail to your wife?" She dropped her hand to her side. "Is Martha working there, too?"

Shifting his mail to one side, Nelson held out his hand. "That's my property."

She held the envelope up to the light. "It's a check."

Christopher abandoned his hopes for fresh air.

"Don't worry about it, Peaches." Nelson reached for the envelope. "I'll take care of it."

"But-t" — she handed over the check — "Mr. Nelson, what's going on?"

Hearing the uncertainty in her voice, Christopher met Jeb's gaze. Against the brass and warm wood of the old-fashioned mailboxes and pigeon-hole sorting system, the postmaster's pale face and twitching, gray eyebrow convinced Christopher that Jeb knew the contents of the envelope. He wondered if the postmaster's pained expression spoke to the magnitude of the secret.

Squeezing shut his eyes, Jeb cleared his throat. "It's nothing, Taylor."

"Exactly!" Nelson tore the envelope from her hands.

She tilted her head and stared at the tall man. Turning, she looked at Jeb. "What's going on?"

The postmaster sighed and closed his eyes. "After Nelson's AIDS diagnosis landed him in the hospital too many times to count, Social Security deemed him unable to work and put him on disability benefits."

The worlds tumbled from his mouth like a pent-up reservoir. Christopher rubbed the side of his mouth and waited.

"HIPPA!" Nelson shouted.

Jeb held up his hand.

"Okay," she said.

"When he got the virus under control, he went to work at the rosin factory and concealed his employment income from SSA by accepting payment in Martha's name" — opening his eyes, Jeb stared at Nelson — "and he doesn't even love her."

Taylor gasped.

"Fucking hell, Jeb!" Nelson stormed past Taylor and slapped his hand on the postmaster's counter. "Can't keep your mouth shut, can you?"

"The last time I checked, you couldn't keep your pants shut!"

Jeb's cheeks colored, and Christopher scratched his chin. *This should be interesting.* He moved closer to Taylor.

"Watch your mouth!"

Jeb pointed. "You're the one keeping secrets, Bill Nelson! You've lived a double life for decades, and everyone with a lick of sense knows it except Martha." He shook his head. "Blood transfusion, my ass."

"You have designs on my wife?" Nelson asked.

"I have designs on you!"

The two men stared at each other.

"I think we need to go," Taylor said.

Her announcement filled the silence, but she remained still.

Dr. Green walked into the room, assessed the situation, and crossed his arms. "Everything all right?"

Leaving the man to referee, Christopher took Taylor's arm and pulled her back toward the door. Ocelot had nothing to do with rosin production. The translucent resin derived from pine trees conditioned the bows of stringed instruments, but it also went into varnishes, inks, linoleum, adhesives and soldering compounds. He had no expertise in the subtleties of the sticky, small-batch compound, but he recognized a tinderbox about to explode. "Let them sort it out."

She planted her feet.

"They don't need a lecture."

She looked up. "A lecture on what? They both look like they're about to cry."

Her blinking expression tugged at his heartstrings. Faced with federal fraud and two men sorting out their lives, she had little need for biblical teachings, moral outrage or condemnation. *She's worried about them.* He tugged her arm again. "Jeb knew about the fraud. One day, it would have come out."

Swallowing, she moved toward the front door. "That doesn't make it right."

"Does it matter to you?" When the shock wore off, Jeb and Nelson might be desperate to hide their secrets, but he wanted her clear of the charged confrontation. *What will Nelson do to keep his secret? What will Jeb do now that it's out?* He pulled her into the bright sunlight. "Come outside for a breath of air."

Looking over her shoulder, she craned her neck toward the two men and their dialogue, but the door shut, and the conversation sank into the background noise of passing cars, swaying trees and humming cicadas. "Their troubles aren't your business."

"Of course they're my business!"

Hearing her outrage, he smiled. "The entire town's your business?"

She raised her chin. "Mr. Nelson was a hard-ass science teacher. He made people cry! Senior year, he went on disability, but I never knew why he left the school."

"No guesses?" he asked. "The town's not that big."

"Plucky told me he had HIV, but I didn't believe her." She looked down the road. "Her mom's a nurse at the county hospital, but why would she share something that private?"

"You thought Plucky was making up the story?"

"I thought she was trying to be outrageous." Turning toward the post office, she sighed. "Turns out, Plucky wasn't the outrageous one."

"Having HIV isn't an outrage."

"No, but Mr. Nelson had this bit he did every year during the lesson on lab safety. He'd take an extension cord and hold up both ends. '*Look*,' he'd say. '*The cord has a male end and a female end, and they only go together one way*.' I'd cringe, because I knew there were gay kids in the classroom, and I wondered how much strength it took to hear that kind of bullshit your entire life and still keep your head above water."

"Did you say anything?"

She shook her head. "I felt too intimidated. What does that make me?"

He smiled. "Young." Her confusion bordered on endearing. Every online post she made had exuded cheerful optimism and playful promotion. The positive bias had intrigued and infuriated him, but her resiliency had earned his respect. *She's exhausted and frustrated. Losing her store and her hometown didn't break her, but losing confidence in her old teacher set her wobbling on the edge. What can I do to help?*

"Why would he lie to the people in this town? And to his employer?" She gasped. "The government!"

He stared at the post office building. "You can't judge people's motives. Just live and let live."

She let her shoulders slump. "I'm sorry you had to see that mess. We're usually much nicer in Ronan."

"I'm sure." He tried to sort out his impulses. *I'm here to clear debris. Dr. Greene can handle maintaining the relationships.* When Taylor looked up, her disappointed expression made him want to do more than clear out the storm's mess.

She walked past him and put her hand on the car door. "Let's get you back to town."

"Are you sure?"

She brushed her eye. "Just give me a second and I'll be right as rain."

He scanned the worn parking lot. Across the road, faded white eves and a worn, gray roof peeked from the shadows of oaks and mature azalea bushes. The forgotten South teased glimpses of beauty, but had the farmers fallen on hard times or migrated north? Dropped pink and white flowers littered the ground. In a few more days, the blooms would brown, mix with last year's pine straw and begin their return to the earth. *Alpha to omega and dust to dust. What will be my legacy?* He cleared his throat. "I'm sure your teacher has his reasons."

She spun and planted her hands on her hips. "You didn't have to be nice to him!"

Suppressing a smile, he held his palms in front of his chest. *I'm not sure what I'd do with tears, but I can handle a spitting wildcat.* "Desperate men steal money."

She threw her hands in the air. "He's not desperate! The rosin factory pays him a good wage."

He rubbed his lip and watched her disappointment turn to frustration. Color tinged her cheeks, and though he could have blamed the sun, her pinched face and narrowed gaze signaled a wave of frustration riding the storm's wake. "People have done more for less."

Her mouth dropped open, but she closed it and bit her lip.

I could help you find something to do with that mouth. A slight sheen of sweat gloss her cheeks, and he realized she had more to say about Nelson's betrayal than she'd let on. "Cat got your tongue?"

Turning, she flexed her fingers at her sides and walked to the car.

"Warm weather got you a little piqued?"

She patted her back pockets and dug in her purse.

"You left your keys on the doctor's counter."

She shielded her eyes from the sun and stormed toward the clinic door.

As he passed him, he cupped her elbow. "I don't have to be nice."

Her gaze narrowed.

"You want to go a few rounds?" He pulled her against his chest. "I can take you." Her eyes widened, and he lowered his lips, brushing them against her soft, salt-tinged surprise. "The question is, can you take me?"

She turned away. "I hardly know you."

Her chest rose and fell, but she glanced at his mouth and wet her lips. He released her elbow and grinned. "Even better. You mad about the theft or mad about the betrayal?"

She sighed. "Mr. Nelson has a roof over his head and a wife who loves him. Walk through downtown Ronan and tell me who's desperate."

Risking his life, he rubbed her arm and remembered the chocolate icing. "He was your mentor."

She nodded. "I've known him my entire life."

He thought of his mentors. They might have his back on the golf course or battle him for auction items, but if his world imploded, he wanted C.Y.'s patience and hardened mettle. "Duration doesn't strengthen relationships, but trouble does."

She toed a rock.

"You'll hear his side of the story and let go of your outrage."

"But he's stealing from the government!"

His lips ticked up into a smile. "Call the tip line."

She sighed. "I liked you better when you were going to kiss me."

He stepped closer. "Did you?"

She sniffled.

The desire warming his blood had nothing on the midday sun, but her emotions ran high, and he wanted her thoughts free and clear before he did more than brush her lips. "Are you going to cry?"

Pulling back, she slapped his chest.

He winced and smoothed the fabric. "Hey, you'll wrinkle the shirt."

She squared her shoulders. "I don't cry!"

He shrugged. "You looked close to it."

She marched toward the clinic door and looked over her shoulder. "Go back to Atlanta!"

A fleeting smile parted her kissable lips. He grinned. "You know Atlanta's only an hour away, right?"

Dr. Greene opened the post office door, stepped into the sunshine and jangled the car keys he had stored in his pocket. "You forget something?"

Taking the keys from his hand, she smiled. "Thank you."

Dropping his chin, Dr. Greene nodded. "I heard the commotion and came over. Those two have a decade of lies to untangle. Everything okay with you?"

She shaded her eyes and smiled. "Of course! I'm fine."

Dr. Greene looked at him.

Yeah, I'm not buying it, either. She can keep actin' like an outraged church lady, but the postmaster's the one with a heavy heart. He shrugged.

"Why don't y'all pick up lunch, go break at the reservoir and stick your feet in the water," Dr. Greene said.

Christopher considered the suggestion, but deep water had gotten him into this mess. Without a flood risk, he might have chosen Ronan for the factory site and built an interpersonal wall so high that Taylor's empathy, sparkling eyes and damn-near-perfect ass would have never scaled it.

Helming Ocelot had ruined his raw appreciation of sun, party boats and country life. The last time a friend had invited him out for a boat ride, he'd spent the day studying houses and wondering how many people lived in the floodplain. *I wish I'd never heard of risk assessment, but I can't spend my life weighing the pros and cons of every decision.* The thought of nearly kissing Taylor made him regret his restraint, but the practicalities of his life kept him grounded.

A dam choked every major Georgia river. Residents loved the resulting public waterways, but few understood the possibility of dam failures and government management. "A reservoir might be just what we need to cool down. Sandwiches are in the car."

Taylor shook her head, walked past him and opened the car door. "We need to get back to downtown."

Approaching the vehicle, he cleared his throat. "You going to single-handedly save Ronan?"

She lifted her chin.

"Pride cometh before the fall," he said.

Meeting his gaze, she rolled her eyes. "Don't quote scripture at me."

"What? You don't like that verse?"

"You're not religious." She shook her head and leaned on the car door. "People shouldn't use quotes of any kind, scriptures included, without fully understanding the source material."

He laughed and braced his hands on the hot roof. "I know people who dedicated their entire lives to studying scripture, and they still have questions. Who's allowed to read and interpret the Good Book? Your uncle and no one else?"

She stared. "I don't take you for much of a church-goer."

He clapped his hand to his chest. "What? I go every Sunday with my mama." *And spend most of the sermon plotting my week.* "Just because I'm not a believer doesn't mean I don't pay attention." *Sort of.* "I'm spiritual. I try to do good."

"And your daddy?"

He spends most of the sermon on his phone. Leaning on the roof of the car, he smiled. "Regular member of the congregation at the Cathedral of St. Philip."

"Huh."

"Why aren't you in a nunnery?"

She frowned.

"You're not all in, are you?" he asked. "You're okay with Nelson's love, just not his lies."

She rolled her eyes.

"Peaches…"

She held up her hand and turned away. "No."

He rolled his shoulders and wondered how fast he could claim a real kiss, squash his intrigue and box up his interest in this woman. "I have a hole in my foot and a clawing hunger in my stomach. You must be hungry, too. Let's fuel up before we head back to town. Your daddy seems like he has Ms. Tina's repairs under control. The crew won't miss you."

"My daddy has called me three times."

"Huh."

She smiled. "Lunch, but only because your crew's probably scratching their heads and wondering what to do without your help."

"Nah, that'd be Dilly."

She laughed. "Twenty minutes, but then we get back to work."

He slapped the roof. "Deal!"

Rolling her eyes, she closed the driver's side door.

He lingered and scanned the cluster of buildings. *Being the boss has benefits. Between the Ocelot dealer and the drivers I bought from Atlanta, nobody needs me onsite to accomplish work.* He opened the passenger door and settled in the bucket seat. *Does that mean I'm redundant?* He loosened his collar and rubbed his face. "So, how far away is this reservoir?"

"A mile up the road. It's a nice lake, but you need a jon boat or something to enjoy it. We'll have to settle for the bank."

He looked out of the window and thought of the last time he'd woken up early, pushed an aluminum, flat-bottomed boat into clear, cool water and waited for nature's rhythms to soothe his mind. *Hell, most of the time, I throw back the fish and just watch the ducks.* "I could do with some time on the bank."

"You're going to lose your bet."

Shifting in the seat, he shook his head and thought of the fleet of black-and-cream machines clearing Ronan's debris. *What do I need to rebuild?* The beautiful woman beside him turned up the radio and rolled down the car window. In a room of Atlanta socialites, her tan-and-blonde hair would blend with the crowd, but beneath the shadows of the pine trees, her blue eyes shone. *I'll tease her, we'll share a lackluster kiss and she'll be out of my system.* Smiling, he gripped this thigh and flexed his fingers. "Don't cash in your chips just yet."

Chapter Nine

Taylor turned onto the old reservoir's gravel drive and replayed the brush of Christopher's lips. *His kiss was chaste and comforting, wasn't it?* Nothing about her response fit into those neat, affectionate boxes. Risking a glance at his honed profile, she wanted to forget Nelson's fraud, the storm and every bad decision she'd ever made. *Wouldn't one terrible decision trump them all? Why am I the only one trying to behave?* She gripped the steering wheel and grinned, but she would keep her legs together and her fantasies to herself.

Up the road, a modernized reservoir charged three dollars for admission, but like her, the birds and fish preferred the old site's solitude. Bass, bream and channel catfish mined the waters, while bald eagles, loons and ducks claimed the sky. She'd built a lifetime of memories at the lake and constructed one of the wood duck boxes in the west side's grassy, shallow waters. Spying a deer on the small, sandy beach, she smiled.

The doe looked at the car and bolted.

Do I belong here? Her skin tingled, and she reached for the knob controlling the air conditioner. Feeling the blast of cold air, she prayed the temperature change would center her thoughts.

She eased off the accelerator, put the vehicle in park and crossed her arms over the steering wheel. Turning her face to the cold air, she breathed deeply and wanted to close her eyes, but she feared losing the day's momentum. *What other lies did Mr. Nelson tell me?* Tears threatened to fall.

"Are we going to eat in the car?" Christopher asked.

Turning her head, she forced a smile. He looked as confident and cocky as the day he'd rolled into town, but somewhere between Ms. Tina's house and Jeb's station, he'd found room to relax his shoulders. "Sure. You want to let the AC run?"

He laughed and reached for the door handle. "No way. The minute I step foot in Ronan, you'll rat me out, and every one of my drivers will laugh me out of town."

Wait until they hear how Mr. Nelson pulled over a fast one. Stepping from the car, she focused on the well-loved scenery. The birds chirped, the trees swayed and her worries would pass. *I'll ask Mr. Nelson to turn himself in or I'll call the tip line.* Setting aside her standards for a teacher and trying to view his deceit from a peer's perspective, she understood why some people hid their desires, but the greed and fraud stood on its own. Reaching into the back seat, she grabbed the lunch bags and wondered how she would tell the bags apart. Pulling out a sandwich, she laughed at the size of the bite mark and tossed that bag to Christopher. "This one's yours."

Catching the bag in midair, he nodded. "Thanks."

She walked toward an old wooden bench, sat and stretched her legs. In the shade, the air felt pleasant and bees buzzed around the small white blooms of a Serviceberry tree. She inhaled the sweet scent and watched a wood duck drift on the water. Three fuzzy ducklings trailed their mother. "This was a good idea."

Settling beside her, he crossed his ankle over his knee and nodded.

Her sandwich tasted as good as she remembered. She cleared her throat and told herself to relax. *He came to Ronan to help, not handle my crazy.* "You have siblings?"

The hand holding his sandwich stilled midway to his mouth. "Excuse me?"

She waved her free hand toward the ducklings. "Brothers and sisters?"

"I know what you meant." He turned. "You're seriously asking me that question?"

"What?" She took another bite of her sandwich.

Rubbing his face, he exhaled and looked over the water. "You don't know."

She flicked breadcrumbs from her fingers. "Sorry... I mean, I recognize your face from the papers, but I know so little about you." She bit her lip. "Big family?"

He shook his head. "Small."

Choosing silence, she watched the ducks' ripples. *So much for more kisses.*

"I had a brother," he said. "He died."

She squeezed shut her eyes and searched for a way to apologize. Here she was, running her mouth about a teacher's lies when he had suffered real loss. She'd always wanted a sibling, but mourning one seemed much worse than her loneliness. "I'm sorry."

"Most people know the story," he said. "They know better than to ask."

She shifted on the bench. "I'm not most people."

He set aside his sandwich and looked at her. "I know."

Leaning her elbow on the bench's back, she rested her head in her hand. Too embarrassed by her faux pas to ask about his brother, she waited for him to lead the conversation.

He turned and looked at the reservoir. "William lived on campus, but he had a car, and he enjoyed driving his friends around downtown. I was still in high school, but if I was at a house party, he'd drive past, lay on the horn and let his passengers whoop and holler."

"Didn't your house parties have gates?" she asked.

He smiled. "Not all of them."

Holding her breath, she worried that William had lost control of the car and struck a bystander.

"After college, William stayed for business school, and I enrolled in the Army."

"You skipped college?"

"I earned a degree after returning from Iraq." He glanced at her. "Does it matter?"

She considered the question. "No, but it's not what I expected."

He cleared his throat. "A Mississippi college kid peeled out of a parking lot, sideswiped a car and hit William's car head-on."

She released her breath and reached for his arm. Beneath her grip, his arm felt solid, but he kept his gaze focused on the lake.

"The asshole's blood alcohol level was 0.2." Shaking his head, he exhaled. "William's death was all over the

Atlanta news, but stuck in Iraq, I felt a million miles from the loss."

"That must have been rough." Too afraid to retract her hand and leave him adrift, she spread her fingers and held the connection.

He nodded. "People cope in different ways. I buried my head in the sand and finished my tour of duty. My grandfather started a foundation to curb drunk driving and underage drinking." He cleared his throat. "Nothing he does will bring back my brother."

She squeezed his arm and pulled away her hand.

Catching it, he held it in his grip. "William was a good man. I'm glad you asked about him." He smiled and released her. "Although the story's a downer, so you might not be glad you did."

She settled her hands in her lap. "I'm sure your grandfather takes comfort in his work. What an honorable gesture."

"Well, he certainly has the connections."

She tilted her head and frowned.

He cleared his throat. "My grandfather's former Governor James M. Durand."

Realization dawned, and she widened her gaze. Jumping up, she grabbed her lunch. "Um, we're done here."

Catching her hand, he pulled her back to sitting. "Really?"

She stared. After two terms, Governor Durand had run for President, but he'd failed to capture his party's nomination. She should have recognized the connection. The Durand family name popped up so often on the news that she'd leaned to tune out the chatter. "I was like, seven when he ran for office. How was I supposed to know he's your grandfather?"

He laughed and released his hold. "Ronan must be more interesting than I thought."

Sinking onto the bench, she crossed her arms and lifted her chin. "I have better things to do than pay attention to Atlanta news."

"Like what?"

"Run a bookstore. Make dinner." She swallowed. "Pray."

He laughed. "Yeah, your hundred thousand followers and I caught on to those trends."

Any thoughts of a playful flirtation vanished beneath the weight of his family obligations and the depth of their conversation. Sitting beside him, she was so far out of her league that she needed a new rulebook. "I don't understand how you can live without faith."

"Tell me why my brother died."

She exhaled. After so many years, his pain felt palpable, and she doubted she could do anything to soothe it. "I can't answer that question. I know in my darkest moments, I turn to God, and I feel comforted. When I walk into a library, I know I'll never read each book, but I love the order and promise of new discoveries. If my family's habits guided their lives, why can't they guide mine?"

"And other people's habits?"

She faced him. "I can only share what's worked for me."

He toyed with the end of her braid and rubbed the strands between his fingers. "And if no one's there? If the books are gibberish?"

She smiled. "I've never come away disappointed."

Dropping her hair, he stood and stretched his back. "We should get you back to town."

The sun cast long shadows across the grass, but she remained sitting. "Why do you keep doing that?"

He looked down.

"Stretching your back."

"It's always been tight."

She stood. "Maybe your body's trying to tell you something."

He looked at her.

His wry smile softened the pain of their midday break.

"You sound like a West Coast hippie," he said.

People I love have called me worse things. Thinking of the night she'd left Josh, she remembered his slap's sting and his accusations' cutting pain. *I'd rather be an 'ambitious whore' than Josh's wife.* She swallowed. "You'll run for office one day, too, won't you?"

"Maybe."

She nodded. "Then take care of yourself. Limping up to the podium won't help your campaign."

He laughed. "I don't limp."

Looking over the water, she nodded. "Not yet, but I've seen my daddy shuffle home after a long day on the job." She turned and inhaled the summer's humidity. The South carried so much potential for life, no wonder the vines climbed trees to reach the sun. "Maybe you should spend less time in the office and more time using the gifts God gave you."

"Your dad didn't give up his profession."

She smiled. "No, but he changed the way he did things."

Nodding, he dropped his hands and sat beside her. "Smart man."

Is he? She looked over the lake and wondered what kept her parents tied to Ronan. She imagined battling the loss of a family member amid skyscrapers and elevated highways. *I'll take nature and good people any day of the week.* She uncrossed her arms. "Has your grandfather made progress with his advocacy?"

He nodded and unpacked his lunch sack. "Learning to drink might be part of growing up, but everyone should survive the experience. Granddaddy lobbied for more public transportation, improved identification cards and mandatory education classes for servers. Instead of turning on the lights and booting people out of the door, staff should screen patrons for excessive intoxication."

"They can't catch everyone."

He inclined his head. "Every person counts."

She thought of the rowdy bonfires on her family farm and the hired limousine that had taken her and her friends to prom. Her parents had made space for her to learn her limits without dampening her fun. "I hope your brother's legacy saves lives." She smiled. "When I went to college, the underage drinking laws were in full force. Cops were always out checking IDs."

Picking up his sandwich, he took a bite. "You can thank my grandfather for spoiling your fun."

She grinned. "We had plenty of fun, but I'm sorry about your brother."

He nodded.

"I'm also sorry for sticking my foot in my mouth."

Laughing, he slapped his chest and swallowed. "Noted."

She finished her sandwich. "Do you drink?"

He nodded. "I do, but I drink responsibly."

He probably does everything responsibly. She considered eating her bag of chips but slouched on the bench and enjoyed the scenery. *Except wear socks.*

Grinning, she felt childish, but the breeze caressed her skin, and the reality waiting downtown hurt too much. "We should get back."

Opening his bag of chips, he offered her one.

"Thanks." She took a chip, bit it and wondered what heavenly whim had merged their paths. *A thousand people could have aided Ronan, but Christopher came. If the Lord has plans for good and not for disaster, I'd feel a lot better if I could glimpse the plan.* She crunched the chip and imaged her uncle telling her to be humble, patient and kind. Digging her foot in the grass, she looked at Christopher. "How long were you in Iraq?"

"Until the war ended in 2011."

She tried to piece together a timeline. "And your brother died?"

"2005."

I was still in middle school. Well, at least God has a sense of humor. After high school graduation, she'd gone to college with her childhood sweetheart, and her world had narrowed. Senior year, between exams and wedding preparations, she'd barely had time to breathe, much less read the news.

"You said you didn't have a brother. Sisters?" he asked.

Wait! He listens? I told Josh I needed more time, but he didn't pay attention to the big requests, much less the small ones. "My parents tried for more kids, but no luck."

He tilted the bag her way.

Taking another chip, she savored the salty crunch and the simple pleasure of sharing a bench. "My dad was the youngest of three brothers. The oldest inherited the farm, the second went to seminary and my dad made his way in the world as contractor." She smiled.

"I guess he should have gone into the military, but he balked."

"Smart man."

She considered him. "You regret your service."

He shook his head. "No, but honoring the commitment was rough."

I'm sure the years toughened you. She let the scene and a full stomach lull her.

He shifted his weight.

She sat straight, gripping the edge of the bench.

"You're no longer spitting nails, but you're jumpy."

She shook her head. "Since the storm, I have trouble sleeping and concentrating. Jumpy doesn't describe the feeling. I'm restless, not scared." She exhaled. "Maybe I'm just running on fumes. The thing with Mr. Nelson set me off. I told myself I wouldn't waste any more time thinking about it, but it feels like one more thing to manage. I keep replaying the sounds of the wind. Plucky and I took shelter in the basement. I didn't see the storm, but I felt it."

"I wondered how you stayed safe."

She drew a quick breath. "You thought about me?"

Running his hand through his hair, he nodded. "Your posts were annoyingly bright spots of light cluttering up my feed. How could I *not* think about you?"

Laughing, she inclined her head. *He seems like the type of man who would help a turtle cross the road. He doesn't need to do it, but he does.* "Well, most people don't rally the troops to help a stranger."

"Ronan needed help."

She swallowed. "Of course... Ronan."

Standing, he offered her a hand. "We've already dug through my past, so yours is fair game, too. Many service people come home jumpy, and PTSD is common. Given what happened to Ronar, you should talk to a professional."

She gripped his hand and let him pull her to standing, but her foot caught on the bench support, and she landed flush against his chest. Beneath his work shirt, his chest felt as solid as his forearm, and she appreciated the quick feel. *I can think of another form of therapy that might help distract me.* Looking up, she smiled, pulled back and brushed the chip crumbs from his chest. "Sorry."

He laughed and shook his head. "Don't worry about it." Picking up his lunch sack and hers, he walked toward the car.

A doe stepped from the bushes.

Stiffening, she waited for the animal to recognize danger and bolt.

A fawn stepped out of the woods.

"Well, aren't you pretty?" he said.

Great, now I'm not sure who deserves my jealousy – Christopher for enticing the deer or the fawn for enticing Christopher.

The pair stepped to the edge of the lake, lowered their heads and sipped the water.

"The water looks good," he said.

"It's clear and cold."

He cocked his head. "How cold?"

She wanted to laugh, but the deer held her attention. "Cold enough to make you squeal."

"Is that a bet?" he asked.

She looked at him. "Do you have a gambling problem?"

He laughed. "I have a lot of problems."

The doe and her fawn retreated to the woods.

She frowned. "You scared them off!"

He unbuttoned his shirt.

The motions stole her focus. *Screw the deer.*

"The doctors tell me swimming is good for my back."

Each button revealed the bronzed hardness she'd felt when she'd landed against his chest. Unable to pull her gaze from the show, she watched him part the fabric and shrug out of the shirt. "You're really going swimming?"

"You are, too."

She blinked. "Absolutely not."

He unbuttoned his jeans.

I'm considering it. She cleared her throat. "You have a hole in your foot."

"If the wound gets infected, I'll go back to Dr. Greene." He added his boots to the pile, slipped off his jeans and stood beneath the April sun in a pair of briefs.

Biting her thumb, she let her gaze wander from the top of his head to his proud toes. She'd seen a few naked men in her lifetime, but now she could go to heaven a fortunate woman. None of the fumbling high school students or lanky collegiates she'd known had looked this good, and Josh had preferred the dark. *Maybe they were too young. Maybe I should spend more time in Atlanta.*

Christopher turned and headed toward the water.

She watched his butt cheeks shift beneath the fabric and considered spending the rest of the day sitting in the sand and enjoying the show.

He looked over his shoulder. "Get in the water, Taylor."

She swallowed.

"The swim will give you something else to think about besides Ronan and your teacher."

God bless Mr. Nelson and his greedy ways. She shook her head. "I'm good."

Raising his hands over his head, he dove beneath the water and came up ten feet away from the shore.

Water glistened on his chest. "Cold?"

He rubbed his arms. "Like a fucking plunge pool."

She laughed.

"Get in."

"I can't." She twisted her long braid around her arm. "I can't go back with wet hair."

Standing, he rubbed his hands over his face.

Droplets cascaded from his arms and ran down his chest. She wetted her lips.

He dropped his hands and shook his torso.

The next time I hear the pledge of allegiance, I'll be the first person to raise my hand and cover my heart. Thank you for your service.

"I promise not to splash you," he said.

She laughed. "What are we, in kindergarten?"

He cocked his head. "If you come swim, I promise your hair will stay dry."

His slow, measured declaration punctured her resolve. Could she swim next to him, two streamlined bodies sliding through the water, and emerged unscathed? Would her memory of the swim linger into old age and bring a smile to her wrinkled lips?

She weighed the consequences. If she returned to town with wet hair, she would need a better cover story than an early afternoon swim. Every person she encountered would imagine she and Christopher had been up to no good. If she stayed on the shore, she would miss the chance of a lifetime, but she would avoid the burn. *Damned if I do, and damned if I don't. I spent my virginity on Josh, and what did that get me? Bedroom eyes and his condemnation.*

Standing, she acknowledged the curiosity that had sent her deep into the library stacks and pushed her to open the bookstore. She'd tried on hundreds of characters, but none had fit. Anticipating the cold, clear water, she rode a natural high that raised her heartbeat and heated her skin. Pulling her shirt over her head, she grinned. *Who said country life is boring?*

He whistled. "Atta girl!"

Slipping off her boots and shrugging out of her jeans, she stood on the beach wearing a white bra and a pair of matching hip huggers. "Keep your hands to yourself. We're not practicing lifts."

Laughing, he sank into the water and submerged his shoulders. "Baby, that movie's older than you."

"So's your back."

He clapped a hand to his chest. "You wound me."

She put one foot in the water, winced and looked at him. "Did you see that movie in the theater?"

Drawing back his palm, he skimmed the surface and sent a wave of water toward her.

The splash tickled the water but fell short of reaching her. Taking a deep breath, she closed her eyes and walked forward. When the water reached her core, she drew her breath and paused. By the time the sensation reached her nipples, she felt the cool weightlessness of submersion and pushed forward until she could tread water. *I'm going to get my kiss, and I'm going to enjoy every slick, weightless minute of it.*

"The water feels good, doesn't it?" he asked.

Grinning, she nodded.

"Are you thinking about Ronan?"

She shook her head.

"Your teacher?"

She smiled. "Nope."

He swam closer.

His strokes looked effortless. *Maybe he joined the wrong military branch.*

"I caught you checking me out on the roof."

She scrambled for a cover story, but the water's allure kept her weightless. Lifting her chin, she focused on him. "You're easy on the eyes."

"Easy enough for an indulgence?"

Heat blossomed in her core.

"Easy enough to let go of you good-girl persona?"

I stopped being a girl the day I left for college. "Do I look like a girl?"

He glanced at her breasts, swallowed and focused on her eyes. "No, ma'am, you don't. You look like a woman who had a shitty day and deserves a reward."

"And you're willing to give it to me?"

He laughed. "Generous as I am, I'm hoping we'll both benefit from this" — he swam closer — "attraction."

She tilted her head.

"No strings attached. No expectations. Just two single people looking for a good time."

He stayed just out of reach. She wanted to grab him, make the first move and retain a glimmer of control, but she stalled. Uncertain how to bridge the gap between playful banter and a full-on assault, she treaded water. "And you're sure you're a good time."

"Only one way to find out." Claiming the sandy slope, he reached for her and pulled her against his chest.

No longer floating, she gripped his shoulders and met his flinty gaze. Between the sky and the water, his eyes looked like mercury, and she wondered how many women lost themselves in his quicksilver gaze. Feeling his hand tighten at her waist, she no longer cared.

He dipped his head and brushed his lips across hers.

His touch warmed her, but she tasted the cool reservoir. Beneath the sky, his airy, transparent manners and moneyed confidence dissipated. She felt heat, and she wanted more. Tightening her grip on his shoulders, she claimed his bottom lip.

His groan encouraged her, and he opened his mouth. Sweeping her tongue between his lips, she waited for his response and the sloppy, wet kisses she remembered from Josh.

Raising his free hand, Christopher cupped her head and countered her bold sweep.

His lush, heated caress wiped clean her expectations. Water lapped against her nipples, and his measured explorations teased her senses. Judging by his kiss, he possessed enough rhythm to dance, kiss and fuck, possibly at the same time. *Good God, what have I done?*

She wrapped her legs around his waist and held on tight, willing to let him lead until kingdom come. Every one of his strokes and murmured appreciations felt genuine and brought her pleasure. She wanted to submit. She wanted to tear free her lips, lean back into the soft acceptance of the water and let him feast to his heart's content.

He broke the kiss. "Stay still."

She blinked. The rhythm of his heaving chest matched her breaths, but she stared at his lips.

"If you keep returning my kisses, those thin cotton panties won't do you much good, and you'll have more than wet hair to explain."

Loosening her legs from his waist, she slid down his body until his erection pressed against her stomach, and the clutch of her hands kept her head above water. "Such as?"

"Why you're knocked up and leaving town to marry a Durand."

She laughed at the absurdity of the statement, but her gaze remained fixed on his lips. *One more kiss. After all that I've been through.* She grinned. *Just one more kiss.*

"Stop looking at me like that."

She looked up. "Like what?"

"Like you want to eat me."

Pinching her lips, she struggled to contain a laugh and released her hold. Treading water, she considered her options. She wanted to climb back into his arms, but she also wanted to wrap up the moment of pleasure and hold it close to her heart. *A whiff of rejection would dissolve the day, and I'm not ready to take that risk.* "What, exactly, was your plan?"

He ran his hand through his hair. "Prove you're crappy kisser and get you out of my system."

She laughed and tossed a handful of water into his face. "Oh really?"

He grinned. "I had altruistic plans too. I meant to distract you."

She licked her lips. "Mission accomplished." Turning, she pulled her body through the water and headed toward shore, but she paused and looked over her shoulder. "I like your brand of therapy, Christopher. Let me know when you're ready for another session."

Laughing, he strode toward the bank. "I told you, no strings attached and no expectations."

When she found the lake bottom, she stood and wrapped her hands across her chest.

"Why did I think I would shock you?" he asked.

She smiled. "I'm a simple, country girl."

He looked at her lips. "Who knows how to kiss."

She laughed. "Yes, kissing made its way to Sparrow County." She reached for clothes, turned her back and unhooked her bra.

He groaned.

Unable to suppress her smile, she kept her back to him and stepped out of her wet panties.

"You're killing me, Taylor."

She looked over her shoulder. "Good."

Biting his lip, he shed his briefs and cocked his head.

"Trying to shock the virgin?" she asked. "You're too late."

"Fuck me."

She laughed and looked away before she did more than kiss him. Pulling her shirt over her head, she wiggled into her jeans and let thick, sun-warmed cotton soaked up the lingering water. Turning, she found him dressed and shook her head.

"Disappointed?" he asked.

She nodded.

He stepped forward.

She stepped back. "You missed your chance."

Closing the distance, he cupped her elbow. "What does that mean? If I'd slid a finger beneath your underwear, I would have found you wet and welcoming?"

Would have? I still am. She raised her chin. "Yes, but time's a wastin'. We have work to do."

He lowered his head until his lips hovered above hers. "I'll happily throw you back in the lake and cede the bet."

She heard the exaggerated promise and laughed. "A plant for a kiss?"

Raising his head, he focused on her. "More."

She met his unblinking intensity and swallowed. "If you build a plant in Ronan, it won't be because we tumbled in bed. The people in this town deserve prosperity. This game" — she cleared her throat — "is between us."

"You're sure?"

Her response died in her throat. The moment he'd walked into her bookstore, surety had become outdated. Shaking her head, she scooped up her wet underwear. "Get in the car, Christopher. You don't want to walk home." She passed the bench and the soft indentations left by the deer. Looking over her shoulder, she smiled, but his hardened intensity stole her breath. He wasn't a flirtatious coed enlivening her spring break. *What have I gotten myself into?* Her heart skipped a beat. *How soon can I find out?*

Chapter Ten

Christopher's dick strained against his jeans, but he would keep Taylor's effect hidden. Trying to get comfortable, he reached for his seatbelt and felt the tension in his lower back. Left unchecked, the tightness could lead to spasms, but he had better things to do than lie on the floor every morning and roll around on a yoga mat. *Like fuck Taylor.* He cleared his throat. "Not today."

She stopped checking her reflection in the visor mirror. "Excuse me?"

"My back's bothering me."

She frowned. "Are you saying I'm heavy?"

"I've had dogs bigger than you."

Laughing, she started the engine. "Thanks, I think."

"No problem." He could see her standing at a podium in a tweed suit, shaking hands with donors and charming everyone in a ten-mile radius, but he could also see her decked in lace and draped across his bed. He shook off the images. A few hours of labor would clear her from his system. Halfway to town, the silence in the car felt too thick. "So, back to Ms. Tina's?"

She nodded.

"You going back up to the roof?"

"If Johnnie hasn't fixed it," she said.

He shifted his weight. "When will you…?"

"Why did you really kiss me?" She glanced at him.

"Why does any man kiss a beautiful, willing woman?" He replayed the kiss and wondered if he'd misunderstood the situation. *I'm pretty sure wrapping your legs around a man signals consent.*

"Boredom?" she asked.

He crafted a pithy response, but the collateral damage felt too dear. "You don't bore me."

She smiled. "Good."

"Why did you kiss me?" he asked.

Her mouth ticked up on one side.

The half-ass side-smile settled his nerves.

"Boredom," she said.

He laughed and scratched the back of his head. "Well, the next time you get bored, give me a call."

She nodded and slowed for downtown's remnants.

Hearing her dejected sigh, he looked away from the piles of debris and the busy workers. The closer they came to downtown, the more she settled into her dogged role. Her blank features and slumped shoulders made sense, but her trembling chin worried him. She looked like a soldier coming upon the remnants of a roadside bomb. The soldiers patrolling in soft-sided Humvees saw the destruction of geopolitical decisions, and some of them never let go. "We're going to fix Ronan."

His promise sounded as pretentious as his presence in Iraq. He'd stalled traffic and disrupted local business in a heavy, oversized, military vehicle. Iraqis had cursed him and spat on the ground, preferring Saddam Hussein's rule to his glorified, American presence. A butcher had looked at him and hacked a knife into a hanging goat carcass. He'd returned the man's gaze. *What am I doing here?*

"Forgetting this work felt good," she said. "I've always believed in the power of make believe."

He felt Ocelot's weight and cleared his throat. "Why don't you drop me at Central Alley and Drake? I'll spend the afternoon managing the cleanup crew."

A man wearing an orange vest stepped into the street.

Stopping to let him pass, she glanced over. "Chickening out?"

"Trying to win a bet." He watched her summon a smile, but the gesture looked sad. "What happened to surviving the Civil War, Reconstruction, a boll-weevil infestation and the Great Depression? If your sass is any indication of the local population, Ronan is strong. You can recover from an itty-bitty tornado."

"Yeah." She swallowed. "I know. It just takes time."

"Hey." He leaned across the emergency brake and tipped up her chin. "You going to cry?"

"Tears are cathartic," she said.

"So is sex."

She laughed. "I, um…"

"Lost your nerve, huh?" He released her chin and grinned. "You come find me in trailer two. I'll help you forget you ever heard of Ronan."

"I doubt that's possible."

He winked. "Try me."

She rolled her eyes. "Get out."

"Peaches, I'm offering to do the gentlemanly thing and let you use me to your heart's content."

"If I come find your trailer, I promise my heart has nothing to do with the visit." She reached across him and unlatched the door. "Now, get out."

Her arm grazed his crotch, and his dick twitched against the friction. *I should have tried the caveman routine. Sloppy kisses, my ass.* Scanning the corner activity, he recognized the Ocelot dealer standing beneath a white tent and nodded in recognition. Dilly stood nearby, holding a tablet. As the car door swung open, beeping machines and the bass discharge of dropped loads permeated his quiet intimacy with Taylor. He sighed, climbed out of the vehicle and hoped Dillan had brought his hard hat.

"Christopher," she said.

Turning, he leaned down.

She held up his phone. "You forgot this."

He reached for the device and let his fingers brush hers. "Can I have your number?"

"Isn't it a little late for that?"

Unlocking his phone, he handed it to her.

She took the phone and tapped her digits into his contacts.

Nodding, he took the device and glanced at the entry for 'Sloppy Kisser'. Laughter slipped past his guard, and he shook his head. "We're quite a pair. Don't forget…trailer two."

She gripped the steering wheel and tossed her braid over her shoulder. "Doubt it."

Nodding, he shut the car door and tried to forget her passionate kiss. *A man can hope.*

"Mr. Durand!" Dillan hurried to his side and presented him with a bag of white socks.

He took it and nodded his thanks. "Where do we stand?"

Dillan consulted his tablet. "A few hiccups, but the machines perform better than you expected."

He always sandbagged his estimates. Watching a loader dump rubble in a waste container, he nodded and savored the pride of a job well done. The company's all-electric, compact track loaders worked without hydraulic components, and the prototype skid steers and excavators used next-generation electric motors. He knew the new machines could compete with traditional hydraulics. *Well, I'm selling those too.* Taking the tablet from Dillan's hand, he scanned the power load and battery performance. Taylor's admonishment about sitting still resonated. "Tell a driver to take a break. I want to try."

"What?" Dillan swallowed. "You want to *drive*?"

He cocked his head. "What? You want to go first?"

Dillan's skin paled.

He thrust the socks back into his assistant's arms and jerked his head toward the tent. "Take a break. I can take care of myself." Waving his hand in the air, he flagged an Atlanta operator who had just dropped off a load. "Let me have a try?"

The man nodded and climbed out of the cage.

Gripping the bar, Christopher climbed into the seat. Ocelot's track loader provided a smooth ride that enabled operators to accomplish careful and exact work. The machine's lower center of gravity kept it stable, which translated into safety for the operator and safety for those working nearby. The tracks lasted longer than tires, and if the electric models met his expectations, Ocelot's developments would tear up the industry. He checked the dashboard, aimed for a pile of debris and grinned.

* * * *

The battery indicator flashed red. Looking up, Christopher noted the onset of twilight and stretched his arms above his head. His muscles protested an afternoon of turning and twisting his torso, but the machine's performance made up for the discomfort. Glancing at the block of buildings and the piles of sorted waste, he climbed down from the machine. "What time is it?"

"Seven," Dillan said.

"Shit." He laughed and rolled his shoulders. "That was more fun than I expected."

Dillan handed him a bottle of water. "You made excellent progress, but the rest of the operators hope you're done so they can call it a day."

He uncapped the bottle and downed the sweet, cold water. "You should have released them at six."

"Uh-uh," Dillan stuttered.

Crunching the plastic bottle, Christopher pulled off his hard hat and scratched his scalp. *I'm glad I don't spend my summers running down tread.* Swinging the hard hat at his side, he made eye contact with the nearest operator and slashed his hand across his throat.

The man grinned and killed the motor on the skid steer.

"How's it running?" he asked.

"Great!" the operator said.

He nodded and walked toward the tent. "We're making excellent progress."

The dealer nodded. "Tomorrow, we should head to the trailer park and let the insurance appraisers do their work here."

He exhaled. *Seven deaths and I've been making jokes about tin-can hookups.* "Sounds good." His stomach rumbled, and he wondered what kind of corporate catering truck waited at the high school.

"Christopher Durand!"

He turned and found Ms. Tina standing in the middle of the street. Creased pants replaced her housedress. He wondered if she'd found an iron or a polyester blend that never wrinkled. "Yes, ma'am."

"Just where do you think you're going?" she asked.

He swallowed. "To eat."

"You come to my house."

He smiled. "That's unnecessary. Ocelot set up a portable kitchen."

She raised an eyebrow.

You know, not that many people can raise one eyebrow. Men, we have shaving to thank for our facial tricks, but women? He looked at Ms. Tina's pleats. "Thank you for the offer, but I'll eat with my drivers."

"'Thank you' is not an option."

He worried she would march down the middle of the street and grab him by the ear.

"Your assistant already brought over your things." She smiled. "Such a sweet boy, that Dilly."

I should have spent more time overseeing operations and less time running the Dirt Dog Rodeo. He swallowed. "My things?"

"Already in the guest bedroom," she said. "Thanks to your crew, I have power."

"You do?" He scratched his head.

"Dillan dropped off a portable generator." She fanned herself in the fading light. "Bless his heart." Her gaze narrowed. "Now get your ass to my house."

Clearing his throat, he wondered whether Ms. Tina's offer came from a deep-seated appreciation or a deep-seated fear the town would learn of her windfall and expect her to open her home. Her offer flattered him, but he should return to the high school and bunk down with his crew. Banter and cold beer would reveal the operators' ticks and grievances. Short of system failures, their official reports would praise the machines, and he needed to identify improvement opportunities before the first generation rolled off the line. *Right out of the gate, we have to be superior.* "Ma'am, I really need to debrief with my crew. I'll take you up on your hospitality, but first let me head back to the high school."

She yawned. "Lawd, you're slow. Tell your crew to come, too. We have more than enough food."

He scanned the street. "Where's Roger?"

"At the house, scavenging bits of fried chicken." Turning, she offered her elbow.

He debated whether to believe her or head back to his truck. Choosing manners over machinery, he took her arm and led her toward her house. True to her word, light spilled from the old house's windows. Devoid of its tarp, the patched roof presided over white columns and a temple-fronted facade. Ocelot operators and townspeople lounged on the wide lawn, and a pile of rose bush clippings sat by the curb. His drivers streamed past him and headed toward three food trucks parked along the street. "Well, isn't that a sight."

She withdrew her arm. "Prettiest house in town, but they're not here for the history. They're here for the food."

Each truck sported a generator and a long line.

He grinned. A decade ago, food trucks had hit the Atlanta dining scene, but he'd torn open MRE's or claimed a spot in the mess hall. The Army's chili mac and cheese had turned stomachs, but the powdered eggs had given him nightmares. *And when they ran out of powdered eggs, they switched to canned eggs. Who the hell flew a can of eggs across the Atlantic?* The hunger churning his stomach was strong enough to make MRE's look good. "Who lured these trucks down from Atlanta?"

She shrugged. "How the hell should I know? Dillan asked if they could park on my street, and I said, 'Why not?'"

He scanned the three trucks and licked his lips. The chef-owned and operated vehicles offered everything from fried chicken sandwiches to lobster rolls and Cajun shrimp po'boys. *I need to give Dilly a raise.* He remembered his manners and turned to his host. "Have you eaten?"

She waved a hand in the air. "I'm on a liquid diet. When you're ready to bed down, come find me on the porch." She whistled.

Heads turned, and Roger came running.

Scooping up the small dog, she kissed his nose.

Roger licked her lips, looked at him and bared his small, white teeth.

"Yes, ma'am." He walked toward the nearest food truck before he became the animal's next course. Rubbing his hands, he considered the menu.

"Mr. Durand?"

Can't a man drool over truffle French fries in peace? He turned and greeted Dillan with a smile. "You did good."

Dillan glanced to the side. "Thanks, but I noticed the skid steer's joystick controls were sticky."

He repeated the comment in his head to make sure he'd heard the man correctly. "You did *what?*"

"I, uh, wanted to drive." Dillan looked left and right. "The dealer said even a moron can drive a skid steer."

"You're not a moron, but I"—he cleared his throat— "was joking when I told you to get behind the wheel. We have immersion classes for office workers who want to get their hands dirty."

Dillan grinned. "I know! I just fired up my email and enrolled."

He bit back a smile. "The controls?"

"Oh, yeah. I talked to the mechanic you brought down. He said most of the time he would check the wires connecting the actuators and hydraulic pump to the joystick, but"—he looked around—"the mechanic said that can't be the issue."

The fries could wait. He rubbed his hand along his jaw. "Sticky all the time or just one direction?"

Dillan skewed his jaw. "I'd say all the time."

He scrolled through his knowledge of the machines. Ronan's residents were observant, and the rough details of Ocelot's new machinery had most likely leaked. *That's fine. Let our competitors sweat.* "I wonder if the joystick's control board has a loose connection. Tell the mechanic to take a look."

"Me?" Dillan scanned the crowd. "Why me?"

"You took the initiative and found the problem. Now, go find the solution, too." Turning toward the food truck, he paused and met Dillan's wondrous gaze.

"Tell the mechanic to lend you a pair of coveralls. The machines are electric, but the dirt and debris haven't changed — and don't leave the machine unattended."

Dillan grinned. "Yes, sir."

Beckoning Dillan to his side, he counted the minutes until he could eat. "What are you having for dinner?"

"I can't decide." Dillan looked toward the crew of operators congregating on the brick steps. "Should I eat what I want or what's good for me? My mama always said to start with a salad."

Laughing, he figured every dietician in the Goober State would take one look at the food truck menu, tally up the salt and saturated fats and turn greener than a raw peanut. "Everything in moderation, but you laid a lot of tread today. I'd say eat what you want."

Dillan rubbed his hands.

He slapped the man's back and urged him forward. "Also, thanks for luring these trucks to Ronan."

Dillan jerked his chin toward the white house. "It was that woman."

At the base of the front porch steps, Rebecca interviewed Taylor under a camera crew's spotlight. He appreciated Taylor's ties to her community, but he doubted she could have summoned Atlanta's best food trucks. Rebecca's platform gave her recognition, but she usually reserved her favors for charity auctions. "Which woman?"

"The blonde."

Appreciation warmed his chest and lifted his lips into a smile. Pulling out his cell phone, he navigated to his feed.

Folks, you sure know how to make a town feel loved! Thank you for all the love and support, but to be honest, hot food would do a body good. My daddy has a fire burning in his smoker, but variety is the spice of life. Bring Ronan something good to eat, and the town will be at your feet. We'll even share with the insurance company reps and the good folks from FEMA.

Scanning the row of winking emoticons, he imagined her debating whether to leave the joke or temper her post. *I'm glad she left it.* He looked toward the opposite side of the street and saw a line of men and women in logo shirts hunched over their food. The insurance reps and FEMA staff looked fearful and kept their conversations low. *Relax, guys, I doubt anyone will yank your food.*

Rereading Taylor's post, he sensed the return of her playful optimism, and neither Jeb nor Bill Nelson had shown his face on the lawn. *I can't take credit for her resilience, but I'd like to think the dip in the lake helped.* He headed up the lawn and grinned.

"Aren't you going to eat?" Dillan asked.

He waved off the man. "In a minute." Keeping out of view of the cameraman and the spill of the lights, he listened to the interview.

"What do you hope to see in the coming days?" Rebecca asked.

Her jeans still held a store tag, but he doubted she would appreciate an intervention.

Taylor lifted her chin and smiled. "I won't lie. The last few days have been hard, but every time I feel overwhelmed, God sends me another sign. Ocelot Enterprises rolled into town and doubled the speed of debris removal. We asked for food, and people came."

"Do you have any outstanding concerns?" Rebecca asked.

Opening her mouth, Taylor paused. "Our community's leadership team needs space to plan for a long-term rebuilding effort. I'm not talking about physical space, but about mental space…breathing room." She blinked. "Sometimes a break is exactly what a person needs. I hope our elected officials have the freedom to think big. Ronan's historical district was beautiful, but we need tougher building codes, live-work spaces and energy efficiency."

Rebecca tilted her head. "Will there been pushback?"

His ex leaned in, no doubt drawn to the smell of blood.

"My daddy patched together half the buildings in this town. Rebuilding what we had will give us peace of mind, but building strength will give us economic advantages."

Her feel-good cameo suddenly had teeth. If the city manager had any sense, he would issue a statement applauding community activism. If the board of commissioners had done their job, they would have strategic plans waiting on file servers. He wanted to break into a slow clap, but he crossed his arms and relaxed. *Points for Taylor.*

Rebecca smiled.

He recognized her aloof shield. *Life isn't a choice between eating what you want and eating what's good for you. A smart man picks the things that satisfy him and keeps him going strong.* Turning his head, he admired Taylor's confident bearing. *Right now, Taylor Lenore looks good enough to eat.*

Turning to face the camera, Rebecca held her smile. "Reporting live from Ronan, I'm Rebecca Ossnock, WSB-TV News."

The crewmember holding the spotlight cut off the beam.

Taylor turned to an older man. "How'd I do?"

Gray hairs threaded his five-o'clock shadow, but even in the spotty light, his strength and reserve cut through the waning light. Christopher took him for Taylor's father and straightened his shoulders.

"Great." The man kissed Taylor's cheek and whispered in her ear.

Laughing, Taylor nodded toward Rebecca. "Thanks for covering our plight. The first time we met, I thought you were out to get me, but every bit of news coverage keeps Ronan in peoples' prayers."

"Oh" —Rebecca covered a yawn— "I'm not worried about you. For some reason, I feel like you'll come out of this situation ahead."

The older man squeezed Taylor's shoulders.

Turning, Rebecca lifted her chin and walked up to him. "Christopher."

He nodded. "Rebecca."

She smiled. "You've always enjoyed the country life."

"And you've always been ready to leave it behind you." He uncrossed his arms. She might be the granddaughter of a former state senator, but he doubted Georgia could hold her ambitions. "Why are you covering the tornado aftermath? Send a local correspondent."

She made a soft, noncommittal sound. The sound grated on his nerves.

"I thought you'd meet Taylor and come to your senses," she said, "but you're still here, and I wanted to see why."

"Why are you?"

She scanned the yard.

On another day, the laughter and takeaway containers might have been a party.

"Taylor Lenore's sweet, Southern appeal is the flavor of the week, but when people watch my clips, she's not the only woman they see." She wrapped her hand around her curled, red hair and settled it over her shoulder. "Every minute of airtime is a minute that could lead to a national opportunity for me."

He loosened his stance. Rebecca's poise and education made her a talented reporter, but without a pull from the top, she would spend her life conducting short, snappy interviews to feed the local news cycle. *Or get married.* "You're done with WSB-TV?"

She exhaled. "Atlanta hasn't been everything I hoped."

The weight of the admission forced him to drop the niceties. *Maybe I should have ended things sooner. Maybe we should have remained friends.* "Rebecca..."

She stepped back and smiled.

Amid the sweat and humidity of Ronan's citizens, her flawless, black eyeliner and curled hair stood out. She had no problem charging into his office and manipulating social events, but she couldn't manipulate his life. He searched for a response. *How do you apologize for failing to love someone?*

"Every woman has a plan." She scanned the assembly, looked at him and lifted her chin. "Clever women have more than one."

Nodding, he accepted her audacity and resilience would carry her to the top. "I hope we remain friends." He smiled. "No matter which coast you choose."

She laughed and glanced at the food trucks. "Have you eaten?"

His stomach clenched. Memories of lunch mocked him but sharing fries in the front seat of the news van held little interest. *Like Rebecca even eats fries.* "I'm working on it."

Shaking her hair down her back, she smiled. "And here you are, standing on this hill. The food trucks are down there, Christopher. Ever since Iraq, you've seemed lost. I thought I could grab your attention, but you're as stubborn as a mule."

"When have you met a mule?"

She ran her tongue along her teeth and frowned.

He watched her ponder the question and held his breath.

Her forehead crinkled, and she grinned. "Atlanta has a zoo."

"I'm sure it does." Whether Rebecca had ever visited said zoo was another question. Looking over his shoulder, he found Taylor and her father deep in conversation.

Taylor glanced at him and smiled.

Speaking of stubborn… He mulled over Rebecca's accusation and turned to say goodbye, but he spied her halfway down the lawn. *I'm not lost. I'm busy.*

A little girl stopped and tugged on Rebecca's skirt.

He had a sneaking suspicion the little girl was the same loud-mouthed fury who'd greeted him at Ronan Reads.

Bending, Rebecca cupped the girl's head.

Friendship and shared memories let him absorb the moment.

"I figured you'd spend the night driving equipment," Taylor said.

He found her standing beside him. "How'd you know I spent the afternoon driving equipment?"

"Word travels." She rolled her shoulders, smiled and winked. "Plus, I asked."

He laughed and matched her smile. *She doesn't do artifice.* Remembering the feel of her legs wrapped around his middle, he wondered what else he could do to ease her burdens. *I could spot her in a crowded Atlanta ballroom. She'd be the only woman meeting my gaze without a hidden agenda.* He tried to focus on the reality of their acquaintance. Taylor Lenore loved Ronan, and he doubted she would commute to Atlanta for a good lay. "I didn't know you were such a multitasker...repairing roofs, keeping track of upstarts and summoning food trucks." He dipped his head. "I'm impressed."

She waved off the compliment. "Shucks. Just a few hungry people in need of spicy food and friendly conversation."

He estimated a hundred people sat on the lawn. "Does your family solve all their problems with food?"

She smiled. "And love."

What a combination. He heard a group of men laugh. "I've focused on workhours, but you've focused on workers."

She wet her lips. "The difference matters."

"I bet we have more in common than you think." He reached for her hand and intended to make his interest clear. *If you want more than a kiss, Peaches, I'm ready to bite.* "But I'll still win our bet."

"What bet?"

The man's gravelly voice froze Christopher's overture. Dropping his hand, he looked up and met her father's aged, blue eyes. "Just a friendly wager with your daughter." He redirected his hand and offered it to the man. "I'm Christopher Durand. Pleasure to meet you."

"Jack Lenore." Jack took his hand.

He felt the strength in the older man's grip. His calloused fingers held as steady and sure as the beams in Ms. Tina's house. Usually the Durand name meant something. He waited, wondering if he and Jack would spend the evening locked in a silent appraisal. *I had other things in mind.*

After a deep breath, Jack nodded and turned to Taylor. "Don't let your mama hear you're gambling."

"Oh, Daddy, it's not for money."

Jack scanned him. "I'm sure."

"Christopher's the man from Ocelot who brought down the heavy equipment," she said.

He bit back a smile. *The man. Not 'the owner' or 'the president'. Jack's about to make me out as a long-haul driver and kick me to the curb.*

Clearing his throat, Jack nodded. "I saw you up on the roof with Taylor, and I appreciate what you're doing for Ronan, but we'll be just fine without your help. My entire life, I've patched up this old town, and I'm proud of every scar on my hands. I doubt you appreciate that connection from your office suite."

Christopher opened his mouth to say something about driving machines, poking around in the research lab or running job sites.

Jack raised his eyebrows. "Ronan's assets are unique to Ronan."

And you're not about to let go of your prized possession. He swallowed and tamped down a challenging smile. "Yes, sir."

Across the lawn, a man shouted, pointed to the ground and claimed the company lost his ticket. His slight frame looked familiar, but Christopher had seen so many townspeople in passing, he struggled to remember names. In front of the shouting man, a utility worker holding a table held his ground. At well over two hundred pounds, the worker looked like he'd graduated from college football, sent his punt returner up in the bucket truck and held the line on terra firma. His slight, shouting opponent didn't have a chance.

"Aw, shit," Jack said. "Brent's been drinking."

Turning, Christopher made the connection and looked at Taylor. "One of your uncles?"

She nodded and leaned closer to Jack. "Do you want me to call Aunt Mary?"

Jack shook his head. "I've got it." He kissed her cheek and strode toward the pair. Stopping near Brent, he threaded his hands and let them hang in front of his belt buckle.

The low, steady posture and wide-legged stance looked restrained but ready for action. Christopher's first supervisor had adopted the same pose.

Brent looked at Jack and frowned, but he continued berating the worker.

Jack listened more than he spoke.

"The storm took down Uncle Brent's church," Taylor said. "Over the last week, I've caught his gaze drifting toward the horizon. Losing so much at one time must feel like an insurmountable obstacle. I'm sure he's frustrated."

"You lost your bookstore."

"But nobody depends on me. My uncle's church on Chapel Hill is in ruins. The winds carried off the steeple, tore bricks from the walls and lifted the roof clear off the rafters. Uncle Brent thought his prayers made a difference. After the storm, he looked defeated, but not defeated enough to stay home. I love his perseverance. He has three kids and a community of believers to lead. He can't hide in the cellar."

"That's not what you did."

She swallowed. "That's what I wanted to do."

He nodded and watched the trio. Jack and the utility worker conversed. Brent crossed his arms and stuck out his chin. "People cope in different ways."

"I've seen him helping others and asking about reconstruction. I assumed he had it together." She sighed. "Maybe not. Maybe I should call Aunt Mary. Maybe I…"

He stepped closer. "You dad can handle his brother."

"Tonight, but what happens tomorrow?" She rubbed the side of her face. "I thought Uncle Brent's distractedness and vague responses meant he had too many irons in the fire, but maybe those weren't the problem. Daddy should take him home."

After a traumatic event, memory problems could be a sign of trouble, but so could a hidden flask. He'd lost William to a drunk driver, but Taylor didn't need his burdens. "Your dad seems like a nice guy."

"Yeah, he has this covered." She glanced at the food trucks. "C'mon. Let's eat while everyone's distracted."

She grabbed his hand and pulled him along like a playground confidant. He let her.

"I'm starving," she said.

And I don't want to be your friend. Feeling the same strength and determination in her grip that he'd sensed from her father, he followed her down the lawn. *Mr. Nelson's lucky if the cops process his fraud without dragging his name through the mud* – his stomach clenched – *fuck, I could eat a horse.* He angled toward the food truck most likely to appeal to Taylor. "I think this one has salads and wraps."

She laughed and tugged free her hand. "I don't want a salad. I want ribs or something I can sink my teeth into."

He flicked his lip. *Maybe I could drive down on the weekends.*

"You know, you do that a lot," she said.

Meeting her gaze, he stilled his hand. "Do what?"

"Rub your thumb across your lip. Do you need lip balm?"

He laughed and pulled her toward the truck that smelled like hot chicken, cool pickles and butter slathered on a rich bun. "Just a tic," he said. "The desert air kept my lips as chapped as the sand dunes."

"I always thought the dunes would be soft." She angled her head. "Like your lips."

Turning his head from the menu, he looked at her. "You think my lips are soft?"

She grinned. "Just like your hands." Kicking his boot, she winked. "How's your foot?"

He considered throwing her over his shoulder and demonstrating his health. Based on the tightness in his jeans, he needed multiple rounds before any part of his body went 'soft'. He cocked his head. "Just Peachy, thanks for asking."

"Stupid nickname." Jerking free her hand, she spun to the ordering window. "Two combo plates, please."

The man behind the window nodded. "To drink?"

"Tea."

"Sweet or unsweet?"

She cracked the knuckle on her thumb. "Sweet."

The man nodded. "Lemon?"

Christopher ran his hand through his hair. *Georgia might be the only state in the union where ordering tea takes longer than ordering a meal.* He wanted to cut off the man's line of questioning, but the worker turned to the tea dispenser, filled two foam cups with sweet, frothy tea and handed them to Taylor. *Don't I get a vote?*

She tucked both drinks in the crook of her elbow and reached for the plastic bag of food dangling from the window.

The smell of fried chicken and crackled black pepper erased his rebellious thoughts. He followed her through the crowd like a gun dog following a trail.

Looking over her shoulder, she smiled. "Anyplace in particular you want to eat?"

In bed. He smiled. "You're the boss."

She laughed and chose a white, painted swing hanging from an A-frame. Confederate jasmine climbed a steal lattice along the frame's sides, and he wondered if Ms. Tina's approach to roses deserved more respect. He sat, rubbed his hands on his jeans and tried not to grab the plastic bag from Taylor's hands.

"Tea?" she asked.

He nodded and set the cup on the swing bench.

Settling on the far side, she placed the food between them and opened the bag.

Steam and the seductive appeal of spicy, fried food rose from the bag. "I could eat everything you have."

She laughed and ripped the paper from her straw. "Well, I'm sure you can go back for seconds."

I intend to. He reached for the first container. Stilling his hand took every ounce of strength he possessed. Looking up, he waited for her to make eye contact. "Luring the food trucks down here was brilliant. I concede the day."

Waving a hand toward the lawn, she picked up her sandwich. "Oh, I told them to send you a bill."

"You did *what*?" He stared, wondering when a siren had replaced sweet Pollyanna. "You should have asked me."

She chuckled. "I'm kidding, but you would have paid the bill, wouldn't you?"

He picked up his sandwich and took a bite. The savory heat and bright spice held up their end of the bargain. After chewing, he swallowed and nodded. "I would."

She set the swing in motion and sat cross-legged on the bench. "I get that about you. Behind all the tough corporate analysis, you're a little bit of a softie."

Her shy smile loosened his heartstrings.

"Who else sacrifices their lips to a sloppy kiss to make a woman feel better?"

"I told you the kiss wasn't sloppy."

She gave the swing another push and tucked up her legs. "But you expected sloppy."

Busted. Wondering what else she'd picked up about him, he kept the swing in motion and let the cicadas fill the silence. When he finished his meal and leaned his arm across the bench's back, the urge to play with her braid surprised him. Figuring his greasy fingers would make a mess and a hundred observers would report on his forwardness, he settled for the swing's artificial proximity. "You worked hard today, too."

She wet her lips and nodded. "Except for the midday break."

His cock stirred.

Lifting a napkin, she cleaned her hands and shifted toward him. "You look at ease."

You have no idea. He adopted the lazy, contented smile of a man with no worries. "I enjoy being out in the country."

She glanced at Ms. Tina's house and raised her eyebrows.

He laughed and settled his hands across his stomach. "Relative country. My family has a hunting camp on the Cumberland Riverbank. Someone back up the family tree grew Sea Island cotton. The fields no longer grow crops, but the acres of pine and spartina grass amaze me. I can spend days stalking quail, turkey, wild boar and deer without seeing a soul. When the squelching mud loses its appeal, I take out flat boats for redfish or speckled trout. In the summer, I go after tarpon."

"Sounds deadly," she said.

He laughed. "We eat everything, but the camp isn't a blood bath. Straight across the river, I can see a sea island where feral horses, great horned owls and wood storks hold sway over tourist ferries. The visitors crawl all over the island, but none of them look over their shoulder and see me among the scrub."

"You want to hide?" She sipped her tea.

He shook his head. "I appreciate the peace and quiet. Don't you have a hiding spot?"

She looked away. "The bookstore."

Shit.

"Taylor, it's going to get better..."

Holding up her hand, she shook her head. "I appreciate what you're doing here. Even when you're stealing kisses, you're looking out for me."

Fucking altruistic monk that I am.

"But you're going back to Atlanta, and I'm staying here. I can't get frustrated every time something interrupts my worldview. I'm glad you love your family's camp. Everyone needs a respite."

"First-world problems."

She smiled. "Exactly."

He thought of Iraq and the damage from the war. *What am I even supposed to call the remnants of the country? Third World? Developing world? Low- and middle-income countries?* He blew out his breath and wondered when he would come to peace with the past he never controlled. "I like golf."

She laughed.

His statement felt so normal and predictable. He wanted to wrap his arms around the stance and defend it until his dying day. *I'd rather wrap my arms around her at the driving range.*

"We have beautiful courses."

He looked up. "You play?"

She shook her head, brushed her bangs out of her eyes, and toyed with the end of her braid. "I used to carry large-format books about the sport."

"Were they green?"

Laughing, she nodded.

"I'll tell you something you probably didn't learn in your books. When golf started, the Scots played coastal areas called 'links land'. Despite the green jackets, we're playing a sport that started with sticks, rocks and sheep burrows."

"How democratic," she said. "But you're right. I didn't know that fact."

"So people get nostalgic and say they're hitting the links, but most golf courses are parkland courses. Unless the course occupies the space between the ocean and agrarian land, it's not a links' course. Don't listen to jackasses in argyle socks who say otherwise."

She laughed. "Do you have a course at your little hunting camp?"

'Little' doesn't begin to describe it. "I've thought about putting in a few fairways." The admission cost him the ease of the warm, summer evening. He and his dad butted heads over the eleven-thousand-acre camp. He wanted to preserve the acres of woodlands, maritime forests and marshes. Richard wanted to flip the property, establish a formal hunting club and sell off residential plots. *I'm sure he'd love to preside over the lodge, just as he presided over the boardroom.* He sighed. Duty and leisure went hand in hand. Links or not, Ocelot's earnings paid the property taxes on his seaside escape, and throwing in the towel would gild his generation but leave nothing for the next. "The night's getting late."

She covered a yawn. "You probably have work stuff."

An endless feed of emails, reports and market analysis waited in his inbox. "Ms. Tina told me I could bunk at her house."

Taylor gasped and faced him. "Get out!"

He straightened. "What? The old pile looks better than my current accommodations."

Uncurling her feet, she stood and stared at the white house. "I've lived in this town most of my life, and I've never seen the inside of that house. You show up and" — she stared at him — "carpetbagger."

Laughing, he shoved aside the dinner boxes and settled her close enough for a whisper. "I tell you what. If you wait until I get settled and climb the ladder to the rear balcony, you can explore the whole damn house."

"Absolutely not. Ms. Tina'd flay me."

"She'd never know," he said. "I'll leave on a light."

Coughing, she slapped her chest and shook her head. "You're forgetting one thing."

He raised an eyebrow.

"Roger."

Biting his lip, he tried not to laugh. "Leave the dog to me."

She tilted her head. "And then?"

Indulging himself, he picked up her weighty braid and tugged it. "The rest is up to you." Meeting her gaze, he smiled. "Don't forget... I'm a generous man."

"Are you now?"

Rubbing the smooth stands between his fingers, he figured his offer had an ice cube's chance in hell, but the fun of issuing the challenge outweighed his reservations. *I'll play by club rules, but I don't see any white stakes marking this course.* Remembering Jack Lenore, he cleared his throat and focused on the woman sitting beside him. "I'll be as generous as you want me to be." He winked. "Come for the tour, and stay for the hanky-panky."

Laughing, she stood and stretched. "I'll think about it."

His dick shot to attention. Keeping his arm along the back of the bench, he nodded and tried to stay cool, but the entire lawn probably heard his heartbeat. Sneaking around was a high school activity, but high school was the last time he remembered having fun. Shaking his head against thoughts of William, Iraq and Ocelot, he scanned Taylor's generous curves and smiled. "Come find me, Taylor. If not here, come to Atlanta."

She eyed the tall white house. "You'll be exhausted."

"I'll never be too exhausted for you." The truth of the statement caught him off guard.

Grinning, she bit her lip. "Leave on your light."

Her bright, inquisitive smile eased the burdens of his day. Generous man that he was, he vowed to use his skillsets to help her forget Ronan's destruction and anything else keeping her up at night. Relaxing into the warm, evening air, he smiled. "I'll wait up for you."

Chapter Eleven

Taylor walked away from the swing and headed for the food trucks. *Don't look back.* She knew Christopher remained on the jasmine-scented swing, his long legs spread in front of him like a satisfied king. His casual, innuendo-laced offer tempted her, but she had better things to do than to sneak into Ms. Tina's house for a quick thrill. *Don't I?*

Grabbing a wad of napkins, she wiped her hands clean and looked at the lawn's dwindling occupants. James and Katie Jesse sat on his trench coat and looked up at the stars. Johnnie and his wife held court with a group of childless friends. She wanted to spend her life in the same fashion. The stability of homemade biscuits, butter and sweet honey satisfied every craving she had. *Why didn't I stay with Josh?* She touched the scar below her eyes and sighed. Balling up the napkins, she tossed them in a trash bag hung from the food truck's side. *Because he wanted me to submit, and I wanted to be heard.*

"Ready to go, Peaches?"

Hearing her daddy's voice, she smiled. Her parents had a stellar marriage, but her mother preferred to spend her evenings in the back garden with the flock pecking at her feet. She often put down her Bible, raised her face to the sky and inhaled with such purpose a person would think God gave awards for soulful, country piety. "Sure, Daddy." Looking past her father's lined, loving face, she caught Christopher's gaze, smiled and linked arms with her father.

"You did good work today," he said. "I taught you well."

"And the rest of the house?" she asked

"A few rotten boards and leaky windows, but we'll shore up Ms. Tina's refuge."

They walked toward their vehicles. "Why won't she let anyone inside?"

Jack laughed. "I figure ghosts claimed the house, or she keeps Roger's corpse in the front parlor."

"No!" Planting her feet, she looked back to the wide porch.

He tugged her back into motion and patted her arm. "I'm only kidding. The house belongs to her. What right do the rest of us have to judge how she lives?"

"You just fixed her rotten boards and leaky windows," she said. "Will you send her a bill?"

He shook his head. "Nah. She donates to the church and the civic associations. God will balance the scales."

Will he? She kept her faith front in center, but the storm's devastation upended her belief that good things happened to good people. "Did you hear about the Ronan Recovery Foundation?"

"Plucky seems like she found a calling," he said. "I'm sure the public appreciates a tangible way to help."

His optimism soothed her worries about the city's reputation. She looked at him and weighed the risks to her own reputation. "I might go over to her house this evening and help her unpack a few donations or write thank you notes." She had every intention of stopping by Plucky's small cottage, but she needed time to process kissing Christopher, and she needed to know what her friend thought about the situation. What she did after she left the cottage remained up in the air.

"Seems late to lick stamps."

She laughed. "Daddy, you don't have to lick the stamps anymore."

"Your mama takes care of that end of the business." He paused and rubbed his whiskers. "Taylor, I knew times are changing, but some things are worth preserving." He looked at the old house. "Ms. Tina's china collection will outlive us all, but I want you to do what's right for you, not what's right for right now."

He would have escorted her to the church, but he would have offered to call off her wedding, too. The half-hearted, gallant gesture would have given her pause. *Did I want someone to step in and tell me I made a mistake?* She rubbed the small scar. *If my father trusts me to make big decisions about my life, he has to trust me to make small ones, too.* "You only get one life, Daddy."

"And God will judge how you live it."

His solemn pronouncement cooled her fire, but she looked over her shoulder and saw Christopher still lazing on the porch swing. His hardened temptation offered illicit thrills with few side effects, but succumbing to his charm could alter her life in ways she never imagined. *Before his fall, Lucifer was the most beautiful angel, but Christopher's a man. I won't inconvenience him, and he certainty won't change my life. At the end of his stay, we'll part ways, and I'll go back to rebuilding Ronan Reads and serving my community.* She blinked and turned away from Christopher's heavy-lidded appraisal. "I appreciate the warning."

Jack nodded and fished out his keys. "Your mama enjoys having you home. She'll wait up."

She nodded and tried not to feel selfish for claiming the loft above the bookstore. "She always does."

Leaning down, he kissed her cheek. "See you in the morning, Peaches."

"Yes, Daddy." She smiled and waited until he drove away. Climbing into her car, she adjusted the vent fan and drove to Plucky's house. The small blue cottage once had a green lawn, but a mix of grasses had jumped the border and crept into the gravel driveway. Beyond the nebulous parking area, a light shone from the storage shed. She put the car in park and walked toward the shed. "Anyone home?"

"In here," Plucky said.

A bulb hung from a wire. Stepping into the yellow glow, she found Plucky surrounded by a mountain of cardboard boxes. "How's it going?"

Plucky kept her head down. "Fair enough. I'm trying to keep track of everything, but people bought way more than I expected." She held up a sheath of printouts and a box cutter with a fresh, gleaming blade. "Ready to pitch in?"

"Sure," she asked. "Point me in the right direction."

"Look up the order numbers, mark off the items and crush the boxes for recycling." Plucky passed her the box cutter.

She sliced into a line of packing tape. "I had a weird encounter with Mr. Nelson at the post office. I think he's collecting disability money from SSA, but also accepting plant salary in his wife's name. He's double-dipping!"

Plucky brushed her bangs from her eyes. "That asshole accused me of cheating in the tenth grade. I had a tampon in my pocket, and he thought it was a cheat sheet."

She rolled her eyes, but then she frowned. "Wait! Did you have a cheat sheet?"

Plucky laughed. "In my other pocket, but when I pulled out the tampon, he turned beet red."

"Plucky!" She drummed up a soft-hearted reprimand, but her phone vibrated with a message.

The food trucks were brilliant, but I'm ready to eat your pussy and hear you scream my name.

"Good grief." She stashed her phone and struggled not to rub together her legs.

Plucky looked up. "What? It's just a few boxes."

"Right." She swallowed. "Sorry... Something caught me off guard." Walking around the box, she unpacked tall, plastic glasses, and tried to find the associated order on the printout. Her phone vibrated dangerously close to her clit.

Watching you swing a pry bar got me going, but the only tool your pussy needs is my tongue.

Need rippled through her core. She dropped the phone and let it clatter to the packed dirt floor.

Plucky looked up. "What the fuck?"

"Um" — scooping up the device, she shoved it in her back pocket and looked at the labels in her other hand — "don't worry about it. Just a few texts from Christopher Durand."

"Figures." Plucky's long, blue-tinged bangs swept over her eye. She tucked them behind her ear and shook her head. "Only you would land Atlanta's most eligible bachelor and not know what to do with him."

She frowned. "I didn't land him."

"Sorry." Plucky shook a cardboard box. "I'm sure he's texting you Bible verses."

"At least I would know how to respond."

Dropping the tape gun, Plucky put her hands on her hips. "Just fuck him."

"No!"

"Why the hell not? Your Bible-licking naivety hasn't done you a lick of good. Josh was an ass wipe. At least with Durand, you know you'll have a good time."

"Why don't *you* fuck him?" She tossed out the line, but the moment it left her lips, she regretted the offer.

"Trust me, I would." Plucky sighed. "When you put on a dress, you look like a glittering show pony. I look like a fat, blown-out donkey."

She gasped. "We wear the same size!"

Plucky laughed. "And yet, I don't have any sexy texts from Durand."

She felt her phone vibrate but ignored the alert. A second vibration forced her to close her eyes.

"Tell me what it says," Plucky said. "Let me live vicariously through Ronan's darling girl."

Pulling the phone from her pocket, Taylor read and reread the texts.

I didn't want you, then I couldn't stop thinking about you. Purge my curiosity.

She typed out her response.

With my sloppy kisses.

One night. No regrets. Prove me wrong.

Closing her eyes, she remembered the hard panes of his stomach.

Plucky ripped the phone from her hands and read the texts. "For the love of God, just go to him. The next time a billionaire walks into the bookstore, give him to me, but don't let this asshole get away."

"He's not an asshole," Taylor said. "Most of the time."

Plucky picked up the tape gun. "You never know what you have, do you?"

"What's that supposed to mean?"

"Your entire life has been too easy." Plucky shook her head.

"You know my demons!"

Plucky laughed. "Sure, Josh the limp-dicked noodle, who slapped you around and hid behind his religion."

She traced the small scar his class ring had made when he'd backhanded her. "I loved him."

Clearing her throat, Plucky took a deep breath, squared her shoulders and exhaled. "You loved the idea of him, just like you loved singing with the Christian Fellowship, standing beneath the spotlight and accepting the town's praise. You can't help your family, but you sure as hell can help what you do with your life. And what have you done, Taylor? You've sold children's books and lattes to a town that always loved you."

"What would *you* have done?"

Plucky threw up her hands. "I don't know, but I never had the chance!"

She replayed her friend's choices. Plucky had shied away from college and leaving her mother, but Taylor had wondered if fear had kept her homebound. Beneath the shed's yellow light, moths fluttered, and years of minor grievances lingered amid the stale sawdust. She believed every person had a chance, but why hadn't Plucky taken hers? "You can still shape your life. We're young and beautiful and free!"

Plucky shoved a box across the dirt floor. "I can work my ass off from nine to five, but the only thing I'll earn is a paycheck. Nobody's going to rescue me."

"Why do you need rescuing?"

"Because this shit town is dying! When's the last time your daddy framed up a new house? When's the last time an out-of-town business came to Ronan and held a hiring fair? We get fast-food joints, gas stations and tax-prep franchises." Exhaling, she planted her hands on her hips. "You can't spend your life preserving and restoring the past's glory. Face the facts... Ronan's on its last leg."

"Come on, Plucky. You want to get ahead? Take a risk!" She felt like kicking a pile of boxes. "I put all my savings into Ronan Reads!"

Plucky laughed. "Keep telling yourself that story."

Her friend's slow condemnation warned her to prepare for the worse.

Plucky braced her hands. "You're Taylor Lenore, Little Miss Georgia Peach Queen and Ronan's pride and joy. This white bread and butter, integrated view of the town is so simplistic it's laughable. You could have opened a cupcake stand and it would have been a success."

"What's wrong with cupcakes?"

"They're frivolous, sugar-loaded monstrosities!" Plucky threw up her hands. "Who the hell pays five dollars for a cupcake?"

She could see the vein bisecting Plucky's forehead. "I like cupcakes, and if I had opened a cupcake stand, I sure as hell wouldn't have hired you to work the counter."

"You hired me to work at your bookstore."

Closing her eyes against the pain of losing a friendship, she knew books, cupcakes and donated oscillating fans were all excuses. "Well, the bookstore's a pile of bricks, so fuck us both."

Plucky exhaled. "I'm sorry. I know what it meant to you."

"You did?"

"You carved out a space where everyone felt safe."

Biting her lip, she nodded.

"But life shouldn't be safe. The only person who feels safe in this town is you. Huge, automated machines comb the cotton plants and smash them into huge, rectangular bales, but who's running the controls? The plantation owners put into place tight-lipped, prestige-soaked barriers to success, and those barriers still linger. Why do you think the old biddies shit themselves over antiques? The slaves are gone, but the oppressive heat and the scarred hands aren't? Who's propping up this fantasy land?"

"It's not a fantasy."

"Tell that to the seven people who lost their lives living in trailers!"

Plucky's chest rose and fell, but her moral outrage fell short of its mark. Taylor heard her yearning for something more, but her aspirations meant nothing unless she took the first step. *I don't want to be the person she's accusing me of being, but I don't want to be her, either.* Shaking her head, she knew the time for second-guessing the past had passed. "I hear you, but I don't have an answer. I run a bookstore. I'll try to do more."

Exhaling, Plucky nodded.

"I can take some of these boxes to the recycling center tomorrow."

Plucky stepped away from her work. "Take as many as you can fit in your car."

"And the rest?" She looked at the leaning towers of cardboard and saw a network of strangers who cared more about easing the suffering of Ronan's residents than up-sizing their coffee orders. *If I fall short, others step up. We thrive as a community. For all her observations, Plucky keeps missing her chance to rally and lead.*

"I'll make sure they get where they belong."

Meeting Plucky's gaze, she nodded and gathered up enough boxes to fill her car. "Okay, I'll see you later." Packing the boxes in, she hoped Plucky found a way to thrive. *Nobody said life would be a crip course, but I won't let regrets outpace my memories. I can't grant unspoken wishes, but I can open my eyes.*

Her phone vibrated.

Will you keep me waiting all night? I can't work with a hard-on as big as Texas.

She laughed and thought about telling him to rub one off in the shower. Plucky's accusations stung, and she needed time to sort the wheat from the chaff. *I can't be the town's golden girl, I can't turn a blind eye and I can't pretend I've never failed.* Josh's leering smile dimmed beneath the force of Christopher's confident grin. Temptation at her fingertips, she sighed and threw away the burdens of perfection for the pleasures of the flesh. *Maybe I'm the one who needs to take a risk.* She grinned. *Let the town talk.*

I'm coming.

On my face?

That's up to you.

Backing down the gravel drive, she turned on the dark, country road and pushed away the rational thoughts threatening to steal her fun. She slowed for Ms. Tina's house, scanned the second floor and looked for a light. Sure enough, a single bulb illuminated the house's rear. Her daddy's extension ladder leaned against the roof, and she wondered if he'd left it there to taunt her or to facilitate the tomorrow's work. *Either way, Christopher is waiting, and I want him.*

A silhouette rose and braced his hands on the railing.

His hard-edged bulk made her wet her lips, but her attraction to him felt like the most natural thing in the world. *Shit.* Putting the car in park, she ached to answer his summons and find out if his gray eyes could deliver their promised ride. Midnight shadows drifted across the abandoned lawn, and cicadas filled the trees with a steady hum. She climbed out of the car and walked around the perimeter of the house until she stood at the base of the ladder. "O Romeo, Romeo! Wherefore art thou Romeo? Deny thy father and refuse thy name."

Christopher laughed. "You keep surprising me. I don't know what to say."

She shook her head and gripped the rails. "Say nothing. The play ends badly."

"Family pride?"

She shook her head. "Foolish youth." Climbing the rungs, she swung her leg over the balustrade and dusted off her hands. The porch light illuminated a green-painted floor and a white bistro set where he'd set up his laptop. A slow ceiling fan kept away moths and mosquitos. Condensation dripped down a cold beer bottle and stained a white linen napkin "You're working?"

"You look surprised."

"Not as surprised as the Roger will be." She scanned the shadows for the dog.

He pulled back a chair and revealed a snoring, white terrier.

Covering her mouth, she tried not to gasp. "You drugged the dog?"

He laughed. "Dillan dropped off a pack of sausages."

Eyeing the animal's round stomach, she wondered if Christopher could buy her complacency with such cheap tricks. "I'm sure Ms. Tina feeds him." The dog looked too healthy and well-loved for her pity. Glancing at Christopher, she wondered if the same adjectives applied. Beneath the yellow light, his eyes shone with the king of the savannah's quiet confidence, and his bare feet gripped the porch. Concrete and steel had replaced scrubland and rocky hills, but she recognized his dominance. The flirty, impulsive kiss at the reservoir brought a smile to her face but climbing into the lion's den upped the ante. She wondered if she could walk away without losing her respect, her reputation or her heart. She swallowed. "So, about that tour."

"Of the bed?"

She swallowed. Recognizing lust was one thing — but acting on it was another.

Pressing a few keys on his laptop, he straightened and led her toward the house's two French doors. Their painted, white mullions looked smooth to the touch. Protected from the weather, the paint lasted longer than the rain-shipped fascia board and railings. *The house isn't falling down. It just needed an intervention to save it from disrepair. Would it shield their activities from prying eyes and eager ears?* "Are you sure Ms. Tina's asleep?"

"I watched television with her for an hour. She's snoring in a rocking chair." He traced his hand along her upper arm. "I had other plans for you."

She swallowed and tilted her head. Somewhere in the house, Ms. Tina's snores sawed over true crime reruns and the air conditioner's hum. She grinned. *Wait until Plucky hears what I'm about to do.* "Deception is an aphrodisiac."

"Is it?" he asked. "I usually stick with oysters."

She laughed and stepped into the chilled bedroom. *Unless Ms. Tina turns out to be a hoarder, anything I see has to remain a secret.*

He flipped on a light.

"Oh!" she said.

"That's what they all say."

"You're awesome."

He laughed and crossed his arms. "Finally, we're on familiar ground."

She shook her head and walked away from him. The 1950s held dominion over the room, and she caught her amazed expression in a wide, beveled mirror over the dresser. Fake flowers occupied a vase, and she'd put down money they hadn't changed in decades. Turning, she found teal paint covering the walls and a diamond-patterned pink area anchoring the bed. The matching white furniture faded into the background against pops of color from a yellow herringbone bedspread, a pink glazed lamp and round pink throw pillows. Raising her hand, she touched the thick, patterned drapes. She could see the frayed, light-damaged lining, but she could care less about their condition. "I wonder if they went to the tropics for their honeymoon."

Christopher pulled the door shut and smiled. "The 1950s were bright."

"Is the entire house like this?"

He shook his head. "The upstairs hall has wood paneling, deer racks and rust-colored carpet."

"That's disappointing." She looked toward the French doors and the warm, spring night. "Maybe we should go back outside."

"They left the downstairs plaster and heavy furniture intact, but they renovated the upstairs for modern conveniences."

Caught between the freedom of the porch and her curiosity to see 1950s 'modern conveniences', she looked back and forth between the bedroom door and the porch. Surrounded by a barrage of colors, she stared at the big, yellow bed. *You could film a porno in here and get a million views – not that I'd ever make a sex tape.* She swallowed. *Sex. That's why I'm here, isn't it?* She swallowed and headed for the door. "Let's see a bathroom."

He stepped into the dark hallway.

Following his head, she peered around the jamb and examined the hallway. A blue glow lit the bottom of the stairs, but she focused on the light at the end of the hall. Her foot sank into the long pile carpet, and she exhaled, grateful to avoid the threat of creaking floorboards. Pushing open the bathroom door, she grinned. Jumbo flower wallpaper with metallic accents and tangerine-colored tiles looked like a precursor to the groovy 1970s, but rounded bullnose edges and black tiled-in accessories made the bathroom pop with vibrant, post-war glamour. "Can you imagine installing this today?"

He shook his head and stayed in the hallway's shadows. "I don't think I'll live to see Modern Farmhouse come full circle to the 1950s."

She looked over her shoulder. "Is that what your house looks like? Modern Farmhouse?"

He scratched his chin. "Something similar."

Realizing he probably had multiple houses, she edged out of the bathroom and decided not to risk waking Ms. Tina for chair railings and plaster ceiling medallions. "Thanks for showing me this room. I wonder if my dad helped install any of it."

"You should ask him."

How would I broach that subject? So, I was sneaking around Ms. Tina's house before I jumped Christopher Durand, and I just wondered... She shook her head and headed for the guest bedroom. Closed doors probably held more bedrooms. *Too bad Ms. Tina and Mr. Roger never had kids.* "At least you haven't seen a ghost."

Following in her wake, he laughed. "The night is young. We'll see what pops up."

She turned and almost bumped into him. "You don't really…"

He took her hand and pulled her toward the bedroom. "Beer?"

She nodded, certain he felt her hand shake. *I should have ignored the challenge in his gaze. I'm a bookseller from Ronan. He's the head of a national enterprise. We're about as different as…* She looked at his ass. *Still just people.* Tugging free her hand, she reached for his back and spread it against his skin. The smooth warmth captivated her. *I didn't climb that ladder for wallpaper. I came for a one-night stand.*

He turned in the doorway, eyebrows raised.

"Why did you come to Ronan?" she asked.

"To find you."

The sincerity of his response sent her tumbling past the last of her boundaries. No matter how many life experiences separated them, she wanted to wrap her legs around his torso and make good on the promise straining his pants. She glanced at his mouth and found the edge of his lips as roughly defined as his jawline. His eyes, now staring so intently into her own, reminded her of late afternoon skies before night edged out the day, and she wanted the night's thrilling comfort.

The tornado had upended her life, but she'd felt a connection with him long before the howling, roof-eating winds. Under other circumstances, their banter would have faded with time, but life dumped him in her lap and challenged her to make something of the opportunity. She could care less whether he'd come willingly or divine machinations had pushed him along. If Mother Nature wanted to taunt her, she would grab her prize and savor her reward.

His eyes darkened as if he could sense the shift in her mood.

"Can you be quiet?" he asked.

She bit her lip and nodded.

"How quiet?"

His rough question ignited the fuse in her chest. She caught him staring at her lips and felt the desperate inches separating their bodies. Claiming his lips for a quick kiss, she inhaled the rich allure of a hardworking man. As airy and transparent as she found his clean-shaven warmth, she tasted sweat on his lips and the strength of his grip. Pulling back before she thought of more than quick thrills, she looked at him. "Quiet enough."

He took a deep breath.

She waited for him to accept the challenge.

"Why?"

She said nothing as they stared at each other. The hardness pressing against her thigh assured her he wanted everything her body offered and nothing from Ronan's golden girl. "You're not from here." She scraped her teeth across her lip. "And when you leave, you'll be a bright spot in my memories."

"What if you come with me?" he asked.

Smothering a laugh, she traced his jaw and smiled. "I don't belong in Atlanta."

"Where do you belong?"

She glanced at the bed. "Right now, I belong below you."

Swooping his arm beneath her knees, he picked her up.

His bruising, heated kiss left her panting. She pressed against his hold, arching for contact as he stood at the edge of the bed.

"You're sure?" he asked.

"You have protection?"

Laughter wrinkled his skin.

"What? I don't want you to drag me off as a knocked-up bride." She sensed he would do it, and the only thing she wanted from him was a night of bliss. *Well, maybe two or three.*

He lowered her to the bed.

Rising on her knees, she pressed her body against his as he traced her spine. Impatient to claim her prize, she stroked his erection and heard him hiss. "Can *you* be quiet?"

Raising an eyebrow, he stepped out of his pants and stood before her in lean boxer briefs.

Reaching for him, she smiled and traced the line between his abs. "If you came looking for little ole me, Atlanta must bore the socks off you."

He captured her hand and pressed it against his erection.

"Trust me, Taylor. I'm not bored."

Retreating from his heat, she pulled her shirt over her head and relished his hungry inspection. Her breasts spilled over her bra, and she thrust her chest forward, willing him to touch her skin.

His slow smile preceded a firm grip.

He cupped her breast and thumbed her nipple. "Last chance to flee."

"Stop stalling." Her breath came in short pants, and she felt the wetness pooling against her skin. He kissed the skin beneath her ear, and his short beard grazed her neck. "You said you'd be generous. You said you'd make me forget." He shifted his hips, grinding his cock against her thigh, and she felt the scrape of denim and cotton making their last stand.

He raised his head. "Is that what you need?"

"Yes." She breathed her submission, willing him to take the lead.

Dropping his head, he buried his face against her neck and stroked her skin. His cock pressed against her thigh, and she shifted, desperate to feel more than promises. "Wait."

Groaning, he pulled back.

She shimmied out of her jeans, unhooked her bra and reached for him.

He held her at arm's length. "You haven't changed your mind?"

Shaking her head, she slid her hand into his briefs and felt the heavy heat that strained against the seams. "I want to feel you before you make me come." *So I can remember. So I can spend the rest of my life savoring this memory and comparing my other lovers to you.* A small-town hero would claim her hand, but she doubted he would warm her bed like Christopher. Falling against the yellow coverlet, she felt the scrape of the 1950s fabric and smiled. *Nothing will top this experience.*

Christopher pulled a condom from his shaving box. He sheathed his cock, climbed on the bed and straddled her.

She arched her back, impatient to feel his touch.

Kissing her until she relaxed, he trailed his hand to her heat and rubbed her clit.

His long strokes matched the rhythm of his kiss, and she arched, using her body and her lips to tell him what she needed. He picked up the pace, and she nodded, feeling the pressure building in her core. Reaching for him, she found him hot and heavy against her hand. She stoked her thumb along his ridge and felt the smooth slide of the condom in her hand. Guiding him to her heat, she raised her hips.

He sank into her depths and closed his eyes. "Taylor."

The heady pressure dragged a sigh from her lips.

Meeting her gaze, he lifted her hips and set a rhythm.

His thrusts filled her core, but she wanted more. Meeting his gaze, she smiled and pushed against his chest.

He withdrew and sat back on his legs. "You're fucking killing me."

"Isn't that the point?" She straddled him, grabbed his shoulders, and seated herself on his heat. Leaning close, she whispered against his skin. "Again."

Gripping her hips, he thrust into her and rubbed her swollen clit.

She chased the delicious friction and moaned.

"No, this is the point," he said.

Dropping her head to his shoulder, she met his thrusts and let her world explode. As she bit back a scream, she sank her teeth into his muscled shoulder and shuddered.

He gripped her ass, his muscles tensed and he huffed as he found his release. Cupping her head, he pulled back and smoothed her bangs from her face. "I didn't think you could do it."

Her body felt too heavy to move. Blinking, she raised her gaze. "Do what?"

"Stay quiet."

Laughter bubbled up in her chest, but she swatted his broad, exposed chest and climbed off his lap. "Well, you have a lot to learn about me."

He pulled off the condom and tied a knot at the end. "Apparently so."

She watched him chuck the condom into the small, wicker trashcan in the room's corner. "If Ms. Tina finds that..."

Stroking his thumb across her lips, he smiled. "Your secret's safe with me."

Am I? Sliding off the bed's edge before she destroyed the mood, she scooped up her clothes and made a mad dash down the quiet hallway. The tangerine and black bathroom looked harshly lit, and she wondered how much the illicit encounter heightened her response. *He can't be that much better than other men. Sometimes, being bad feels good.* Glancing at the mirror and the reflected hallway, she grinned. *Really good.*

A few minutes later, she walked down the hallway and schooled her breathing. If Ms. Tina were out of the house, she might have run back to the teal bedroom and hopped on Christopher for round two, but by definition, one-night stands had to end. Glancing at a closed door and stalling to calm her heartbeat, she wondered if Ms. Tina had decorated the other guest bedrooms in vivid shades of purple and jade green. She pried open the door, flicked on the light switch and stared.

Mirror-backed shelves lined the walls. On each shelf, toys sat in repose, their scratched faces, nibbled ears and painted edges infinitely reflected in the mirrored room.

She stepped back and tilted her head. The toys spanned the decades from pink-cheeked, porcelain dolls to grinning, harlequin clowns and fatigued, plastic soldiers. "Ghosts would have been better."

Backing out of the room, she reached for the light switch and came face to face with a purple-haired pet she'd taught to swear. "Fuzzball!" She reached for the long-lost toy, brought it to her nose and expected the sweet, babyish perfume she remembered from the country mall. Instead, she smelled dampness and dust, but an unmistakable homemade earring dangled from the toy's right ear, and she knew the creature had belonged to her.

Tucking the toy under her arm, she scanned the other trophies and wondered if they'd belonged to a long list of Ronan's youth. *How many times did I search the lost and found bins or peer at my friends, wondering who'd pinched my pet?* Her discovery tipped the scale and sent Ms. Tina's sweet eccentricities into the red zone. "Kleptomaniac crow!"

Turning off the light, she reached for the door. *What if she knows it's mine? What if she realizes I took it?* The prized, purple bundle felt like a hot potato. Kissing Fuzzball on the nose, she set it back on the shelf and sighed. "I'll come back for you."

She slipped into the teal bedroom, found it empty, and padded out to the porch.

Christopher sat shirtless in front of his computer. He smiled, closed the screen and looked up. "All good?"

She grabbed her shoes and walked to the railing. "I have to go."

Standing, he reached for her. "So, not a big cuddler."

Cuddling sounded like the perfect end to her day, but her life wobbled on uncertainties. "If we do this again"—she waved toward the bed—"I'm staying to cuddle and fuck you until you kick me out."

His eyes narrowed, and he reached toward her. "Taylor, stay."

Twisting out of his grasp, she threw her leg over the balustrade. "I can't."

He ran his hand through his hair and skewed his jaw.

She blew him a kiss and climbed down the ladder. *I don't know what Ms. Tina thinks she's doing, but she gave me an excuse to leave Christopher Durand speechless.* Reaching for the next rung, she smiled and lowered her foot, searching for solid ground. *What a night.*

Chapter Twelve

"Morning, Ms. Tina." Christopher filled a cup of coffee from an ancient drip pot and handed it to his hostess. "Sleep well?"

Ms. Tina yanked the cup to her chest. "Not a well as you, I imagine."

He wondered if the floorboards had given them away.

Yawning, she turned to the refrigerator, opened the door and swore. "I need a buggy, a bag boy and a damned grocery store."

Based on his midnight quest for a snack, the appliance held a shriveled lemon and a carton of milk. He stirred a spoonful of sugar into his cup of coffee and sipped. "I hope you don't mind, but I sent Dillan to pick up breakfast."

She straightened and peered at him. "From where?"

"The donut shop in Honey Tree Village." Her gaze widened, and he congratulated himself on adopting Taylor's people-focused mantra. *I've always put people first, but I assumed they could take care of their basic needs.* "I didn't know if you liked donuts, so I asked him to pick up kolaches, breakfast sandwiches and croissants."

She sipped her coffee. "You're a good boy, but you'd do better with a pot of chicken mull and a few sheets of egg bread. You're probably too young to know that food."

Pressing together his lips, he made a noncommittal noise and recalled his experiences with the savory chicken soup endemic to this region. "I've had a few bowls of mull at fundraisers and other big gatherings."

"Good. Some things shouldn't change." She patted her robe's pocket. "Your mama taught you to make it?"

"No, ma'am."

Her hand stilled. "Shame. So, you need a wife who cooks."

"I eat just fine."

She shook her head and located the cigarettes. Pulling one from the pack, she looked at him. "Mull's easy enough for men to make. Boil a whole chicken, pull the meat from the carcass and churn the meat through a grinder." She thumbed a lighter, her fingers repeating the rhythmic motion until the flame lit.

He wondered how many of her breakfasts began with coffee and a smoke.

Putting the cigarette in her mouth, she cupped the end, lit it and exhaled. "Thicken the broth with milk and butter, cook it down, and return the meat to the pot. Before you go crazy with the salt, split the wrapper on a long line of buttery soda crackers and crumbled them into the soup. You'll see it's good eatin'."

Opening his mouth, he searched for a way to thank her for her concern.

She pointed the lighter at him. "Nancy Lenore makes the best chicken mull around. Instead of marrying that carpenter, she shoulda opened a restaurant and kept us all fed."

The cigarette bobbed so much that he worried it would fall out of her mouth. "What kind of restaurant?"

Picking up her mug, she turned toward the back door and mumbled.

He caught little of her response. "What'd you say?"

She waved her cigarette in the air. "Can't smoke in the house."

Setting his mug in the sink, he rinsed out of the coffee. "Sorry... I thought you said something more about Ms. Lenore's restaurant."

"I said, she shoulda called the restaurant 'Chicken Bitch'."

The screen door slammed.

He laughed and imagined Ms. Tina and Greta going head-to-head over a recipe book. If he offered Greta a bowl of mull, she would take one bite, put down her spoon and smile. Ms. Tina's response might be as colorful as her upstairs bath.

The two women had graduated high school around the same time, but he doubted they would have been friends, and the divisions in his state bothered him as much as the Iraqi War. More than once, Greta had taken him and William across the river to 'run errands' in her community. She'd picked up a sack of fresh corn, settled on her mother's porch and spent the afternoon catching up on local news.

He and William had fended for themselves. At first, they'd hung around the porch, peered in the windows and tried to read the old newspaper papering the interior walls. After a while, Greta had called them little devils, shooed them off the porch and told them to make their fun.

The neighborhood children kept their distance, but he and William had loved baseball and footraces as much as they did. Hours later, when the aroma of smoked poultry, sweet corn and tomatoes had slipped down the street, they'd known to return to Greta's cottage for okra stew and fried corn cakes. *No wonder we slept like rocks. How many divisions can exposure and friendship cure?* Taylor and Plucky had clashed, she'd told him, but he hoped they found a way back to a meaningful friendship. He didn't care much for the sour-faced blackbird, but Taylor's expressive face revealed her emotions and he wanted to sooth her pain.

He replayed her late-night ascent and the way her nerves had almost gotten the best of her. Once she'd made up her mind, she climbed into his lap knowing exactly what she wanted. *Did she spend the rest of her evening yearning for more? If she hadn't bolted, I would have gladly given it to her.*

Shaking his head, he dried his hands. *I don't have time to daydream about women.* In twenty minutes, Dillan would arrive with enough breakfast pastries to feed every member of the Ocelot crew, the volunteers working on Ms. Tina's house and anyone who showed up hungry.

Stepping outside, he found Taylor and Ms. Tina sharing two rocking chairs. Upwind of the cigarette smoke, Taylor looked well-rested, chipper and absorbed by Ms. Tina's running narrative. The drop in his stomach had nothing to do with hunger. He cleared his throat. "Hi, ladies."

Taylor looked up and smiled.

"Good morning," he said.

"Good morning, Christopher," Taylor said.

He cocked his head and savored her blush.

Ms. Tina snorted.

Turning to the older woman, Taylor rested her elbow on the rocker and tucked her chin into her hand. "Ms. Tina, how come you and Mr. Roger never had kids?"

"Didn't happen." Ms. Tina stared out over the grass. "We saw every doctor within a hundred-mile radius, said our prayers and waited. Then we waited some more."

Taylor nodded.

The probing questions took him off guard, but she and Ms. Tina had history. You don't get to know people by smiling and looking away. Leaning against the kitchen doorjamb, he bit his lip. *Their history's not so close that Ms. Tina lets her in the house.* He tried to steer the conversation toward a neutral topic. "Your husband found a job down here. What'd he do?"

Ms. Tina stubbed out the cigarette in a brass ashtray. "Ran the bank." She waved a hand toward the old house and shrugged. "A lot of good it did him. Dead by fifty."

"I'm sorry…"

She whistled.

The piercing sound reminded him of live ammunition, and he winced.

Roger, the terrier, came running from the house, nosed open the screen door and jumped into Ms. Tina's lap.

She lifted the dog and let him lick her face. "And where were you last night?"

Christopher picked at his nail and felt his cheeks warm.

Taylor cleared her throat. "But you could have adopted a baby."

He cocked his head and wondered why she dwelled on the subject.

Ms. Tina stoked Roger's fur. "I kept hoping I'd fall pregnant, and I worried I would love a biological child more than an adopted one."

He straightened. "That's ridiculous."

Both women looked at him.

He looked back and forth between their stares. "All parents have favorites. Kids survive. I did." He spied Dillan behind the wheel of his truck and walked toward the steps leading off the porch. Passing Taylor, he grazed her arm and hoped she knew how their encounter occupied his thoughts. The contact sent a bolt up his skin, and he pulled back his arm. *No strings attached. No expectations. Just two single people looking for a good time*

She looked up. "You weren't the favorite?"

Her question pulled him from his self-admonishment. "Not even close. But William tried harder, and I was slow to catch on."

She nodded.

Roger growled.

Ms. Tina shushed the dog.

None of them knew how much he missed William and wished he could have traded places with his brother. Living another's life felt like a penance, but ever since he found Taylor, he wondered if he had something left to learn. Turning from the porch-bound trio, he fled toward Dillan. "Mission accomplished?"

His assistant hurried past the old, forking magnolia tree and stopped at the base of the porch steps. "The owner appreciated your heads-up on the order."

He nodded.

"How many'd you get?" Ms. Tina asked.

Her scratchy yell probably woke the neighbors.

Dillan put his foot on the first step, leaned on his knee, and grinned. "Plenty."

Leaping off Ms. Tina's lap, Roger rushed to the edge of his domain and nipped at Dillan's foot.

Jumping back, he held out his hands. "Hey! I bought those hot dogs!"

Ms. Tina rose from her rocking chair. "What hot dogs?"

Scooping up the animal, Taylor deposited the animal in Ms. Tina's arms, linked her arm with his and pulled him down the steps. "Just a taste, Ms. Tina. That's all."

Caught between two worlds, he planted his feet, but Taylor's insistent grip felt determined. *I've seen her swing a hammer, but I didn't expect such a force of nature. What happened to the sweet, indie bookstore owner with a quick verse?* Remembering the way she'd used him the previous night then left him wanting more, he brushed the edge of his lip, caught the action and leaned close to her ear. "Did you bring me any lip balm?"

She swatted his arm and released him.

Dillan frowned.

She smiled at the man. "Show me what you brought."

"Twelve dozen donuts, kolaches, breakfast sandwiches and croissants."

"Aww, that's so sweet. Bring it out to the high school. I'm sure the Ocelot crew will appreciate the breakfast."

Dillan skewed his jaw and jiggled the keys in his hand. "No, ma'am. I bought twelve dozen of each kind. Mr. Durand said we're feeding anyone who's hungry."

She turned to Christopher. "You bought six hundred pastries?"

He shrugged.

"Cheater!" She planted her hands on her hips.

Laughing, he pulled out his phone. "I had help." After Dillan had driven the mechanic crazy diagnosing the skid steer, he'd rounded up the rest of the Ocelot drivers, broken down pallets and put together rough tables to support the pastries on order. *The kid has initiative. Maybe he won't plateau in HR after all.* By now, the Ocelot drivers should be ready to serve the pastries beneath the white tent at the corner of Central Alley and Drake. A few thousand people lived within Ronan's city limits, but the breakfast load would make a sizeable dent and give his employees an altruistic high. He leaned close to Taylor's ear. "You want a ride?"

She pulled away. "I've already eaten. And once people pick up their pastries, they'll be right back here working on Ms. Tina's house." She glanced at the ladder. "Some of us have work to do."

"Aww, you're going to miss the fun."

She frowned.

"Sore loser?"

She narrowed her gaze.

"I'm feeding people. How can you be mad?"

"You're playing dirty," she said.

I'd like to play dirty with you. He winked. "Just picking up tricks as I go along."

"Our bet wasn't about the size of your bank account. I said I could muster more good than your mechanical envoy. You scoop and dump"—she lifted her chin—"and leave the people to me."

He walked to the truck bed and lifted the top of a white, cardboard box. The breakfast foods' sweet and savory aromas drifted across the lawn.

Taylor's nose twitched.

"You sure you don't want a ride?" he asked.

She glanced at his boots. "How's your foot?"

Laughing, he held up his hand and caught the keys from Dillan. "Trust me, Taylor. I can perform." Unwilling to spend the day bantering on Ms. Tina's lawn, even if his opponent was a breath of fresh air, he waved to Ms. Tina and jerked his chin toward his assistant. "Come on, Dilly. Get in the truck."

* * * *

Christopher dished out his share of the breakfast goods, checked on the Ocelot equipment, fielded phone calls from his management team and wondered how soon he needed to return to the office.

His phone vibrated.

Lifting the device to his ear, he smiled. "Miss me yet?" C.Y.'s polite laugh said volumes.

"You done playing hero?"

He thought of Taylor and shook his head. He'd come to Ronan to confirm her safety, check the performance of the electric research machines and do a good deed, but right now, he preferred the local view to Ponce de Leon. "I'm working remotely."

"I've heard that phrase before," C. Y. said.

"How'd it work out?"

"A bunch of bugs on their backs in bed, skimming executive summaries and scheduling tee times."

Taylor said the county has a decent golf course. Heading for the truck, he figured he could find greens near any Georgia town. A driving range and a putting green said nothing about Ronan. "Ever since I came down here, Dillan does my dirty work. I should let him run the company." He gave C.Y. space to respond. "Or did you want that job?"

"I'd double your profits."

Looking at the stack of flattened pastry boxes, he nodded. "Probably. But at what toll?"

"Your morning email alarmed the research staff. Why did you tell them to investigate the control boards instead of going through me?"

He climbed into the cab and shut the door. "When I called you, you didn't pick up the phone."

"It was five in the morning, Christopher."

"I didn't know massage firms scheduled services that early."

C.Y. snorted. "This isn't how hierarchies work. You should trust your direct reports."

"I trust you."

"Then why the circumvention?"

He glanced in the side mirror. A final Ocelot machine pushed downtown's rubble into a pile. The rest of the crew filled their stomachs and dispersed to rural locations to complete their tasks. In another day, the high school and the outlying homes would resemble the historical district. History had scarred them, but they were ready to rebuild. "I want to know whether the control boards were cheap or sloppy. Did you cut corners or did an engineer make a mistake?"

"I don't make mistakes," C.Y. said.

"Everybody fucks up. As soon as the electric drive machines roll into dealerships, operators will push them to their limits. We have to solve problems before those machines hit the floor."

"I'll take care of it."

He turned the key. "No more glossy performance reports. If there's a problem, I want to hear about it, even if you're at fault."

"I hear you."

He nodded and hung up the phone. Cruising toward the high school, he came across a familiar car parked on the roadside. Steam oozed from the hood, and Taylor bent over the engine, leaving her sweet ass on full display. He slowed to a stop and rolled down the window. "What's going on?"

She raised her head. "What do you think's going on? My car overheated."

"You need water?"

Wiping the sweat from her forehead, she shook her head. "I probably have an oil leak. Maybe some of the oil spilled on the engine block. As soon as it burns off, I'll let the engine cool, add more oil and get on my way."

For any other stranded motorist, he would have nodded and rolled up the window. Instead, he opened the door and climbed down from the truck. "Want a donut?"

She wrinkled her nose. "No takers?"

He winked. "I saved you one."

"You did not."

Shrugging, he leaned against the truck. "I saved myself a donut, but I'm generous."

She rolled her eyes and kicked the front tire. "Of all the things…"

The wind shifted and carried the smoke into his face. Turning his head, he caught the sweet smell of antifreeze and worried the oil leak might be more serious than she thought. If the engine block had cracked and antifreeze had mixed with oil, the necessary repairs would total her car. "Let me give you a lift to the mechanic's shop. They can tow your car and take a look."

"I don't need a tow."

"Taylor, I've been around machines most of my life."

She raised her chin. "So have I."

"That doesn't mean either of us wants to spend our day hanging out on the side of the road."

"I have it covered," she said.

Meeting her gaze, he hoped manners would undercut her pride. "Please? Your daddy can run you back out here with a case of oil." Her gaze narrowed, but victory felt out of reach. "The donut has a vanilla bean glaze."

She licked her lips but turned and looked down the empty road.

"Why won't you let me give you a hand?"

Glancing at the rear of the sedan, she shrugged.

He straightened and peered into the backseat. Stacks of flattened boxes filled the backseat. "Where were you going?"

"The recycling center. Plucky's so good with technology. She brought in all these donations, and I'm just" — she shrugged — "plodding along like a donkey."

I've never seen a sweeter ass. He pulled her into her arms and felt her hiccup. Beneath the sting of smoke, he caught her honey-laced scent. "Tears of frustration?"

Pulling from his embrace, she brushed her eye. "I don't cry!"

Smoothing her cheek, he noticed a small, crescent-shaped scar beneath the corner of her eye. Anyone with means would have asked a cosmetic surgeon to smooth it away, but he liked the subtle imperfection. *Maybe she bumped into a table corner as a kid.*

She turned away from his touch and wiggled out of his arms.

Hardheaded woman. Maybe she doesn't want the town to know where she gets her kicks. He opened the car's back door and pulled out the first stack of boxes. "Come on. Grab the rest and I'll take you to the recycling center. When we're done, you can meet your dad for repairs."

She skewed her lips and looked at the truck.

"Vanilla bean," he said.

Brushing past him, she grabbed the next stack of boxes. "You can't solve every problem with food." She looked over her shoulder. "Or sex!"

His smile grew. "Oh, I appreciate a challenge."

When he dropped the last of the boxes in the bed, he climbed into the cab and found her biting into his donut. "You going to share?"

She tore off a piece.

Leaning across the divide, he cupped her chin and stole a quick kiss. "Delicious."

She shoved the offered piece into her mouth. "I agree."

Her pleased grin disarmed him. Whatever distance had kept them apart on the naked asphalt had dissolved in the cab's intimacy. He put the truck in gear, found his bearings and searched his navigations system for the recycling center. In occupied the same road as the post office. "You all done at Ms. Tina's house?"

"She's back in business."

Mourning the loss of the extension ladder, he wondered where he and Taylor could meet up. Having tasted her lips and felt her muscles clench around his dick, he wanted to explore the subtleties of her response and what made her tick. "You going to tell me why you fled last night?"

"Personal reasons."

He glanced at her. "Things can't get much more personal than sex."

"You're going to think I'm stupid."

Fun, beautiful and stubborn, but I haven't seen stupid. "Try me."

She exhaled. "Okay, you remember those a purple-haired pets they used to sell? You could teach them tricks, and you could almost believe they lived?"

He nodded and turned onto the road for the post office.

"Well, I saved up my money, bought one and thought it was the neatest thing." She tapped her nails on the door. "Then I lost it."

The tapping might drive him crazy, but he understood she had something on her mind and wondered how the story explained her scramble down a ladder. *Maybe I'm out of practice.* "Sucks."

Pivoting in the seat, she shook her head. "But I didn't lose it. It's in Ms. Tina's house! With a bunch of other kids' stuff. She stole it!"

"Aren't you too old for toys?"

"I'm sentimental," she said.

I can tell.

He slowed the truck for the post office parking lot, skewed his jaw and wondered if country life might be simpler than he thought. "Maybe we can stop and check on Jeb."

"That'd be nice."

He turned into the rough parking lot. "You're upset because twenty years ago, she picked up your toy and didn't return it?"

"Why is she hoarding toys?"

He shrugged, chose bright sunlight over feminine outrage and climbed out of the cab. "Beats me."

"People in this town are decent. We go to church, we look out for each other and we leave our doors unlocked. We don't" — she puffed out her cheeks and walked toward the post office's glass door — "do whatever Ms. Tina's doing with those toys!"

"You make them sound like sex toys."

She tripped on a pothole and glared.

Trying not to laugh, he offered her a steadying hand.

"I have it!"

Hearing the indignation in her voice, he recognized the moral certainty underpinning her life. *Work hard, dream big and good things will happen to you.* He thought of Iraq and shook his head. *Sometimes people spend their lives fighting for the right to sleep peacefully and feed their families.*

Shading her eyes, she scanned the small cluster of businesses. "How many other kids lost their besties to that klepto crow?"

He repeated the phrase and laughed. "Aren't you being a little harsh?"

She pursed her lips, but a bubble of laughter slipped from her throat, and she smiled. "Maybe."

Returning her smile, he recognized how much he enjoyed her optimism and her playful, fun-loving attitude. *Let Ms. Tina explain what happened to the purple monster.* He imagined that conversation and grinned. "You can't confront Ms. Tina, can you? That's what has you so bent out of shape. You wouldn't know about the toy room unless you were in the house." He winked. "With me."

Mumbling under her breath, she walked toward the post office. "Maybe I should trade your donut for a drink."

He followed her into the air-conditioned haven. The transition from sunlight to polished wood messed with his vision, and he ran into her back. Grabbing her hips for support, he grinned and stepped to the side.

She stayed rooted to the spot.

Looking around her, he saw a pile of boxes listing from the arms of a petite woman. Vaguely recognized the woman's blue-black hair, he moved to lighten her load.

Taylor gripped his arm. "Heya, Plucky."

He looked toward Jeb for confirmation.

The postmaster nodded.

"Oh! Hey, Taylor." Plucky slid the boxes to the polished counter, turned and cleared her throat. She brushed her hands clean and smiled. "Thought you'd be at Ms. Tina's house today."

"A little car trouble. My friend, Christopher, helped me out."

My friend, eh? Feeling all eyes on him, he nodded his head toward Plucky. "Nice to see you again." Plucky smiled, but her gaze stayed flat and focused on her friend.

Taylor released his arm, walked toward Plucky's boxes and picked up the first one. She shook the cardboard container.

A muted sound emerged.

Setting it aside, she picked up a second box and shook it.

Plucky grabbed the box and lowered it to the counter. "Come on, Taylor. You're worse than a kid at Christmas."

Undeterred, Taylor picked up a third box. "You're up to no good, Plucky Kennedy. Ain't no reason for you to be mailing boxes."

Hearing dusty dirt roads and lazy summers in Taylor's exaggerated drawl, he wondered how much self-awareness lay dormant behind her pretty blue eyes. *Beware the 'ain't'. Ms. Tina looks like a nice, old broad, doesn't she?*

"My business has nothing to do with you," Plucky said.

Taylor reached over the counter and grabbed a letter opener.

He looked at Jeb.

The man shook his head and shrugged.

Slicing the tape on the third box, Taylor parted the cardboard.

Plucky lunged and closed the flaps. "Get out of my stuff!"

Taylor had inches on her friend. He leaned against a pillar and wondered if Ms. Tina cared to bet on the brawl's outcome. *My money's on Taylor.*

Using her shoulder to block Plucky, Taylor pulled a dehumidifier from the box. "Fancy reading light." She dropped the machine on the counter, braced her hands on her hips and faced her friend. "I knew the foundation was too good to be true. You're stealing from people who need your help, and you tricked me into helping you."

Plucky swallowed. "Nobody wanted the dehumidifier. It's too small."

"So you're returning it to the manufacturer" — Taylor turned the box — "in Key West? Plucky, the only things they make in Key West are cocktails and hermit shell crabs."

"Quit being ugly!" Plucky said.

"*I'm* the one being ugly?" Taylor's jaw muscles clenched, and she backed up. "The Ronan Recovery Foundation is a fraud" — pinching the bridge of her nose, she pushed out slow, deep breaths — "and I've been telling everyone in town how great it is."

"Go back to your mama and daddy." Plucky reached for the packing tape. "They've always taken care of their little princess."

"Jealousy never suited you." Taylor thrust her hand over the cardboard flaps. "Green's the definition of ugly."

"Oh, listen to Peaches! She'll tell us how to straighten our lives." Plucky slammed the tape gun against the polished counter. "Grow up!"

Jeb winced.

Christopher crossed his arms. *Oh, good, they're calming down.*

"We've always been equals," Taylor said. "I pick up the trash, I mop up the spilled coffee and I treat you like my friend."

"But at the end of the day, you keep the profits."

"Who else should keep them? You? You didn't take the risk!" She sighed and closed her eyes. "I understand wanting more, Plucky, but this isn't the way to get it.

You're so clever and talented. Don't sell yourself short."

Plucky ripped the box off the counter and turned toward the door. "The fact that people buy shit for complete strangers isn't my fault. They want to improve someone's life? Fine!" She pivoted and faced Taylor. "They can improve *my* life. I want to pay someone to make my goddamn coffee without feeling like it's a fucking luxury!"

"Plucky!"

"Taylor!" Wobbling her head from side to side, she pantomimed Taylor's expression. "Grow up!"

He stepped forward.

Taylor turned to Jeb. "Mail fraud is a crime. Tell her, Jeb."

The postmaster nodded. "The potential prison penalty is very high. Each offense counts. If the fraud scheme involves federal disaster relief" — he shook his head — "sentences get long."

"Oh, come on!" Plucky said. "It's a dehumidifier!"

Christopher could have heard a pin drop. *Mail fraud and petty theft aren't worth a life, but they might be worth a friendship.* He moved toward Taylor's side.

She kept her body turned toward Jeb. "How many boxes in the last week?"

He scrolled through tablet screens. "Maybe twenty."

She pivoted and stared at her friend. "Twenty?"

Plucky cleared her throat. "Twenty-three."

"How much money were you hoping to make?" Taylor asked.

Plucky adjusted her grip. "I'll pay back the money."

"To who? The people who bought items from your wish list or the people who you falsely represented?"

She took a deep breath. "Shut down the foundation and give the money to disaster relief."

Plucky rolled her eyes and headed for the door.

"And put in your notice," Taylor said.

Looking over her shoulder, Plucky paused and looked like she might cry.

If I were Taylor, I'd pay an accountant to check the books at Ronan Reads. The Ocelot employees who came up for disciplinary hearings were often repeat offenders. He had shortened the three strikes rule to two strikes and you're out. Intending to reinforce Taylor's mandate, he strode ahead of Plucky and opened the door. A mascara-tinged tear rolled down her cheek. *Is she crying because Taylor caught her or because she lost the income?* He softened his stance. "Do you need help getting out to the car?"

Shaking her head, she squared her shoulders. "I got myself into this mess. I can get myself out of it."

Jeb came around the counter and turned over the 'open' sign hanging in the window. "I've been trying to retire for five years, but nobody wanted this position. I'm done. Let someone else sort Ronan's mail."

"Jeb, no." Taylor gasped. "You're an institution!"

"You've always been a sweetheart, Taylor, but life will go on without me. Key West, on the other hand" — he sighed — "maybe I can't go on without it. Go sort out your beef with Plucky while I close up."

Christopher wondered if the postmaster would be Ronan's last defector. He glanced at the parking lot, and when he looked back, he saw Taylor resting her head against Jeb's shoulder. The older man held her with one arm. Her tearstain blossomed on his government-issued shirt. Christopher wanted to be the man offering her comfort, but he frowned. *I have no reason to claim that honor.*

Drying her eyes, Taylor pulled away from Jeb's chest and cleared her throat. "I don't cry."

"Of course not," Jeb said.

She walked past Christopher, and he hoped Plucky's head start gave her enough time to hit the road before Taylor stepped into the parking lot. He rejected Plucky's fraud, but he wanted to spare Taylor the pain of any more confrontations. Stepping into the sunlight, he sighed. *No such luck.*

Taylor and Plucky stood six feet apart beneath the blazing sunlight. Taylor held her phone.

"What are you doing?" Plucky asked.

"Canceling the foundation," Taylor said. "I won't be part of your lies."

His phone vibrated.

Due to an outpouring of support, the Ronan Recovery Foundation has closed its wish list and has stopped accepting donations. The organizer thanks the online community for its generosity and ensures donated items will end up in the hands of a Ronan resident recovering from the storm. God told us to love your neighbor as yourself—Matthew 22:36-40—and I want y'all to know we're feelin' the love!

He liked the message and hoped the little heart conveyed his support.

Plucky looked at her phone. "You're such a bitch."

Taylor laughed. "You're the one dragging people into your selfish schemes. How dare you dump this fraud on Jeb? You know what he's been through with Mr. Nelson. His social media feed likes every designer from Atlanta to New York. I've always felt safe with him, but he's about to abandon Ronan for a place where people don't fuck over each other!"

Wincing, Christopher wondered if he should demote the head of HR and put Taylor in charge of labor relations. *She doesn't mince words, but her concern comes from her heart. She's as worried about helping Plucky as she is about righting wrongs.*

"When Jeannie Mae told me she'd seen you at the post office, I hoped she'd made a mistake and the Ronan Recovery Foundation had nothing to do with her confusion. I thought maybe you'd found a book rep or a distributor willing to take back titles." Shaking her head, she looked at the ground. "Silly me."

"Silly doesn't begin to describe you," Plucky said. "You're a walking caricature of a doll."

Taylor raised her head. "Look who's talking. You scammed people for a latte!"

"Get over yourself." Plucky crossed her arms. "You didn't know what I was doing, and even if you did, nobody would hold you accountable for my actions."

Exhaling, Taylor rubbed her forehead. "Maybe I did know you wanted more. More than once, the till came up short five dollars. I attributed the shortfall to multitasking and moved on with my day, but I should have asked you what happened. People don't get fat overnight, and they don't steal five dollars to change their life."

"I'm not fat!" Plucky said.

"I never said you were!"

Plucky looked away.

Taylor dropped her hand. "You could have asked for a raise."

"You're hardly raking in the dough. You pay me more than minimum wage, but" — Plucky sighed — "I wanted more."

He smiled. *Maybe they'll hug it out.*

Taylor cocked her head. "How much more?"

"Enough to tell myself we're equals. Enough to hold up my head and have the church ladies meet my gaze instead of casting judgment on my attire."

"They judge everyone!"

"But they don't tell you when they see your mistakes." Plucky slapped her hand against her chest. "They tell me! They hold out an impossible, golden standard, and I'll never measure up to it. I don't have the resources or the allies in my back corner, armed with town secrets and ready to wield them in my defense."

"Life shouldn't be a war," Taylor said.

"But it is!" Plucky hung her head. "And I'm losing. For a second, I wanted power. I wanted the ability to surprise people and leave in a cloud of dust." She flung wide her arms. "But here I am, in little ole Ronan."

Taylor looked at him.

He nodded and stood just out of reach but ready to come to her aid if she needed him.

She faced Plucky. "I just don't know why you'd choose yourself over everyone else."

Plucky laughed so hard that she bent over and braced her hands on her knees. Looking up, she shook her bangs from her eyes. "My entire life, people chose themselves over me, and you're no different."

"Give me one example," Taylor said.

Plucky straightened. "The principal sent you to Girls' State. You knew how much I wanted to go."

He frowned and recalled his memories of the high school event. For three days, he'd shared a hotel room with strangers, sweated in an air-conditioned conference room and tried not to laugh as his peers slipped sexual innuendos into their prepared speeches. Half the time, the speakers had laughed before they finished their lines.

"You never said anything," Taylor said.

"I was the president of the youth legislature club! Who else in our graduating class knew about parliamentary procedure and rules of order? The only thing you knew how to do was raise your hand, ask questions and nod like the world made sense."

Taylor threw up her hands. "The event sucked. I had to wake up at six in the morning to read my notes, apply lipstick and make sure I did Ronan proud. You would have hated it."

"I would have had something beside poverty and parliamentary procedure to pad my college essays!"

"Great, so now it's my fault you never went to college."

Christopher shifted his stance.

"You never asked," Plucky said.

"About what?" she asked. "The event?"

"Anything!" Plucky said. "The event. The accolades. The raises. You never asked if I wanted more." She turned and walked toward a car.

The thing looked uglier than a crushed opossum.

"Plucky, wait!" Taylor said.

Lifting her hand, Plucky gave her friend the middle finger.

Taylor stopped short and watched Plucky spin her tires, kick up a cloud of dust and peel out of the parking lot. Turning, she walked toward him.

He'd heard every word of the argument, but he watched her hips sway and knew he wanted her at his side. "Come to Atlanta."

She stopped and tilted her head.

The invitation surprised him as much as it surprised her. Dropping his chin, he inhaled. "Come to Atlanta, Taylor. Just be yourself. I'm not asking you to change." The second request felt more confident than the first, as if he only needed time to wrap his mouth around the words. "You don't belong here."

"I do," she said.

Ronan might charm day-trippers, but the town's faded glory stemmed from natural resources and a legacy of rich men presiding over farm workers. A hundred years after its heyday, the town had an inadequate labor pool, poor entrepreneurial skills, weak institutions and a grudge against the Manufacturing Belt. *Why did I consider building a factory here?* Trailers, poverty and inequality existed in every town. As soon as locals peeled back the curtains, the prosperous, powerful, racially harmonious 'New South' crumbled into wizardry and cover-ups of. If she would leave Ronan and give Atlanta a try, he would buy her enough purple-haired animatronic pets to fill a new bookstore.

"No," she said.

He scanned the dusty parking lot. *Why the hell not?* He cleared his throat and tried a different approach. "You deserve a little vacation."

She crossed her arms. "Oh, were you offering? I thought you issued a command."

He exhaled. "Taylor, I'm definitely making you an offer."

"You're offering me the easy way out."

He narrowed his gaze. "Take it."

She scanned him from top to bottom. "I want to get in your truck, strip off my bra and let it fly out of the window."

He nodded and reached for his keys.

"But sex can't solve every problem."

He exhaled. "One date."

She nodded. "Maybe."

Closing the distance, he looked down. "Maybe?"

"When this is all over." She looked over her shoulder where Plucky's dust dissipated in the wind. "Then maybe you can take me out."

The offer felt like a lifeline. He tugged her toward the truck. "Come on. I'll buy you a drink, and we can talk more about your bra."

"Christopher, the nearest bar is thirty miles away."

"I'll buy you a tall boy."

She laughed.

Finding relief in the sound, he popped the tailgate and let her set the conversation's pace.

She hopped up next to him and swung her feet. "What am I going to do about Plucky?"

He rubbed her back. "You're sweet, aren't you? You worry about so many people you forget to worry about yourself."

"I have everything I need."

Except me. But I'm the one who needs her. I'm the one who needs a ray of sunshine, a mischievous grin and a body than makes a man want to sin. He grinned. *Good thing I'm writing the rules.*

"Why're you smiling?" she asked.

"Just thinking about our date in Atlanta." He tipped up her chin and pressed a kiss to her lips. Relieved not to taste the salt of tears, he pulled back and smiled. "I didn't know how much I needed someone in my life like you. In the face of all this bullshit, you're generous and kind."

"Is that all?"

"And smoking hot."

Smiling, she cupped his hand against her face and pulled away. "Christopher, you know I can't move to Atlanta."

He heard the tone shift and raised an eyebrow. "Why not?"

She shook her head. "I belong in Ronan."

"You don't know what you're turning down. We can get your bookstore back up and running. With your social media following, half your customers probably come from the metro area. Until you find a place of your own, you can stay with me. Greta will take care of you."

She frowned. "Who's Greta?"

"My housekeeper."

Shaking her head, she exhaled. "That's not my life. I've never met a housekeeper."

"She used to be my nanny."

"Even better," Taylor said. "Just take me back to my car."

He replayed Plucky's defense and wondered if his silence overlooked Greta's unspoken desires. "Greta's the person who bandaged my knees and read me bedtime stories. If she wants to keep working for me, she has a job for life."

Taylor looked at him. "Would you pay your mother a salary?"

Holding her gaze, he turned over his recent interactions with Greta. Besides giving C.Y. a hard time and berating him for staining his tuxedo, she greeted him with the same smile he recognized from his childhood. "Would you put yours out to pasture? The last time I checked, menopause didn't wash away pride and self-respect."

"Ask her," Taylor said. "Don't wait until your life explodes."

He nodded. When he returned to Atlanta, he would ask Greta if she wanted to stay with him or retire back to the Sea Islands with a fat pension. *Hell, maybe she's always wanted to open a business. She could give Chicken Bitch a run for its money.* He settled his hand on Taylor's thigh and felt her strength. "You left Ronan for college?"

She sighed and looked down the road. "Yep."

"Then you can do it again."

"But I always meant to come back," she said. "I own a business. I want to rebuild Ronan Reads."

"And I meant to run for governor and lead a life of public service. Dreams change, and inexperience is the only thing holding you back from an urban outpost of Ronan Reads. I've seen the world, and I came back to Georgia. You can see Georgia and still love Ronan."

She shook her head. "It's not the same."

"Why not?"

Hopping off the tailgate, she rubbed her arms. "My family needs me. This town needs me."

He heard her conviction, closed his eyes and remembered her slipping from his arms. *What if I need you?* He understood loyalty and prioritizing family needs, but until he'd met her, his life had never felt like a tradeoff. When she said she would never leave home, he believed her—but he refused to give up.

Chapter Thirteen

"Come to Atlanta," Christopher said. "Please. Give the city a try."

Taylor brushed her hair out of her eyes and wondered how many times she would repeat herself before the temping man absorbed the message. Exasperated, she cleared her throat. "Absolutely not. This thing between us" — she waved a hand in the air and ignored the pangs of fear creeping up her spine — "doesn't depend on us living in the same city."

He rubbed his hand over his face. "Taylor, I can't drive down here every time I want to see you."

"I can drive to Atlanta."

"Your car's a piece of shit."

Staring, she waited for him to make a grand gesture, but she feared the arrogant asshole would dismantle her pride's remnants. In front of Rebecca's microphone, she had said Ronan would rise into the beauty and charm of Buckhead, but in her nightmares, the plywood and torn shingles coalesced into shoddy construction. Ten years from now, the seams would show, and Ronan's residents would regret their hasty decisions. *I'm staying to fight for the town my friends and relatives deserve.*

"At least come spend a few weekends with me. I'll send a car to get you."

Tilting back her head, she stared at the dark, gathering clouds. An afternoon shower would cool her emotions, but rumbling thunder brought her back to the dark basement where she and Plucky had held each other and feared losing their lives. Tears welled in her eyes. She blinked and kept her face averted. "No."

"Why the hell not?"

She heard his exasperation and wondered what would make him lose his cool. Wetting her lips, she inhaled. "Why don't you move here?"

He frowned.

"Work remotely. Drive into the city for big meetings. What do you do all day, anyway?"

Laughing, he rubbed his brows.

"What's so funny?"

He dropped his hand. "How am I supposed to run a national company from Ronan? Not even Ronan... The shell of Ronan. Show me your conference rooms and jet hangar."

She narrowed her gaze. "How am I supposed to run a neighborhood bookstore from Atlanta?" She jabbed her finger into his chest and hoped anyone peering through windows enjoyed the show. "Why should I give up my life? You have more flexibility to change yours."

Cupping her hand, he pulled her finger to his lips and kissed her hand. "You're ridiculous."

The warmth of his lips eased her anger like a hot compress. She leaned into his touch. Remembering her cause, she yanked away her hand. "My mother says I'm a drama queen."

"I'm sure she's right."

His concession eased her frustration. "But you still want me to come to Atlanta."

He wrapped an arm around her waist, pulled her close, and dropped his head. "You make me smile, Taylor. You're so pure and sweet, but your emotions and fierce opinions light a fire that's hard to quell. I know you love Ronan, but you need a bigger stage."

His whispered suggestion sent a thrill coursing through her body, but she remembered sitting in the audience while Josh preached. Far from home, she struggled to merge his words with his actions. Wiggling out of Christopher's embrace, she squared her shoulders. "Don't think you can sweet talk me into a move" — she narrowed her gaze — "or weekend visits. I'll come to Atlanta for a date, but you'll come here just as often. Baby steps, Christopher. Life in Ronan moves in baby steps."

He threw up his hands. "Fine. I've never been much for phone sex, but if you want to get your kicks over a video feed, I'm happy to help."

Rolling her eyes, she marched to the passenger side of the truck. *This thing will last a month, then he'll find someone new to warm his bed.*

"Taylor..."

She turned.

Holding up his phone, he snapped a picture. "If we're going digital, I need pictures. Your pouty lip does something to me."

She refused to look at his pants. "Spend time in Ronan and I'll do more than pout."

"So many promises."

Hearing the frustration in his voice, she searched the cracked parking lot and the empty country road for an anchor. Travelers passing old buildings with faded white eves and worn gray roofs saw leggy azaleas, towering pines and weeds growing between cracks. She saw history and loyalty.

Despite the town's faded glamour, Ronan's residents refused to let the town fade into the forgotten South. They built up childhood dreams, bought bake-sale cookies and cheered from little league stands. She knew how to repay them. Christopher's offer tempted her, but let Plucky be the woman who abandoned her hometown when something better came along. Looking over her shoulder, she recognized Christopher's easy confidence and generous heart. Something better had come along, but Ronan needed her more than he did.

A piece of plastic wrap skittered along the broken asphalt.

She reached to pick up the trash.

Coming around her side of the truck, he grabbed her hand and held it tight. "You're mad."

She bit her lip. *Atlanta might as well be Hades. I never expected temptation to wear such a charming grin.* Shaking her head, she avoided his gaze and prayed Rebecca's polished reserve had worn off on her. A lifetime of polite encounters had trained Taylor to avoid saying 'no', but she knew her mind, and she refused to give up her identity. "I'm not mad. I'm frustrated. Your refusal to move here makes sense, but you have to understand I can't give up Ronan."

"I get it." He squeezed her hand. "We'll figure out a solution."

Releasing her breath, she nodded. "Does problem solving make you popular at Ocelot?"

"My family name makes me popular."

She cracked a smile.

He tucked her hair behind her ear. "But problem solving earns me respect. We'll find a way to see each other."

Reaching for his face, she stilled her hand and held it at her side. "You can't solve your way out of this problem. We're from two separate worlds."

He cupped her cheek. "Atlanta's an hour away."

"It might as well be another continent." She stepped back. "Why don't we spend the next few weeks enjoying the ride and see where it takes us?"

"I don't have a few weeks."

Her heart skipped a beat, and she bit the inside of her cheek to hold back tears. "A few hours. Take me back to my car then go shower at Ms. Tina's house. This evening, the high school's having a parking-lot fundraiser. Come enjoy it. When I win our bet, you'll have a reason to return to Ronan."

He stoked her cheekbone. "I already have a reason."

Pulling free, she turned her back on him and opened the passenger door. *As soon as he leaves, he'll forget this interlude and go back to the life he knows.*

"Taylor..."

Turning, she looked at him. "You said you'd put Ronan at the top of the list for the new Ocelot factory." Raising her voice, she hoped the wind strengthened her words and buried her fears. "Come meet your future workers at the fundraiser."

"You'd do anything for this city."

She swallowed. "You stayed in Ronan to win a bet, didn't you?"

He ran his hand through his hair. "Taylor."

The long, slow caress of her name sounded like a dying man's last words. *I'm learning to say no, but disappointment hurts.* Aching for a solution, she feared the compromise she would accept.

"Taylor..."

"Stop saying my name!" Squeezing her eyes closed, she held up her hand and focused on the span of their acquaintance. *I've known him for three days.* Clearing her throat, she blinked in the bright sunlight and forced a smile. "Don't be a sore loser. Ms. Tina has twenty dollars on the line."

"She can afford to lose it."

She lifted her chin. "According to the papers, so can you."

Shaking his head, he rounded the hood, opened the driver's side door and climbed in.

At every light and stop sign, the electric motor quieted and the cicadas overwhelmed the truck cab's silence. He pulled up next to her stranded car, put the truck in park and reached for his seatbelt. "I'll wait with you until your dad shows up."

Dropping her phone into her purse, she shook her head and reached for the door. "I'll be fine. This is Ronan."

"I can't leave you on the side of the road."

She hopped down. "You weren't the first person who stopped to help, and you won't be the last."

"Taylor..."

"Have your assistant unload the boxes for the recycling center. I'll figure out what to do with them."

"My assistant?"

"You have one, don't you?" she asked.

He frowned. "Dillan likes you."

"Dillan hardly knows me." Slamming the door before Christopher gained the upper hand, she waved and walked toward her car. Heat radiated from her sun-baked hood, but she leaned against the hot surface, looked to the phone in her hands and waved off his hovering presence. When he finally drove off, she let the tears fall.

* * * *

"Is this fundraiser going to work?" Principal Bettina Levatino asked.

Taylor unfurled a tablecloth and smoothed the thin plastic over a white folding table. Municipal crews had cut utilities and fenced off the high school buildings, but Ocelot's crew had finished the debris removal. Their relentless power had cleared the scar between the parking lot and the football field and opened up room to rebuild. Principal Levatino would nurture the scar until it healed. "I believe you can do it."

Nodding, Bettina surveyed the parking lot.

The BBQ Relief Riders had arrived from Nashville with enough food to feed every soul within a hundred miles. Cement-filled coffee cans held tall metal poles, and a network of thick-bulbed patio lights waited for a spark of electricity. On a makeshift stage, an Ozark string band warmed up, and Rebecca stood in the spotlight, ready to emcee the night.

As the gathering grew, Taylor beamed. The more people mingled over food and community, the more they believed in Ronan's future. *The fundraiser has to be a success.* She turned to Principal Levatino. The woman's straight black hair defied humidity, and the crease on her jeans stood tall. "You talked the teachers into the auction?"

"Every last one of them," Bettina said.

"You sent out the press release and alumni blast?"

Bettina crossed her arms and tapped her fingers. "Who's the teacher?"

She reached for the next tablecloth. "How could you fail?"

Watching volunteers unfolding chairs, Bettina dropped her hands. "How much does the community have left to give?"

The note of uncertainty registered. She set down the tablecloth and looked at the gathering from the principal's point of view. "Bettina, you scared the shit out of us for four years, sent us into the world and told us to do good. Now, the good's coming back to you. Ronan is more than its downtown. Sparrow County has plenty left to give, and Georgia" — she watched Christopher stride across the parking lot, wondered when he would leave and choked on the state's name — "won't let you down."

Bettina cupped her elbow. "You sick?"

"Nope, just tired." After spending the afternoon burying her emotions, her eyes felt dry and her body ached. No amount of BBQ and beer would buffer Plucky's fraud. The only thing she could think to do was double down her efforts. By making better connections, finding out what people needed and being the person God and her parents expected her to be, she'd do better. In the meantime, she would count down the agonizing minutes until Christopher left and she no longer felt his unexpected, velvety touch. The fading sunset and the generator's dull hum softened her pain's edges, but she refused to admit her feelings for Christopher outweighed her purpose in life. *Humans form emotional attachments to people who help them. I'm a human.* The patio lights flipped on, and she startled.

Principal Levatino patted her back. "That's it. I'm getting you a beer."

She intended to chug it.

Christopher stopped beyond her arm's reach. "How does this fundraiser work?"

You buy fifty acres, build a farmhouse and learn to love the land. In another life, he'd grown up down the road and thrown footballs with the older brothers she'd never had. He'd teased her about high school crushes until she'd stolen a kiss amid the ethereal magic of fireflies. Surrounded by the friends and family she loved, she would have chosen him over any other man, but her fantasy world had never existed, and she refused to trade her life for glimpses of make-believe. *What does he see when he looks at Ronan?* She imagined his coastal spread and knew her dreams of success were a joke to him. *He'll never settle in Ronan.* Clearing her throat, she nodded toward the stage and savored the moment. "We're putting Ronan's teachers in jail."

He scratched his head.

Damn if he didn't look cute. She let down her guard and grinned. "During the fundraiser, the teachers sit on the sidelines, miss the party and try to look pathetic. As soon as their students and former students raise enough money to spring them, they're free to join the fun." The teachers congregated at the base of the platform. Fifteen stools sat on the stage, and her mother would occupy one of them. "Patrons can buy the teachers drinks and food, but the teachers can't leave their stools until they make bail."

"How much?" he asked.

"Fifteen."

"Fifteen dollars?"

She cleared her throat. "Fifteen thousand."

He raised his finger and counted the faculty and staff. "You plan to conjure up a quarter of a million dollars by planting people on a stage?"

Wetting her lips, she nodded. "'Conjuring' isn't the right word."

"What is the right word?"

She smiled. "Crowdsourcing."

Turning, he offered her a slow clap. "I underestimated you."

Bettina handed her a can of beer. "Didn't we all?"

She popped the top and toasted the principal. *I can do this.*

Josh climbed onto the stage and took the microphone.

Shit. She swallowed. His sweet, full cheeks and floppy blond hair made him look like an earnest schoolboy, but she knew the strength of his reproach. *He broke the rules for his pleasure, and when I wanted more than servitude, he threw the rules in my face.* Finishing her beer, she wiped her lips.

Christopher leaned close. "You're white as a ghost. Who is that?"

"My former fiancé."

He cocked his head.

Josh smiled. "Let us open this fundraiser with a blessing."

The crowd bowed their heads.

"Good and gracious God, we recognize life is a blessing. As we mourn those we lost, we thank you for your generous love. Encourage us to be persons of honesty and integrity, to listen to the needs of our community, to recognize generosity in the smallest gift and to proclaim the Gospel. Amen." Stepping back, he waved.

The crowd cheered.

"Local boy?" Christopher asked.

She swallowed and her throat felt parched. "He grew up here, but he leads a mega-church outside of Savannah."

"Maybe he and Rebecca can get together," Christopher said.

Choking back a laugh, she tried to imagine a less likely combination. "She'd eat him alive."

Christopher rubbed her lower back.

She flinched. Feeling his hand still, she sighed. "I'm sorry."

"You're still mad?"

She glanced at him. "Exhausted."

He nodded and left his hand at the small of her back.

For a moment, she leaned into the touch and closed her eyes, but she'd promised Bettina to help with the fundraiser. Smiling at Christopher, she stepped away from his heat and turned to the principal. "What next?"

"Find the football team," Bettina said. "They promised to set up chairs."

She nodded.

"Amen, I say to you." The fiddler leading the band raised his bow. "Evening, folks." He drew his bow across his strings and called the show to order. "You ain't here for the key of me, so let's start this show."

The crowd cheered.

Feeding off the energy, he pulled the microphone to his lips. "We're here tonight to raise money for Ronan's high school and the teachers impacted by the storm. I have fifteen brave souls ready to take their seats, so break out your digital wallets, spam your friends and free the staff."

A crowd member put two fingers in their mouth and released a commanding whistle.

The fiddler signaled a crew of wizened musicians ready to play guitars, mandolins, dulcimers and autoharps. "We don't rely much on sheet music, so our weekly jam sessions pass our techniques to the next generation." He nodded toward Rebecca. "That pretty lady promised to record our show." He winked. "Just 'cause there's snow on the roof, don't mean there ain't a fire in the fireplace."

Rebecca laughed.

Taylor dropped her empty can.

"I'd come down the mountain just to get a look at her, but since I'm here, we might as well give you a good show. Here's *Seneca Square Dance*."

The fiddler set the melody, and the acoustic players layered in their sounds. As the microphone amplified the lively tune, couples turned to one another and found their rhythm.

Christopher turned to her. "Do you dance?"

She shook her head.

"Not at all?"

Swallowing, she admitted how much she wanted to lose herself in a night of spinning laughs, raucous stories and promising stares. "I'm a terrible dancer."

"Weren't you a pageant queen?"

She smiled. "I sang the national anthem."

He laughed and tugged her toward the line for food.

She smiled at everyone and introduced Christopher as Ocelot's CEO. A few people involved with Ms. Tina's house cast her knowing glances, but most volunteers and locals thanked Christopher for his resources. Proximity forced him to respond to the crowd's appreciation. He answered their questions but remained by her side. Each step she took in the line brought her closer to a good meal, a fresh beer and a quick goodbye.

At a table for eight, she and the group tucked into the food.

"Oh, Peaches sent out the call, and we've been recording teacher stories for the last three days." The speaker, a former star of the high school basketball team, flexed his shoulders. "I chipped in forty dollars to free Coach O, but I figure he'll need more than my cash to bail his ass out of jail."

Christopher turned to her. "You organized this fundraiser?"

She shook her head. "Principal Levatino came up with the scheme and managed the logistics I helped spread the word."

"How did I miss this?"

Looking toward Rebecca, she wondered how anyone in the southeast could have missed the event. The anchor had mentioned it on the metro news, and the Ronan Reads social media post had more than a thousand shares. "You've been busy working and managing logistics. Think 'telethon meets social media'. It's a concert with a purpose." She grinned. "But self-deprecating humor and self-shaming will rack up the cash."

"Shame?"

She set aside her plate. "The teachers with the most embarrassing stories will get out first because their stories will go viral in Ronan's extended community. Right now, everyone knows we need a laugh."

The fiddle player adjusted the microphone. "Our next song is an ancient tune from England called *Jeannette and Jeannot*. For this beautiful ballad, I'm turning over the microphone to our divas."

Two middle-aged women clasped their hands across their instruments, played and sang. Their pure, alto dirge epitomized longing and grief.

You are going far away, far away from poor Jeannette,
There is no one left to love me now, and you, too, may forget.
But my heart will be with you, wherever you may go,
Can you look me in the face and say the same, Jeannot?

Taylor shifted her chair and turned her back on the melancholy sound.

"Our next sound is an anthem for people going through hard times. Banjoist Ola Belle Reed wrote *I've Endured* about overcoming hardships during the Great Depression. I figure the good people of Ronan know something about finding strength."

She exhaled. *What happened to happy songs?*

Christopher stood. "Dance with me?"

Hesitating, she felt her dinner mates' appraising glances and nodded. *One dance.*

He led her beneath the patio lights and pulled her close. "Why do you do this?"

She blinked. "Do what?"

"Push yourself. Throw everything you have into helping people. Who's helping you?"

She thought of Mr. Nelson and Plucky as two hiccups in a blissful life. Then she looked at Josh glad-handing the city manager. Her ex-fiancé had been more than a hiccup. He was a shameful reminder that shiny packaging could hide rotten fruit. She rubbed the scar near her eye and looked at the expanse where her high school had once stood. "What other choice makes sense? The minute we throw in the towel, we have nothing left to lose. My family has my back, and that's more than most people can say."

He shifted her body until she pressed against his frame. "You believe in people."

She nodded.

He stepped forward and carried her into the tune.

Feeling him claim the lead, she relinquished control. "Why haven't you run for governor?"

He exhaled. "I can't run on a name."

"You don't have a platform? Ideas? Ways to save a dying town?"

"Taylor…"

She stiffened and stepped away. "Don't ask me to give up my dream without defending yours."

He pulled her back into position and resumed the dance. "Populations thrive on high employment. The last fifty years brought so many improvements, and we invented whole new industries to add value. Now, we need to modernize the industries we have before we lose our foundation. Grid improvements, electrification and well-paying manufacturing jobs are the next wave."

"You talk like a president."

"But I love Georgia." He looked over her shoulder. "Our state can produce batteries and advanced vehicle technologies as well as anyone else on the planet. The feds can spend billions upgrading plants and subsidizing car-buying, but I want Georgia to make the parts and design the motors. Ocelot's new fleet of vehicles proves our capabilities, but I don't want to run a fleet of small companies. I want to manage the regulations and infrastructure for improvements. American manufacturing is a thing of the future."

Laying her head against his chest, she listened to his heartbeat. Given his line of work, she expected a platform of fixed roads and repaired bridges, but his progressive, electric agenda sounded aspirational. Her father would hate a conflux of factories and unionized labor, but having glimpsed Christopher's vision of the future, she bet half the fundraiser's attendees would apply for Ocelot manufacturing jobs. She thought of rebuilding Ronan, but she accepted his board horizons. "What happened to the free-trade gospel? I thought everyone in politics wanted to address climate change and rein in corporate power?"

"Federal."

His response rumbled against her cheek, and she smiled.

The song ended, and he tipped up her chin. "Economic regionalism doesn't win elections. I need the peoples' heart."

She swallowed. "Efficiency and cost effectiveness aren't enough?"

"No, and every job in the state has spillover economic benefits. Think about tossing a stone into a lake. How far will the ripples extend?"

She thought of their reservoir dip.

"You were right, Taylor. Everything comes back to people—happy household, happy life."

Squeezing shut her eyes, she feared loving him. *I thought I would die happy in Ronan, but if I know what I missed, can I be happy?* She cleared her throat. "Good. Great. Do it."

He blinked. "What?"

Stepping out of his frame, she counted the remaining teachers. Her mom's vacant seat warmed her heart, and she knew the extended community would free the others. "Start a committee. Call up the Secretary of State, get the signatures and submit the forms."

"Taylor, running for governor isn't that easy. You have to have people…"

She smiled and held up her hand. Despite his refusal to sacrifice his life on the altar of love — or at least lust — she believed he cared about people over money, politics and religion. Living in Ronan, she understood how globalization hit small towns. If he could balance the state's budget, support low-wage workers, fight inequality and attract industry, he had her vote. *I bet he looks amazing in a suit, too.* She cleared her throat. "People won't be the problem. Go marry Rebecca, pop out two-point-five kids and take charge."

"I don't want Rebecca. I want you."

She swallowed.

Waiting, he raised an eyebrow.

"Mind if I cut in?" Jack asked.

Jerking away from Christopher, she turned and clasped her hand to her chest. "Jesus, Daddy, you scared me."

Jack kept his gaze on Christopher and pulled her to his side. "Mr. Durand, it seems like all we do in this town is work and feed you, but my wife's making supper tomorrow night, and if you're free to join us, we'd be grateful."

"Daddy, that's unnecessary."

The men stared at each other.

"Daddy…"

Christopher nodded. "I'd be honored."

"Really, supper's unnecessary," she said.

Christopher turned and smiled at her. "I'd like to spend time with your family."

"You would?" She scrambled to rearrange her thoughts and let a glimmer of hope grow. Her mother's scarred dining room table came from her side of the family, but her father presided over it. Their family debates often eclipsed dinner and spilled onto the front porch. They rarely held back, but Christopher could handle them. "I mean, I'd like you to come."

Christopher nodded. "Done."

Feeling her cheeks warm, she turned and exhaled. *Can I do this again?* Looking over the crowd, she saw the last teacher stand and wipe the sweat from his face. *I feel you, brother.*

As the teacher descended the stairs, the audience cheered.

Taking a bow, the fiddler smiled. "That's all for us. Don't let the mountain king knock you down. Keep your good eye on the devil, know his kingdom and know his pain. We're all survivors, and as long as you keep gettin' up, you can trust the Lord you're gettin' better."

The patio lights flickered.

Someone loaded a popular rap song, and the high school students cheered.

Josh stepped away from the spotlight's glare and walked toward her.

His loopy grin looked as welcoming as the harlequin clown in Ms. Tina's toy room.

"Mr. Lenore," he said. "Taylor."

I never came first, did I? Taking Christopher's hand, she pulled him away from the father who loved her and the man she'd thought she loved. *Thank God the pageant coordinator taught me how to make an exit.*

"Peaches, wait!" Josh said.

For a year, she'd built Ronan Reads, accepted her neighbor's questioning glances and refused to explain what had happened between her and Josh. *If I acknowledge what happened between us, the story will spread, I'll upstage Principal Levatino and I'll never forgive myself.* Smiling as if she just won the pageant crown, she looked over her shoulder and met Josh's gaze. "Have a nice life."

His eyes widened.

Feeling like a queen, she squeezed Christopher's fingers and held her head high.

Chapter Fourteen

"You want to tell me what's going on?" Christopher asked.

Tilting her head, Taylor smiled. "We raised money to help people rebuild their lives. Beautiful night."

He followed her toward the fenced-off lot housing Ocelot's machines. "I'm talking about Dipshit." The amplified music drowned out the night bugs, but he trailed her through his company's orange construction fencing, security lights and shadow-casting trailers.

"Great guy. Knows the Bible by heart."

Planting his feet, he spun her to face him. "I don't believe you."

"Hmm." Planting her hands on her hips, she looked at the night sky and inhaled. "That's the problem, isn't it? To succeed in life, you have to believe in many things — God, the government and love." She closed her eyes. "Which one will fail first?"

Stepping into her space, he wrapped his arms around her and folded her against his chest. "Which one failed you?"

She sighed. "Love."

The breeze carried off her whisper, and he stroked his thumb along her arm. His rhythm was slow and soothing as a caress, but the tension in his arms stemmed from coiled fury. Whatever the former fiancé had done to her, he would find a way to undo it.

"My mother sticks to the Bible's teachings like fridge magnets. She believes in submission and the whole nine yards. Plucky made fun of her and called the scheme sexist, but I believed it could work. I saw so many crumbling families that I hoped supporting Josh was the time-honored answer. When he proposed, I couldn't wait to start our lives together. We spent the night in bed, woke up the next morning and said our prayers for a life of happiness and bliss."

He tightened his grip.

"But we never talked about the important things. A marriage should mirror the love between Christ and the church. When a husband submits to the Lord, he has a servant's heart. Josh didn't have a servant's heart, and he wanted a servant. He wanted me to cook, clean and birth babies. All the time in high school and college I spent daydreaming about Ronan Reads"—she exhaled—"he must have laughed."

Turning her against his chest, he stoked her spine.

She cupped her cheek and fingered the small scar beneath her eye. "When I stood up for my dreams, he slapped me and his senior ring left a mark. I called my mama, but she said men had the right to discipline their wives."

He forced himself to draw a breath. "You broke off the engagement."

"Eventually." She dropped her hand and cleared her throat. "For the longest time, I made excuses. I know you don't believe in God, but I do, and I spent a lot of time talking to church counselors about unity and Ephesians. As graduation grew closer, I understood submission and obedience weren't the same thing, but I felt so helpless and desperate for a solution. I did the only thing I knew how to do. I ran home."

Out of his depth, he skewed his jaw and wondered how to broach a topic he barely understood. The women in his life shunned physical violence, but they had enough resources to rebuild their lives in any corner of the world. For all her entrepreneurial spirit and kindness, Taylor had barely stepped foot outside her hometown. "How many times?" he asked. "How many times did he hit you?"

She looked up. "The number doesn't matter. Eventually, I worked up the courage to leave him."

It matters to me. Given a little privacy, I'll return the blows. "I don't understand why you came back to Ronan and your family. I would have done anything to get my daughter out of that situation."

She sighed and looked toward the dwindling festivities. "I don't think my mama's right, but she gave me the wisdom she knows best. She and Daddy love me."

He turned her in his arms. "Here's my wisdom, Taylor. You're so much more than your mother's girl. Your heart and love for your neighbors make you beautiful, and you should spend the rest of your life doing what you do best." Pressing his lips against hers, he hoped warmth and gentleness soothed her regrets and promised her a future.

Pulling away, she traced her lip.

He tipped up her chin. "I've seen enough violence in my life to understand how pain lingers. I'd never ask you to give up your faith, but I'd never strike you, either. I didn't realize how hard you'd fought to build Ronan Reads. Asking you to move to Atlanta was a mistake."

Lit by the fundraiser's glow, her smile bloomed, and she draped her arms around his shoulders. "Dance with me."

He dropped his hands to her waist. "I thought you said you were a terrible dancer."

She ground her hips against his thigh. "I thought you said you could lead."

Throwing back his head, he laughed, centered her against his thigh and hoped his jeans kept his cock under control. Dropping her hips, she mimicked the bedroom roll, and he groaned. *At least we're in plain sight. Given a wisp of privacy, I'd show her how a real man worships the woman he loves.* The sentiment caught him off guard. He missed a step and dropped his hands from her ass.

"What's wrong?" she asked.

"Nothing to worry about." Watching her teeth scraped against her lips, he cleared his throat. "I should get you back before your father whips out a marriage license."

"That only happens in movies."

Jack's appraising gaze suggested he knew what else happened in dark rooms. *Wouldn't I guard my kid, too?* The responsibilities of fatherhood sent him backing toward the safety of patio lights and watery beer.

She tilted her head, and her hair skimmed her breast.

He wanted to peel her shirt from her arms, raise her breast to his lips and suck her until she ached. That echoing emptiness could hurt, but it could also bring pleasure. He wanted to fill her until she screamed his name, and the entire town marked his claim. *William would have fucking loved her, but she's mine.* He blinked. *Isn't she?*

"Cat got your tongue?"

"Something like that." He closed his eyes and exhaled. She danced her fingers up his chest, and he memorized her sweet floral scent. "We should go back to the fundraiser."

"I have another idea."

He opened his eyes.

"You know, I see you riding around in your big 'ole truck" — she smiled — "but what does all this stuff do?"

"Stuff?" He cleared his throat and focused on the fleet of electric lifts, track loaders, skid steers, and excavators. "You want to touch a truck?"

She batted her eyes. "I want to touch *your* truck."

He feared his jeans would fail. "Taylor, as much as I'd like to take you up on that offer, I don't think this is the time or place..."

Turning, she disappeared into the shadows.

"Taylor?" Scratching his thumb along his lip, he exhaled. "Fuck me."

From the shadows, she laughed. "That's the idea."

Shaking his head, he followed her and hoped Dillan would erase the security feed in exchange for a fat check. *Wait. If Taylor's onboard, I'm keeping that file.*

"You coming?" she asked.

He grinned and found her seated on the platform of a boom lift. "Did I mention I have a very nice house in Atlanta?"

She laughed and unbuttoned her shirt. "I'm sure you do."

"And that Ocelot has this lot under surveillance?"

Her finger stilled, but she moved to the next button. "I'm sure you can take care of that issue."

Gripping her side, he traced a hipbone. "Are you saying goodbye?"

She looked down. "We knew this thing between us wouldn't last."

He claimed the other hip and pulled her forward until her legs straddled his hips. "Why do you keep calling it a thing? What's wrong with a relationship? Love doesn't always fail."

Shaking her head, she reached for his shirt and tugged it from his jeans. "I don't want you to fail, Governor."

He laughed. "Only you could make that word sound dirty." Feeling her touch against his bare chest, he tabled his objections. *She's a grown woman, and if she wants to taste a goodbye, I'll give her something to regret.* Stepping back, he crossed his arms and pulled off his shirt.

She licked her lips. "The moment you went for a swim, I knew you were trouble."

"What took you so long?" Gripping the edges of her shirt, he pulled the fabric over her head, unhooked her bra and dropped his head to her peaked, rosy nipple. Drawing the bud in his mouth, he sucked until he felt her push against his control.

She gripped his shoulders. "Christopher."

Releasing her nipple, he raised his head and claimed her mouth. Her grip on his shoulders tightened. His kiss channeled every ounce of frustration and disbelief that accompanied him through Ronan.

Relaxing her hold, she pushed against his chest and reached for his belt.

He shook his head. "I didn't have time to savor you at Ms. Tina's house."

Looking up, she smiled. "Who says I want to be savored?"

In the shadows, her grin shone, but he feared becoming a memory.

She wrestled with his belt buckle. "Get naked."

He let her pull off his belt, but he pried the thick leather from her hands. "You first."

Scooting off the platform, she shimmied out of her jeans and kicked off her boots. "How's your foot?"

Adding his boots to the pile, he scanned her curves. Amid the shadows, she stood proud, and he ached to sink into her warmth. "My foot's the last thing that should worry you."

She laughed and reached for him.

Shaking his head, he dropped the leather belt, captured her hands and traced her spine. "Turn around."

She tilted her head. "Why?"

After pressing a kiss to her mouth's corner, he skimmed his five-o'clock shadow along her jaw, turned her and trailed a hand down her back. "I think you want to get caught." Cupping her ass, he parted her cheeks and imagined sinking into her heat. Stroking his dick, he considered claiming the first release and spraying his cum along her beautiful back. Aware of his surroundings, he inhaled and slapped her ass. "And I think your back's sexy as hell — especially this stretch of soft, bare skin before your sweet ass." He bit his lip and thrust against her thigh. "You undo me."

Looking over her shoulder, she grinned.

He picked up his jeans and laid them over the hard edge of the platform. Ocelot's cabs had leather seats and air conditioning, but if she wanted to fuck in the wild, he would happily facilitate her release.

He curled his hand around her hip.

She arched into his touch.

Splaying his other hand on her back, he guided her over the edge of the lift bed. Nestled against her plush ass, he wanted to thrust and take her, but he wanted her wet and begging for relief, too. Sliding his hand along her arm, he held her wrists and dropped his other hand to trace her wet folds. "How long have you thought about this?"

"Since the minute you rolled into town."

He growled, stroked her clit and heard her gasp. "And how long were you going to wait?"

"Forever."

Her whispered admission sent him over the edge. He wanted to turn her, cradle her face and tell her she would never wait again, but she needed something more than kindness, and he vowed to give it to her. "Stay still." Releasing her hands, he pulled a condom from his wallet, sheathed his dick and ran his hand down her back. "Taylor."

"Christopher." She wiggled her ass.

"Shit." Gripping her shoulder, he centered his hips, guided his finger into her depths and brought her wetness to his lips. "You taste so good." Lining up with her entrance, he slid inside her with one long, slow thrust and felt her shudder. Her muscles clenched his dick, and he held her fast, trying to go slow.

"More." She pushed against him, and he sank deeper. "I want more."

Released from his constraints, he held her hips from the edge of the platform and rocked into her heat. Each thrust brought them closer, and he strained to hold back, pleasure her and show her she meant more than an illicit fuck.

She braced her weight against the platform and hung her head. "Yes. Yes!"

Her cries sent him over the edge. Flooding the condom, he held her hips, wrapped his arm around her waist and pulled her body tight against his chest. Panting, slick with sweat and humidity and holding a woman gilded by moonlight, he wondered if he had ever been happier. Slipping from her, he closed his eyes and took a deep breath. When he opened them, he caught her bright smile and marked this memory.

"Where is he?" C.Y. asked.

Shit. C.Y.'s insistent demand sounded more appropriate for a crowded gym than the shadows of a work lot, but Christopher calculated he had about three minutes to get clothes on someone. Reaching for Taylor's shirt, he spun her around and yanked the thin cotton over her head.

"What the hell?" Struggling, she shoved her arms into the sleeves and pulled out of his grasp. "I liked you better with bedroom eyes."

"Then you should have let me fuck you in a bedroom."

She giggled.

He handed her his shirt to clean up.

"I don't care if he's the CEO. Find him. *Now*," C.Y. said.

Taylor's eyes widened, and she yanked her pants from his arms. "Who is that?"

"Ocelot's Vice President of Energy & Transportation." He offered her a boot. "Nice guy. Met him in Iraq."

Hopping in place, she shimmied into her clothes, tugged on her boots and leaned against the boom lift. "Oh, I want to meet him."

He rubbed his temples and wished he had worn an undershirt. "Like this?"

She grinned. "Why not?"

"Dilly, where the fuck is Christopher?" C.Y. asked.

"Maybe you should check near the skid steers." Dillan raised his voice. "Mr. Dong, if you could just wait a moment."

Slapping a hand over her mouth, Taylor smothered a laugh. "Mr. Dong?"

I knew I loved this woman. He swatted her ass, slipped on his jeans and guided his feet into his boots.

"I gave you one assignment, Dilly. I told you to keep him out of trouble."

"Sir, I don't work for you," Dillan said.

Christopher threaded his belt and cinched it around his waist. *I'll double Dillan's salary.* Checking to make sure Taylor was ready, he stole a kiss and hoped the artificial lighting hid her flushed cheeks and swollen lips. Letting loose a whistle loud enough to turn a pack of dogs, he stepped into the cone of a security light. "Looking for me?"

C. Y. marched up to him. "Where the fuck have you been — and where is your shirt?"

He cocked his head. "Scouting Ronan. Collecting performance data from the new fleet." Thinking of Taylor, he grinned. "Making friends with the locals."

"We need you back in Atlanta. Your father has occupied your office, and he won't give anyone peace. Between your early morning emails and his nine o'clock daily meetings, I don't have time to get shit done." C.Y. exhaled. "Doesn't your family ever quit?"

"No." He digested C.Y.'s complaints. Running the test machines in Ronan kept him busy, but he'd made up the difference late at night. The workload dogged him, but he had persevered for the chance to finish the job and savor Taylor's company. He doubted his father's motivations stemmed from the same desires. Robert's reluctance to release his hold on Ocelot would hold back the company. Frowning, he turned to Dillan. "Why didn't you tell me my father's been rampaging through the office?"

"Uh, I, uh… You looked like you were having fun." Looking back and forth between him and C.Y., Dillan fainted.

An orange traffic cone buffered his head and kept him from knocking the asphalt. Staring at his assistant, he exhaled and turned to C.Y. "See what you've done? You've startled the poor thing."

C.Y. jerked back. "Me?"

"Oh, for the love of God." Taylor strode out of the shadows and cradled Dillan's head in her lap. "Call the paramedics to come have a look at him."

C.Y. frowned. "Who's the woman?"

She looked up. "Who the hell are you?"

He inclined his head. "My name is Dong, C.Y."

"Well, Mr. Dong, see yourself to a cell phone and call 911," she said.

C.Y. turned to him. "Did she give me an order?"

I doubt it will be the last one. He nodded.

Dillan moaned.

C.Y. crossed his arms. "Who is she?"

He opened his mouth to reply.

"My name is Taylor Lenore." Beating him to the punch, she brushed Dillan's hair from his face. "And this sweet baby needs our help."

He envied the man, but he doubled down on his pledge to hire fifty-year-old project managers. When Dillan opened his eyes, he gripped the man's hand and pulled him to standing. "You okay?"

Looking back and forth between him and C.Y., Dillan swayed.

He tightened his grip.

"I should have come down sooner. Bum-fuck Ronan is at the top of your list for the new factory, and you're in flagrante with a country girl. She'll either turn up pregnant or sell her story to the press." C.Y. shook his head. "Dude, you're losing your touch."

Abandoning Dillan to gravity, Christopher swung and decked his friend.

Catching himself on all fours, C.Y. grinned. "I was right. We are *so* fucked."

Taylor stared at him. "Ronan was at the top of your list?"

He rubbed his fist. "The site has merit, but the Ocmulgee River spills its banks too often, and I can't afford to let the factory flood."

"Tell her you're soft on Georgia," C.Y. said.

He kept his gaze locked on her. "She knows."

Shaking her head, she turned her back on the conversation and walked toward the fundraiser.

"Taylor, wait!"

She paused.

Jogging to her side, he cupped her elbow. "I told you Ocelot intended to build a new factory. I told you Ronan might be a contender. I didn't make promises."

Shrugging out of his grip, she sighed. "I thought I could make a difference."

"You can't battle nature."

"How would you overcome the river flooding?" she asked.

"Berms and pumps." He rubbed his jaw. "Georgia's politicians spent the last century arguing over water rights. Even the Supreme Court justices tired of hearing about our water wars with Florida. I believe the engineers can design a flood-proof building, but who's to say what the next fifty years look like? Water from the Apalachicola-Chattahoochee-Flint river basin provides drinking water to most of Atlanta. What happens if it slips its banks?"

"We're just talking about the little ole Ocmulgee."

"It's little today, but demographics change. Infrastructure ages. What if the reservoir fails?"

"Worrying about the future will paralyze you. Where do you want to build your life?"

He stared.

Shaking her head, she walked off.

"Taylor, wait!"

She paused and looked over her shoulder. "You want to manage the state's drinking water supply? You want to juggle priorities and weight the risks to agriculture, power generation and manufacturing sites?" Planting her hands on her hips, she narrowed her gaze. "Stop holding back and make the run!"

Before he could answer, she flipped her hair over her shoulder and strode off. Speechless, he stood in the shadow of his grandfather's achievements. Ocelot's equipment moved the world, but he feared casting a net so far that he could never pull in it. Seeking reassurance, he turned to his friend.

On his feet, C.Y. brushed his palms. "What did I say?"

Torn between knocking C.Y. flat on his ass and chasing after the woman he loved, he exhaled and turned to his assistant. "Find me a clean shirt."

Dillan nodded and scurried into the darkness.

"Where *is* your shirt?" C.Y. asked.

"I let Taylor use it to clean up."

C.Y. inclined his head. "Such a gentleman."

He rubbed his fist. "Shut up before I deck you again."

Laughing, C.Y. slapped his back. "You're the boss."

He watched Taylor disappear into the crowd. *The boss of* what?

Chapter Fifteen

Standing at the farmhouse kitchen counter, Taylor stared at the plucked carcasses of two chickens. 'Processing' sounded more removed than 'slaughtering' and 'butchering', but she knew what the softened words obscured, and the physical labor turned her stomach.

Tightening her apron strings, Nancy sipped her water and picked up her sharp knife. "Tell me about him."

She swallowed. "Christopher?"

Nancy looked up. "Yes, Christopher. Every person in town mentions him in the same breath they mention you. Tell me about the man from Atlanta."

Replaying Christopher's heated caresses in the shadowed parking lot, she felt her cheeks warm and wondered if she would ever wear a backless dress without thinking of him. Ocelot pulled him back to Atlanta, and she doubted he would come for supper.

"You met him at the bookstore then he came down to Ronan to help with the recovery. We clicked, I guess."

Nancy raised her eyebrows. "You *clicked*?"

She nodded.

Shaking her head, Nancy flipped the bird, reached along the breastplate and removed the heart.

She winced and averted her gaze to the glass bowl set aside for giblets. Within minutes, the liver and gizzard joined the heart. The intestines and undesirable organs landed in a separate bowl.

"What does Christopher do?" Nancy asked.

"Like you don't know."

"Young lady, don't you sass me."

She exhaled. "He runs his family's company."

Nancy set down the knife. "His grandfather was the governor."

"Yeah, about that." She traced her thumb along the age-softened wood countertop. "Was he a good governor?"

Picking up her poultry shears, Nancy cut off the carcass' neck and set it aside for soup stock. She flipped the bird again, pried out the preen gland and removed the feet. "He was good enough. Why?"

"Christopher mentioned running for office."

Shaking her head, Nancy carried the bird to the ice-filled sink, submerged the carcass and braced her hands on the edge of the sink. "Taylor, honey, that man's never going to settle in Ronan, and you're never going to be happy anywhere else."

"I know." She frowned and stared at her mother's tense shoulders. "I don't have an answer, but he's so generous and even-tempered and" — she exhaled — "out of my reach."

Turning, Nancy shook her head. "No, that's not the case. He'd be lucky to have you, but I don't know if you can manage him. You had a hard enough time with Josh."

"Josh was a selfish asshole."

Nancy gaped.

She swallowed and thought about her mother sitting in the pink gingham glider every night. *Having one child might be worse than having none. You can't dilute your love.* "I love you, Mama, but I don't know what's going to happen. I need you to trust me and let me figure out my next move."

Wiping her hands on her apron, Nancy leaned on the counter. "You know I put everything I had into raising you." She picked up the sharp knife and made a slit on the second bird. "But I raised you for a purpose."

Watching her mother process the carcass, she swallowed and wished the scene played out like a made-for-television movie. Far from being cold and uncaring toward her flock, Nancy mothered the chicks, ferried scraps to the adult birds and eased their slaughter. Pressed, she would admit how much she loved their soft, clucking affection, but she embraced their end as much as she embraced their pinfeathers. *I'm not a sacrifice.* She cleared her throat. "I appreciate everything you and Daddy did for me, but you have to trust me."

Pausing, Nancy looked up. "I didn't raise you to grow old at my side, Taylor Lenore. I raised you to do good. '*Many women do noble things, but you surpass them all. Charm is deceptive and beauty is fleeting; but a woman who fears the Lord is to be praised,*'" she said, quoting

Proverbs 31:29-30. "You came back to Ronan for a reason."

Taylor had heard the proverb her entire life, but she wondered if fearing the Lord would be enough to soothe her soul. *I don't need charm and beauty, but I need to do something good for the world. Pecking around Ronan's dust won't be enough for me. I need more.*

"If you think Christopher Durand is the man who'll make you happy, then stop sneaking around town and put your heart into the relationship. Go to Atlanta and live the high life. Your leavin' might break your daddy's heart, but he'll survive."

Startled, she looked up. "Daddy?"

Shaking her head, Nancy yanked out the second heart. "You and your father are two peas in a pod and as accepting as lambs. You've always been Daddy's girl."

She looked past the Cherokee roses and the soft, sweet decay of the fallen blooms. Jack bolstered her dreams. He stood in the wings at the pageant, rigged up lights so they could work deep into the night and came to her rescue with adhesive bandages and jumper cables. *He could learn to love Christopher, too.* Inhaling, she watched Nancy lower the second bird into the ice bath. "What are you making?"

Drying her hands, Nancy brushed a halo of wisps from her eyes and tossed her apron in the washing machine. "Fried chicken, collards, cream corn, okra and mashed potatoes. Welcome to the country, Christopher Durand."

"What about the smothered green beans?"

Nancy pursed her lips and released a smile. "Good catch."

She laughed. "What are you really cooking?"

"Mushroom Asiago chicken with thyme." Nancy pulled a bin from the cupboard. "And mashed potatoes."

Her mother's mischievous grin gave her pause. *She wouldn't poison Christopher, would she?* "I don't remember that dish."

Nancy reached for the spray disinfectant. "Peaches, you've been off at college and on your own for a few years. What do you think your daddy and I do all day? We cook, we drink and we pray." Nancy winked. "Mostly."

She held up her hand, looked away from her mother and groaned.

* * * *

Staring at stacks of Nancy's rose-painted china sitting on a white lace tablecloth, Taylor counted eight chairs around the table and frowned. "Mama, who else is coming for supper?"

"You, me, Daddy, Uncle Brent, Aunt Mary, Charles, your friend Christopher and" — Nancy counted the chairs and repeated the names — "Ms. Tina!"

So much for an intimate family dinner. No wonder she had me iron all the napkins. Taylor cleared her throat and reached for the dinner plates. Setting them out, she tried to ignore the butterflies in her stomach, but she wanted Christopher to like her family as much as she liked him. A stronger feeling coiled in her heart like a small glow. Afraid to smother the flame, she explored the idea of love and let visions of happiness prance through her subconscious. Too many things had to go right before she and Christopher could do more than trade jabs, steal glances and get their kicks. Biting back a smile, she surveyed the formal place settings. *No wonder Mama prepped two chickens.*

Uncle Brent, Aunt Mary and Charles arrived first. Her cousin, the youngest of three boys, would graduate from high school in a month. She hated how the tornado had destroyed his senior year's pomp and circumstance. After everything his class had weathered, she accepted his sullen expression and the petulant way he kicked an errant weed in the driveway. *I'd feel pissed off, too.*

Leading the charge into the house, Aunt Mary breezed through the front door carrying peach cobbler and a gallon of home-style vanilla ice cream. She handed off the items and waltzed into the kitchen. "Nancy! It smells like heaven in here."

Juggling the dessert course, Taylor leaned toward her uncle for a kiss and smiled at Charles. "How you doing?"

"Sucks," he said.

"Charles, watch your mouth. There are ladies present."

Uncle Brent's half-hearted reprimand made her smile. Like everything else pertaining to his third kid, he loved his son, but his corrections lacked force and righteousness. *Give him grace and take on as many of his burdens as you can handle.* She shifted the dessert to her left arm and swung an arm around Charles' shoulders. "You get a summer job?"

Looking away, Charles nodded. "Don't tell my dad, but I'm caddying up near Atlanta."

She frowned. "Your mom knows?"

"Of course."

"What did your dad want you to do?"

"Stick around Ronan and help rebuild the church."

She sighed and dropped her arm. "I can see why you chose golf."

"Peaches, bring that ice cream to your mother before it melts," Uncle Brent said.

Smiling, she carried the cobbler into the kitchen, set it near the refrigerator and put the ice cream in the freezer

"I heard he's rich," Aunt Mary said.

Nancy cleared her throat.

"What?" Reaching for a wineglass, Aunt Mary uncorked the bottle and filled her glass. "I liked Josh, but if you're gonna make a trade, good choice, girl. Trade up!"

"We're friends." Taylor's insistence fell flat.

Her mother and her aunt smiled.

"Of course you are," Aunt Mary said. "Friends who could share a mansion in Buckhead, pop out cute little Durand babies and invite your ole Aunt Mary to stay at the beach house."

She frowned. "I don't think he has a beach house as much as a camp."

Aunt Mary sipped her wine. "Oh, Peaches, don't mind me." She winked. "I'm flexible."

Clearing her throat, Nancy slid a bunch of asparagus toward her sister-in-law. "Nancy, do me a favor and snap off the ends. Peaches and Christopher are friends, and no one said anything about her leaving Ronan."

She met her mother's gaze.

"Yet," Nancy said.

Drawing a breath, Taylor filled a glass with ice and let the freezer door's thud cap the conversation.

Beep! Bbbeeeppp!

Taylor peeked out of the kitchen window. Ms. Tina's old sedan barreled down the driveway. The woman drove like a speed-happy drunkard, but she gripped the wheel at ten and two. "I'm surprised Christopher let her drive."

Aunt Mary laughed. "Like the man had a choice."

Jack waited by the front door. When the bell rang, he opened the door and shook his head. "Damn. Ms. Tina, you look like you glued a dead bird to your head."

Brushing past her host, Ms. Tina handed him a bottle of wine and waved off his comment. "Jack, you wouldn't know a pheasant if it landed on your windshield." Approaching Nancy, she raised her cheek for a kiss. "I don't know why you married that man. His biscuit's not done in the middle, if you know what I mean."

Laughing, Nancy led her to the kitchen. "He is who he is, God love him."

Left among the men, Taylor waited for Christopher to enter. When he stepped past the threshold and removed his hat, her heart skipped a beat. His gaze met hers, and she took pleasure in the small smile gracing his lips.

Nancy walked back into the room and dried her hands on a dish towel.

He turned to her. "Mrs. Lenore, thank you for having me."

"I'm so glad you came."

Extending his hand, he shook Jack's hand and handed him a bottle of whiskey. "I don't know what you like to drink, but this one's a favorite of mine."

Taylor wondered if he'd gone to the liquor store or sent Dillan. Either way, he'd made the effort, and she loved him for the small act. *Play it cool.* She cleared her throat. "Can I get anyone a drink?"

Uncle Brent raised his finger. "Bring me a beer, Peaches, if you don't mind."

Her father and Christopher nodded.

Charles crossed his arms.

"Chuckie?"

"Come on, Peaches. You know he won't let me drink," Charles said.

Uncle Brent turned to her father. "If it's all right with you?"

"Your kid," Jack said.

Charles grinned. "Come on, Peaches..."

He stretched the vowels like a screech owl.

"...I'll help you make drinks."

Rubbing her ear, she left Christopher with her father. Uncle Brent and Aunt Mary chatted with her mother. The butler's pantry bridged the dining room and the kitchen. Although it would never house a butler, it offered enough space to uncap beers, store beverage napkins and power an ice machine. Finding a neat stack of napkins on the bar, she rolled her eyes. *Mama thinks of everything. How many times did she forget to set out napkins before the nicety made her checklist?*

"So, you fucking him?" Charles asked.

She kept her eyes on her task. "So, you smoking weed every chance you get?"

Charles laughed. "You know, you shoulda been a boy."

She pulled three beers from the beverage fridge. "Why's that?"

"We woulda gotten along better."

"We get along just fine." She leaned a hip against the counter and smiled.

"But we're the last ones standing." He glanced toward the living room. "And when we're old, we'll be the ones cleaning up their shit."

Hearing the dejection and disappointment in his tone, she set down the cool bottles and pulled down three pint glasses. "What's bugging you, Charles?"

"Life."

She nodded, uncapped the beers and filled the glasses. "Anything in particular?"

He tugged his earlobe. "I thought all I had to do was graduate high school, take out a loan for college, get an MBA and work my way into a fat corporate position." Reaching for a beer, he chugged it. "When's my life going to start?"

When you take responsibility for it. Picking up the other two bottles, she left Charles in the wet bar but looked over her shoulder before she crossed the doorway. "This is the hardest summer of your life. You know something's coming, but it's not here yet. Try to be patient. Learn to play golf." She smiled. "If you land that fat corporate position, you'll need to know the difference between a putter and a driver."

He laughed. "Do you know the difference?"

She glanced at Christopher and found him deep in conversation with Uncle Brent and her father. "No, but I'm willing to learn." Carrying the beers and napkins toward the men, she met each one's grateful smile and dispensed the glasses.

Christopher's hand brushed hers. "Thanks." He took the last beer, reached around her back and anchored her to his side.

She tried not to breathe and upset the unexpected position. *I thought we were playing it cool.* Feeling his fingers brush her hip, she released a grin. *Apparently not.*

"How many dealerships in your network?" Jack asked.

"We have a shade over sixty primary locations. The dealers span twenty-five states and run coast-to-coast," Christopher said. "Ocelot is a part of the country's infrastructure. If you need equipment, we'll get it to you."

Uncle Brent nodded and sipped his beer. "Your granddaddy started the business."

Christopher nodded.

She wanted to beam with pride, but she had no role in his success.

"Where'd you go to college?" Uncle Brent asked.

She stilled. Remembering how Christopher had skipped college in favor of Iraq, she expected him to diffuse the question or parlay it into a discussion of his military service.

"I earned an online degree through a university in North Carolina. The executive MBA caters to goal-oriented, seasoned professionals, but it works for jaded veterans, too."

Jack and Uncle Brent laughed.

Beyond his confidence and capability, his self-effacing honesty shone as his most desirable asset. He pulled double shifts to cover his responsibilities to Ocelot and his interest in Ronan, but given a choice, she would claim his time and trust God to find his rest.

Charles walked out of the wet bar holding a beer bottle.

How many empty bottles will I find in the recycling bin? Slipping from Christopher's grasp, she nodded to her cousin and decided to pull him into the conversation.

Mr. Nelson and Plucky had committed fraud, but she'd refused to mete out punishment. Her cousin was blood, and the sooner the family supported his efforts, the sooner he would find peace among his kin. "Charles is caddying this summer near Atlanta."

Uncle Brent choked on his beer. "Since when?"

"Since I needed something more to do than push a broom," Charles said.

Eyeing his son's beer, Uncle Brent shook his head. "You've grown up too fast."

"Have I?" Charles tipped back his beer.

Christopher turned to the teenager. "Which course?"

She left the men in the living room, walked into the kitchen and found her mother and Aunt Mary side by side over a tablet.

"Nancy, the man's company makes forty billion dollars a year." Aunt Mary tapped the screen. "B for billion."

Taylor cleared her throat.

Her mother locked up. "Peaches, I was wrong. You're in over your head."

She exhaled. "But I like him."

Aunt Mary rolled her eyes and looked at Nancy. "She's your daughter, all right. Once she sets her mind on something, nothing come hell or high water will turn her back."

"What does that mean?"

Sipping her wine, Aunt Nancy grinned. "Hardheaded and beautiful."

Nancy rolled her eyes. "Peaches, just because a man shows interest doesn't mean he's planning to get down on one knee."

Taylor raised her chin.

"And he doesn't strike me as a God-fearing man." The oven timer beeped. Straightening, Nancy turned toward the appliance.

Aunt Mary nodded.

Seeing her two role models shoulder to shoulder, Taylor poured herself a generous glass of wine. "He's a regular member of the congregation at the Cathedral of St. Philip." She sipped her wine while the women she respected exchanged wordless expressions. *Whether he pays attention is another manner.*

Nancy tilted her head. "But is he a believer?"

Weighing the consequences of her response, she chose honesty. "No, he's not."

Both women frowned.

Their nearly identical, disapproving expressions reminded Taylor what Ronan expected of her. She cared about their souls and the souls of others, but she didn't need a pulpit and a weekly sermon to know the power of living according to God's word. If Christopher wanted to spend time with her, he would spend time with *all* of her. In between tangled limbs and lazy afternoons, her passive evangelism would highlight the door to salvation. Whether he stepped through that door was entirely up to him, but she refused to reject him before he sinned.

"Well, I'll be," Aunt Mary said. "Dinner's ready."

Seated at the table across from Christopher, Taylor settled her napkin in her lap, located his long legs, and settled her feet against his ankle. The skin-to-skin contact soothed her, and she hoped it soothed him. At the head of the table, her father presided over the salad bowl. At the foot of the table, her mother claimed the bread. *Who will say the blessing?*

Accepting her husband's subtle nod, Nancy thanked God for their bounty, the gift of Ocelot's assistance and the pleasure of a shared meal. "Amen."

"Jeb said you've been by the post office a few times," Aunt Mary said.

Nodding, Taylor lifted her fork to her mouth and took a bite.

Aunt Mary cocked her head. "Dr. Greene heard you and Plucky get into it."

She swallowed and smiled. "You know us girls."

Charles snorted.

"What's all the drama?" Aunt Mary asked.

I can't expose Plucky's mistake or Mr. Nelson's fraud. Scanning the table, she settled on Christopher's minor infraction. "City boy stepped on a nail and punctured his foot. I drove him over to the clinic for a tetanus shot."

Christopher shrugged and lifted his beer. "True."

Aunt Mary sipped her wine. "Hmm." Turning her fork from edge to edge, she picked up the utensil and set it back down. "Why were there so many outgoing boxes in the post office lobby? I'd recognize Plucky's handwriting slant any day of the week. Girl never learned to hold a pencil correctly."

"Mom, this chicken is delicious." She took another bite.

"Why, thank you. I grew the thyme…"

Slapping the table, Aunt Mary dropped her chin and pointed. "Taylor Lenore, you're hiding something, and nothing stays secret in this town."

She stared down her aunt, but her heart jumped in her chest, and she struggled to swallow the chicken. Feeling light on oxygen, she rubbed her throat and looked to her mother for help.

"Don't you pull that choking routine with me!" Aunt Mary said.

Nancy tilted her head. "Peaches, are you okay?"

Christopher stood and rounded the table.

Slapping her chest, she forced the chicken back into her mouth and spit it into her napkin. "Jeb's retiring and moving away!" Squeezing shut her eyes, she felt Christopher's hand on her shoulder and waited for her family's reaction.

Ms. Tina snorted.

Aunt Mary laughed. "Is that all? Peaches, everyone in town knows that man's gay, and he's been itching to leave Ronan since he reached the age of majority. We've known he fancied men since he spent recess complimenting the teachers' shoes. What he does with that information is his business." She sighed and took a bite. "I thought you had real gossip."

She pried open one eye and stared at her aunt. "Everyone knows?"

Nodding, Aunt Mary sipped her wine. "Apparently, everyone but you."

"I thought this town couldn't keep a secret."

"It can't," Nancy said, "but some things aren't worth mentioning in polite company. Let the man mind his business.

"You don't care." She frowned. "Next you'll tell me that Jeannie Mae's cheating on Johnnie."

Nancy looked at her husband.

"Oh, come on!" Taylor said.

Jack shrugged. "I don't care who licks whose bits. I just don't want to hear about it."

"Jack Lenore!" Nancy covered her eyes.

Charles laughed and finished his drink.

Eyeing her son, Aunt Martha speared another bite. "But what's with all the boxes?"

Taylor swallowed. "Something to do with Plucky's foundation." She felt Christopher's squeeze, looked up and smiled. "I'm okay, thanks."

Frowning, Jack tracked Christopher reclaiming his seat.

"So, what do you think of Ronan?" Ms. Tina asked.

Christopher set his napkin in his lap. "I think the town has a lot of features. It's close enough to the airport to ship freight, the community members work hard and before the storm, the officials and I had discussed a manufacturing facility." He scanned the table. "We still have issues to discuss."

"Oh, brother." Standing, Charles walked toward the butler's pantry. "I've heard that line."

"I'm glad you're here," Ms. Tina said. "We don't need another poultry processing plant." She shook her head. "Nine dollars an hour. Hell. I couldn't pay a maid that much."

Jack lifted his fork. "Too bad you don't make mail trucks for Jeb. The Postal Service awarded a ten-year contract to manufacture a new generation of US-built vehicles. Ronan needs that kind of long-term investment."

Taylor opened her mouth to defend Ocelot.

"I don't make ten-year commitments," Christopher said. "I make lifelong commitments. Ocelot has never closed a facility. Once we're part of a community, we stay and support growth. That contract with the postal service is shortsighted. The manufacturer will produce fuel-efficient internal combustion engines or battery electric powertrains, but in ten years, electric vehicle technologies will make the *new* trucks look like dinosaurs. For less than $10 billion, the US Postal Service could convert its delivery vehicles to an all-electric fleet." He picked up his fork. "How many times do you want to spend that much money?"

Jack bristled. "Ronan doesn't do billions."

"No, but the federal government does," Christopher said.

She considered looked at the two men she loved and realized that for their future to work, they would have to learn to sort out their grievances. Like Charles, they might as well start now.

"I doubt all the carrier parts will come from the US," Uncle Brent said. "Chinese companies will stamp out components, and the contract winner will assemble the vehicles on our shores." He sighed. "We'll still lose jobs. The US shouldn't have normalized trade relations with China. We let them ramp up production of export goods, when we should have locked them out of American markets." He adjusted his seat. "Am I right?"

Looking up at the ceiling, she swallowed and abandoned her hope of getting through the meal without drama. "Is there a middle ground?"

Uncle Brent laughed. "China's stealing our technologies. Robotics, electric vehicles, biotech" — he waved a hand in the air — "they're making everything we need through a program called Made in China 2025. It's a unitary, state-controlled economy. Soon we'll have to ask permission to use our own stuff."

Heat flooded her cheeks, and she vowed never to wave her hand in the air again. Fearing Christopher would take the bait and mark this supper as his last meal with her family, she smiled and cleared her throat. "Uncle Brent, where do you find time to read so much?"

"The Internet!"

Aunt Mary laughed. "Don't get me started."

"Tell me about your Sunday sermon." She sipped her wine. Nancy told her never to talk about religion and politics, but religion might save this family meal.

Uncle Brent pointed at her. "Don't change the topic, young lady. I want to hear what your friend has to say about international competition."

"Brent, put down your hand," Nancy said.

"Don't protect her." Uncle Brent turned to his wife. "She's an adult."

Jack stood. "She's also my daughter."

Looking across the table, Taylor met Christopher's amused gaze and swallowed. She saw spots and knew she had sweat through her shirt, but he looked as cool as a cucumber. *Maybe all his family dinners work like this? People give and they get, but at the end of the day, they love each other.*

Stumbling into the room carrying the peach cobbler, Charles lifted a spoon to his lips, took a bite and heaved his stomach's contents of all over Ms. Tina.

"Oh, hell," Uncle Brent said. "Mary, take care of your son!"

Wiping the vomit from her eyes, Ms. Tina exhaled and stood. "Well, I never!"

Her remaining family members sprang from their chairs. Chaos erupted around the dining room table. Covering her face with her hands, she inhaled, dragged her palms down her cheeks and met Christopher's gaze. "I'm sorry."

He grinned, crossed his arms and sat back in his chair.

Ms. Tina flung her hands to her side, and vomit flew on the carpet. "I knew I shoulda stayed in Washington!"

Closing her eyes, she nodded. *Christopher probably thinks I have porcelain dolls and livestock trophies in my bedroom.* Remembering Ms. Tina's stolen treasures, she surrendered her claim on her childhood. *Ms. Tina can keep Fuzzball. She earned him.* Opening her eyes, she met the woman's spittle-soaked gaze and cleared her throat. "Please, take me with you."

Christopher threw back his head and laughed.

Chapter Sixteen

Christopher surveyed the dining room and debated how the evening would end. Ms. Tina looked like she might strip, and Brent looked like he might spit. *I'm not sure which outcome would be worse.* He hoped Ms. Tina could drive herself home, but he owed the older woman a debt for her kindness. *All I wanted was a slice of cobbler and a chance to win over Jack Lenore.* Standing, he placed his napkin on the table. "I'm sorry, Ms. Tina. I shouldn't have laughed, but I know how much Taylor loves Ronan."

Ms. Tina wrinkled her nose. "Not as much as I love a hot shower and a good smoke." Shaking her head, she walked toward the front door. "You don't see me laughing."

"Please, wait!" Nancy hurried to her side. "Let me give you fresh clothes."

Pausing, Ms. Tina looked over her shoulder. "What am I going to wear, Nancy? Your bathrobe?"

Nancy covered her mouth and dropped her hand to reveal a grin. "It's chenille."

The older woman's expression wavered. Seeing his opening, Christopher walked to her side. "Why don't you give me the car keys? I'll turn on the air while you get changed."

Ms. Tina scanned the room.

Mary cupped her arm around Charles' dry-heaving shoulders, Jack restrained his brother and Taylor skidded into the room carrying a mop.

"Absolutely not. You help with the cleanup," Ms. Tina said.

"Are you sure?" He lowered his voice. "I have all the time in the world."

She shook her head. "That's what you think, but time doesn't keep." Pausing on the threshold, she watched Taylor wring out the mop. "Get what you need before it slips from your hands."

"Ms. Tina…" Jack said.

Holding up a hand, she strode past her host and his brother. "Save it." She nodded to Nancy. "Thanks for the food. I always said you were the best cook in Ronan."

Nancy inclined her head.

Turning, he walked to Taylor's side and laid his hand on her back. "What can I do to help?"

"I've got it." She rubbed her neck and kept her gaze on the mess.

He wanted to be the person rubbing stress from her shoulders. "But I want to help."

She exhaled and used the mop to corral the mess. Meeting his gaze, she jerked her head toward the table. "Collect the silver and set it in the kitchen sink." A small smile softened her embarrassment. "I don't think anyone will finish their dinner."

"I dunno, Mom." Charles gripped his stomach. "Must be a stomach bug."

Brent jerked free of his brother's grip. "Don't give me that crap."

Jack grabbed his brother's arm and pulled him toward the front door. "Let the women handle it."

"Why? You see how she has handled it so far? He's a mess!"

"And where were you the last eighteen years?" Jack asked.

"What is *that* supposed to mean?" Brent jerked free of his brother's grip.

Picking up the place settings, Christopher carried the knives and forks into the kitchen. Nancy's countertops looked as tidy as a cooking show. He thought about his attempts at cooking and wondered how many meals a person needed to cook until scraps and dirtied pots made way for organized efficiency. *Hell, maybe Greta deserved more than a pension for putting up with me and William.*

Taylor carried the mop and bucket into the kitchen, opened a door to a laundry room, and dumped dirty water down the utility sink. She wiped her brow. "Not exactly how I wanted the evening to end."

He set the silver in the sink and leaned against the counter. "What was your plan?"

Washing her hands, she turned and grinned. "Whiskey?"

Letting a laugh escape, he rubbed his lip. *She's flushed and embarrassed, but she's never looked sweeter.* "Whiskey?"

"I figured you, Daddy and Uncle Brent could retire to the porch and sip a whiskey. The sunset's pretty this time of year. Maybe Charles would choke down a glass, and you guys could tease him about his tolerance."

"I think his tolerance might be higher than yours." Watching her blush, he walked across the room and stroked her cheek. "Everything's fine, Taylor. Accidents happen."

She looked up. "Tell me the last time someone threw up on your houseguest?"

Cupping her soft cheek, he dropped his hand. "I don't have houseguests."

"What?"

She looked at him as if he'd failed US history. Running his hand through his hair, he stepped back and leaned against the kitchen counter. "Greta's not the type to plan menus and harass florists."

"Neither am I."

"My mom did, but that style of entertaining went out of fashion. When business guests come into town, I take them out to eat. Social media has opened up everyone's lives, but I barred the door. I don't want pictures of my flatware on *The Constitution*'s style page. I don't want people judging the intimate choices I make in my home."

Settling in the space beside him, she plugged the sink and ran hot water. "How can you run for office and expect that level of privacy?"

Soaking up the mix of jasmine and sweat rising from her skin, he watched her plunge her hands into the water and fish out a fork. Her thigh brushed against his. His pulse skyrocketed, but he doubted she noted the contact. *She's effortless, but I only want more — more of her optimism and selflessness, more of her belief in goodness and her ability to fight for causes and make me laugh.* He shifted his weight. "My grandfather maintained his privacy. He kept his home in Buckhead, but he took up residency at the governor's mansion. The residence is a pile of 1960s Greek Revival bricks. Every dinner looks the same. The house belongs to the state, not to the man."

"Or woman."

He inclined his head.

Exhaling, she set the fork on a dishtowel. "That house isn't me, either."

"It could be." Choosing between subtle and honesty, he peeled back the years of competitiveness guarding his heart. "Who do you want to be?" *Do you want me?* His unspoken question lingered on his lips. The minute he'd arrived in Ronan, she pushed him away, but chance had drawn them together. Given his choice, he would take a lifetime of dishes and brushed thighs to hold her close.

"I don't know what I want." She braced her hands on the edge of the counter. "I thought I did. I thought I knew where I belonged."

"My grandfather said, '*A man should be loyal to his God, his family, his country and his political party*'."

She smiled. "Well, you have room."

He tugged her away from the sink and settled her between his legs. "I have room for you." Pressing his lips against her sweet mouth, he let his kiss counter her arguments. Then he pulled back. "Give me a chance, Taylor. Let's make this thing between us" — he smiled — "whatever it is, work."

She smiled. "Maybe."

Cocking his head, he recognized the teasing glint in her eyes and anticipated the catch. "Maybe?"

She stroked his cheek. "When I saw you in the bookstore, I thought you looked like a nomadic cowboy. Your skin was so tanned that I wondered if the sun had hardened it into armor."

It did. A thousand sun-baked days kept me from my obligations. "Now?"

"Now, I know you're a softie, but damn, you're good-looking."

Laughing, he turned her and swatted her ass. "Brat."

She slipped out of his reach and scraped her teeth across her lip. "Sometimes."

If he believed in a God, he would give thanks for the woman dancing across the dull linoleum. Her hips swayed as she walked into the dining room, and for the first time in a long time, he felt like something belonged to him. Though he would never possess and tame her, he intended to cherish her with all his heart.

Nancy watched her grinning daughter pass and zeroed in on his face. "You don't deter easily?"

He shook his head. "No, ma'am."

She nodded and placed a stack of dishes near the sink.

Moving to give her room, he cleared his throat. "Can I help you wash up?"

"How many dishes have you washed, Mr. Durand?"

"Enough to know the process."

She smiled. "I don't mind getting my hands dirty, but I'd be happy knowing Taylor didn't have to."

He nodded. He would take honesty any day of the week.

"Go help her clear the table. When she shoos off your efforts, find Jack on the front porch. You might as well get to know him."

Smiling, he moved toward the dining room and paused. "Mrs. Lenore."

"Call me 'Nancy'."

"Nancy." He swallowed. "I'm not sure how this thing between Taylor and I will work out."

She narrowed her gaze.

"She might split her time between Ronan and Atlanta." He hoped the amendment clarified his position. Geography couldn't confine his feelings for Taylor, but her mother's love might clip its wings before it took flight.

Shaking her head, she turned her back on him and reached for a scrub brush. "If that's that hardest problem you two face, God blessed you."

That easy?

"But Taylor won't give up easily." She shut off the water. "She loves this town, and Ronan's citizens love her."

"I hear you."

She nodded. "Smart man."

He strode to Taylor's side like a gladiator claiming his prize. "Your mama likes me." Taylor looked skeptical, but he reached for the breadbasket and the butter dish.

She brushed away his hand. "She's being polite."

"Polite?"

"Mama once told me my butt looked like two dead rabbits in a paper bag."

Laughing, he felt the butter dish slip from his fingers, but he tightened his grip. "What were you wearing?"

"Tight black pants and a crop top."

The thought of her dancing on the football field stole his focus, and the butter dish clattered to the table.

Fractured pink and white porcelain unfolded across the lace tablecloth like fallen petals. "I'm sorry." He reached for a shard. "I'll buy her another one."

She darted toward the shattered dish and blocked his attempt. "Careful... You'll cut yourself!"

Her sweet, protective gesture warmed his heart, but he wondered who would protect her. Gripping her arm, he pulled her to standing and looped his left arm around her waist. When she tried to pull free, he tightened his hold. "You don't think much of me, do you?"

"No, I just..."

"You mocked my truck, my footwear and my ability to clean up messes."

"Christopher, you're a guest."

He held onto her and stacked the shards in a neat pile. "I don't want to be a guest. I want to be family."

She bit her lip.

"We're going to make this work." He cupped her cheek. "If a tornado can't come between us, nothing can."

"I didn't like you." She hiccupped. "I mean, before the storm."

"Not even a little?"

A second hiccup escaped. "You seemed so cocky and sure of yourself. My whole life, I've been a pleaser, but you looked like you could take on the world. How did you end up in Ronan?"

He pressed a kiss against her forehead, dropped his hand from her waist and scooped up the shards. The shattered porcelain weighed little, but he gripped it lightly and held the threat away from her body. "You lured me here."

She put her hands on her hips. "I did not."

Another hiccup. Smiling, he turned toward the kitchen. "I'm Atlanta's hottest bachelor."

"Oh, brother. I told Plucky you had attitude."

He paused and looked over his shoulder. "So, you talked about me?"

"Maybe."

Her smile looked as pleased as a cat. "What else did you say?"

She hiccupped. "I told her I'd do you."

"Honesty...at last!"

She rolled her eyes. "Asshole."

He hoped Nancy's dishes blocked her from overhearing Taylor's foul mouth. *I have plans for that mouth.* Looking for a trash can, he scanned the cabinets for a pullout handle.

Cupping his hand, Taylor uncurled his fingers and lifted the shards from his palm. "Don't throw away the dish because of a few cracks. Mama loves that discontinued pattern" — she smiled and set the remnants on the counter — "and Daddy has enough fast-acting adhesives to repair a house."

He nodded and followed her into the kitchen.

Glancing at the butter dish, Nancy paused, but she resumed washing salad plates.

He ran his hand through his hair. "I'm sorry, Ms. Lenore."

Nancy shook her head. "Don't worry about it."

She's being polite. Taylor's observation pushed him toward a livelier apology, but he accepted the house rules. *Manners smooth over life's rough spots. If Taylor wants to glue together the pieces, I'll apologize for my clumsiness with flowers and a case of wine.*

Linking hands, Taylor pulled him toward the back door. "Let's go find that glue."

He followed her into the humid backyard and submitted to the steady chirps of night bugs and the soft calls of frogs. Beyond the house light, a gooseneck fixture illuminated the chicken coop. Subdued coop chatter made him think of Greta's Sea Islands home. *I hope she and Taylor get along.* He imagined Taylor playing on the old, metal swing set in her yard and wondered if she wanted kids. *One thing at a time.* The breeze shifted, and spring's decay reminded him of summer's marathon. *We don't survive the heat, we endure it.* Intending to savor Taylor's heat, he pulled her close.

She chewed her bottom lip and avoided his gaze.

"What now?" he asked.

"You almost fit in."

"Almost?"

Looking up, she smiled. "You'd almost fit in anywhere, wouldn't you? That's part of your charm."

He traced his thumb across her lip and dropped his gaze to her mouth. "I don't want to be anywhere else."

Capturing his hand, she kissed his thumb and drew it into her mouth.

The quick scape of teeth sent him into overdrive, and he pulled her flush against his erection. "Good?"

Releasing him, she laughed. "Like butter."

Shaking his head, he held her against his chest and teased apart her lips for a real kiss. She yielded and tipped it back, clutching his arm as she leaned into his support. He followed her submission, chasing her pleasure and her throaty moans until his breath came in deep pants. His desire to touch her, kiss her and show her how he felt threatened to override his logic. Tearing free his lips, he stared.

"Now who's quiet?" Her words came in short bursts.

"Give me a quiet spot, and I'll give you a reason to yell."

She wiggled out of his grasp and walked toward the garden gate. Looking over her shoulder, she scanned him from head to foot. "I'll hold you to that promise."

He adjusted his pants. "Tease."

She blew him a kiss.

Working from home isn't an option. I'll never get anything done while she's around. Lengthening his stride, he caught up and swung his arm around her shoulder. "When the dust settles, I can't wait to take you out on the town and take you home to bed."

"In Buckhead?"

He nodded and scanned the yard. *Wherever home might be.* Rounding the corner of the house, he followed her toward the front porch's steady light and fluttering moths. Lost in his plans for the next weeks and the logistics of commuting, he kept his head down and let her lead.

"That's not how it works," Jack said.

"I underinsured the church." Brent sighed. "I can't afford to rebuild what we lost."

Taylor stiffened.

How much is this going to cost me? Suppressing a smile, he tried to care about the money, but he would surrender every penny in his bank account to keep her at his side.

"You don't have to do anything," Brent said. "I talked to a guy out of Mobile who'll prepare the damage estimates and qualify the church for federal public assistance grants. He'll inflate the repair estimates and get FEMA to pay out enough money to rebuild the whole structure. That tornado might be the best thing that ever happened to this town."

Taylor slapped her hand over her mouth and crouched.

Lowing himself to the ground, he felt the tension in his lower back. Despite the tightness, he stayed by her side.

She gripped his thigh.

Her grip's tension grounded him more surely than the overheard conversation.

"Take up a collection," Jack said.

Taylor nodded.

At least her immediate family's honest.

A rocking chair creaked on the worn boards.

"It won't be enough," Brent said. "The guy from Mobile said religious institutions have special protections. If he can show the repair costs exceed more than fifty percent of the cost of a new building, FEMA will pay for a full replacement."

"The walls are still standing," Jack said. "How're you going to get to that level of damage?"

"Water damage and foundation repairs. Vague photographs, inflated square footage estimates and upgraded cost estimates for the items we lost."

Christopher rubbed his jaw.

Jack whistled. "That's a hell of a risk. Just build back what you can afford."

"You weren't there, brother. I rode out that damn storm in the back office. As the wind tore at the walls, I huddled inside the room with my books and robes, and I felt God testing me."

The rocking stopped, and heavy footfalls traversed the porch.

"I'm still here. I have to rebuild. The church must go on."

"I won't be a part of it," Jack said.

"Just keep your mouth shut. If anyone asks, you never had time to visit the destruction."

The footsteps descended the steps and paused.

"I'm only telling you so you can steer clear of the assessment," Brent said. "Leave the rest to me. Everybody else has."

Taylor shook her head and looked at him. "For a rich-enough prize, even true men will turn thief."

Her whispered proclamation broke his heart, but he followed her lead.

"I won't let him do this. He'll regret it for the rest of his life." She stood.

He reached for her forearm. "Taylor, I know he's your uncle, but you don't want to get involved in this mess. He's past desperate."

She pulled her hand free. "He's still family."

He exhaled.

Rounding the corner, she stepped into the light. "Uncle Brent."

"Shit, Taylor. How long you been there?"

Coming up beside her, Christopher crossed his arms and watched Brent's face pale. "Long enough."

Shaking his head, Jack walked down the steps.

His footfalls sounded heavy and resigned. For the first time, Christopher caught the resemblance between the men. The older brother had inherited the farm, Brent had gone to seminary and Jack had made his way in the world. *People don't have to be slaves to age-old trades, but more often than not, they follow the tracks their ancestors laid down.*

Jack edged closer to his daughter and gripped her arm. "Brent's feeling desperate. Given a good night's sleep, things will look different in the morning."

Taylor raised her chin. "Will they, Uncle Brent?"

Brent narrowed his gaze and crossed his arms. "No, Taylor, they won't. And you'll stay out of my business." His fingers curled against his forearm.

Prepared to protect Taylor, Christopher shifted to her side.

Flanked by men who loved her, she stepped forward. "You can preach from the field as beautifully as you preach from the altar. You have options."

"You've always stuck your head where it don't belong. Go back to the kitchen and help your mama."

She rubbed her neck. "Mama doesn't need my help, but you do. If I'm hearing you correctly, you're talking about defrauding the government. What's Charles going to do while you're in jail?"

"Taylor..." Jack said.

She looked at her father and raised her eyebrows.

Shaking his head, Brent shook his head and faced his brother. "You never could keep ahold of her, Jack. You spent too much time indulging her tomboy whims and pretending she was a son."

Jack frowned. "She's my child."

Brent spat. "The two of you are a pair."

"Three," Christopher said.

Brent narrowed his gaze. "Don't you have better things to do?"

Well, getting Taylor the hell out of Ronan holds a lot of appeal. He scratched his chin. "Oh, I'm here for the money. The False Claims Act allows private citizens who know of individuals defrauding the federal government to file lawsuits and recover funds on the government's behalf. Whistleblowers are entitled to fifteen to twenty-five percent of the recovery. How much are we talking?"

Brent sneered. "You're not going to drag your name through the courts for a hundred thousand dollars."

"I'm guessing your friend from Mobile cast a wide net." He smiled. "And don't worry about my reputation. I'll file the lawsuit under seal. I'll ruin you to protect Taylor."

Brent lunged and grabbed his throat.

He gripped the man's forearms and squeezed with his considerable strength.

"Don't hurt him!"

Taylor's cry sent his self-preservation into overdrive. Seeing Jack pull her away from the tussle, he focused on Brent and shifted his grip. Finding the man's pressure point, he squeezed until Brent yelped and loosened it. Leveraging the slack, he pulled Brent closer, upset his balance and swept his legs from under him.

Brent landed on his back, sputtering and slapping his chest.

Unwilling to give him time to regain his balance, he dropped his knee to Brent's chest and held him to the hard-packed earth. "Don't talk to her again." He dropped his voice. "If you threaten her, my lawyers will be the least of your concerns."

Brent choked and nodded.

Releasing his hold, he stepped back and turned to Taylor and her father.

Jack released her.

Facing the trio of men, she rubbed her arm, turned and ran into the night.

"Shit," he said.

Brent coughed.

He ignored the man and looked at Jack. "Where's she headed?"

"Higgins' fields." Jack rubbed his jaw. "She'll be safe there. I'll get the truck."

Shaking his head, he eyed Brent and brushed the dirt from his knee. Remembering the desperate look in Taylor's gaze, he piled on Nelson's double-dipping, Plucky's fraud and Brent's inflation schemes. Every betrayal chipped away at her vision of Ronan, and she clung to the old town's romance like a proxy for her life. *Why can't she see the future coming over the horizon?* If Ronan fell, she would fall with it. He understood why she fled, but she had options. "No need. I'll go after her."

"How're you going to find her?" Jack asked. "It's pitch dark in those fields."

He pulled out his cell phone. "When she's ready to talk, she'll answer." Turning his back on the men, he walked toward the fields and gripped the phone. *Please, let her answer.*

Chapter Seventeen

Taylor followed a path through Mr. Higgins' cotton fields. She had spent the first two decades of her life watching him load boxes of seed into planters and keep the tractors moving. *I'll spend the last decades of my life doing the same thing.* Domed dirt beds kept the leaves dry, but this early in the season, the young plants looked so helpless that she blamed her swollen eyes on their flat-leafed vulnerability. *You're going to make it.* Tears dripped down her cheeks, and she wandered through the backcountry fields. Christopher offered sunflowers and organic gardening mix, but she needed heat, light and freedom to move. *As soon as he returns to Atlanta, I'll have everything I need except the town I loved. Did it ever exist?*

In the middle of the field, a gnarled oak tree cast shadows over the rows. The tree had presided over generations of crops, and barring Mother Nature, it would preside over generations to come. She dug her fingers into familiar grips and scrambled to the first large branch. Resting her back against the rough bark, she exhaled and replayed Uncle Brent's confessions.

No matter how she diced his plan, his actions were morally wrong, technically illegal and downright pitiful. *I'll never be able to look him in the eyes again.* Squeezing shut her eyes, she wondered if she should report him. *Isn't FEMA dismissing his claim better than lawsuits and jail time?* She kept her knowledge of Mr. Nelson and Plucky to herself, but how long could she look the other way and pray for interventions?

Above the cotton fields, she put herself in Uncle Brent's shoes. *He has three kids and a congregation that relies on him.* Hating her sympathy for the man, she imagined her mother overhearing the conversation. *Nancy'd grab him by the ear and march him into town. No, that's not right. She'd lecture him with Ezekiel and pray for his soul.*

Her phone buzzed with a message from Christopher.

Where are you?

I'm fine. I'll see you tomorrow.

That's not the way this works.

She frowned.

You have masculinity issues and a hero complex.

You like me.

Her fingers hovered over the screen.

I do.

Inhaling the humid night air, she let her feelings for him wash over her like a cooling shower. She never thought she needed a hero, but when he came riding into town with a fleet of dozers, her heart hesitated, and she gave him the chance he deserved. *I won't throw Ronan Reads under the bus, but the town didn't win that bet. I did.*

Head toward the old oak tree in the middle of the cotton field.

Can I miss it?

She smiled and thought, *only if your time in the city has short-circuited your brain.*

No. Come find me.

She wrote, 'I'm sorry I ran. I should have stayed to fight. I should have known better,' but she deleted the words and waited. Half the state considered 'white trash' a badge of honor, and the other half considered the term offensive. Where did her family fall? The question occupied her thoughts until she heard someone approach.

"Taylor?" Christopher asked.

Bracing her hands on the rough bark, she swung her legs over the side. "Hold on. I'm coming down."

"Don't bother," he said. "I'm coming up."

Waiting, she listened to the katydids and cicadas. Lightning bugs flashed near the field's perimeter.

"Taylor?"

She looked down and saw his shadowed form at the base of the tree.

"How the hell do I get up there?"

She bit back a laugh. "There's a scar about six feet off the ground. Use it as a handhold and hoist yourself up."

He groped the truck and swore. "Of all the women..."

"Do you want me to jump down?"

"No!" Cocking his head, he jumped and grabbed the branch where she sat. Walking his fingers along the bark, he hoisted himself, threw a leg over the limb and shimmied into position. "Nice view."

"You're not even out of breath."

"Are you offering to help?" he asked.

His banter amused her until the reason for her flight constricted her chest. Wrapping her arms around her legs, she rested her head on her knees. "I'm sorry."

He let his legs swing on either side of the branch. "For what?"

"For putting you in that position," she said. "For making you defend me."

Running his hand over his face, he sighed. "Taylor, I love you. I've loved you since the moment you tried to send me back to Atlanta with my tail between my legs."

She looked down. "You've spent too much time inhaling exhaust."

He scooted forward. "No, I know exactly what I'm saying. I know you love me, too. How many times have you made exceptions to your rules?"

Lifting her head, she looked at the stars. Hercules the Kneeling Giant presided over the northeastern sky. The ancient Greeks said the weary, star-studded hero took his knee beside the slain dragon or rested after battle. Either way, she sympathized with his disillusionment and refused to sentence Christopher to a hero's ending. She exhaled. "That's the problem, Christopher. There shouldn't be exceptions. Every time I make allowances, I make room for sin."

"You make room for humanity."

She exhaled and looked at him. "Is there a difference?"

Rising to his feet, he held his arms wide and walked the branch like an Olympic gymnast. Stepping around her, he set his back against the tree trunk, sank to his bottom and pulled her against his chest.

She relaxed into his warmth. *One last memory.* His chest rose and fell against her back, and she took comfort in the steady rhythm.

He stroked her arm and settled his hand across her sternum.

The heavy weight slowed her heartbeat. Exhaling, she closed her eyes and dropped her head against his shoulder. The oak's leaves blocked the starlight, but judgment waited outside the canopy, and she would protect the people she loved by continuing to love them, but also by turning them into the authorities. Psalms 26.2 seemed appropriate. *"Test me, Lord, and try me, examine my heart and my mind."*

Christopher drew a deep breath. "I won't question your religion, but I won't let it define our love."

She closed her eyes. "That's a relief. Otherwise, we were doomed from the start."

He laughed. "You love Ronan, but deep down, you think you owe the town a debt."

Shifting in his embrace, she looked at him. "My college professors warned me about men who tell me what I'm feeling." A mosquito buzzed her face, and she twitched her nose.

He raised his hand and crushed the bug in his fist.

Poor bug. Sequestered in the mighty oak, she sighed. *Poor me. I'll never forget this year.*

"You don't owe this town a debt. Communities raise children."

She nodded. "This community is worth rebuilding."

"I agree."

Tilting her head, she wondered what he'd looked like before William's death and the mantle of running Ocelot. *He wouldn't have been the fresh-faced college graduate manning the phones at party headquarters. He would have been the quiet observer in the back of the room. When he stood, the room's occupants would have noticed. That's where he belongs, and I belong here.* "I have to stay in Ronan. Uncle Brent will come to his senses. The rest of the problems you've seen" — she frowned — "people feel desperate after the storm. Maybe Ronan Reads was too big. Maybe I should work out of the schools."

He stroked her cheek. "Ronan Reads wasn't too big. Think bigger."

She looked away. "I reached too far."

He exhaled. "Taylor, don't let a few bad apples spoil your love for this town and your ambitions."

Shaking her head, she leaned away from his chest and created distance where she only wanted warmth. "That's not what the phrase means. One bad apple *can* spoil the barrel. I'm not blameless, but I'm trying. How can Ronan succeed if everyone who cares leaves town?" Swinging her legs over the side of the branch, she considered the ground and wondered if she could make the jump. Leaving Christopher would hurt, but Ronan felt too small for his ambitions, and she refused to be another burden. "I know you can't stay here, Christopher. Go."

"What does Ronan need?"

She frowned. "Jobs. Prosperity. Faith."

"The Ocelot plant will help."

She cupped his rough cheek. "You can't build a plant in every city that catches my eye."

"Ronan did more than catch your eye. It shaped you."

She exhaled. "Into a fraud?"

Turning, he pressed a kiss against her palm. "I see a woman who's beautiful, passionate and loyal."

She closed her eyes. "And naïve."

"No." He tipped up her chin.

She inhaled.

"Full of hope," he said. "Jobs and prosperity relieve stress, but you know what Ronan's citizens need. You pull together resources and find common threads. If anyone can find ways to eliminate blight and poverty, it's you. Come to Atlanta. Stand by my side. Hell, run with me."

She frowned. "Georgia elects its lieutenant governor on a separate ticket."

"So, we'll rewrite history and run together," he said. "One platform for two candidates. If anyone can improve the functionality of the state government and help bridge the rural divide, it's you."

"Maybe I should run for governor."

He laughed and tugged her into his arms. "Maybe you should."

She shook her head and inhaled his clear scent. Housing options, employment opportunities and neighborhood associations looked good in hundred-page reports, but rebuilding her community had to be her first priority. "Even if that kind of partnership were legal, I want to stay here. I want to show Uncle Brent, Plucky and Mr. Nelson they have other options."

"How are you going to do that? Sell a lot of books?"

His question almost undid her. Far from blaming him for the outburst, she loved him for the futile frustration of wanting something he couldn't have. "A variety of federal and state funding sources exist for housing and community initiatives." She swallowed. "Ronan could be a case study. You could help."

"I don't build houses, Taylor. I build machines. If I'm elected governor, I build coalitions."

"Of course you do." Swinging her legs, she dropped down from the tree limb. Her ankle turned, and she winced, but she refused to make a sound. "I have to stay here. I have to stay until the end."

Lowering himself to the ground, he folded his arms. The distance between their heartbeats felt too vast for a simple caress.

"I get it," he said. "I stayed in Iraq until the end. That doesn't mean staying was the right decision."

Scanning the field, she saw the bumping headlights of an old truck and knew the old oak tree's solitude had ended. Whether Jack or Mr. Higgins sat behind the wheel mattered little. Someone she loved would open the door, and she would get in. If Christopher were smart, he would get in with her, and they would go about their lives. She turned to him. "You didn't stay in Iraq to serve. You stayed to ignore the pain of your losing your brother."

He swallowed. "That's not true. The conflict wrecked me. The coalition forces should have done better. *I* should have done better."

"When did you leave?"

"When the war ended. When the kids came within an arm's length, demanded handouts and laughed at my pocket change and candy."

He would carry candy, wouldn't he? Fighting the tightness in her throat, she shook her head. "You're making excuses You stayed so you wouldn't have to face your loss in Georgia. You stayed so you wouldn't have to face your family and define your terms. You care about people. I can see it when you tease Dillan, flatter Ms. Tina and coddle me. Well, I've faced my loss. It hurts like hell, but I'm not confused about where I belong."

Reaching for her, he pulled her against his chest. "You'll let this town destroy a chance at happiness?"

"It's the only choice that makes sense."

He dropped his forehead to hers. "That's not true."

She closed her eyes and inhaled his airy, transparent warmth. When heat singed the back of her neck and Ronan felt too small, she would remember him and the strength of his appeal. She would wish they had stumbled into the same college lecture hall or spilled their drinks at a bar. She opened her eyes. "It is true. To make a relationship work, we both have to change, and we both have to be true to ourselves."

The truck came to a stop, and the highlights cast the oak's long shadow over the fields. Mr. Higgins opened the door, stepped from the cab and scratched his head. "Peaches, that you?"

She stepped away from Christopher. "Yes, Mr. Higgins."

He set his shotgun against the tire.

In Ronan, the silhouette made perfect sense.

Christopher moved in front of her.

Gripping his arm, she stepped around him. Mr. Higgins was as trustworthy as a steel plow, but he chewed tobacco and left cups of spit fermenting in his center console. "Just a lovers' spat. Give us a lift on the tailgate?"

Mr. Higgins nodded. "Get in." He pulled out his phone. "She's safe, Jack."

Christopher stalled, but she pulled him toward the truck and felt the moment he relented.

Mr. Higgins paused with one foot in the cab. The dome light illuminated his smile. "Plenty of better places to get your kicks."

She laughed. "Why does everyone think I'm sneaking around to get laid?"

"We were all young once." He climbed into the truck.

Not everyone is Ronan is bad. Releasing the tailgate, she planted her butt in the middle of the tailgate and patted the cold metal to her side. "Hop on up."

Christopher looked toward the oak.

"The ride's not so bad," she said. "I've had worse."

He grazed her cheek. "But you could have had better."

Amid the old truck's exhaust and vibrations, she pulled away from his touch, crossed her legs and dropped her head in her hand. The cotton plants would grow, and her memories of him would fade. "We all make mistakes. You gave up your dreams for your family."

He nodded, sat beside her and took her hand.

The truck's taillights cast a red glow. She watched the road dust swirl and wondered when she would see him at a press conference. Would Rebecca stand at his side, or would he choose another woman to smile and wave like a dutiful wife? The distance between them felt like the life she never lived.

Mr. Higgins slowed for Ms. Tina's house.

Releasing her hand, Christopher jumped down and braced his hands on either side of her legs. "Come in."

She lifted her chin. "Go home. Shower off the dirt, write the press release and entrust Ocelot to someone who wants to run the company." Wanting one more kiss, she glanced at his lips, but tightened her hands on the tailgate's edge.

Ms. Tina opened her front door. "That you, Higgins?"

Her yell probably woke the whole neighborhood.

Mr. Higgins rolled down the side window. "Just running errands, Tina."

"It's damn near ten o'clock."

"Go back to your shows!"

Ms. Tina slammed the screen door.

Christopher sighed.

Pulling a fresh tube of mint lip balm from her back pocket, she offered him the salve. "I found an extra."

"Taylor…" He rubbed the plastic cylinder between his fingers. "Just come to Atlanta for a weekend."

She shook her head, turned and rapped on the rear window. "All good."

Straightening, Christopher released the tailgate.

Mr. Higgins nodded and put the truck into gear.

As he pulled away, she watched Christopher shake his head, turn and climb the front lawn. *Go be the leader this state deserves.* Passing through the line of roses, their wicked spikes ready to tear clothes, he paused and looked over his shoulder. She looked away and prayed for a warning before he returned.

Without his steady presence, she scrambled into the truck bed and scrunched her hair. Before college, she'd enjoyed taking risks and revving her engine, but stealing kisses, speeding down empty roads and courting conflict were teenage rebellions. *Ronan Reads was my dream. But what if Ronan Reads wasn't enough?* The lieutenant governorship was beyond her experience, but she'd spent most of her life in Ronan, and she'd learned a thing or two about how the town functioned.

Mr. Higgins slowed for a stop sign.

Beyond his truck's headlights, the commercial district waited like an empty slate. She rapped the window. "Let me off at the bookstore."

"Peaches, it's late."

She raised her eyebrows.

"I'll have to tell your daddy."

Standing, she hopped over the edge of the truck. "Don't worry, Mr. Higgins. I'll tell him myself."

"Daughters." Shaking his head, he shifted into drive. "Thank God I never had one."

She walked past the bare sidewalk and the damaged tree standing sentinel outside her store. The store's brick walls remained, and the stout floors would survive another hundred years, but she relished the chance to upgrade the air conditioning system and install a tankless hot water heater. *Ronan's historical district was beautiful but staying in my lane was too easy. Everyone needs permission to fail and recover. We need to build for the future.*

Grinning, she realized she could have a servant's heart and still make waves in her town. She might beat Christopher to office, but he'd inspired her. She picked up a handful of red dirt and rubbed her fingers through the clay-rich soil. *I'll have to start small, but I know everyone in this town, and they know me.*

The city manager acted like a mayor, but elected commissioners handled policymaking and legislative decisions. She figured she could win an election and serve as a commissioner, but streamlining operations and overseeing department heads might be more up her ally. *And if I fail?* She let the dirt fall from her hands, pushed open the door and stood in the middle of the moonlit floorboards. Looking up to the night sky, she inhaled and closed her eyes. *Leaving Ronan would be easy, but this town made me, and I can make it better.* She grinned. *Mama thought she was raising a chicken, but wait until she hears me crow!*

Chapter Eighteen

After ignoring Ms. Tina's shrewd gazes, Christopher climbed the stairs to the second floor and listened to the night bugs from his host's upper porch. *I love Taylor, and as soon as I sort out my life, I'll make sure she knows I love her. I won't let her go.* Within an hour, he made three phone calls. He called his dad and announced his intent to run for governor. He called C.Y. and offered him a promotion. Finally, he called Greta.

"You going to marry this girl?" she asked.

"If she'll have me."

"Thank the heavens! I thought my work'd never be done."

He cleared his throat. "So, Ronan's a nice place to live."

"You're out of your mind, Christopher Durand."

He rubbed his jaw. *Probably.*

"I'm going back to the seashore." Greta ended the call.

Feeling adrift, he fired up his laptop and plotted his next steps. If he stayed away from flood risks and uncertain outcomes, he wouldn't achieve his dreams, and his heart told him that he needed Taylor. Before claiming her, he would establish himself where she belonged. Acreage in Ronan came as cheap as furrowed land. He scrolled through listings for horse farms and hunters' retreats. For a few million dollars, he could own a hundred acres of flat land with an internal road system and mature timber. For a million more, he could bypass the flood plain, claim the high ground and sleep at night. *But what does Taylor want?*

The thought of buying a house without her input made him smile, but he wasn't buying a house, he was buying his future. Pressing 'Send' on an email to his corporate realtor, he leaned back on the porch chair and rubbed his eyes. Figuring life owed him a laugh, he scheduled a meeting between C.Y. and his father and pressed 'Send'.

Sleep still refused to come.

At five, he pushed himself through a workout, showered and paused in the hallway. The door to Ms. Tina's toy room stood ajar. He frowned and carried his bags down the steps.

In the middle of the kitchen, Taylor's toy sat on the table.

He grabbed the shaggy, purple offering and dropped it in his bag.

"Early start?" Ms. Tina asked.

Caught red-handed, he smiled. "Thank you for your hospitality. The next time you come to Atlanta, please let me return the favor."

She snorted and walked to the coffee maker. "You can't control everything in your life. I wanted kids."

She reached for a filter. "It never happened. Collecting those forgotten treasures was a hell of a lot cheaper than therapy, but I held out hope." She shook her head and filled the coffee basket with grinds. "Then I couldn't stop."

"Should we lock up the Ocelot giveaways?"

She laughed. "When my husband died, I faced life's realities. You know, the devil fans complacency, but you strike me as a capable man. Taylor gives you lip? You sit her down and talk about the facts. Maybe you'll learn a few things." She pressed the brew button, turned and braced her arms on the countertop. "If everyone in this town weighed risks like uptight Northerners, nothing would get done."

Walking across the kitchen, he handed her a business card. "Sage advice. Can I hug you?"

Slapping the card on the counter, she turned up her cheek. "I'd rather have a kiss."

Dipping his head, he complied and thought about the flood risk that kept him from Ronan. His project manager deserved a raise. Taylor deserved whatever she wanted. He'd never met a woman like her, and pulling away from Ms. Tina's papery-soft cheek, he understood Taylor's community role models. "Thanks, Ms. Tina."

"Get off with you before the sun comes up and we put you to work."

He nodded, let himself out of the house and jogged down the steps.

"Wee-tah-kah-loo. Fuck-you."

The toy's chirping condemnation brought a smile to his face. Pulling it from the bag, he set it on the dash. *At least Taylor will have to see me again to retrieve it.*

He met Dillan in the high school lot. "Let's roll."

Dillan nodded, whistled and jerked his thumb toward the road leaving Ronan. The convoy of eighteen-wheelers and RVs occupying the high school parking lot roared to life and moved into formation.

Christopher rubbed his ear. "You riding with me?"

Glancing at the nearest rig, Dillan nodded.

"Final choice, Dilly?"

His assistant looked toward a rumbling eighteen-wheeler.

Watching the man's cheeks color, he shook his head. "You're not licensed to drive them, but you can ride shotgun."

"Your coffee's on the tailgate," Dillan said. "Do you need me to get it?"

I need an hour of sleep. He shook his head. "Go ahead. I'll take up the rear."

Nodding, Dillan waved his hands and ran for the convoy's nearest rig.

He plucked his coffee off the truck tailgate and climbed into the cab. Unscrewing the mug's top, he sipped the liquid and watched the vehicles roll out of the parking lot. One by one, they moved into formation and heralded Ocelot's power.

Lingering in the near-empty lot, he looked at the high school's outline. *Did we do good?* Believing Ocelot's presence had made a difference, he nodded and pulled onto the state route. *We don't survive. We endure.*

He slowed for a red light and watched a crow bisect the shaded intersection. Sparrow County's roads were empty enough for a Chinese fire drill, but sheriffs hid behind billboards, and he had little patience for moving violations. Peering through a filling station's rusted, metal pumps, he saw Taylor's car coming toward the intersection. *Maybe she came to find me.* He grinned.

Pulling into the gas station, he put the truck in park and crossed his arms over the steering wheel.

Taylor slowed for the traffic light.

He waved. *She doesn't see me.*

A second truck approached the intersection from the opposite direction.

He honked at Taylor and waved again.

She glanced at him, startled and waved.

Beckoning her toward the station, he held up the old toy and saw her laugh. *At least I can do one thing right.* Reaching for door handle, he glanced at the second truck and swore it picked up speed. The truck's lift kit and gleaming grill gave it a full-speed locomotive's ominous appearance. Narrowing his gaze, he checked the red light and looked at Taylor.

She turned her car's wheel toward the station.

"Get off the road!" Torn between blocking the intersection and running her into a ditch to protect her, he laid on the truck's horn. Three long, hard blasts failed to stop the oncoming truck or alert Taylor to the threat. *Please stay in your shitty car.*

The second truck crossed the center line. Squaring up like a missile before a target, it occupied the road and headed straight for the woman he loved.

He put his truck in gear, fumbled for the accelerator and smashed the pedal to the floorboards.

The second truck crossed the intersection.

Electrons connected, and his truck shot forward.

Taylor slammed the brakes.

The truck driver glanced at him, overcorrected and jerked the wheel hard to right. His truck spun and fishtailed toward the gas station. Striking a large, horizontal propane tank, the truck came to a rest and steam seeped from the engine.

Slamming on the breaks, he jumped from his truck and ran toward Taylor.

She climbed from the sedan and stumbled toward him. "What's going on?"

Fear cleared the exhaustion from his limbs. "Stay down!" He tackled her, wrapped his arms around her body and rolled on the hard asphalt. The material tore his clothes, abraded his skin and left tiny pebbled embedded in his muscles. Panting, he held her against his chest and exhaled. "Shit."

Fighting his hold, she turned and stared. "That's Uncle Brent's truck. What's going on?"

He followed her gaze and looked at the steaming wreckage. Beyond the shattered windows, Brent slumped against deployed airbags. Blood trickled from his head. "I don't know."

She struggled to free herself. "We have to help him."

He shook his head. Acrid smoke burned his eyes, and he replayed a horror reel of wartime explosions. "Call the police."

"Christopher! That's my uncle."

He tightened his grip and watched flames crawl up the side of the truck.

"Christopher!" She struggled.

The flames grew and heated the pressurized liquid inside the vessel. As the temperature rose, the liquid boiled and the tank failed. A towering explosion sent a ball of flames higher than the pine trees. The gas station's windows fell in showers of glass, and heat rolled across the asphalt. He gasped and felt a sharp pain in his ear. As the light and heat seared his eyes, he held firm to Taylor and watched for movement in the truck. When the authorities came and took his statement, he would meet her gaze and tell her the truth. Her uncle never moved.

She stopped fighting him.

Feeling the resignation in her deep breaths, he released her and let her roll to the hard asphalt.

She sat back and stared at the flames. Blood dripped from her forehead. "What happened?"

He wiped away the blood.

She winced but stared at the flames.

Horizontal tank dispensers helped fuel heavy industry, but left untended, they succumbed to rust and elemental exposure. Modern tanks depended on concrete barriers and metal cages, but the impromptu barbecue pit on the far side of the gas station looked too rusted for advanced controls. *When's the last time the Fuel and Measures Division came out here?* He exhaled. "The pressure in the tank exceeded the safety relief valve. Instead of venting excess pressure to the atmosphere, it blew."

She dropped her head in her hands. "No, I mean, what happened to my uncle? He headed straight toward me."

Given his experiences in Iraq, he knew the propane tank would burn for hours, and they were lucky to have avoided falling shrapnel. He wrapped his arm around her shoulders. "I don't know."

The fire breached the truck's gas tank, and a second explosion rocked the intersection.

The assault blasted his eardrums, and he wondered when he would hear completely again. Debris fell on the convenience store's roof, singed bushes and rained as soft, gray ashes. Even if his back tensed up and left him homebound, he would bear the ringing and hold Taylor and keep her safe. Reaching for his cell phone, he dialed for help, laid the phone on the road and let the speaker convey the ring.

"Nine-one-one. What's your emergency?"

"Car wreck and BLEVE on the corner of…" He looked at Taylor.

"Woodcreek Road and State Route 3," she said.

"Injuries?"

He swallowed. The technical term for the explosion clued in the emergency dispatcher, but it meant nothing to Taylor. She'd feel the loss, and he hated to hurt her. "One fatality."

Taylor hung her head.

"Ten minutes," the dispatcher said. "Stay on the line."

"What am I going to do?" she asked.

He ended the call, shoved the phone in his jeans and stood. The blast's heat stung, but he steadied his stance and held out his hand.

Looking up, she took his grip.

He pulled her to standing and led her to the roadside.

She hobbled and leaned against his frame.

"You're hurt," he said.

"It's nothing."

"Do you want me to carry you?"

Shaking her head, she reached toward his face and brushed his cheek.

Beneath her soft touch, he felt rough grit

"You don't look fit to carry anything."

He raised his eyebrow.

"I'm sorry. I just can't lean on you." Limping, she pulled away from him and sank her back against a wide pine tree. The needles at her feet cushioned her fall, but a soft grunt escaped her lips.

Sliding down beside her, he looped one arm around his knee, stretched out his other limb and watched the truck burn.

"Will the station burn?" she asked.

"The old tanks are underground. As soon as the propane burns off, the flame will die back."

"And the truck will smolder."

He pulled her against his side. "Taylor…"

"Don't say it."

He looked at her. "Say what?"

"That this disaster was an accident—that Uncle Brent lost control." She rubbed her hand over her face. "He aimed for me, didn't he? He took up the whole damn road and hit the gas!" Jerking free, she planted her foot and started to stand. Her ankle wobbled, and she swayed.

Tugging her back to sitting, he held her hand and gave her as much space as she needed.

She dropped her head against the pine tree and stared at the green canopy. "I shouldn't have said anything at dinner. I should have let Daddy handle him."

The truck's tires melted, and the metal wheels glowed. "I didn't hear Jack telling you to stop."

"He would have!" She turned her head and faced him. "I know it."

"Do you?"

She exhaled.

"Every day is a choice, and you have to choose your path."

She shook her head. "Fuck you. When are you going to make your choice? How long will you let other people to run your life? You want to talk about choices? Make yours!"

He watched the truck burn. "I made it, Taylor. I choose you. You want to stay in Ronan and be Little Miss Georgia Peach Queen? That's fine by me. I'll adjust."

"*You'll* adjust?" She rubbed her cheeks and pushed her hair out of her eyes. Climbing to her knees, she planted her good foot and stood. Instead of striding off, she swayed and bit her lip. "That's not what I want!" Hobbling toward the convenience station, she looked over her shoulder. "I didn't ask you to come here. I didn't ask for your help."

"Well, hell, Taylor, here I am." He exhaled. "Take me or leave me."

Her lip quivered. Shaking her head, she looked away and took another step.

"Taylor, you're hurt."

She turned, pulled off her shoe and threw it at him. "You tackled me!"

He dodged the ballistic and bit back a smile. *I also saved your stubborn life!* Taking a courageous breath, he stood and drew her against his chest. "I did — and I'd do it again."

Her resistance flared, and she stiffened in his arms. "You won't have the chance. I belong here. I said I could muster more good than your mechanical convoy, but the town's a fraud. Every plate of brownies and good-natured smile covers a secret. What am I going to find next? A human trafficking ring?" She shook her head and pushed off his chest. "Go back to Buckhead. Have a nice life."

Catching her hand, he brought it to his lips. "I won't be happy without you."

She traced his lower lip.

The soft, lingering touch felt too much like a goodbye.

Dropping her hand to her side, she sighed. "You have more to offer the world than your money and your pedigree. You're steady, and you think outside the box. You solve problems most people don't have time to address. Go back to Atlanta and tackle big-picture issues. Leave me in Ronan to do what I do best."

"I always wanted to build the factory in Ronan," he said, "but I had to accept the risk."

She looked up.

He held her gaze. "Ronan isn't perfect."

She snorted and looked away. "I know."

He rubbed her upper arm, willing to let her flee. "I need multi-generational partnerships. I need layers of history and rebirth. A dot-com bloom and a slow fade to black do nothing for me. My company builds things that last. I can be true to that legacy and still embrace the future. Can you?"

Watching his hand stroke her arm, she looked up. "I want you to stay. I'm just so afraid you'll see me fail. You won't ask me to change, but what if you change your mind?"

"I won't." He pulled her close. "I'll stay as long as you'll have me. I want to run for office, but times are changing and I can do it from Ronan." Tipping up her chin, he smiled. "You may not like the campaign trail."

She cleared her throat. "About that..."

The wail of sirens approached. Two police cruisers and a fire engine pulled into the intersection. Half the first responders picked up their radios. The other half stared at the blown-out propane tank, the truck's smoldering shell and the debris field littering the intersection.

An officer strode across the blacktop with the full-bodied swagger of a man whose ego outgrew his stature. "What in the hell?" His gaze widened. "Peaches, that you?"

She nodded and settled against Christopher's side. "Morning, Officer Davey."

He lifted his radio to his mouth. "Send out an ambulance. Peaches Lenore is bleeding."

She looked at her fingers. "I'm fine." Taking a deep breath, she squared her shoulders. "I mean, I'm not fine. Uncle Brent tried to run me off the road and defraud FEMA. Bill Nelson conned the government into doubling his wages, and Plucky pulled a fast one on the nation."

Officer Davey pressed the button on his radio. "Blunt force trauma."

She shook her head and looked at the wreckage. "We have work to do."

"Peaches, we'll get you a glass of water and somewhere to sit." He looked at Christopher. "What the hell are you two doing standing on the side of the road?"

He shrugged. "The lady wanted to take in the view."

"She's delusional."

He opened his mouth to respond.

She stepped forward. "I'm not, and the next person who tells me what to think is getting a swift knee to the balls."

Mirroring Officer Davey's move, Christopher stepped back.

She turned and looked at him.

He raised his palms.

Frowning, she shook her head and stuck out her hand. "Give me the keys to your truck. I need somewhere to sit and call my parents."

"They're still in the ignition."

She nodded and walked past the crowd of first responders.

Several called her name.

Officer Davey shook his head. "That girl always had a mind of her own."

He smiled. "I wouldn't have her any other way."

Chapter Nineteen

"I can't do it," Taylor said.

Lounging on Ms. Tina's second-floor porch beneath a lazy ceiling fan, Christopher looked up from his laptop. "Do what?"

"Stand behind a microphone and deliver this sanctimonious speech!" She waved the edited papers in the humid, evening air. "How am I supposed to give the eulogy for a man who tried to kill me?"

He closed his laptop and sat up. "Brent was your uncle."

She squeezed shut her eyes and took a deep breath. When she opened them, pollen still littered the painted green floor, and Christopher still looked like a conditioned athlete presiding over the white bistro set. She scanned the shadows at his feet and found Roger drooling on the man's toes. *The dog has good taste.*

"Read me what you have." He lifted his beer and set the bottle back on the linen napkin. "I like listening to your voice."

"You do?"

"Among other things."

Seeing his gaze darken, she chose pleasure over pain. "Like what?"

"Hearing you moan."

She walked toward him and traced the collarbone peeking from his shirt. Since the accident, she'd occupied Ms. Tina's upstairs bedroom and given her parents time to come to grips with her choices, but she had no interest in coming to grips with Christopher's shirt. Unbuttoning the next button, she spread her fingers on his smooth chest.

"What about the speech?" he asked.

"What speech?"

He laughed and stilled her hand. Shrugging out of the shirt, he tossed it on the floor, grabbed her hips and settled her against his bulging cock.

Roger stood, took one look at them and wandered into the bedroom.

Yes, again. With her legs straddling his lap, she rubbed against his heat and pressure. The thrill of surviving the tornado and the near-miss had ebbed, but she struggled to get enough of him. Savoring the moments when they collaborated on their passions, she let steel beams and exploratory committees occupy different sections of her mind. He occupied her heart. "I've never had sex without a condom."

He grunted and tightened his hold on her hips. "Never?"

She shook her head.

"Don't you want to wait until life settles down? Marriage, picket fences and the whole nine yards?"

Shaking her head, she looped her hands around his neck.

"Geez, Taylor, you can't say things like that and expect me to think straight. At least, let me take you to the courthouse. I don't want to fear for my life every time your father cleans his gun."

She laughed and pulled her sundress over her head.

He cupped her breast and trailed his hand down her abdomen. At the sight of her curls, he stopped. "What happened to the panties?"

"What panties?" She grinned.

Standing with her legs wrapped around his waist, he shifted her to one side, dropped his pants, and reclaimed the bistro chair. "Last chance."

She lowered her legs and stood. Poised above his heat, she held his gaze and lowered herself onto his cock. The slide and friction of skin against skin stole her breath, but the intensity of his gaze anchored every thought. Wanting more, she picked up the pace and watched him lose focus. Feeling in total control, she claimed every inch of him and held off her pleasure.

"Taylor!" Burying his head in her neck, he rubbed her swollen clit and clenched her ass as his control broke.

She felt him come and reveled in the connection, but her vision blurred, and she clamped her lips together to stifle her scream. Shaking in the aftermath of her release, she leaned back against his palm and arched over his legs.

He held her hips, shifted forward, and pressed a kiss against her abdomen. "Exhibitionist."

Closing her eyes, she'd never felt so accepted and so loved. Lifting her hand, she let him pull her back to sitting and looped her free arm around his neck. "You love me."

"As much as you love me — maybe more — but quit stalling and finish your speech."

She laughed and climbed off his lap. The cum running down her legs threatened to derail the moment. *Now what? I can't dash down the hall to the bath.*

He picked up his shirt and slowly cleaned the mess. "On second thought, maybe we should practice." His gaze darkened. "I wasn't at my best."

She tilted her head. "Oh, really?"

"Not even close."

The admission thrilled her, but the man she loved was a night owl, and she planned to use every square inch of the bedroom. "Hold that thought."

He groaned.

"And stay in your chair."

"If you're going to boss me around, try putting on clothes." He tossed over her sundress.

Laughing, she slipped her arms through the openings and spread her draft papers on the table. "I shouldn't have called the speech sanctimonious. It's just, after meeting with the neighboring priest, I felt like I had a grip on my emotions but" — she shook her head — "maybe I don't."

He nodded toward the rumpled bed. "I can think of several ways to help settle your emotions."

Lifting the corner of her mouth in a slight smile, she shook her head and stared into the darkness beyond the porch railing. The honey and lemon subtly of magnolia blooms floated on the breeze. Ms. Tina claimed a horticulturist had dated the tree to 1848, but Taylor wondered if *she* was full of shit. A hundred and fifty years ago, Ronan had grown from the junction of two railways, and she would never know whether its inauspicious, mosquito-infested birth had stemmed from pride or greed. In her uncle's case, greed and desperation had won, but she believed stress had eroded his rationality. *What did Uncle Brent love?*

"Taylor?" Christopher asked.

She looked at his chiseled profile and the shadows cast by the overhead light. *The sun didn't bake the life out of it. It cured him until he was ready to roll. I told him we didn't need big businesses to bail out our economy, fix our roofs or complement our eyes, but we do need a fighting chance. I can't preach and I can't stabilize our economy, but I can love people and keep them on track.* "You really want to hear this eulogy?"

He smiled. "I'll hear it one way or another, won't I?"

She picked up the first page. "Did we let down Brent Lenore? Did we fail to see his pain?" She met Christopher's gaze. "Too sophomoric?"

"Keep going."

She nodded. "How many of you saw Uncle Brent mumbling to himself, flying into a rage or nursing a drink after the tornado? Uncle Brent didn't drink When he said he felt like he was having trouble getting his life back under control, we should have listened. We should have sent him to a doctor or a mental health professional. We should have done more than pray.

"I pray God will forgive my sins and grant me eternal life, but I want you to remember Uncle Brent's life on this earth, too. Remember the times he kneeled with you, celebrated your marriages and consoled your grief. I don't need to play video and audio clips to remember his laugh. You don't need facts and transcripts to remember his sins. We're all sinners, brought together by tragedy to pray for God's mercy upon another sinner." She looked up. "Too heavy, right?"

"Religion isn't my thing," he said.

"I know…"

He held up a hand. "Hear me out. You're focusing on your uncle's life and what it meant. If you want to get up there and preach fire and brimstone, nobody will stop you."

She frowned. "I don't preach."

He raised his eyebrows.

"I don't" —she sighed — "mean to preach. I mean to help."

"I know you do, Taylor, and the town knows it, too, but brevity is the secret to a good speech."

"What would you say?" she asked.

"Fuck Uncle Brent." She clapped a hand over her mouth then asked, "Are you sure you want to run for governor?"

He stood, pulled her to standing and held her close. "Yes." Dropping his head, he breathed deeply and buried his nose in her hair. "I planned to woo you, but I didn't know how much I needed your heart until I almost lost it. A kinder man would thank Brent for pushing my emotions to the brink, but I'm not kind. I don't enjoy taking risks." He tightened his hold. "If you're my weakness, I'll guard you with all my heart."

Tipping up her chin, she looked at him. "And if I'm not?"

His lips hovered above hers. "You are."

"Taylor!"

Ms. Tina's summons rang through the house.

Raising his head, Roger howled in response.

Taylor rubbed her ear and stepped away from the man she loved. "People will think we're massacring the poor animal."

He adjusted his pants. "Not if they know you."

"Come help me unload the dishwasher!" Ms. Tina said.

A threatening footfall sounded on the steps. Shaking her head, she turned toward the door, looked over her shoulder and met his gaze. "Some things never change."

He scanned the secluded balcony. "And some things change for the better."

* * * *

Taylor gripped the podium's edges. Beneath a cloudless blue sky, a tent shielded her neck and a crowd of mourners. Birds chirped and wildflowers crowded the clearing, but the solemn occasion brought tears to her eyes. Her uncle's flower-draped casket looked as sincere in the field as it would in a stained-glass alcove. *Maybe more.*

She cleared her throat. "Uncle Brent loved football. He said his love for the sport began in high school when Coach Griffin"—looking up, she met the old man's gaze—"asked the team to kneel before every contest. He asked God to help his team play a fair game, avoid harming the opposition and guard their bodies from serious harm. He asked that the most deserving team win. Then he led the team in a prayer. Usually it was the 'Our Father', but Coach wasn't strict. If someone had something to say, Coach said, 'Amen!'"

Coach Griffin wiped a tear from his eye and nodded.

"Nobody warned my uncle about keeping his mind safe in the storm's aftermath." She straightened her spine. "By now, news of his fraud scheme has leaked or passed between neighbors like whispers of a lottery win. I don't know if Uncle Brent would have gone through with his plans, but the Mobile firm has questions to answer. So do we.

"Did we let down Brent Lenore?" Looking up from her notes, she faced the crowd. "Did we fail to see his pain? How many of you saw him mumbling to himself, flying into a rage or nursing his drink? Uncle Brent didn't drink. When he said he felt like he was having trouble getting his life back under control, we should have listened. We should have sent him to a doctor or a mental health professional. We should have done more than pray. This week, I realized that staying comfortable is the same thing as staying complacent. For Ronan to thrive, we have to keep moving and keep helping each other."

A couple at the back of the crowd stood and walked away.

She didn't care if they left to grieve or pass judgment. *I get to say my piece, and they get to say theirs.*

Fearing she would lose more of her audience, she flipped the page. "I believe prayer works miracles. I also believe silence is a sin. How many of you heard about Uncle Brent's death, opened your Bibles and prayed? Thank you for your prayers." She clasped her hand against her chest. "My family appreciates each and every heartfelt gesture, but the next time your neighbor flounders, I want you to conclude your prayers, set down your Bible and find a way to help."

Her voice felt strong and true. "Complacency is not an option. A few thousand people live within our city limits, and each one of them counts. Each soul is precious and beautiful. Uncle Brent was precious and beautiful, too, and his town will miss him. His children will miss him." She paused. "I will miss him."

Charles rose and walked away from the tent.

Too many times since Uncle Brent's death, he had asked about his role in the tragedy.

"*No, precious,*" Nancy had said. "*You have one foot in your youth, and one foot in your prime. The only thing we ask of you is decency and respect. You're no more responsible for your father than I was for mine.*" She'd patted her nephew's shoulder. "*And we all know he strayed far from the Lord.*"

Free of doctrine, Taylor abandoned her papers and spoke from her heart. "Before the storm, my life was too easy. Prayer and psalms were too easy. Now, I know better. I want you to remember the quality of Uncle Brent's life. Remember the time he kneeled with you, celebrated your marriage or consoled your grief. I don't need to play video clips to remember his laugh. You don't need facts and transcripts to remember his sins. We are all sinners, brought together to pray for God's mercy upon another sinner.

"I don't know how to talk about the tornado and the destruction in our lives, but I do know how to talk about the future. Ronan isn't a blip on the map. It isn't an exurb. It's a place, and the people who live here need more than prayers. We need economic opportunities, quality education and hope. I hope in the Lord, but I also trust every one of you. So did Uncle Brent. If we let him down, shame on us. If we find meaning in his death, we're making progress. Amen." Stepping down from the podium, she paused and met her mother's gaze.

Nancy nodded.

She released her breath, kept her head high and reclaimed her seat.

Christopher offered his hand.

Gripping his fingers, she let his steady presence calm her jitters.

He leaned close. "Taylor Lenore for president?"

"Just city manager." Her whisper felt too loud and irreverent for the service, but she looked straight ahead and watched Charles mount the makeshift stage, mount a stool and strum his guitar.

"My daddy had a lot of things to say over the years, but when he preached, his favorite hymn was *Abide with Me*." Charles strummed the guitar, and his voice rang over the amplification system.

When the song ended, the presider recited his prayers and the mourners stood.

She scanned the sea of black hats and somber, gray suits. "Where's Aunt Mary?" Frowning, she released Christopher's hand and pushed through small groups until she found her aunt standing near the rear of the tent. "Aunt Mary?"

Aunt Mary turned and nodded.

"What's wrong?"

"He loved you so much, Peaches, and what he tried to do was so wrong." Taking both of her hands, she held them fast. "How can you ever forgive us?"

She pulled her aunt close for a hug. "I was terrified." Her whispered truth stung. "But I was also bewildered, and someone saved me. I don't know if Uncle Brent had a change of heart, Christopher intervened or God had a plan, but I'm alive and so are you." Looking over her shoulder, she saw Christopher talking to Charles and her father. "We're going to make it."

Aunt Mary nodded and drew a deep breath. "No more secrets."

"We'll take the good with the bad."

"Then we need to talk about how this town works."

Taylor swallowed. "After the wake?"

Aunt Mary nodded.

Returning to Christopher's side, she slipped her fingers into his hand.

"If I've learned one thing at Ocelot, it's that we have to balance technology and manufacturing. If one side gets ahead, the other struggles to keep up." He squeezed her fingers.

"Ronan's a far cry from a manufacturing hub," Jack said. "In the highly industrialized and mechanized society you praise, progress razes the places I hold dear."

"Ronan can't be a museum," Christopher said.

She reached for her father's arm. "We're reclaiming as many materials as we can salvage. Those old beams in the bookstore weathered the storm."

He sighed. "Life was easier when I had a plane and jigsaw."

You also worked yourself to the bone and needed a shoulder replacement. "We'll find a way to make it work, Daddy."

He skewed his jaw. "Some things needed to go. If I see one more 1950s avocado bathroom..." He shuddered.

Christopher laughed. "Did you work on Ms. Tina's house?"

Jack rubbed his jaw. "Man, I haven't been inside that place in years."

Glancing at her, Christopher winked. He cleared his throat and looked at Jack. "Investors recognize Ocelot for its growth and prosperity. When we decide to locate a new facility or consider expansion, we look for prospering and growing communities like Ronan."

Taylor bit back a smile. *What's all this 'we'? As far as I can ascertain, Christopher runs that company like a battalion. When he says, 'Jump', Lord, they jump.* She thought of the office he'd created in Ms. Tina's spare bedroom. Most days, he worked from Atlanta, but on Fridays, he returned to Ronan with tales of C.Y.'s pushback and Dillan's insolence. Seeing him walk up the lawn, her heart swelled.

"The generator production facility will comprise three hundred thousand square feet and employ more than three hundred workers." Christopher looked at Charles. "By the time you finish college, we'll need onsite managers and production leads."

Charles nodded so many times that he looked like the hula girl in her sedan. She thought about swatting Christopher's ass, but the solemnity of the occasion stayed it. *When everything's said and done, couples marry, corpses rest and communities mingle.*

"Taylor tells me you're planning to run for governor," Jack said.

Charles' jaw hung open.

Christopher nodded. "In due time. I have a house to build, and a community to learn." He rubbed his lip. "The presence of an Ocelot's manufacturing facility will attract other facilities, contract trainers and specialized companies. If I were an investor, I'd invest in land."

Charles stared. "You just signed a purchase agreement for six hundred acres."

Glancing at him, Christopher nodded. "Growth brings together students and individuals from the banking and financial industries. I worried about Ronan's flood plain and proximity to transportation, but the final decision depended on people. The workforce, the local leadership and recovery effort made the difference in my decision."

"Bullshit," Jack said.

She struggled not to laugh.

Christopher brought her hand to his lips. "Taylor helped."

Scanning the crowd, she felt at home and planned to thrive with him by her side. *I hope the people of Ronan seize their opportunities and thrive, too. I worried Ronan held my soul, but the town never had it.* Seeking Plucky in the crowd, she met her friend's gaze and let a small smile soften the enmity between them.

Lifting her chin, Plucky nodded and swept her bangs across her forehead.

She shook her head, looked toward downtown and felt the sun warm her cheeks. *I can't rebuild this town myself, but I can help.* She grinned. "Let's get on with it."

Christopher dropped his head. "Is that an invitation?"

"We're at a funeral!" She looked around to see if anyone overheard him. Seeing a sea of community members coming together in grief, she gave thanks for the tornado, but the next time God wanted to reset her life, a flash of lightning would do.

"So, later?"

She rolled her eyes and turned from him.

He caught her hand.

Smiling, she chewed her lip and grinned. "Definitely later."

Want to see more from this author?
Here's a taster for you to enjoy!

Lost in LA
Amy Craig

Excerpt

Wylie stood in the shadowed hallway of the two-bedroom apartment, her fist clenched as she brainstormed ways to fight an eviction notice.

Dottie, her roommate, was texting her from the security of the bathroom.

Couldn't she face me? After four months of cohabitation, Wylie knew very little about the woman. She mostly found it funny when the overpaid nanny confiscated candy from her sugar-restricted charges, retreated to the bathroom and savored the contraband where no one could see her. Today, Wylie struggled to find humor in the situation. Breathing through her frustration, she released her fist and sank to the floor. "The wrappers in the trashcan give you away," she whispered. "We both know what you're doing in there."

She looked down the hallway and focused on the living room couch where Dottie's orange-and-white cat luxuriated on the corduroy fabric, as smug as its owner. White mini-blinds cast stripes of sunlight on the room's beige carpet, valance drapes and dusty brass fixtures. As a native of Santa Monica, Wylie understood that the furnished apartment on Montana Avenue and Fifth Street relied on its location to attract tenants. The nineteen-hundred dollars a month sublease let her walk to the beach where she taught yoga, but the cat paid nothing for his sunlit pleasure. *Maybe I'll take you with me. I could hold you for ransom until Dottie adds me to the lease.*

The cat yawned.

You're right. You're not worth the trouble.

Steam seeped beneath the bathroom door, as nebulous as her counterarguments and self-doubts. Ignoring the tacky feel of the semi-gloss paint, she leaned against the bathroom door and pulled her fingers through her long blonde hair. *This is what I get for being too trusting and naïve. I should have put my name on the lease. I should have known better than to get myself into this mess. I could find Dottie a boyfriend. A girlfriend. Whatever. Threaten to reveal her undocumented cat. Light her bed on fire.* She laughed and released her hair to cover her mouth. *Shit, that wasn't appropriate.*

She rapped on the bathroom door. "Dottie! Let's talk about this situation like grown women. I'm this close to finishing two-hundred hours of professional certification and landing a full-time job with benefits. What am I supposed to do now? Live on the streets?"

Her ostensible roommate remained silent.

"There has to be another alternative."

The faucet ran as Dottie added hot water to her tub, ignoring their shared utility costs and the environmental impacts of her two-hour bath. "What's done is done. Cousin's in and you're out."

Wylie exhaled, finding it impossible to reason with a woman who lacked the courage to face her. "This isn't right. Don't you have to give me some notice or something? Don't you even feel bad about what you're doing?"

"Not really."

She hung her head. *It doesn't matter if she stays in that bathtub until the floor caves in. Her name's on the lease and she calls the shots.*

"I know I promised you a year —"

Wylie's hope soared.

"But we all thought my cousin would fail her semester at UC and have to repeat it. Maybe, like, twice. Now that she's graduated, she's decided to come to Los Angeles to pursue her acting career." The plastic snap of a toiletry bottle echoed in the tiled room. "My aunt called and told me this morning. What am I supposed to do?"

"Tell your mom you already have a roommate? One who's never been late paying rent?" She considered kicking down the door and upending the bubble bath all over Dottie's head. "A roommate who changes the litter box for the cat you're not even supposed to have in the apartment!"

"Leave Snickerdoodle alone."

Wylie eyed the cat. "I love animals."

The cat stood, repositioned himself and presented his ass to Wylie.

Wylie stared at the bathroom door. "This is bad karma!"

"Sorry, kid."

"Your cousin will never make it to her auditions on time." Her words sped up and she stood, hoping her hard-won native logic could override the aspirations of a wannabe actress. "Your cousin needs to live in one of the San Fernando Valley neighborhoods. The Central and Eastside neighborhoods would be even better if she's looking for a deal."

"She's a trust-fund kid."

"She might decide this apartment isn't a good fit. I don't want you to end up with zero roommates. Maybe she could sleep on the couch for a while." Water sloshed on the other side of the door and Wylie crossed her fingers, hoping her magnanimous offer cloaked her desperation.

"That's the thing. My cousin wants the second bedroom. My aunt already wired me six months of rent."

Of course she did. Wylie bit her lip and decided to play her final card. "I guess I could take the couch."

The bathwater stilled.

Wylie clung to a moment of hope.

"You'd still have to pay me the same rent."

The counteroffer hit Wylie like a rogue wave. Her eyes widened and she slapped the door in disbelief. "You can't charge me the same amount you're charging for a bedroom."

"Why not? My name's on the lease. We're not friends, Wylie. Take it or leave it."

She opened her mouth to accept a month on Dottie's fur-strewn couch.

The other woman pulled the plug on the bathwater. "You know what? Scratch that. I don't want to put up with three women sharing one tiny bathroom. It's not like we're desperate."

Tears streamed down Wylie's cheeks as she hung her head and let her hair shield her face. The draining water sucked away the last bit of her hope. *Right now, I'm the definition of desperate.* She cleared her throat, determined to retain her pride. "How long do I have until your cousin shows up? Like, a week?"

"She'll be here in the morning."

Wylie stared at the bathroom door. "Are you serious?"

"Honestly, I thought you'd be gone by now."

She wiped away her tears. "Funny. I'm still here."

"You should probably leave tonight and make a clean break."

Laughter bubbled up in Wylie's throat, displacing her desperation. "This is not helping me out. This is, like, the definition of not helping me out."

"I guess you can stay the night. I'll use your deposit to pay for a cleaning service."

"You're funny, Dottie. Fucking hilarious."

The woman remained silent for a minute. "Sorry, kid."

Wylie retreated to a bedroom full of mismatched furniture and cursed her stupidity. She shoved her clothes into her duffel bag, folded a set of sheets and crammed them on top of her clothes. *People have done more with less.*

Dottie emerged from the bathroom wearing a towel and a hair turban straight from the archives of the home shopping channel. She tossed an envelope of cash on the bare mattress. "Here's your deposit. I hope everything works out."

Wylie stared at the clumsy script bearing her name, Wylie Winidad. The sight of the familiar envelope brought tears to her eyes and she shook her head, realizing Dottie had never felt the need to deposit her hard-earned cash. "Thanks, I guess."

The woman nodded and retreated without saying another word.

Wylie picked up the envelope of money and shoved it into her purse while she considered her predicament. *Why do bad things happen to good people? I've done everything right since my parents left town. How am I going to scrape together the money I need for a deposit on my own place? I need to figure out a way to take care of myself, but there's no way I'm calling my parents. Most of the people I know have moved away and like...grown up.*

She thought of her mom and dad ensconced in an Oregon complex full of California refugees. *'They'll be the hardest years of your life,'* her mother had said, boxing up a lifetime of dishes and serving pieces. *'You're only twenty-six years old. Instead of fending for yourself, why don't you tag along with us?'*

'Because I belong here.'

'Oh, honey, you'll always belong with us.'

Wylie blinked away the sting of tears. *'Thanks, Mom.'*

The next day, her parents had driven up the coast in a rental truck full of furniture and left her in Santa Monica with a wardrobe of frayed designer jeans, a jumble of high-priced loungewear and the athletic gear she needed to host her beachside classes.

She'd gotten drunk with Natalia to celebrate her independence. Clinking glasses, they'd toasted having everything they needed. Most of their sporadic interactions involved yoga classes and cocktails, but Wylie knew her best friend would let her crash for a few days if she happened to be in town. Unfortunately, the spunky yoga enthusiast worked as a studio scout and her social media feed showed her scouting battle sites on the Horn of Africa. *Who would let me in? Nobody. I have nobody left in this town.*

She wheezed as the reality of her situation set in. The muscles in her airways tightened and stress impeded her breathing. *Now is not the time for an asthma attack.* She focused on calming her rapid inhalations, but the muscles in her neck and chest tightened as panic set in. The pain of the clenching muscles echoed through her body. Doubling over, she scrambled for the rescue inhaler in her purse and dumped out the contents of the bag. The metallic inhaler caught her eyes. She pumped the cartridge, slumped to the floor and waited for the rush of the short-acting bronchodilator to relieve her systems. *What would I do without my medicine?*

Twenty minutes later, her breathing slowed and she wondered when the misery of this day would end. Trusting her heart rate to remain stable, she struggled to her feet and hefted her duffel bag, testing her strength against an upset stomach and shaky limbs. *I can do this.*

Dottie sat on the couch in a pair of pajamas, her turban in place while she watched a cooking show with the cat.

I'm surprised she's not hiding in her room.

The cooking show went to commercials.

Dottie looked up. "Do you need any help with your stuff?"

Oh, so now you're helpful? Wylie shook her head, dropped the first duffel bag by the front door and returned to the bedroom to grab the second one. She straightened her spine as she walked between her former roommate and a television chef demonstrating how to make pasta. "Adios, Snickerdoodle. It's been swell."

The cat's eyes remained closed.

About the Author

Amy Craig lives in Baton Rouge, Louisiana USA with her family and a small menagerie of pets. She writes women's fiction and contemporary romances with intelligent and empathetic heroines. She can't always vouch for the men. She has worked as an engineer, project manager, and incompetent waitress. In her spare time, she plays tennis and expands her husband's honey-do list.

Amy loves to hear from readers. You can find her contact information, website details and author profile page at https://www.totallybound.com

Home of Erotic Romance

Sign up for our newsletter and find out about all our
romance book releases, eBook sales and promotions,
sneak peeks and FREE romance books!